S0-BJB-271

THE FISHERMAN'S QUILT

Margaret Doyle

THE FISHERMAN'S QUILT

A Novel by Margaret Doyle

THE FISHERMAN'S QUILT

All right Reserved @ 2004 by Margaret Doyle

No part of this book may be reproduced or transmitted in any form or by any means, graphic, electronic, or mechanical, including photocopying, recording, taping, or by any information storage retrieval system, without the written permission of the publisher.

Port Gamble Publishing
PO Box 582
Eastsound WA 98245
www.FishermansQuilt.com

ISBN:0-9761099-0-5

Printed in the United States of America

"North to Alaska" by Russell Faith, Bob Marcucci and Peter Deangelis
Copyright@ 1960, renewed 1988 Universal-MCA Music Publishing, Inc. (ASCAP)
All rights reserved. Used by permission.

"I Am Woman" by Helen Reddy and Ray Burton
Copyright @1971 Irving Music, Inc. on behalf of Itself and Buggerlugs Music Co (BMI)
All rights reserved. Used by permission.

"United We Stand"
Words and Music by Anthony Toby Hiller and John Goodison
@1970 (Renewed 1998) EMI BELWIN MILLS LTD.AND EMI APRIL MUSIC INC.
All rights for EMI BELWIN MILLS LTD. Controlled and Administered in the US and
Canada by EMI MILLS MUSIC INC. All Rights Reserved International
Copyright Secured Used by Permission

"Love is Everywhere"
Words by John Denver, Joe Henry, Steve Weisberg and John Martin Sommers
Music by John Martin Sommers
Copyright © 1975; Renewed 2003 Cherry Lane Music Publishing Company, Inc.
(ASCAP), Dream Works Songs (ASCAP), Anna Kate Deutschendorf, Zachary
Deutschendorf and Jesse Belle Denver
All Rights for Dream Works Songs, Anna Kate Deutschendorf and Zachary
Deutschendorf
Administered by Cherry Lane Music Publishing Company, Inc. (ASCAP)
International Copyright Secured All Rights Reserved

CONTENTS

CHAPTER ONE

THE BIG MOVE
In which we move our household to Kodiak and settle in a shack

Matt flew back home to Seattle on the midnight flight. Drunk and bleary-eyed, he was always the last one off the plane. He had a fishing job lined up in Kodiak on the *American Eagle*.

"So we have to get up there in two weeks, before the king crab season starts. We gonna make this happen, Mama? Head up the Alcan?"

"All right! Chelsea, babe, we're headed 'North to Alaska, going north, the rush is on,'" I sang the old Johnny Horton hit to our baby.

As we drove home to our little cabin on Lake Alice, Matt turned to me. "I managed to rent a small house in Kodiak for us to stay—nothing fancy, but it won't be long until we find something better." He put his big paw of a hand over mine and said, "You sure you want to do this?" His black brows came together over his light brown eyes, and I wasn't sure if I saw appreciation or uncertainty in them.

"I want to see you more, Matt. I can't stand these long separations. Chelsea is four months old and we've been together a total of ten days since she was born. I want to be a fishing family. And driving up the Alcan highway will be an adventure."

Before we left, we had Chelsea baptized, or as they called it then, "dedicated." Matt was the first of his high school crowd to get married and be a father. His best friend Jamie came over and teased Matt.

"So how are you adjusting to fatherhood? How does it feel to be the old man?"

Matt threw a teething biscuit at him. "Don't feel left out. You can be Chelsea's godfather."

Without even asking me.

I broke in. "I thought you were proud of being a pagan, Matt, and I refuse to believe in original sin. I hate the idea that our innocent beautiful baby has a black ugly sin."

Then Jamie said with his smug finality, "Yeah, but if she does, it's a good idea to get rid of it, right?"

So, though Jamie's bossiness drove me wild, I figured I might as well take advantage of his intrusion to celebrate my baby. It made me mad that Jamie always found a way to barge his way into our lives, but if something did happen to Matt and me, I would want Jamie and Gail to be the ones to take care of Chelsea. They both loved kids and had a good sense of humor and a stubborn, if idiosyncratic, integrity.

When Matt and Jamie went out for some beer, I called the priest at Holy Innocents Church in Monroe.

"And are you a parishioner, Mrs. Hunter?"

"Uh, no."

"Then why is it you want your child baptized?"

"We're moving up to Alaska, and I kind of wanted to protect her, you know, send her off with your blessing."

"I'm afraid I can't perform the sacrament if you're lapsed."

Lapsed. They always have the great word for putting you down. I thought they'd be delighted to have me back in the fold. Again that sniggering, called-upon-the-carpet feeling.

Instead we had the ceremony across Puget Sound at Mom's village church in the woods near Shine. We partied and played with dainty black-eyed baby Chelsea and said our formal farewells to the family.

"Matt sure picked the right girl," his mom said. She shivered, "He's lucky to have a wife who wants to go with him to Alaska."

Lucky? This is going to be a ball—cozy little home, free from the rat race, money to "live like Vikings," as Matt would say.

After everyone left and we were still at Mom's, I worked on finishing the fancy quilt I'd started before Matt and I married. It was made of satins and velvets from my old hippie dresses, pieced in a scalloping wave pattern. I backed the quilt with slippery gold taffeta. It was kind of messy, but the overall effect was pretty, from a distance.

The day before we left was one long party. My sister Tricia and her kids came over first, then Gail and Jamie, then more of Matt's friends from high school and from the canneries in Alaska, and Peggy, his sister, when she got off work. We ran back and forth, in and out of town. I took an old chair to trade for a black velvet jacket at an antique store. The jacket was smooth and glossy, maybe a little ratty, but I could sew the tears. As I turned in front of Gail and Peggy, Gail said, "Nora, that jacket goes perfectly with your pale skin and beautiful dark hair."

I said, "I just love the idea of bursting in the door, wearing this coat and smelling of cold frosty air and perfume."

"What a romantic you are!" Gail laughed.

Peggy smiled thinly and said, "Or a showoff."

But nothing could slow me down. We took my little cocker mutt Goldie to the vet and my piano to be stored in Glenn Mayhew's house. Glenn was an Alaskan fisherman, too. He and Matt lived together before Matt moved in with me. Now Peggy was living at Glenn's house, "keeping" it for him while he was away fishing.

Finally we all met back at the cabin to eat take-out Chinese food with our fingers because the knives and forks were already packed.

The night went on and on, with me muddling through, sorting out the mess and giggling, passing the baby around until I put her to bed, while Matt and his buddies drank beer and threw each other in the lake.

I was packing some garlic into a box of kitchen spices about two in the morning when Jamie came up to me and grabbed my hand. "Come on, Nora, we've got to do some dancing and talking before you leave." I was afraid Matt would be jealous and give me a hard time, but Jamie said, "Nora, you and I have been friends for a long time. Maybe Matt needs to be educated."

Jamie pulled me by the wrist, me still clutching garlic in both fists. We went up to the road behind the house, where we could hear the music from the radios blaring and the guys yelling down at the dock and the dogs barking all around the lake.

"Remember after Sam died, when you asked me, 'Jamie, who's going to love me?' and I told you it would all work out? You didn't believe me then, did you? But didn't it all turn out? And now you've got an old man and a baby girl and you're doing just fine, aren't you?"

"Yeah, but Jamie, you said 'We all do' when I asked you who'd love me, and you did, and now I'm going to miss you."

"You're not going to miss us—you're going to Alaska!" and he started twirling me around in the street and we laughed and stumbled and the huge garlics I'd brought with me flew out of my hands and went spinning into the night.

Doug Bradley passed out that night on the single bed in what had been Chelsea's nursery. Matt and I collapsed upstairs sometime before dawn without even knowing Doug was there until he woke us up the next morning. Suddenly he was looming over us, reeking of beer and cigarette smoke. "Hey Captain, you got any smokes on you? The real thing, not the hippie stuff."

3

Matt tossed him the pack off the table next to our bed and said, "Get out of here, Bradley."

Gail came back over to see us off and to take away baskets, garden tools, car wax, and other miscellaneous junk we were leaving behind.

After the men had systematically packed the big pieces we were taking with us—stereo equipment, Oriental rug, lamp, rocking chair, boxes of books and clothes and blankets—I attacked the rear of the Jeep, cramming every empty space with candles, knitting needles, pillows, stuffed animals, and all the other charms and trinkets that would be abandoned if I didn't find a cranny to stash them.

When, for the last time, I walked out of the small log cabin where Matt and I had lived, I looked through the bare windows and saw the house, stripped of my possessions but still mysterious, furnished with the landlord's black Chinese tables and cabinets. It had the look of Oriental elegance and harmony I loved— shibui.

It looks so bright and spacious, why do people pack things around anyway? Why not move free and unfettered?

But I had packed my most precious belongings, leaving behind my warm-hearted sister, my eccentric mother, my antique piano, and fun-loving friends. Now we were Pioneers to the Last Frontier, where I would carve my niche out of the wilderness with my baby, my dog, my music, my rocker, and my husband.

We looked like a gypsy family, with Goldie and baby on my lap, patchwork pillows surrounding us, baskets and bells swinging from the roll bar, and a lampshade perched between my knees and the dashboard.

"You're going to change, Nora," Gail said. "I can see you getting real religious. Be good to Goldie. Don't leave her out in the cold."

"I wouldn't do that, Gail," I protested, and felt guilty in advance.

Would I neglect Goldie? Would I turn out to be a bad mother?

On our way out of town, we took the baby for her last shots at the clinic, filled up the gas tank, and stopped for the first purchase of cocaine we ever had to buy. With Matt and now Chelsea to stabilize my life, it had been a long time since the all-night jams. We justified it this time to stay awake for the long drive north—our defiant and celebratory gesture good-by.

Once we hit the freeway, I felt tired and washed out. We stopped in Bellingham two hours later for dinner. No problems at the Canadian border, but we got lost in Vancouver for an hour. We had a late snack in Hope, and then Matt stopped for me to drive at Cache Creek Crossing, but I couldn't stay awake.

4

It felt like the wheel was pulling away from my hands like a wild horse breaking for freedom, so Matt took over again.

For miles and miles there was nothing but wilderness and the highway, a uniform forest of trees on either side of the road and mountains in the distance. We stopped at a gas station at Fort Nelson and as I hopped out, the tin box of chocolate chip cookies that Mom had made clattered to the asphalt.

I realized then how casually I'd kissed Mom goodbye. With the crumbling cookies by the gas pumps, I knew it would be a long time before she would make cookies for me or hold Chelsea or dispense her irrational wisdom that always made me so impatient.

I remembered Tricia and me standing with our arms around each other at Lake Alice, tears running down our cheeks as we said goodbye.

"Oh baby sister, what will I do without you?" she'd said.

What would she do without me? Tricia is such an unusually good person—so funny and unmaterialistic, there is no one like her. How will I manage without her?

As I sat by the gas pumps, missing Tricia already and hugging Chelsea to me and hoping someday she'd have a sister to love, Matt walked by and saw me crying. "What's wrong?"

"I'm thinking about Tricia. I just wish the good fortune that's come to me would come to her, because she's so deserving of it. She has such a frustrating time with Lou and his little meannesses that he can't really help."

"Meannesses?" Matt smiled. "Like?"

"Like calling her 'broad' when she hates it and making fun of her, that she's flat-chested. I always have to restrain myself when I talk to her about how you and I love each other—it sounds like bragging."

"Saying goodbye isn't so easy when you get right down to it, is it? Maybe Tricia's just got to spend some time paying her dues without you."

We drove on, seeing lots of camper vans loaded down with moose carcasses, and when we stopped for gas at Pine Mountain, the lady station owner offered hunters' lodgings that were really just plywood shacks. Moose meat hung alongside a shed to freeze-dry. Further back on the property were five cages the size of outhouses. Inside the cages black bears loomed, sad but still threatening.

About eight o'clock, 30 hours after we'd started out, Matt drove into Wonowon, where we finally stopped right off the highway. It was snowing.

Our motel room reminded me of the Bates Motel in *Psycho*. It was about ten feet wide with a small sink, a tiny bathroom with a flimsy steel shower, and two mismatched iron-framed beds. But we were too exhausted to care.

We left early the next morning and before too long, on an ice-covered slope, the jeep started bumping and rocking unevenly. Matt pulled over and discovered we had a flat, so he fixed it off the freezing cold highway, while I nursed the baby.

The icy mountain passes were terrifying. I'd get nervous and begin to sweat, close my eyes, and clutch Chelsea. To make matters worse, every time we slid on a patch of ice and almost went over a cliff, Matt yelped, "Whoopee!" I felt like crying and throwing up at the same time.

It brought back the days when Sam used to frighten me, driving his Porsche at breakneck speeds over the mountain roads east of Seattle. That seemed like ages ago.

Matt, Jamie, Fitz, Doug—the good old boys—had all lived with Sam and me in a huge ramshackle house named Hotel Universe. Sam and I spent our days roaming through bookstores and curio shops, renovating vans, hiking through woods, shopping for funky wardrobes and organic food. We spent our nights cooking saturnalian feasts, prowling darkened nightclubs, and exploring the fantastic and scary corners of our minds.

Then Jamie and Doug were drafted into the army and sent to Germany. Sam and the others started selling dope and hash from the connections Jamie and Doug made overseas. Sam and I dreamed of building greenhouses and making music once we were rich. But after the dope-selling business got off the ground, the good old boys bought fancy cars and turned their sights on the bigger bucks and bigger status of cocaine-dealing in South America.

I joined in the glamorous outlaw aspect of it, too. Sam was handsome, dramatic, and thrilling—anything was possible with him. The drugs weren't acid or heroin, nobody was going crazy or turning into a junkie. We all were making our fortune. But where were the greenhouses? In the back of my mind I heard, "There is no such thing as a secret shared." Sooner or later, we'd get caught.

So we overestimated our sophistication and soon a bunch of flashy parasites started mooching off Sam and Jamie, who called each other "godfather" and prided themselves on controlling every situation, taking care of everything and everybody.

Matt was put off by the showiness and sloppiness of it all—trashing hotel rooms and snorting lines of cocaine off tabletops in restaurants. He drifted in and out, crashing in one of the bedrooms when he wasn't fishing in Alaska.

One night Sam and Jamie were waiting for a big load of cocaine. They were already uptight, and when the washing machine backed up into the sink and overflowed, they started screaming at me. Matt hauled into the room, reached into the sink, and pulled out whatever was blocking the drain. The water started gurgling away, and Matt told them, "Clean up your own act before you go tearing into Nora—she's got more class than all the rest of you put together."

Somebody stood up for me.

By then Sam and Jamie's personal drug cabinet included something called "sippy-sippy," which made them more silly and reckless than ever. Gail took Jamie to Europe to dry out, but Sam wouldn't clean up his act, though he tried to buy a legitimate niche in the record-producing business. The "artists" took his money and cocaine and let him sit in on their recording sessions.

Sam and I moved to a cabin in the woods and I planted a garden and bought a piano while Sam sped on life's fast lane. He played cops-and-robbers games in his silly little Porsche until one night when he finally drove off the side of a cliff.

Months later, Matt reappeared. Among all the glib promoters and self-proclaimed artists, Matt was a solid rock with a "salt of the earth" job. He was independent, he was responsible, and he said he loved me. We spent the summer at a cannery in Alitak on the south end of Kodiak Island and got married before wintering back at Lake Alice, where Chelsea was born.

We drove on and on.

"Our baby is such a sweetheart, Matt. I love her so much."

Her plastic port-a-crib was wedged right behind my seat. A jaunty little gingerbread doll with corkscrew curls bobbled from the roll bar, amusing Chelsea for the longest time. And dumb old Goldie would pop her head over the side of the crib and Chelsea would coo and reach for the dog. Then I'd nurse Chelsea or dandle her on my lap until she was ready to sleep again. "You don't realize what a wonderfully good baby she is, Matt. Look at her sleeping like a sweet baby kitten."

He glanced at Chelsea over his shoulder. "Just think in a few years some dirty old biker will be licking her ear." It was such an obscene comment I wanted to cry.

At Rocking Moose Lodge, while Matt was patching the tire, I went inside for breakfast. The lodge's dining room was warm and busy. A girl in a long dress, who spoke with that soft, precise Canadian accent, served me. I fed Chelsea some applesauce, and four hunters came in and ordered about thirty bottles of liquor.

We drove on, planning to stop at Whitehorse for a drink. At Lake Watson, we went into a store, where I got a pair of pink sunglasses. On the way out of town, I persuaded Matt to stop again and leave our "Monroe is Alive in '75" button at the place where everyone posts license plates or bumper stickers or something from their hometown. When we got back in the truck, I sat on my sunglasses and broke them.

As we drove north, I started singing to Chelsea on my lap, my favorite pastime.

"I hope it won't be too long before I can get my hands on a piano." Matt nodded. After going through all the lullabies I knew, I sang "Someday Soon" and changed the last lines to:

> *He loves his damned old fishing boat*
> *As much as he loves me*
> *Someday soon, going with him*
> *Someday soon*

and yodeled at the end. Matt said, "Very good, Mama," and took my hand.

"Maybe we can ship my piano up from Glenn's house. I wonder what's going to happen when he comes back home to Seattle after the season. Won't your parents have a fit if Glenn moves back into his house while Peggy's there and they're living together?" I asked Matt.

"Glenn's been asking her to marry him for years, but she says he's too square," Matt said.

"I bet they'll get married, " I said. "I can't see Glenn telling Peggy to move out."

Matt grunted. "Glenn doesn't have much soul, but he's harmless. Peggy doesn't have anything better to do."

"Matt, that's no reason to get married, and it sure won't see you through the hard times."

"What hard times, Mama?" He took my hand and brought it to his lips and kissed it.

"There's bound to be hard times, Matt."

We stopped again in the afternoon near Lake Tielsen at a peaceful clean coffee shop in the back of another quiet lady's kitchen. I ate raisin pie while smelling fresh bread baking in her oven and listening to a clock chime with muted hammers.

My home is going to be just like this.

We pulled off the highway at the Yukon River so Matt could fulfill one of the Sourdough Requirements by pissing in the river. Whitehorse was so cold and bitter and end-of-the-world that we didn't stop, though shortly after we drove through town we heard a Dairy Queen ad on the radio and it comforted me to know that civilization as I'd known it existed up here. The land looked like it had been burned, scorched in a forest fire. I drove around Destruction Bay as Matt dozed. "Destruction Bay," I said to him, "Do you think it's an omen?"

"Oh, don't be so superstitious."

We left without breakfast the next morning as the sun was rising. It was cold and windy and we drove down terrifying icy mountain roads into Beaver Creek.

We stopped for breakfast at a roadside cafe. A couple from Colorado came in and their baby had a cold, but they didn't have any warm clothes on her. They were headed in the direction we had just come from. "What's the road like that you just traveled?" I asked one of them.

"The stretch we just came is terrible. We were slipping all the way on ice you can't even see." But it wasn't as bad as the whoopee passes, although my stomach was still in kinks.

The Canada-Alaska border was high in the mountains. Matt got out of the Jeep, but I sat still with baby in arms and dog on lap, as the inspector crawled in. He looked for dope in all the places Matt had especially cleaned out, sure they would give us the once-over and determined to be clean. "We're not smoking that shit anymore," Matt said when I asked him where we would get marijuana in Alaska.

After the border it was good old U.S. highway, clear and wide for the most part. After the British Columbian and Yukon wilderness, uninhabited and rustic, I felt like a time traveler, returned back to the America of asphalt and plastic and shopping malls.

Then I drove up and down curvy mountain roads into Anchorage, but it wasn't scary. I could hold onto the wheel and see lights and houses. But there were massive cold glaciers in the near distance.

I can't think of anything bigger or less interested in me than a glacier.

On the road between Anchorage and Homer, I saw hunting country—log-cabin lodges and dense forests full of bear and moose. I wanted to live in Homer when we passed through it. It looked like a neighborly Wild West town with log cabins and flower boxes. We drove through the business area and down the spit to the ferry terminal. We stopped at the Salty Dawg lighthouse tavern for a beer. It was dark inside, with sawdust and dogs on the floor and a jukebox glowing benevolently from a corner.

After buying ferry tickets for Kodiak that night, we went back to cruise the town. I bought a dress and told Matt it was the last dress I'd ever buy. We had time to drop off our dirty clothes at a laundry and have dinner and go back to pick them up—thirty dollars! Matt said, "We've got to get out of here. We're spending money like niggers."

Waiting in line for the ferry, we ran into a fisherman friend of Matt's and his wife—Skip and Fran McEnnis. That evening, after we'd boarded the ferry, with Chelsea asleep in the cabin, we went to the lounge. A blond teenage boy dressed in a homemade collarless shirt, with knee-boots pulled over his pants and a colorful hand-knit wool cap on his head, was sitting with Skip and Fran. He was already glassy-eyed and he slurred his words. A disapproving older man, dressed in the same way as the boy, looked on.

"Who are they?" I asked Matt.

"There's a Russian community called Old Believers at Seldovia. They've got jobs working on a carpentry project in Kodiak."

After a couple of drinks I checked on Chelsea, still asleep in the cabin. When I went back to the lounge, Fran was sitting outside the lounge with the young Russian's wife. She looked foreign and afraid, dressed in a flowered skirt with a kerchief tied over her hair. She was holding a baby and she shook as she cried. Then three older Russian men entered the bar and came out carrying her teenage husband. He had passed out.

"When he wakes up," Fran told her, gesturing with a smile, "you hit him with the cast-iron skillet."

Back in the bar people were singing and yelling. A guy who looked just like Paul Bunyan, with dark beard, plaid shirt, and suspenders, was playing the guitar and singing with a huge smile on his face, but when he stopped the music, he spoke with a painful stutter. I didn't realize the Army still had a cavalry, but that was where he'd learned to be a horseshoer. His wife was a marine biologist and it seemed like their marriage spanned centuries. "L-l-l-little house on the p-p-p-prairie m-meets F-f-f-f-flipper," he stammered.

The rowdy night went on and on. Under my feet I could feel us crossing the Gulf of Alaska to Kodiak. The boat seemed like a huge ice skate skittering rhythmically across the deep rocking sea. At four a.m., the ferry docked in Kodiak and Skip McEnnis was missing. We ran up to his cabin and woke him up and shoved him in his car.

As we drove off the ship, I glanced back. The ferry was berthed in the middle of the channel between town and Near Island. It looked like a huge boat in a small bathtub.

The Baranof House sat right above the dock.

That's the kind of house I want.

It was a 200-year old frame house, built by the Russians when Kodiak was their fur-trading colony. Surrounded by grass and trees, it had a sun porch wrapped around the front, and a cared-for, tended look, painted white with green trim.

Across the street was a two-story building where the post office and Native headquarters were located. The summer before, Matt and I had to go to the clinic in the Native headquarters and have blood tests taken before we were

10

married, and I remember being horrified to see a bloody bandage in the cement stairwell.

Past the Baranof House, we turned onto Mission Road. In the dark starry night, I saw the blue onion domes of the Russian Orthodox church and the widening channel to the outer islands, which the '64 tidal wave had washed right over before slamming into the town. But soon, one mile from the ferry dock, we were "home."

I knew to expect only a plain small house. With my sleepy baby in my arms, I walked down wood steps to a rabbit hutch of a dwelling. The main room to my left was painted a flat blue, furnished with a sofa-daybed and a scarred wooden bureau. The corner where the living room met the leg of the kitchen was occupied by a small oil stove and a steel dinette table. The kitchen, straight ahead of me, had a metal-cabinet sink and cupboards and a small-scale stove and refrigerator. Between the stove and cupboards was a narrow entry to the bathroom. The floor of the bathroom was dark shiny green and the walls were painted a gleaming royal blue. Another narrow passageway, between the sink and the cupboards, led to the bedroom, again painted a cold blue, which led to a smaller bedroom, occupied by iron-frame bunk beds.

We made the bed and crashed. Matt began to snore right away. "My man is here," I thought, and felt comforted, secure.

Then it hit me.

What a move I've made! I can't just call up my friends or go over to Tricia's or Mom's or have lunch downtown; now I'm going to have to be the Mommy and stay good-natured and take care of everybody and make things happy and beautiful and mellow.

I cried like a baby.

Well, we'll just have to work hard, make our fortune, and go back to Seattle.

Matt didn't wake up, even when I backed up to him under the covers.

Maybe this was just meant to be so I can develop and become a better person, and Matt and I can grow even closer and maybe things will be better for Tricia if I'm not around. Who knows where your future's going to head? You just have to think it's going to be better.

Matt slept on.

"You've made the bedroom look like a bordello," Matt laughed and put his arms around me as I did the dishes at the metal sink.

"Do you think it's too much?"

"No, Mama, it's nice. Someday we'll have real stained-glass windows instead of plastic pictures from a calendar...."

"And real curtains instead of purple towels, but the quilt and the rug look good, don't you think? Rich and warm and alive."

We glanced from our bedroom into the small room where Chelsea lay asleep, a tiny little bundle in her steel army bunk.

I ran out of clean clothes for Chelsea, so I wrapped her in my socks and sweater with a scarf tying it all together until I went to the laundromat. She looked like a baby Buddhist monk with her bald head and serene smile and the sash-bound robe to her toes.

The Washtub was right across the road from the boat harbor, where some two hundred boats were docked on three "fingers" that stretched out towards the rock breakwater that protected the harbor from the weather. I dragged pillowcases of wash into the big clean laundromat and put Chelsea in one of the laundry bins while I loaded the washer.

Filthy, bedraggled fishermen came in and took showers in another part of the laundromat. They looked like completely different men when they left, clean and combed, with their eyes open.

While the clothes were drying, I roamed next door to the Wanderers bar with Chelsea in my arms.

Now, with motherhood, I no longer frequent the taverns. I have my own living room.

Inside the Wanderers was a console piano. "Does anyone play this?" I asked the bartender.

"Nah, not really."

"Do you think they'd sell it?" I wanted to play it, but I was afraid to ask.

I imagined having a piano to pound again, and then got carried away thinking of forming a business called Suds, a combination laundromat-bar-daycare center where I could perform for babies and their mothers.

"Nah," the bartender said. "The owner lives Outside. He don't want to be bothered."

I left, feeling dumb, and held Chelsea closer to me.

Two men, Sloopy Don Stevenson and Robbie Wade, came to the front door. "Matt Hunter here?"

I invited them in and gave them coffee, and when Matt got out of the shower, they offered him a job as cook on the *Sea Lion*, Robbie's boat. Robbie and Sloop were both slight and blonde with squinty eyes, but Robbie was just a little taller than me while Sloop was over six feet.

"Fish and Game set a fifteen-million-pound quota for king crab around the island," Robbie said. "Season'll probably last until Christmas. We're fishing around Compass Rose and the west side. Should make it to town about once a week."

"Who you delivering to?" Matt paused from toweling his hair dry.

"New England, over in Gibson Cove."

Robbie lit a cigarette and held it over the palm of his hand while I looked around for an ashtray. "I need a crewman since two guys quit on me when I went to help Davidoff—you know Leo Davidoff?"

"*Maggie J?*"

"Yeah, that's his boat all right. She hit the beach at Viekoda Bay. The Coast Guard picked the crew up from the beach, and the next day we went out there along with the *Ocean Empire* and the *Starlight*, tied lines to the *Maggie J*, and got her afloat. God, she took a pounding, but she's a tough little boat."

"So I'd cook, huh?"

"Oh, you know, just round out the crew and throw some steaks on, mash potatoes, the regular stuff. Gloria says I'm a picky eater, but I don't have time to fuck with it. 'Scuse me." Glenn nodded at me and ground out his cigarette. He got up, scraping his chair across the floor, and shook Matt's hand. "We're on the last finger, leaving tonight around eight. See ya down there."

That night I wanted to go to the Beachcomber to celebrate Matt's job before he left. It was a huge 200-foot ship that was beached in a vacant lot just beyond us on Mission Road. It had been converted to a bar with a dance floor.

"Nora, I'm not going out drinking before I start fishing."

"Just one to celebrate."

"No, it's too scuzzy and degenerate. I'm not taking you there."

We drove down Mission Road to the boat harbor. I carried Chelsea, and Matt carried his duffel bag down the steel ramp to the three-fingered boat dock. Goldie whined and was scared to follow us down the metal grillwork of the ramp, so I took her back to the Jeep while Matt waited. We went to the far side of the dock, with the cannery barges moored on the other side: the *Pacific Pearl*, the *King Crab*, the *Royal Reefer*.

The *Sea Lion* was a 90-foot blue-and-white scow with the pilothouse in the stern of the boat. After squeezing between the locker and four smokestacks, we climbed the outdoor stairs and entered the galley.

It was like a neat, compact apartment. Behind the galley table were two cabins, one of them for Matt. I saw his rifle already on the lower bunk, and Sloopy Don's gear on the top bunk. Then to the left, up two stairs, was the captain's stateroom where a little double bed took up most of the cabin, and the pilothouse, where you could look out, not just to the seas, but also to the booms and deck where all the work is done. It seemed so much less awkward than a boat with the house forward. But a boat looks prettier, more balanced when the pilothouse is ahead of the deck.

13

I'm alone at last in Alaska. It's so quiet at home, now that Matt's gone. I'm thinking about parties and old friends and wondering what to do next, now that it's up to me instead of following somebody else. I want to surround Chelsea with a beautiful harvest feeling, a mellow secure childhood. I wonder about me, do I have what it takes?

Last night I dreamed I owned a rooming house, old and funky, with transoms above the doors and tile floors and wood paneling like on ships. There were lots of people there and I worried about meeting Matt later.

I hope I can get a carpet for the bathroom at tomorrow's rummage sales. I hate walking barefoot on the naked floors. It's not the cold here—it's the wind. When I walk down Mission Road towards town and see mountains coming out of the water I feel like I'm poised at the top curvature of the globe, ready to lift off, and then I get an earthbound feeling. It's stark here, elemental, not exciting or lush. I'm longing for something and I don't know what—distraction? I hate to think I'm hooked on the rat race.

Maybe I should stop thinking and roll up my sleeves and actually do something: scour the beaches, learn Russian, write some songs. I think the temporary solution will be giving up cleaning house, totally except for cooking. The future is so far distant, I might as well forget about it for five or ten years—maybe twenty!

Matt pulled up in a taxi one night just as I was headed for bed.

"We just came to town to deliver, then we're going back out again."

He held me close and I burrowed into him. "I'm so glad you're home. We missed you. Let's just stay in bed all day tomorrow."

"No, Mama, I'm just home now because the cannery's unloading another boat. They'll take the *Sea Lion*'s crab first thing in the morning. I've got to set the alarm for five-thirty."

I dreamed that I was pregnant and pulled up to a dock on a raft. I tried to jump onto the dock. I could hardly clear a foot. I stood on the inflated side of the raft and still couldn't jump to the dock, where a doctor was trying to find a blue-baby kit in his supplies. I finally got onto the dock, but the doctor sent me in another boat to a hospital. I saw all these boats pulling into dock and wondered how Matt was going to know I was there. I was so worried and then I woke up and I was still worried.

Matt stirred in his sleep, too. I said, "What are you dreaming of?"

"Oh, a boat," he said. "The *Carrie Lynn* is for sale. She's such a pretty boat. I'd love to have her."

He left the next day.

That fall was unusually cold and snowy, even for Kodiak. I'd take Chelsea for little walks down unpaved Mission Road and curse the drivers who spit gravel onto us because they wouldn't slow down. Matt wanted to get out of our "rabbit hole" as soon as possible, but there wasn't much choice of places to live.

The TV station hooked up our reception and we were able to see videotapes sent from Seattle, about a week delayed. They showed the World Series and got the tapes mixed up, so they played the beginning of the game and then the final innings and then the middle of the game.

There was only one channel for shows and another channel for the "Scanner." It worked like classified ads, with short messages flipping across the screen to the sound of the only radio station. Paul Harvey reported three times a day and the marine forecast was broadcast hourly to the tune of "Sailor's Hornpipe." There was a talk show with country-western singers discussing the difference between "real" country and "Hollywood" country.

I watched Dinah Shore every afternoon, disdainfully at first—she was so bourgeois—then eagerly. One afternoon a black singer was her guest, talking about growing up in the ghetto and how her mother would point out houses with clean windows or neat gardens and say to her, "Hope lives here."

Before we came up, Matt told me that land was $100 an acre and we could build a log cabin, but the only houses available were a log house for $150,000 and a flimsy Aleutian home, one of the houses in the development between town and Pillar Mountain, tiny little mongrel huts shipped up from somewhere Outside after World War II. They were originally meant for Guantanamo Bay in Cuba and looked like the wind would blow them away. They all had the same floor plan, though people remodeled them, making living areas out of the garage, or jacking up the one level and adding a second story underneath. But the Aleutian homes neighborhood looked like a shantytown, with dirt roads, rickety sheds for fishing gear, abandoned vehicles and snowmobiles parked out front, and no trees or shrubbery. At least our rented shack had some individuality.

It was snowing as I went to bed one night, missing Matt, hoping he'd surprise me in the middle of the night. I slept until I heard soft footsteps come down the wood stairs and a knock came. I knew it wasn't Matt. "Who's there?"

"Uh, my name is, uh, Diane. I was just wondering if you have a knife."

"You want a knife? What do you want a knife for?" I said from behind the door, my toes curling on the icy floor.

"Well, I've got some cocaine here, but I have to chop it up. Do you have a razor?"

Even our belligerent crowd down in Seattle wouldn't have done this. She wasn't showing off to be obnoxious; she had to get her coke chopped up so she could get it up her nose. Her recklessness scared me.

"You want a razor blade to chop up your cocaine?"

"Yeah, I just came from the Beachcomber."

"No, uh, no—I don't have a razor. My husband's out fishing."

"Oh...."

I heard her footsteps climb up the stairs and crunch away on the snowy street. What kind of cocaine could have made its way up here? I wondered. It must have been stepped on a hundred times, probably with Drano.

I haven't met many folks here. Sometimes I see Skip or Fran McEnnis or the horseshoer and his wife on the street, but no real friends yet. That takes time.

I spend a lot of my time knitting—a sweater for Chelsea and an Irish fisherman's scarf for Matt's Christmas present. I enjoy knitting, even unraveling tangled balls of yarn. The tedium of it lulls my mind, yet I'm doing something and it's got some continuity to it.

The Katmai volcano across Shelikof Strait on the Alaskan Peninsula has been trying to erupt the last couple of days and the air seems foggy, but actually it's superfine volcanic ash and inside it looks like I haven't dusted for years, like Miss Haversham's house.

I went to the Baranof House and among the samovars and stuffed otters and fish traps, looked at old photographs of Kodiak. I was hoping to buy some to take home to decorate the walls, but there weren't any copies available. There were pictures from the last Katmai eruption in 1912, and it looked like two feet of snow blanketed town.

It started snowing on Halloween and hasn't gone away yet. It's been really cold too, 14 degrees today. I read that we're due for a severe winter this year, and being so close to the ocean, the wind is ferocious and makes the cold seem even more penetrating. Goldie's out in the snow now, barking for me to come and play with her. Fat chance.

My secret to bundling up is putting on layer after layer of clothes, wool preferably, until I can't bend my knees or elbows, hoisting Chelsea on my back in a pack with her drooling down the crack between my neck and my collar, and staggering outdoors.

So I am pretty happy here. I love being able to see Matt on a casual working week basis, instead of not seeing him for months and then getting so excited when he comes home that I'm all tied up in knots.

I love having my little girl too. She is such an accepting baby, like right now she's dangling in her Jolly Jumper, smelling the bread baking in the oven and grinning at me as I sit and pay no attention to her. As long as the house is warm and I keep it clean, I feel like I can keep on top of the rest. Hope lives here.

The landlord forbade us to have any pets, so whenever a knock came to the door, I'd rush to put Goldie into the closet until I found out if it was the landlord or not. Late one afternoon, I went to the library where I discovered Bobby Short records. I left Goldie roaming outside the library, and it wasn't until I got back home that I realized she was missing. I went back in the twilight to retrieve her and saw a shivering little city-dog greet us nervously. Gail's parting words about neglecting Goldie plucked at my conscience.

Matt was out fishing on Thanksgiving, so I made a chicken dinner for Chelsea and myself and told us that it wasn't an important holiday. Chelsea bounced in her swing in front of the refrigerator where I'd taped pictures of chimpanzees and rainbows to stimulate her imagination. After I sang torch songs with Bobby Short, I rocked Chelsea to sleep with the Clancy Brothers' Irish folk songs.

October winds blow wild and rough
In the Castle of Dromore
Take heed, young eaglet , 'til thy wings
Are feathered thick to soar....

The king crab season around the island ended early in December. We were wrong in thinking we'd have enough money to fly home for Christmas, just as we were wrong in thinking we could buy land at $100 an acre. But it was nice to have Matt home the whole month of December, even though we didn't have any money to spare.

One afternoon, while Chelsea napped, I traced pictures from my childhood fairy tale book, rolled out salt dough, and cut the pictures out with a knife. I carefully baked the ornaments and then colored them from a child's watercolor paint box. I made fairy bears, mermaids, trolls, and flute-playing gremlins for the tree.

Another day we drove out to Cape Chiniak to find our own Christmas tree. The day was snowy and cold, and we tramped knee-high through snow across the rocky fields. It was almost dark at three in the afternoon when we cut the little tree down and dragged it back to the Jeep. We decorated the tree with the salt dough fairies and a few ornaments I'd bought at the Christmas bazaar.

Christmas Day was very quiet and holy. We had presents by the tree, simple homemade gifts: Matt's scarf, a small carved bear for me, a sweater for Chelsea, lots of toys and trinkets from the relatives. Matt's mother sent us all brown-and-white checkered lumberman's jackets for Christmas, like the three bears. My Mom sent a set of twelve fragile glass-etched cordial glasses.

We all napped in the afternoon, wrapped in the warm and binding smell of the turkey cooking in the oven.

Matt's sister Peggy called to say she and Glenn had just announced to the family that they were getting married. "We're combining it with a gambling trip to Las Vegas over New Year's," she babbled happily.

I'd put everything I'd been baking for Christmas on the table, and we sat down to an intimate family banquet. After dinner we drank liqueur, listened to records, and went to bed.

CHAPTER TWO

WINTER BLUES
In which I contract cabin fever and misbehave;
we return to Seattle for two months

The tanner crab season began in January. Slimmer, more spidery-looking than king crab, the tanners were less expensive and sold mostly to the Japanese. The fishermen used the same seven-foot-square cages of rope and iron bars as they did for the king crab, but set wood "doors" to trap the smaller crab.

Robbie Wade did so well during king crab, despite the days off helping fix the *Maggie J*, that he stayed home to remodel his house. So his brother, Fred, ran the *Sea Lion*. It bothered Matt when Fred's wife would call to say, "Fred wants to go out tomorrow morning. Be at the boat at four."

"What is she, his secretary?" Matt grumbled.

It bothered me that his wife went out fishing with them, and even more, that Matt said her figure was as good as mine.

The boat took weeklong trips to set and harvest the pots and bring the crab to the canneries in town for freezing. Matt stayed in town just long enough to sleep and eat one meal before going back out around the island or across Shelikof Strait to the Alaskan Peninsula.

At first, Goldie slept curled up next to Chelsea on the iron bunk bed. She kept Chelsea from rolling off the edge of the bunk.

But one night I heard the springs creak from the baby's bunk and then the dog growling. I jumped up and ran to the bedroom. When I got to the bedroom door, Chelsea had her head up and was chortling, reaching out to Goldie. Still, I thought I'd better get the baby her own bed so there wasn't a turf war on the bunk. I ordered a crib from Sears.

When the crib came to the post office, I lugged the huge boxes into the jeep and drove home. With Chelsea still strapped in her car seat, I dragged the boxes down the steps into the house. I shook out all the 157 nuts, rods, springs, and screws on the dinette table and started to cry.

Then I brought Chelsea in and we had some lunch and I put her to bed and sat down fresh, determined to decipher the puzzle. For a person who'd never been able to figure out combination locks, it was an engineering feat, but reading directions helped tremendously. I made one big mistake and put a side up backwards, so I unscrewed a thousand bolts and undid it and screwed them in again right.

"I am woman, hear me roar...."

At times of frustration with Chelsea, I look to the pair of framed Madonnas that Mom gave me at Confirmation—the Madonna of the Streets and the Gran Duke Madonna. Misunderstood, threatened—she knew how it felt. "Hail Mary...," I began, for the first time in sincerity since grade school.

Sundays always seem to expose the reality of life to me—a composed, mellow mood, sitting in a cloud-darkened room and choosing not to turn on lights as twilight rapidly changes to dark.

Yesterday Chelsea went down for a late nap. I made a cup of tea and turned on Masterpiece Theater *and settled myself. It was the series "Shoulder to Shoulder," the story of the suffragette movement in England. The righteousness of their cause was obvious, but oh God, I hadn't considered their sacrifice. I prayed that I'd never have to become dedicated to a struggle as unpopular as women's rights, knowing guiltily, of course, that I benefited from their commitment.*

It was cold and drizzly outside and the television episode concerned the hunger strike and forced feedings in prison. The suffragettes' determination to resist, their rebellious spirit and frail ravaged bodies disturbed my composed, restful Sunday, a day to contemplate things holy, things non-material and not of this world. The day when you sit home, the world leaves you alone, and you can most feel the essence of yourself.

One wintry day I stopped at a "Plants for Sale" sign by the road that led past the old Russian dock to the canneries, Northern Pacific's electric-blue barge next to Whitney-Fidalgo's bright yellow building.

I found a little fairy-tale house surrounded by car and boat machinery. I walked on a narrow plank path to the door and the lady let me into her tiny neat house with plants climbing all the paned windows.

Chelsea was struggling to get out of her backpack, but the little house was so crowded, I couldn't cut her loose. The lady had a plate of sandwiches and a chocolate cake with a cherry on top on the table. "I'm expecting my mister home for lunch pretty soon," she said. "He owns the machine shop down the road."

With the sunlight streaming in on her neatly arranged little haven, a noontime meal on the table waiting for her man, it was like a beautiful, cozy dream. I got two little containers of geranium starts and left.

I slipped on the ice walking back home and fell heavily to the pavement. Chelsea was in the backpack and her cheek hit the aluminum frame. I disentangled Chelsea from the backpack, took a deep breath and comforted her and then collected myself and stepped carefully back home. When she got a black eye from the fall, Chelsea looked like an urchin-baby with her two snaggly bottom teeth and bruised face.

Matt came in late one night and said we'd go for a drive around the country the next day. In the morning, though, Sloopy Don called and asked Matt if he wanted to go hunting.

I was disappointed, but also glad that Matt was making buddies, and Sloop seemed like a nice guy. When we went over to his trailer, he told me how his mom would chase him out of the house when he was a bad little kid and he would play with his dog in the kennel until his dad came home.

Before Matt left, I handed him a coffee can and asked him to get me some sand from the beach for my plants. While Matt was gone, I stayed home and made raisin pie, patting myself on the back for being a good sport, wondering if Matt would invite Sloop in to join us for dinner, or if we'd all go out when they got back from hunting.

Matt walked in just as it was getting dark and said they'd gotten a deer and that he and Sloop were going to butcher it in the basement. So they dragged it down the outdoor stairs on the side of the house and into the basement.

After Sloop left, Matt went to the hardware store and came back home with a bucket and a mop and some floor cleaner. He got on my case about the house.

"I was ashamed to ask Sloop into the house. It's a mess, Eleanor."

He'd call me Eleanor when he was mad at me, and I hated it. It made me feel like a kid getting into trouble again.

"It's not a mess, Matt. It's just cluttered." I thought it looked homey, although maybe in a poverty-stricken way. The Oriental rug was too big for the living room and ran up the wall at one side. The curtains were a striped Moroccan rug and an Indian bedspread that kept out the cold. I'd tacked artwork and liner notes from record albums on the walls and hung clothes over three chairs in front of the oil stove to dry. A glass gallon jar of homemade yogurt was stewing on the shelf next to the stove.

I guess the bad things were Bobby Short on the stereo crooning Gershwin songs and the Christmas tree still up in the corner. When the door slammed, a rain of needles would shower down, but I thought it amused Matt.

I was stung, especially since I'd thought it was our private joke. But when Matt thought other people were looking, he was ashamed of me.

I drove past the Island Bakery and it was all shut down, with a chain and padlock across the front door. The bakery was one of the few places I could go and feel comfortable—also the tiny bookstore where the owner constantly argued over the phone with his mother about why he wasn't out fishing with his father, and the furniture store, filled with beautiful, expensive things.

The bakery had that pure flour-and-yeast smell, and even though mud and slush covered the linoleum floor where the customers stood, the baking area behind the glass and aluminum counters was clean. I'd go in the bakery to absorb the smells and warmth.

The last time I'd been in there, someone complimented Chelsea and the talk turned to babies and the baker popped up. "Babies, babies, babies! Whatever happened to zero population growth! Doesn't anyone care that we're all going to starve to death by the year 2000?" He looked at me as if I was the one eating his share.

How come my baby provokes zero growth comments?

When I picked up my mail at the post office, I heard people talking about what happened at the bakery. They said the owner went on a binge one night and smashed all the machinery and destroyed everything.

"Now what's going to happen? Will we all have to bake our own bread?" I asked the postal clerk.

"No, they'll fly it in from Outside, like everything else."

There were two churches across Mission Road from us—the Seventh Day Adventists and Jehovah's Witnesses. Every Saturday morning an evangelist would knock at the door to preach to me. At first I took their pamphlets and thanked them. I read one, but the talk of Last Judgment and damnation awoke all the old Catholic memories of wickedness and guilt.

I saw a piano in the Jehovah's Witness meeting room and called on the minister to ask if I could practice on it, but he said, "No, it would get too involved."

Once a week some Mormon missionaries came to visit. They always wore white shirts and ties and dark suits and looked so formal and clean-cut for Kodiak. We discussed religion, mostly theirs, which I admired for its Swiss-like organization and brotherhood. I agreed to read their Book of Mormon, but it seemed like I'd just gotten past the first chapter when God gave a message for somebody to kill somebody else.

How can you tell if it's a holy vision or a crazy hallucination?

I asked the missionaries. "Who's to judge the holiness of Joseph Smith's mission against the evil of Charles Manson's? What if you're wrong in your sincerity?"

"Well, Joseph Smith is the founder of Mormonism. As the Bible says, 'By your fruits ye shall know them,'" the missionary said.

They brought me their women's magazine to read, and it made me long for a kindred spirit in homemaking and child raising. I didn't realize myself how strongly I felt, until they asked me to join their Ladies' Society. "Don't you see, if I join them and become friends and share experiences, I'll feel like a hypocrite, I'll have to believe in things that don't make sense to me, or just be a fair-weather Mormon, along for the ride?" I started to cry. They squirmed and looked uncomfortable.

It struck me as a lot of convoluted thinking, building on social need to determine the doctrine by which we condemn each other. I was already trying to square the convictions I was raised with and what my conscience told me. Why did I have to join their religion to be friends?

I got a flat tire while I was at the post office. I just left the Jeep there, and was so relieved when Matt got home in the middle of the night and said he would fix it after unloading crab the next morning.

I saw the missionaries in town while I was grocery shopping the next day and they said they'd noticed the Jeep sitting there with a flat. "Do you need us to help you change the tire?"

It felt so good to say, "My husband's fixing it." I almost felt a little cruel, I said it with such relish, but I didn't know how I could face them if they did me favors and I still rejected their religion.

A few weeks later, Matt came home one night after midnight. I'd gone to bed and locked the door, as usual. I woke up to hear muffled pounding, threw on my bathrobe and ran to the door, looked through the curtains and let Matt in. Doug Bradley was standing behind him. "Look who I found at the bar," Matt said. We were standing in the kitchen, Matt hugging me through the thick padding of my bathrobe. "Robbie's got a full crew on the *Sea Lion*, but I think I can find Doug something on another boat."

It was so good to have someone I knew from the old days come visit me and see my life through eyes that knew me before Kodiak. Doug slept on the sofa. The next morning over coffee, Doug said, "Well, Nora, you've got your dollhouse and your little dolly and Matt's out wrestling the sea. Looks like everybody's happy."

"I really miss my piano. I wish I could get it up here," I said.

"That'll cost Matt a fortune," Doug said.

"If it keeps a smile on her face, it's worth it," Matt hollered from the bathroom where he was shaving.

"Yeah, I guess keeping a smile on her face is too big a job for you, Hunter—here she's locking you out of your own house at night."

23

I didn't say anything then, but later I asked Matt what that crack was all about.

"Well, why are you locking the door on me? Who did you expect to see when you looked through the window?"

"Matt, that's not fair. If you're worried about me, you should stay home and keep a close watch on me. I'm going to lock the door if you're not here. Who knows what could come to my door?"

"Right. I guess you're the only one who knows that."

"Matt, I married you for life. You're mine and I'm yours and I'd kill you if you were messing around."

"I like the way you turned that around, Mama," Matt chuckled, and backed me into the wall before he put his arms around me.

"Matt, don't torment me like that. I want you home, I don't want you ever to go, but if you have to fish, you have to go. Don't make me out to be the one who's pushing you away."

We get to go home! Matt says after tanner season ends Robbie is going to switch engines in his boat and will pay for Matt to work in the shipyard in Seattle for the next couple of months. And of course Chelsea and I get to go, too!

We talked to Glenn and Peggy, who want us to stay with them in their house in West Seattle, so Chelsea and I will fly down and Matt will join us when he brings the Sea Lion *down.*

The tanner season finally wound down. Robbie and his wife Gloria, Fred and his wife Jennie, and Matt and I went out to dinner at the Kodiak Inn, overlooking the boat harbor. Photographs of the '64 tidal wave lined the halls and there was a picture of the *Sea Lion* sitting dry between the hotel and the hardware store, washed half a mile uptown by a wave.

It was the first time in months that we had been out. I got to dress up, go out in public with my husband and our friends, and I blew it. When the waiter asked us what we wanted to drink, I ordered dirty mother doubles with vodka and Kahlua and cream that tasted like milk shakes, but they went straight to my head and I rattled on and on. I was having such a good time that I didn't even know Matt was mad until he signed the check, got up, and left without a glance at me. I trailed behind him.

He yelled at me in the Jeep as we went to pick up Chelsea at the babysitter's. "Just what the hell are you trying to do, come across like some tramp? What were you doing, telling them how free it would feel to run naked through the woods?"

I cried all night. The next morning my eyelids were swollen and puffy. I felt wrung out like a dirty washcloth. Finally Matt said, "Well c'mon, it's not the end of the world."

He doesn't understand shame. I just want to squirm out of my body. I want to wipe out their memory of me.

"If I could just go back and make it never to have happened," I wailed to Matt, after catching another look at my bedraggled self in the mirror.

"Well, we've all made fools out of ourselves at one time or another," Matt shrugged and his shoulder hit the doorjamb when he went out the door. He left for one more trip on the *Sea Lion* to bring in the last of Robbie's pots and store them at the New England yard.

I can't seem to shake the mood I'm in. I want to be happy. I know I can be happy, but I seem to be increasingly depressed and frustrated. My spirit feels depleted and I just can't find anything to restore it. Last night I woke at three. I had some ice cream and started crying and first I thought, "At least now you can cry without upsetting Chelsea," and then I realized, "It's okay, loneliness is a valid thing to cry about."

Then I thought the answer was to become like a child who has no say in what happens to her. I remembered the numb "whatever happens, happens" feeling I had after Sam died.

I keep thinking of the old places in Seattle like Volunteer Park, the Art Museum and Conservatory, the ferryboats, the Public Market, the mysterious alleys and backyards of Capitol Hill. Chelsea is so comforting in Matt's absence, but her needs are so absolute. When I see her asleep, I long to love her and nourish her, but when she's awake, it upsets me to have her wriggle when I'm changing her or struggle when I'm trying to get her in her high chair. My good humor sounds so false and my stoicism seems so cold, and I just fight the situation. Maybe when she's a little older, she'll be more fun, but in her waking hours now I'm constantly trying to figure out what she wants, taking things out of her way, or shushing her screams.

I don't know me these days. I don't know why I'm so upset and lifeless. I don't have faith that things aren't a big deal, that it doesn't matter, that it will all work out. I sweat the small stuff. I think if I just had some kind of way of letting it all out. But then I get into scenes like when we went out to dinner. I just wish Matt were home.

We stayed with Peggy and Glenn in their little house in West Seattle overlooking Puget Sound. The guest room was all white and gold with Peggy's bedroom furniture from her parent's house. There were green plants and it looked all bright and light and airy. Chelsea slept in a crib in Glenn's office across the hall from our room.

Glenn was getting the *Destiny*, Karl Lundquist's boat, ready to take up north for the salmon-tendering season. Glenn had been running it the summer that Matt and I got married in Alitak. One night that summer, Glenn had a party on board, and early in the morning some drunk beat in another guy's head with a lead pipe and he had to be med-evacced out by the Coast Guard helicopter.

The next spring, Matt fixed the *Destiny* all up while I was pregnant with Chelsea, with the understanding that Karl would let Matt run it that summer. I helped Matt paint the deck a few days before Chelsea came and fell getting off the boat, so I went through childbirth with skinned knees.

Then, when it was time to head north fishing and Matt had the *Destiny* all ready to go in perfect shape, Karl stepped in and took over, making Matt just a crewmember. Karl could do whatever he wanted; he owned the boat. Matt had arranged for Jamie to go along with them as cook that summer, and Jamie, never one to be humble, bickered with Karl the whole time with Matt impatiently caught in the middle.

While Matt worked on the *Sea Lion*, he and Glenn would leave together in the morning for the shipyards across town. Peggy would make breakfast and I'd clean up. Then Peggy would shower while I took Chelsea for a walk in the old stroller that Mom brought over. I loved our strolls. In the morning we'd feel all fresh and wakening, seeing all the different houses where the different people lived, watching the ferries plow through the blue Sound, smelling the green and damp nudges and the tender flowery hints—California under a layer of dew.

I met Maureen and Tessa, my old friends from high school, for drinks at F.X. McRory's one night. Tessa had left her husband and Maureen had lost a lot of weight and the two of them talked about their shrinks. I told them my problems with Matt working so hard and being so distant and they encouraged me to see a counselor myself.

The following weekend we spent across the Sound at Mom's in Shine. Jamie and Gail came over Saturday, and Matt and Jamie left to get beer. Gail and I waited for hours for them to come back, but they were gone all day.

Matt and Jamie and Gail had all lived together at one time, when Matt was going to tech school and Jamie worked at his father's tavern. Gail reminded me of how wild Matt could be. "I remember the night Matt came home drunk and pulled us naked out of bed and then made us go back out drinking with him. He did an Al Jolson routine on top of the bar."

"He never cuts loose like that with me. It's like he thinks I'm his warden. I'd like to have fun with him too."

I showed Gail the bucket of crab teeth that had been soaking and decomposing for a week.

"Good God, that reeks! What are you saving them for?"

"They're ivory, Gail. I'm going to clean them and make necklaces out of them."

I talked her into sitting there on the grass and pulling the guts off the teeth.

Gail had beautiful hands and fingernails. "My hands smell like crab."

"But it's not a rotting, stuffy, gagging smell, it's a clean rough smell, a deep sea smell. I don't mind that—what I'd hate is spending all my days in the tavern with that dark, wet, beery smell."

She stopped cleaning crab teeth to drag on a cigarette. "We're getting out of it."

"You are?" If she could get Jamie out of his dad's tavern, maybe fishing wasn't the only life for Matt.

"Yeah, I talked him out of it. We went to Hawaii for a couple of weeks last winter, and I said to Jamie, 'Isn't this wonderful? No drunks, no fights, no employees, no cleaning, no family hassles. Let's sell the tavern and live off what I make at the clinic and leave all the drunks and the druggies behind.' He agreed and now the tavern's up for sale. And he's going to quit dealing, too."

"Wow, Gail—I never thought he'd leave his dad's tavern. I mean, the coke and all is so dangerous, but the tavern at least is legal.... "

"Maybe he can go fishing with Matt if the money gets tight."

"Oh, but Gail, he'd be gone so long, you'd miss him."

"Not if he was bringing in money—clean money."

We waited for them to return all afternoon. About eight that evening we heard them drive up. I was so mad I thought I'd explode. Rather than do that, I took a bath. I heard Gail: "Where'd you rats go?"

"Rats, huh?" I heard Matt say.

"Yeah, you dirty rats," she said in a gangster voice, and giggled.

I sizzled in the tub like water dropped on a hot greased pan. *We wait all afternoon for them to show up and now its some big joke and everybody's happy?*

When I got out, Matt tried to show me the fish he'd caught. I closed my eyes and refused to look at it. Jamie said, "Oh, Nora's pouting."

"You could have just called us to let us know not to sit around all day waiting for you to show up. Next time we'll just leave." But I didn't want to leave. I wanted them to have fun with us, to want to be with us.

I picked Matt up at the shipyard after work one night and we had dinner at a Hungarian restaurant on the way home. Chelsea was such a good baby. Matt stuck her bonnet on backwards so it looked like an aviator's helmet. The owner came over to us, beamed at Chelsea and said, "Good baby," and I felt so squared away in my little family.

For my birthday, Peggy looked after Chelsea so that Matt and I could go to Twin Lakes in eastern Washington for the weekend with Jamie and Gail in our car, and Doug and Rita Bradley and Fitz and Lisa Paisley in their car.

Before we left, Peggy helped me make chocolate chip cookies and potato salad, and then I picked Matt up at the boatyard. We met everyone else in the parking lot of the dental clinic where Gail worked. I felt so liberated and fancy-free.

"*Free at last…*" I sang.

"Right, Nora, with just a husband and baby," Gail said. "Here, have some Southern Comfort." She handed me the bottle and we passed it back and forth, sipping until she passed out.

Matt and Jamie, in the front seat, saw a deer on the road and slowed down. "Hey, we could get it. Bring some meat home," Matt said.

"Yeah, okay! Pull over here, Matt," Jamie said.

Gail roused to protest. "C'mon, you guys. Don't shoot Bambi. Leave him alone."

"Hey, it would be great," Jamie said as Matt pulled off to the side of the road.

Oh hell, are they really going to do this? Are Gail and I going to sit in the car while they go off on their Great White Hunter scheme? These guys play a game where they're the bad boys and we're the mommies who are supposed to yell and warn them, and they act up anyway to show their independence.

But I didn't want to kill and butcher a deer. That wouldn't be fun or right. The male macho brain would take over and it would turn into a big mess. I had to say something.

"Oh sure, you guys are going to track that deer all the way from the highway and then butcher it and put the bloody carcass in Gramma Hunter's white car—I'm so sure."

Jamie shook his big shaggy head. "Why sure, Eleanor. Matt's mommy loves him. She won't care." He laughed and then Matt floored the accelerator.

When we finally stopped at the resort, it was nearly midnight. Rita got out of her car and snapped at Doug, "You've been on my case the whole trip. Why don't you quit drinking? You might be less belligerent."

"You just shut up, woman."

Matt fished most of the weekend, and I slept most of the weekend. Doug and Rita continued the fight they had begun on the way and their mood began to infect everyone. It rained off and on all day Saturday.

Finally, Sunday morning, we started packing to go home when the men got the bright idea to try another fishing spot. By then I was climbing the walls to get home again; I missed Chelsea terribly.

After three hours on the road home, I started crying. I ached to hold my baby again. I was in the corner of the back seat and at first no one noticed. But when Matt looked back at me in the rear-view mirror, he was shocked. "What's the matter?"

"I just want to be home," I bawled.

"Well, take it easy, we'll be home pretty soon."

But not before we stopped at another fishing spot and got out of the cars. Rita said to Doug, "Drink, drink, drink! I'm so sick of your drinking. That's all you live for!"

Jamie tossed his empty bottle into the brush and took another from under the seat. He said, "Hey, who wants a swig? Dougie, you bad boy?"

Doug took the bottle from Jamie, downed a great swallow and grinned triumphantly at Rita. I thought of apes establishing their dominance with hostile grins.

A Monday morning with Chelsea all screwed up. Who's her mommy? Will she go again? Where is she now?

I feel ugly and am thirsting for a shower and a clean face. But Chelsea's up and must be watched.

Glenn and Peggy, Jamie and Gail, and Matt and I were playing poker at home. Matt's folks gave Glenn and Peggy a plot of land to build a house on and they were all excited, talking about house plans throughout the game.

The pot got higher and higher and Matt won a couple of hundred dollars in one hand. He jumped up from the table, laughing madly like I'd never heard him before, and strutted in the kitchen to get a bottle of beer. We were all rowdy, but I felt a little pang that he didn't even look at me, that he felt so untied to me.

Much later, after Jamie and Gail had left and Glenn and Peggy had gone to bed, I came into the living room. Matt was sitting in a chair by himself. I almost felt like an intruder when I knelt down in front of him and said, "Don't you feel kind of bad about your Mom and Dad giving Peggy and Glenn that land? Kind of like the kid that got left out?"

"Yeah," he sighed, "but no one's ever given me anything and no one ever will."

My poor old loner.

With his winnings from the card game, Matt took us all to dinner in Chinatown a few nights later. Afterwards we roamed around looking for nightlife, getting sillier and more obnoxious. We went to a lounge in a hotel and I was getting nervous about how wild we were. The rest of the crowd was listening politely to the piano player. But I thought we enhanced the atmosphere, livened it up.

The bouncer, a big square-set man with a little head, leaned over our table and said, "You folks are disturbing everyone else. Quiet down." We got up together and left.

Up the street was a nightclub where we could dance and rock on. We were all crushed in a booth on a mezzanine, raised three feet above the dance floor. I sat closest to the railing, opposite Matt. I noticed a group of tough-looking men eyeing me. I got nervous. "Gail," I said, "they're going to ask me to dance."

"Show them your ring finger," she shouted back to me, clapping in time to the music.

That's no help. Matt will just get mad at me. Why can't they see that I'm with a group? I belong with my husband. Maybe Matt will forbid me to dance with a stranger.

A guy with a grizzled beard in a studded black leather jacket approached me, leaned over the railing and asked me to dance. "No, uh no," I said, and then, without annoyance or passion, just to punctuate my refusal, I picked up my glass and tossed my drink at him. He stepped back in surprise and turned to his friends.

I looked to Gail. "What do I do now?"

She stopped clapping, took a drag on her cigarette, started clapping again and smiled brightly. "Just keep laughing," she said through clenched teeth.

Another man from the crowd approached me and flicked his lighter under my chin. "You think you're hot stuff, bitch. Don't you try that shit again."

I looked across at Matt, whose grinning white teeth reassured me. Later I asked him, "What were you thinking?"

"Oh, I was just seeing my teeth going down my throat."

"Oh, you don't understand," I said to the stranger. "See, I'm from Alaska, and we're here on vacation with our friends...."

"Don't ever!" The group of men moved away.

Why did I do that? Why did that turn out so bad? Why did he come on to me, not Peggy or Gail? Was I asking for it?

Without anybody saying anything, we got up as if going to the restrooms and Gail led the way out the side exit. She leaned back against the door and fell out. She regained her balance, but a pearl-handled knife fell out of her pocket and clattered down the steps.

"Do you believe that?" she laughed. "I almost killed myself."

"Well, Nora tried to get us all killed," Peggy said, and I felt terrible.

We met the men out front by the cars. On the way home I died over and over, Peggy saying from the front seat, "You just needed to show off a little." I was so glad to hear her excuse me, her jibe didn't even sting.

The next day I called Maureen and asked her where she'd found her counselor.

I went to the mental health clinic behind a big shopping center. Scary and irreverent thoughts were bouncing around the unpadded walls of my mind.

She entered the clinic, never to come out again.
No, no, it was a dental clinic she went into.
I've always known she was crazy....
Isn't West Seattle where Frances Farmer got her start?
If she's so smart, why can't she act normal?

It looked like every other medical clinic inside. A small, middle-aged woman who was the picture of cool hands and common sense took me to an office, where we sat and talked.

"My behavior is embarrassing and scaring me, and I have nightmares where those who know me best are laughing at me, refusing to understand. I feel unconnected and invisible all the time, and I feel so sad I start crying without warning."

She said, "The bad news is, with only four weeks before you go back to Alaska, counseling can shore you up, but not fix what's wrong. You've gone through a drastic change of being around a large number of people with no sense of responsibility to being alone with a great responsibility. It's obvious you're living too much for that baby. You have to get out by yourself at least once a day for an hour."

"But I have lots of hobbies. I read and sew and knit...."

"Out of the house. By yourself."

"Once a day for an hour sounds like so little, but it's so much, arranging for a sitter and finding something to do. There's nothing to do besides fish, go to bars, and get into trouble. If Chelsea doesn't come with me, how can I barge in somewhere alone?"

"You've got to do it. The good news is your reactions are normal, natural, given your isolation. You don't need electric-shock therapy or mood elevators. Every new mother is lonely."

After my counseling sessions, when I'd come back to Peggy's, I'd tell her I'd been shopping, but Matt would listen while I gave him a detailed retelling of each meeting.

"You didn't tell her what a brute I am, dragging you up to Alaska with me?"

"No, Matt. She did seem surprised that you go fishing for fun whenever you're not working on a boat. She said it's the classic busman's holiday. But it's me—I'm the problem. I feel so alone. I don't blame you."

"I don't think a shrink can tell you anything about yourself you don't already know."

"Maybe not, but at least she tells me I'm not crazy to feel crazy, and she doesn't expect me to feel mellow and together."

My brother Jack came by one afternoon while Chelsea was napping. Jack had on his painter's overalls and carried a six-pack of beer. We sat on the deck, drinking beer and watching the billowy clouds bounce around the sky over the Olympic Mountains and the boughs of the huge pine trees swaying in the wind.

"You know, I'm glad to see you married to Matt. He's a good man and those other guys you were hanging around with were up to no good." Jack seemed to forget that he was the one who had fixed me up with some of those guys. "It's okay to be alone, but it's better to be with someone."

I was touched. This was the brother who used to brag that he never hit me as hard as he could have, and here he was talking to me like he cared about my happiness. "Yeah, but Jack, which is worse—to be independent and alone or to be married and alone?"

"Yeah, that's the hell of it, all right."

Where have I been, in a fugue of some strange sort? I could weed the dandelions out of the lawn or stroll Chelsea in the early morning. My day is so full of doing, doing little things. And more and more little kid things. Right now, I have to open the gate for barking Goldie. I just refused to put away some clothes so I could sit down and think. Not tomorrow, for tomorrow's Saturday and everyone will be home, but Monday I will begin to creep down to the cellar during the baby's morning nap, to write music and plan my strategy in the coolness by the dark wood table.

Peggy came rushing in one evening at 6:30. "Glenn! Is Glenn home?" she asked Matt.

"He was working on his power block when I took off," he started to explain.

"Goddamn him. He said we'd go out to dinner at 6. Where the fuck is he?"

"Hey Peg, lighten up. You just blew in yourself."

"I got caught in traffic and raced to get home."

"Well, maybe he's stuck in traffic too."

The phone rang and Peggy said, "If it's Glenn, tell him I'm not home."

I stared at Matt as he answered the phone and said, "No, Glenn, she's not here, I don't know where she is."

"You lied for her," I said. I walked out the door and down the street.

I wouldn't dare ask my brothers to fend for me against my mate. They would laugh at me if I did. All Peggy does is party and shop and shower and go out for lunch every day. No, that's not fair. She keeps the house and yard in perfect condition, but where does she get the nerve to be mad because she and Glenn got their wires crossed?

I came back and Matt said, "Well, after all, we are staying at their house."

I looked at the card Glenn had given Peggy, sitting on the mantel. It said, "You and me against the world," and I said to Matt, "Yes, I know, that's why I came back."

The following Monday, the *Sea Lion* left for its northward trip. "You heard the rumor going around about Robbie?" Matt asked me as I drove him to the dock.

"No, what?"

"Oh, he has a teenage girl working on the boat, and they're getting it on."

"Really? How shabby, how lowlife. Does Gloria know?"

"Hell, no."

"So she's going around like everything's okay and everybody else knows what's going on. I'd hate to find out everyone but me knew that my husband was cheating on me. God, if he's left his wife, the least he could do is let her know."

"This girl's no Lolita."

"What does she look like?"

"A dyke—stocky, stubby-fingered, hairy legs."

"What's the attraction?"

"Oh, she thinks Robbie's God. He does take good care of his boat," he added thoughtfully. "Jan wants to be a fisherman, make the money and everything else. She stays out of the way, does the job. I don't even know for sure if there is anything going on with her and Robbie. He just gave her a chance."

"Why she'd want to prove herself as tough as the next guy is a mystery to me. I mean, I can see cooking on a boat, and writing down the weights, painting and other chores. But coil those shoulder-wrenching ropes and climb down in the tanks and have fish guts fly in your face? Yuk."

"Oh, I know you couldn't do it. You hate to get your fingernails dirty."

"Well...."

"I like that in you." He parked the car and got his duffel bag out. "C'mere, Mama, give me a good squeeze."

Chelsea and I flew back to Kodiak the next weekend. Before I left Seattle, I bought fifty records and several plants. I struggled with two months' worth of baggage as I made my way through the airport towards my gate, odds and ends straggling from my bulging purse.

We flew into Anchorage with three hours between flights to change Chelsea and check on Goldie in her kennel in the luggage area.

The plane took off for Kodiak, and it seemed to me it was laboring under its heavy load. After half an hour, the pilot announced that Kodiak might be too foggy to land, but they'd fly in and give it a try. When we got near, it was impossible to see the mountains, the islands, or the water, but the plane approached the runway, with Pillar Mountain behind it, three times and circled around each time. My nerves were honed to fish line by the time we gave up and headed back to Anchorage.

The thought of spending the night in the airport filled me with dread, but then, like angels, Robbie's wife Gloria and her four kids approached me. They looked like a gang of street hoods, all slight and skinny with pale faces and masses of curly hair.

"Hi there, Eleanor, you stuck the night here, too?" Gloria asked and then directed her kids to relieve me of my burdens. "Kim, take that basket. Allison, hold her baby for a little bit. Larry, grab the diaper bag."

"Oh thanks, Gloria. What are you going to do?"

"Let's get rooms at the Airport Inn for the night. We'll have dinner there, too."

Fourteen-year old Allison looked me straight in the face as she reached out for Chelsea. "Why are your eyes so red?"

And Gloria said, "She's worn out, honey."

At dinner the kids chattered and Gloria talked about them working on the boat during the summers, helping their dad, and about Jan, as if she were just another of her kids, her strange tomboy daughter, getting a start on the *Sea Lion*.

Maybe there's nothing going on. Gloria may be a hick, but she's a woman, whereas Jan is just one of the strong kids a captain gets to work on his boat.

At four the next morning, we trekked out full of hope to get the first flight to Kodiak. I perked up when I heard the ticket agent announce the good old chauvinist rule: Women and children first.

But though I squeezed my eyes tight and gripped the armrests until my fingers were bloodless and sang "La Marseillaise" over and over to myself, the plane was unable to complete a landing after two tries.

34

As we headed back to Anchorage, I felt nervous and exhausted, dirty and ugly.

I went back to the nursery to change the baby, and water and air the now-lifeless plants. Accompanied by Gloria and her kids, we went to the luggage area, my eyes burning and my head pounding.

A blonde lady with a rough sweater over her big Teuton frame watched us with interested amusement. When Goldie rolled out in her kennel on the conveyor belt and we were puzzling what to do with her before the next flight, the lady said, "If you'd like to go ahead and get something to eat at the restaurant, I'll be glad to watch your dog. I'll make a rope leash and take her for a walk. She's a sweetheart."

After breakfast, we boarded the plane for Kodiak again. This time, on the third approach to the runway, we made it. The sweaty, smoke-filled cabin burst into applause.

CHAPTER THREE

SUMMER IN THE RABBIT HUTCH
In which we return to Kodiak and fishing normalcy

It felt good to be home in the rabbit hole. Matt tendered salmon all summer long with the *Sea Lion*. Only 58-foot or smaller boats could actually fish salmon. Boats over that length got tendering contracts with the canneries and took the salmon from the smaller fishing boats in brailers that held up to a ton of fish, tallied the weights, and replenished the fishing boats' fuel and water and groceries. Some tenders would trade books or music tapes with the fishing boats, or collect their mail to take to the nearest post office so the smaller boats' crews could stay out fishing.

The *Sea Lion* delivered their salmon to a cannery in town, so Matt usually came home once a week. A high quota of salmon was expected, and the Department of Fish and Game kept the fishing periods open from Monday through Friday. My ears perked up when the Fish and Game announcements came on the radio, because if the fishing period closed, I could know to expect Matt home.

With a cup of coffee in the cold of the early-morning sunshine, I feel like I'm in France, only I'm eating Polish sesame candy instead of a croissant. Baby Chelsea's rustling in her crib—I bet she thinks she'll get up early too.

Tomorrow's the day our boat's due home. The Sea Lion *has a heavy throttle to its engines. Sometimes I think I can hear it coming down the channel. Then I run up to the road and if I see a blue and white scow with four smokestacks, I know Matt's home.*

I've decorated the kitchen wall of our little home with copper molds and star-shaped tin cake pans, and I love the gypsy gleam of it when I enter the front door. I've torn down the curtains for the summer light. The biggest window faces Mission Road, but the grassy bank in front of the house rises so steep that, standing in the living room, I look out to a wall of green. On hot summer days, I open the front door and the bare spacious breeziness of it all pleases me. It feels like small-town America. I put Chelsea's high chair on the pallet-board porch and let her muck in her dinner to her heart's content.

Today I hope we get a chair for Matt like the black rocker I saw at a garage sale for $20 yesterday. I'm thinking of asking Doug Bradley to bring me a bird when he comes up later this month to go out with Matt on the Sea Lion.

Matt will be tendering salmon all summer long. When he came home last time, he walked in as I was picking up the bedroom and pushed me on the bed, where he manhandled me till Chelsea protested and we all wrestled together. "You look good, Mama," he said, "like you never had a baby."

I feel like the fisherman's wife in my fairy-tale book, in my little house under the hill.

We went to bed soon after Chelsea, while it was still light out. Matt got up to leave at three in the morning for the next opening and the sky was light again—it never got darker than a dusky twilight.

A basket-weaving class started with a reed-gathering expedition at the Buskin River Beach, halfway to the airport. The blonde girl from the airport was there.

"Hi there. You got your baby, but where's the golden dog?"

"Left her at home today. Thank you so much for helping us at the airport."

"Hey, we gotta stick together while the guys are out fishing, have some fun. My name's Karen."

"I'm Nora, this is Chelsea," I pointed to the papoose in my backpack.

Karen was easy to get to know. She loved to talk, and when we went into the house she shared with Scott—a little shack above the boat harbor—I was back in the good old hippie days with incense, candles, beaded curtains, velvet cushions, and plants everywhere.

We smoked pot at her kitchen table, looking out past the boats lined up at the piers, past the islands scattered along the coastline towards the ocean. After my first drag I relaxed and, glancing around, saw my reflection in a big copper bowl hanging on the wall.

"That's a beautiful bowl, Karen—where'd you get that?"

"Oh, Scott's wife left it here when she ran off with his best friend."

"Are they still married?"

"No, she dumped him good, but she's crazy," Karen's eyes closed as she dragged on the joint before passing it back to me. "It really hurt him, though. I was working up at the court and he just lapped up any attention. We started going out, and I was still working and he was lying in bed smoking a doob one day and I said, 'I just hate getting up in the cold and going to work' and he said, 'Don't go then, move in with me,' so I did. Boy, is she sorry now."

For the first time since moving to Alaska, I felt a kindred spirit in Kodiak, instead of the 50s conformity and the obsession with money and things I'd felt from everyone else.

Karen said, "Scott's the youngest skipper in the fleet, but in five years or so, Matt will be up there running a boat, too."

That's just because we're newcomers and Matt's father isn't partners with him in owning a boat, like Scott's father is. Five years, hell!

Our second anniversary came and went with Matt out fishing. Karen had a tea party for her mom, who'd come up from North Dakota. They looked like the cast from "I Remember Mama," both tall with thick blond hair, ruddy skin, and blue eyes. Karen held herself proud and talked with complete confidence.

I dolled Chelsea up, but she grossed out Karen's mom by eating the dry dog food from the dish on the floor. I guess I grossed out Karen's mom by allowing Chelsea to do that.

"For heaven's sake, child, you're not letting her eat dog food are you?"

"I think it feels good in her mouth, kind of gritty, massaging her gums—she's still got teeth coming in."

"But dog food? For a baby?"

"I vowed long ago never to fuss over what my kids eat, and it's not like dog food's the only thing she eats," I said.

It was good to meet Karen's friends and realize they might be my friends too—Robin, who looked like the Vermont Maid in the maple syrup ad, with her bright, open face and thick brown braids. She was married to Neil O'Hara.

Robin said, 'Neil grew up on a farm but he always wanted to be a fisherman. He worked out of Gloucester after college and then a friend wrote to Neil about Kodiak. So here we are. I'm a nurse, and Neil's fishing, but he'll probably go back to med school someday."

Karen said, 'Everyone calls Neil 'Kid Nelly' because he looks so big and sweet—wait till you see him. He and Scott fish together, and Neil plays Irish folk music loud—he says it attracts the fish."

Robin laughed and shook her head. "That man, he drives me crazy. It's a good thing he fishes: I couldn't take him on a daily basis. Aren't you glad you're married to a fisherman? I just love it when Neil's gone and I can do whatever I want."

"But I thought Matt would be back in town every couple of days, not gone for weeks and then home for hours," I said.

"It's different when you have little ones," Karen's mother said, and I wished I hadn't let Chelsea eat the dog food.

I spent so many quiet summer evenings alone after Chelsea went to sleep, thinking that maybe there was a place for me in Kodiak's nightlife. One night Karen called me to go out to a movie with her—it was an old John Wayne movie, but it was a chance to get out.

We went early and sat in Solly's dimly lit bar, waiting for the next showing. Bearded, glowering fishermen hunched over their drinks or yelled at each other across the room between drags on their cigarettes. When Karen ran outside to check the line for the movie, a drunken Native came up and hovered over me, swaying back and forth. I jumped up and ran over to the phone booth, pretending to make a call, but I didn't know any numbers to dial.

I'd always fantasized about jumping up on the bar and singing all the raucous songs I loved, like "My Boyfriend's Back" and "Love the One You're With," but instead I was anxious to get out of there into the safety of the theater darkness.

I saw a house advertised on the scanner that we might possibly be able to afford, and when I knocked at the door to look at it, there was Robin. Neil stood behind her, tall and slim with curly blond hair and the biggest friendliest smile and twinkling eyes.

Robin showed me the house, wearing a beautiful quilted bathrobe. "That's a beautiful robe, Robin."

"Thanks, Nora. I made it from the bedspread the landlady left here. Then she wanted me to pay for it—can you believe it?"

"Wasn't she mad?"

"She wasn't very happy about it, in fact, she expected me to give her $50. What bullshit! I just laughed." Robin turned and walked down the hall.

After I'd seen the house, Robin said, 'We don't want to settle here; eventually Neil's going to medical school, so we're going to rent a trailer on Mission Road."

Trailers always seemed transient and tacky to me, not a home. I wanted a real home with sturdy walls and a fireplace and a fence around the yard so the kids could play safe.

But when I went to the bank to see if we could get into the house Robin and Neil were renting, the banker told me we didn't have enough money for a down payment.

One weekend day, Matt was unloading the *Sea Lion* in town. I always felt at loose ends anyway, but especially when he was home and we weren't together.

I wandered around the house while Chelsea had her morning nap, then took her to Baranof Park and tried not to cry while she played in the gravel. It was all just so gritty and tough.

I went down to the boat harbor to find the *Sea Lion*, with Chelsea on my hip. Matt climbed up the ladder on the side of the dock to me.

"What's up, sweetie?" he said.

"Matt, can't you come home? I'm so lonely and I'm just wandering around and I don't know anybody and the library's closed and I don't need anything at the grocery store." Tears started coming.

"I know, I know you're lonely. We'll be through here in a little while and then I'll be home, okay? Here—" he handed me a five dollar bill. "Why don't you buy a six-pack and take it home?"

I went home and put Chelsea down for a nap. The sun was shining, streaming down the grassy bank outside the front window like a river of green warmth. The day was still and I sat in the rocker and heard a thin fluty sound. Random notes sweetened the silence. I looked out the side window to the house next door and saw a little Korean boy playing a recorder, like some shepherd calming his flock.

Matt drove up and came in. "Shhh…" I said. "Listen." But the little boy had stopped and fled. Matt put his giant mitt of a hand out to me and we went into the bedroom.

"Oh Mama, you can be so sweet," Matt murmured. He rolled over and pulled me on top of him, stroking my hair and kissing my face.

Afterwards, when Chelsea woke us all up from our naps, we went downtown to buy Matt some boots and get dinner at a restaurant. But after buying the boots we looked at each other and Matt said, "Let's go back home and fuck some more." So we drove back home and plopped Chelsea in front of the TV while we went back to bed. "This is a good summer," Matt said.

It wasn't his fault that he had to go back out at midnight. We snuck out of the house, leaving Chelsea asleep with Goldie to guard her. I drove him to the boat harbor, where Doug Bradley was waiting on deck. He cast off the lines as soon as Matt jumped on board.

Finally the fishing slackened off and the *Sea Lion*'s charter with the cannery ended. Robbie and Matt and the rest of the crew put away the tendering equipment and started rigging the pots to get ready for the king crab season.

"This year we're going out to the Bering Sea," Matt said when I picked him up at the boat harbor one day in August. "There's a huge quota out there and we're going to nail it."

"How long will the season last?" I asked Matt.

"Oh, about a month. It opens in September, but we have to head out there next week to gear up and take the pots out."

"That will be two months you'll be gone!"

"Well, it'll probably be over before that."

"Matt, I've missed you so much just when you're out for five days. We moved up here so you wouldn't be gone for months at a time. Please…"

"Look, Nora, if we do well, I won't have to work again till tanners in February or March. We can get a nice house and go traveling. We can have some adventures instead of just work. I'd love to take you to Bali and Samoa."

"With Chelsea."

"Yeah, we'll take Chelsea. I just want to get ahead and make some good money and get someplace. It won't be so bad. This way I'm not home long enough for us to fight. Just keep busy, don't think about it."

That night Matt woke up writhing and groaning in bed. "What's the matter?" I asked.

Matt said, "My eyes are killing me. I think I got flash burns from welding."

"What do you mean?" I thought of the time I'd scratched the corneas of my eyes—it felt like hot needles burning into my head. Would Matt go blind?

We called the hospital and then drove up to the emergency room. A tall handsome man with grey hair, wearing a white lab coat, strode up to where Matt was lying on a table. "I'm Dr. Copstead. So you were welding?" He leaned over and pried Matt's eyelids open

"Yeah," Matt grunted.

"And no welder's helmet?"

"Nah."

"I'm going to put some drops in. You should feel better in the morning. Guess you'll wear a helmet next time."

"Yeah, for sure."

After he left the room, and Matt was struggling upright, I heard the doctor grumble to the receptionist, "These fishermen think nothing can happen to them and they don't bother to protect themselves." I gave Matt my arm and led him back to the Jeep and home.

In the morning Matt was back to normal, and off to work.

One day we drove out towards Cape Chiniak to fish. The spawning salmon jumped out of the bays and rivers. We drove over low bridges with signs that said "No Fishing," but out towards Chiniak a stream ran parallel to the road and we could see fish slithering in the shallow run.

We jumped out of the Jeep and chased the fish up and down a stretch of the creek. Matt and I tried to catch the fish barehanded, but they always slipped right out.

"He's coming back your way, Matt!" I yelled as the fish we were after changed direction. Matt ambushed it back to me and then came running as I stomped on it with my boots.

Matt was laughing at me and grabbed me with the squashed fish between us.

"What a fisherman you'd make, Mama. Let's take your bounty home."

I fried it for dinner. "This fish tastes like rotten mush. What's so great about salmon?"

Matt said, "Ah, it's a spawned-out, water-marked dog."

"Huh?"

"This salmon's laid its eggs—it was about dead when we caught it, and the water beating against it bruises the meat."

"Killed at home, domestic violence."

"That's just the way it is, Mama."

"If you're a salmon."

We went to the rodeo at Bells Flats, past the airport and Coast Guard base at the head of Women's Bay. There were cattle ranches further out at Saltery Cove and south of Kodiak Island on Sitkalidak Island, with real cowboys who'd get silver belt buckles for rodeo prizes.

Since it was raining, Matt and Chelsea and I sat in the Jeep beside the grandstands and drank beer. We let Chelsea have one, and she turned into a silly little slob. "Nothing more funny than a drunk baby," Matt said.

Then she passed out and as the afternoon grew misty and ghostly, I felt guilty.

What if she never wakes up? How many of her baby brain cells are drowning?

I always thought I would be a better mother if I didn't care too much, if my instincts were more primitive than psychological. I'd taken my cue from Goldie, who fed her puppies and kept them warm with her. She'd put up and put up with their puppy nonsense, climbing all over her, and when she'd had it, she'd rear back and snarl or nip at them.

But this is different. Maybe I'm too straight, but I can't just let anything happen to Chelsea.

Before Matt left for the Bering Sea we went for a picnic. I wore a sundress that I'd made from a floral tablecloth, and envisioned a pastoral farewell scene in a wildflower-strewn meadow or under the sheltering arms of a giant tree by a river.

At the airport we turned onto a dirt road and drove out towards Anton Larsen Bay. The dust rose in clouds from the road and its choking dryness enveloped us.

At last we parked, then walked through woods with brush and undergrowth clawing my bare skin or tripping me. Alongside a stream we found a spot by a tree that wasn't too densely overgrown with briars, bushes, vines, and moss. But it was damp and uncomfortable, and my seat was wet when I got up.

The next night, before Matt left, we had a fancy dinner at home. After I put Chelsea to bed, we turned out all the lights and lay on the sofa and listened to Dylan's *John Wesley Harding* album until midnight. I drove Matt to the boat harbor and when I hugged him goodbye I realized that hug would have to do me till he got back home. "I'm going to miss you so bad. How can I make you come back soon?"

"C'mon Mama, I have to leave. We need to get through Whale Pass when the tides are with us."

I almost wrote November, I'm in such a daze; the weather's so damp and dark. Sometimes, like tonight, I feel responsible for all the dreariness in the world, weary from boredom and non-importance. Reasons? Peggy wrote that she and Glenn don't want my piano cluttering up their basement. Tricia won't risk Lou's wrath to talk long-distance to me on the phone, but she manages to let me know that I could not get the same meaning from the Psalms as she and her friends do. They have their own meanings for God and dying.

Mom is thinking of moving to Canada to see if she could get Canadian social security for the 35 years she lived there before moving to Seattle. I'm afraid she'll drown in the misery and crabbiness I always felt at Grandmother's house, that moving to Canada will imprison Mom in frustration forever, like they never got over the Depression.

Everyone close is moving on and the feeling that I've missed out is moving in. When I grew up, I thought everyone got married, had a family, lived in a neighborhood, and stayed together. They didn't leave.

I guess I just feel sad because Matt's gone and I'm almost afraid to sleep for the nightmares that always come. I have lots to do but am torn between tearing up the town and walking tiptoe through it.

I want my piano and friends that I can talk to without shocking them.

CHAPTER FOUR

WAITING OUT THE DEEP SEA
In which I long in vain for Matt's return; I find diversion in religion;
I seek companionship

The Deep Sea *sank last night in Whale Pass. There were four adults and six children lost. The* Deep Sea—*it sounds so ominous and unforgiving. To think you're safe and making an ordinary trip and then what happens to first let you know you're in danger and what happens between that moment and your last moments alive? What's it like to realize you're living your last moment?*

I always thought you could prepare to survive; there would always be something you could do to make it through. I guess the part that twists me up inside is the drastic change, like with one event all your years of trying to live a certain way amount to nothing. Sometimes change comes faster than destiny.

I called the landlord to ask if I could paint the living room and bathroom. He came over and we agreed on a light beige for the living room and pale apricot for the bathroom.

I'd paint after putting Chelsea to bed. Karen stopped over one evening as I was moving ladders and covering the floor with newspaper. She pulled her heavy sweater off over her head, her blond curls slowly cascading down. "Why didn't Matt help you paint while he was in town?"

"He was working on the boat and I wanted to relax and have fun with him when he had some free time. But now I'm thinking what have we moved here for if I'm still alone so much while Matt's fishing?"

"He's not going to appreciate you, if you do everything for yourself."

We heard Chelsea giggling in her crib, so we tiptoed in to look at her. She was curled up on her back, tickling her own toes. We snuck back out into the living room and I said to Karen, "It's times like this that I ache for her Daddy to see her—I miss Matt so much already."

"I'm glad Scott's out fishing, he thinks all I have to do all day is cook meals for him before he drags me back to bed. I get so tired of him chasing me around the house."

Bragger.

"I'm going to take swimming classes at the pool if I can find a babysitterfor Chelsea. Something to do."

"The Lamey girls live right on the corner. They'll sit for you." Karen looked their phone number up in the book for me.

I went to the high school, where the pool was, and signed up for adult swimming lessons.

"So, you had lessons before?" the instructor asked me.

"I can't remember…. I guess so, but I've always been a weak swimmer. I want to learn the strokes and the breathing and get strong. If I ever have to survive on the open seas, I want to do what I can to increase my chances."

Karen and I, with Chelsea on my back, took Karen's German Shepherds for a walk to Cliff Point between Monashka Bay and Mill Bay. We smoked a joint on the cliff head. As always, I felt sort of dreamy and distracted and woozy. The air had that Arctic bite to it, even though the day was sunny and beautifully clear, as I looked out to the rocky islands between us and the cold ocean. Smoking dope hardly seemed to affect Karen at all, but I thought every idea that came into my head was brilliant.

On the way back, I rubbed my eye and a contact lens fell out. We dropped to our knees and looked and looked through the grassy path.

Let this be an omen of our friendship. If we can find my lens, then we're meant to be friends.

"Aha!" Karen said and plucked the flimsy plastic lens from invisibility.

Afterwards Karen and I drove out to Bells Flats where a lady had a greenhouse, and we bought some tulip bulbs. If there was something to do, Karen would find it.

Later, while Chelsea was having her nap, I planted the tulip bulbs by the roadside in front of our house. I looked up and noticed a young woman walking by with an infant bundled up under her arm. I looked closer and she looked at me. It was Robin. She was wearing boots and a heavy knit cap against the sniping wind, but she still looked neat as a pin, not round but sinewy, angular.

"Hi, Nora! So this is where you live."

"Whose baby is that—not yours, is it?"

"Oh no. I'm looking after Vanessa while her mother works at the cannery. They really can't afford a baby and with both parents working, they never see her."

"She looks kind of cold. Is that blanket warm enough?"

Robin just laughed, "She's fine."

"Would you like to come in for a cup of tea?"

"Thanks. I'll come in, but actually I've given up caffeine. It's not good for your heart or your kidneys and it causes breast lumps." We clomped down the stairs and into the house. "Someday Neil wants me to get my boobs enlarged."

"He does? You're fine the way you are." I appraised her trim all-American-girl looks.

"He wants me to be the blond beauty queen type, and I figure, if it'll make him happy, why not?"

"Well, anyway, I love my tea and coffee. It's smoking cigarettes I worry about. Luckily for me, when I tried it, it just made me dizzy and nauseated."

"You ninny, that's getting high. That's why people smoke."

Robin told me how she and Neil had met at a hospital where he was a medical student and she was a nurse. "He'll go back and become a doctor, but right now we want some adventure, to get away from cities and schooling."

"Yeah, we do too—Pioneers on the Last Frontier."

The department store held a sewing contest, where the entrants modeled their outfits in a fashion show. I picked up some white material at a garage sale, and made Chelsea a white flannel sailor dress with lots of complicated tailoring, red piping, and a dickey set in with snaps and tacked-on stars. When the contest judging came, I dressed Chelsea in her outfit and myself in my Ukrainian embroidered blouse, long velvet skirt, and leather boots.

Lots of women entered the contest, but I was so proud of Chelsea and myself. I was surprised that we didn't win anything, but a thin lady with short straight hair and bangs came up to me when I held Chelsea in my arms and said, "You look like a couple of Russian princesses."

After hearing that, I'd pretend to be the forgotten Russian princess of Kodiak that the czar had exiled to the fur-trading colonies. I'd make Russian tea from a concoction of instant tea, instant lemonade, and Tang. I bought an Ivan Rebroff record, and practiced drawing the Russian alphabet. I longed for a samovar and a balalaika.

Matt called from Dutch Harbor and said I could send Mom the money to buy an airplane ticket to come up and visit Chelsea and me. The weather turned wintry the day she came, and the heater core in the Jeep began overheating again. So we mostly just visited at home. Funny how moms can go through your house after you've cleaned it and find all the hidden grime and dust balls. Mom was enchanted with Chelsea; it was so nice to have someone else enjoy her sweet babyness.

We visited Gloria one day when the wind was blasting. Mom noticed the piano in the dining room. "Oh look, Nora, they have a piano!"

"Yes, isn't it pretty?"

"Do you play?" Gloria asked.

"She certainly does!" Mom boasted.

"How about lessons? Do you give lessons? I would love the kids to play, but it just sits there."

"Well, yes, I guess I could give lessons."

"Okay, great! How about starting with Allison? Would you rather bring the baby with you or have one of the other kids go to your place and sit?"

"Maybe it would be better if one of the other kids came to our house—less distracting."

"Okay then, we'll get some music in this house!" Gloria set coffee and cookies on the table and sat down. "Listen to that wind!" She shook her head. "Robbie called on the radio and said the winds have been going 120 miles an hour where they're fishing."

"I've always liked the wind, blustery and invigorating outside and being safe inside," I said.

Gloria shivered. "The wind scares me, like a warning."

"But it's nice and cozy here." I grabbed Chelsea away from the glass windows of their gun cabinet.

"With all the kids in school, I'm getting restless. I'd like to get a job somewhere."

"Do you think you will?" I asked.

"Robbie would have a cow, he'd never let me. He thinks the kids need me to be home all the time. And he prides himself on providing for us. 'I'm not out here in the Bering Sea working my ass off so the whole fucking town can see you bringing home the bacon.' That's what he said when I volunteered at school. He likes being a Highliner."

I glanced at Mom to see how she took Gloria's language. "What's a Highliner?" Mom asked.

"The top fishermen, the guys who bring in the most crab," Gloria said.

Once we were back home, Mom said, "It seems like fishermen are more concerned with what the neighbors would say and the creature comforts their families enjoy than with their own feelings about what they want. It's as if the luxuries for their wife show their success."

"When I complained to Matt about him always working, never relaxing or enjoying what he's got, he said, 'You'd leave me in a minute if you didn't have a big house and a good car to get around in and trips to Seattle.'"

"Well, you knew what you were getting into when you married a fisherman; I guess the sea gets into their blood."

"I hate that expression—what about their home or their children or even their wife getting into their blood? Is the sea and fishing some wonderful obsession that means more to a man than family, than life?"

"Oh, poor baby." Mom took my hand to comfort me, but I snatched it away and we both felt lonely.

I took Mom to a dinner show at the Harvester, the big, barn-like restaurant on Mill Bay Road. After dinner, the Russian Dancers performed. "I love the way the men throw the women around when they're dancing," I told Mom as we watched the simple, wild dancing of the men in knee-high boots and the women in full black skirts and embroidered blouses.

Fred Wade's wife, Jennie, came over to our table. I was still embarrassed by the St. Patrick's Day dinner where I'd gotten so drunk and made Matt so mad.

"I suppose Matt's out with Robbie on the *Sea Lion*?"

"Oh yeah, it's been awhile, but Matt and I are planning on a big trip when he gets back, if he does well in the Bering Sea."

She laughed and said, "I'm living with my sister now. Isn't that the way it goes? One year you spend half the year on vacation in Mexico, and the next year you're back living with the folks." She didn't seem to remember the shameful incident from the spring.

One night I had Robin and Karen over to meet Mom. Karen came up with a plan to get involved in the Christmas bazaar. "You know, the newspaper's changing from the old typesetting process. I've got a line to the old printer's trays, with the narrow little shelves that hold the type. We can get them free and paint them and sell them cheap—there's so many of them we can't lose!"

Robin chimed in, "And we can sew Christmas tree ornaments and bake goodies for a bake sale!"

"I can use my star-shaped cake tins to make Christmas fruitcakes," I said.

Robin sat by Mom and said, "You live so close, down in Seattle, you must come up here all the time to see Nora and Chelsea. My folks are coming from New York next summer to see us."

Mom said, "They must be rich! All the way across the continent!"

"Well, they want to see Alaska while we're here. We'll be back in New York in a few years."

Later Mom said, "Well, Robin's having an adventure before she goes back home, but you and Karen are in it for the long haul, aren't you?"

It made me feel funny, like Robin is fickle, or like my life is just a flash-in-the-pan adventure for her.

Mom and I looked at a pre-fab house for sale, kind of a cross between a trailer and a ranch house, with an itty-bitty yard and a Franklin stove. The house was about a block from Baranof Park. Although it was above the channel and seemed to get a lot of sunlight, the atmosphere inside the house seemed sad. Maybe it was the dark brown carpet or the wood paneling or the house not being warm enough. But I thought with a little heat and paint it could be livable, and it did have a fireplace and a yard. "Where are the people who lived here before moving to?" I asked the real estate person who showed us the house.

"Well, uh…actually, the man is moving out of town."

"Oh, did they split up or something?"

"No—well, she was very unhappy and…uh…she…uh…died."

Mom whipped around. "She died? How?"

He sighed. "Apparently she took an overdose of pills, and washed it down with a bottle of whisky. She was very depressed."

We both gave up on pursuing that house any further.

"Still, I wish I could get in touch with Matt," I said to Mom.

"What if you had an emergency, and had to talk to him?" she said.

"Well, I guess I'd call Gloria and ask her to call the boat on their marine radio, but Matt doesn't want me calling except for real emergencies. He's never told me how to get in touch with him—we just write letters."

"Oh, poor baby. But how would you contact him if you did want to buy a house? How are you going to have a real home if he's never here?"

When I drove Mom to the airport to go back to Seattle, she said, "I hate to leave you honey. I wish I could be more help. It must drive Matt crazy to leave his wife and baby for so long. I know you miss him."

Last night when I went to bed, I hoped, as always, that I'd be awakened by Matt's footsteps and knock on the door. I woke up around two and felt skinny and bloodless without him to hug like a big tree that I can hardly get my arms around.

I got out of bed and went into the living room and turned the TV on. There, in Kodiak, in the middle of the night, was Toby Dammit, *Fellini's movie about a heedless sports-car racer pursued by a malevolent little girl bouncing a red ball. I'd seen the movie in college when I took some mescaline. It duplicated my scariest childhood nightmares of the evil nuance, the terrifying glance in the midst of normalcy.*

It's weird that soon after I first saw the movie, Sam came into my life—a man who, in looks and character, was Toby Dammit—*tall, blond, wild-eyed, and arrogant. Toby Dammit died when the little girl lured him into a car crash. Sam died alone in a car accident.*

49

It was as if I was the only one in the universe watching Toby Dammit; that it wasn't on other people's TV sets even if they were awake and watching TV, like a televised fortune-teller.

Today was the worst day—okay till I took a nap and thought about Matt. Went to Gloria's, nobody home. Robin not home, nor Karen. Chelsea wouldn't hold my hand and ran into the street when we went to Baranof Park. Called Gail and Peggy, but felt like I got the brush-off, didn't feel any better afterwards.

Damn it, why do I feel so low? Really depressed.

We finally got our own mailbox, so I no longer had to wait in the General Delivery line. I got my last bill from the mental health clinic in relative privacy.

As I left the post office, I saw a girl carrying a little boy about Chelsea's age. On the spur of the moment, I spoke to the girl, "Does your little boy need a playmate as much as my little girl does?"

She said, "Well, yeah, why don't you give me your phone number and I'll come over later." She wrote down my number on her grocery sack and left.

Donna came over after naps with Andrew, who was four months older than Chelsea. "Look, they have the same melted-chocolate eyes," I said.

We set the kids on a blanket on the floor and watched them kind of face off, watching each other tinker with Chelsea's toys.

"So how old are you?" I figured she was about my age.

"Fifteen."

"Fifteen?"

"Yeah, I know, too young. But all us kids just messed around...."

"Up here?"

"No, this was down in California. And I got caught. But I'm glad I have Andy, even though it's hard. He's so sweet, such a little lover."

"Is his dad with you?"

"Oh no, I always knew that would never happen. No, my sister lives up here, in Larson Bay."

"Where's that?"

"Oh, one of the villages. Her husband's Native and they have a little boy a little older than Andy, and they're going to have another baby. So what about you? You're married?"

"Oh yeah, to a fisherman...."

"I figured. I'm on call at the cannery, live in a little tiny trailer. But it's okay."

I heard a car stop in front and then roar away. I looked out the window to see Doug Bradley coming down the steps. "I was visiting in the neighborhood and decided to come by to visit you, say goodbye before I head for the airport. Look, I brought a bottle of wine, too, and some snow."

Wow, to have two friends visiting me at the same time! I feel rich. Wonder if Donna snorts coke or if she's shocked?

"You running a daycare now, Nora?"

"Not yet, no. This is my friend Donna, and her little boy, Andy."

"Hi. Well here, let me draw this line. Got a mirror?"

Donna picked Andy up off the floor. "Oh, don't give me any," she said. "We're gonna go pretty soon."

I must have looked worried, because she said, "No, Nora, it's okay, I just don't feel like it and I better get home in case the cannery calls for an evening shift."

"What do you do with Andy?"

"Oh, I've got a sitter lined up." She wrestled him into his little jacket. "I'll give you a call, maybe we'll do something."

Shortly after Donna left, Karen stopped by and the three of us partied.

"I just love this, everybody dropping by. This never happens!"

Doug drew another line of cocaine, and Karen brought out a joint. I got distracted, trying to watch Chelsea and make her dinner and keep tea on the table after the wine was all gone. Karen drifted out the door and I put Chelsea to bed.

I began to feel queasy as I listened to Doug drone on and on. The room was swirling and I couldn't keep my eyes open.

"Are you falling asleep, Nora?" Doug said in a soft voice.

"I'm just a lightweight, but I can never turn down a drink or a line. I'm sorry." I struggled up off the sofa and said, "I have to go to bed now." I staggered into the bedroom and flopped on the bed, wondering if throwing up was inevitable.

Doug came into my room. I was hanging on to the mattress for dear life. Doug put his head down beside me and said, "Come on Nora, move over. I'll make you feel better."

I gotta get him out of here.

"No, Doug, if you do anything, Matt will kill us. Just go home, please. I'll be okay."

Doug stood up and patted my back. "No, Nora, we're friends, Matt's not going to kill his friends." I heard the chain of bells on the front door peal out as Doug left the house.

Even in my distress, I was afraid of what Doug thought of me.

What a chicken you are! Why didn't you just tell him you don't want him sleeping with you instead of saying it would bother Matt?

Because you're afraid he'll think you're a goody-goody. You're scared to stand up for yourself.

Thank God Doug left. I want my Matt.

I woke up before morning and stumbled to the bathroom. I could hear Chelsea's baby steps behind me. I vomited and sank down in front of the toilet. I clutched the bowl with both hands and threw up again.

I must have passed out momentarily, because I heard Chelsea's voice calling me from a distance, though she was right next to me.

Why, if I can't control myself when I drink, do I continue to drink? Why can't I hate the taste, or at least remember the hangovers? I'm no better than the doomed Natives that litter the plaza downtown, falling down in front of the smelly dirty bars.

Karen called, and for once I didn't resent the feeling that she was checking up on me. "Please come over and help me. I can't bear to fix Chelsea lunch." She came and laughed at me as I walked around, bent in half, my eyes barely opened and my arms clutched across my stomach for the pain and sickness.

Early in November I was up at Gloria's, giving a piano lesson to Allison, when Gloria burst in with her two sisters. Their cheeks were windburned and they were laughing as they dumped sacks of groceries on the kitchen counters. "Nora, did you know Robbie's home?" Gloria called to me.

"He is?" I jumped up so abruptly the chair flipped over backwards. For all my watching the channel and trying to decipher the Fish and Game reports in the newspapers, I never expected Matt to just be home with no warning like this. I wanted to run down to the boat and grab him. "Where are they? Where's Matt? Are they here or down at the boat harbor—oh, I've got to run home and pick up Chelsea! She's going to be so glad to see her Daddy again."

Gloria said, "Oh no, Nora, it's just Robbie. He left the boat with Matt running it. They're still fishing near Dutch Harbor." Her sisters looked so embarrassed and so sorry for me that I almost started crying right there. "I'm sorry, Nora," Gloria said. "Robbie thinks the world of Matt or he would never have left the boat with him to come back. Matt will be home too, pretty soon."

She touched my arm and I forced a smile. "Oh, I just thought, it's been a while and I thought any day now Matt would be home and when you said Robbie was home I just thought—well, that maybe Matt was home too. It's okay, I just miss him, and so does Chelsea." I couldn't look Gloria in the eye. I knew if I started crying I wouldn't be able to stop.

The lesson was almost over, so I left a little early. When I got home with Chelsea the house seemed so cold and empty.

"I accept being married to a fisherman, Chelsea, but in the last year, we've had your Daddy home so little. I wish he didn't feel that if we were together more, we wouldn't get along.

"I don't know what I'm doing wrong. I try to make friends and use the time I'm alone, but on sunny days, or when we go to the park, or I make dinner, or paint the house, I wish I had someone to do it with, to share your sweetness with me. Nobody knows how cute you are."

I read Mother Goose rhymes to her until I started crying and when I tried to rock her, she screamed at me to let her go. I put her in her high chair and got her dinner that she promptly threw on the floor and then wriggled when I tried to wipe the food from her face and fingers. So I got her down from her high chair and sat down to read *The Hite Report*. Then Chelsea began whining for something in the kitchen, so I got up and poured her some juice that she then spilled all over the floor. While I was cleaning that mess up, she ran to the sofa and crumpled the pages of my book.

"I know, Chelsea, I'm so bad to be so selfish, to complain about this. But other women have so much more and they're not bad when they complain or assert themselves. In fact, they get what they want and are called reasonable. Their husbands say, 'I love you,' and remember them on Mother's Day. Maybe if I smoked cigarettes I'd be more content."

Karen came over to get ready for the Christmas bazaar. We worked on the printers' trays, tearing the fiberboard backs off and covering them with gift wrap, or spray-painting the frames.

Robin joined us, too. She was wearing a long dress of calico material, and looked like a character from the Old West. We sewed up the fabric she'd cut out for Christmas tree ornaments and stuffed them, and baked bread and Christmas cakes. The homespun festive feeling was irresistible, and I felt content, normal.

"Scott says if I leave any more pins on the floor for him to step on, he'll spank me," Karen giggled.

"Did you and Matt live together before you were married?" Robin asked.

"Yeah, but we both wanted kids and didn't want to upset the families, so we eloped here in Kodiak."

"When I get married, no one will cheat me out of a big wedding," Karen said.

Robin waved the wooden spoon she was using in the air and said, "I wore my mom's wedding dress and made my wedding cake and we got married at home. I really liked that."

"I wore blue jeans at my wedding, and we went on our honeymoon to Mexico when I was six months' pregnant," I said, when Robin interrupted me.

"The honeymoon was the best part. We just stayed home and it nearly killed my dad to see Neil and me going together into my bedroom every night."

Karen said, "You guys are just exhibitionists. Have you ever seen them making out at parties?" She looked at me.

I shook my head no, and said, "I'd be too embarrassed if I kissed Matt in public and he pushed me away. Wouldn't you just die?"

Robin said, "No, I'd just laugh and kiss him again!"

As I comforted myself with my exiled princess fantasies, I began to long for the spiritual, magical element of church rituals. But to join the Russian Orthodox congregation, to attend their services and become involved with their religion, would be a betrayal of my own heritage. How could I listen to Tommy Makem and the Clancy Brothers after such a defection? Worse, to sit among the Kwasnikoffs and Pestrikoffs with my Anglo-Irish name would render me once again an outsider, a second-class citizen. Might as well be back with the judgmental Catholics.

But as I prayed to Mary, the Mother of God, for strength and saw my identity as a reflection of hers, I felt I could quietly slip into St. Mary's Church and let my thoughts ramble down any spiritual path they chose. I could luxuriate in the peace and quiet and let my hand lotion sink in. So I went to Mass for the first time in five years.

The pastor was Father Jack Reagan, Irish just like the old priests. He preached the familiar sermon for money. I tried to mesh the words of the Creed, spoken aloud, with my beliefs, and at first resisted the parade to the communion rail. But the idea of the universality of the Church, the oneness of humanity, and the strength in a church full of people was something I needed and wanted to believe in. I soothed my conscience, when I recalled my rebellion and lapses, with thoughts of the laissez-faire attitudes of European Catholics, untouched by Puritan scruples. I went up and received communion, too.

After church one Sunday, Father Reagan asked me if he could visit me. When he came to the house, I showed him the books on Ireland that I'd checked out at the library. He told me of a neighbor who belonged to St. Mary's and who had small children, and asked if I'd like her to call on me. "Oh Father, I'd hate to feel like a case," I demurred.

"Oh, that's it, you don't want to be a case," he repeated and chuckled. "Well then, listen, dear, you must come to a cultural event we're having, a dinner put on by the Filipino parishioners."

About two weeks later, I called Fran McEnnis and asked her if she'd like to go to the dinner with me. She was aghast. "The Flips eat dogs!" she protested.

"Oh Fran, no, they don't."

"What about all the neighborhood dogs that have disappeared? Everybody knows the Flips eat dogs."

I still wanted to take the chance to socialize, so I asked Robbie's daughter, Allison, to baby-sit, and got ready to go alone. When I told Allison where I'd be, she wrinkled her nose and said, "All those Filipinos—wikkedy clakkety dink dink dink—I hate the way they push into line."

"But we're all the family of man."

"Huh? They're not my family. I don't got no Filipinos in my family."

I walked into the church social hall and looked around the room. Not a face I knew, not a word I understood. The idea of struggling alone through the evening made me break out in a sweat. I chickened out. I drove out to Monashka Bay and the end of the road and then turned around and drove back through town in the other direction to the airport. Finally I drove home.

When I walked inside Allison said, "Short dinner?"

"Oh well, kind of, but it was great. Those people were nice."

At the Christmas bazaar, Karen and Robin and I all wore long dresses and set up our booth next to Cluckers, the poultry farm owned by Frank McAllister. His son Nick was taking orders for Christmas turkeys and geese. He was handsome and looked like my brothers—tall and lean with wide blue eyes and short curly black hair that had threads of grey in it.

"So you're a turkey farmer?" Robin bustled around our table, setting out the baked goods and ornaments.

"No, it's my dad's business. I'm a pilot for Peninsula Air Taxi. But I'm in town a lot and I coach the kids' Little League."

"Oh, do you have kids?" Robin asked.

"No, I don't have any, but I sure like them, and those kids in the Little League are great. It blows me away how uninterested their folks are. Most of their dads don't even see them play—ever." He waved his arms around the room. "This is what it's all about—having a good time, making stuff for everybody to enjoy, everybody buying each others' stuff they've been making all fall."

"I know, but when people come up to buy the printers' trays we've been fixing up, I feel guilty charging them money for what we got for free. I just want to give them away," I said.

"Never get rich that way, but that's okay. You'll have lots of friends."

Karen, Robin, and I all took turns manning the booth and walking around, seeing what everyone else had made. When Karen took Chelsea to buy her some candy, Nick leaned back in his chair and said, "Here I am, sitting next to the three most beautiful women in Kodiak." I could feel my cheeks blush and I dropped the Christmas bread I was holding.

When it was my turn to roam, I bought a colorful batik picture of a samovar. I stopped at a booth where a girl with long braids and her little boy in Superman pajamas were selling three-in-one stuffed dolls. The handmade dolls were decorated like the Russian matrushka dolls—a mother doll with a little girl in her pocket with a tiny baby doll in her pocket.

When I turned around from buying the doll, I walked into Nick McAllister and dropped the doll. He picked it up for me. "You have a hard time keeping things in your hands, don't you? Where's your little doll baby—back at the booth?"

"Yes, Karen is so good to her, and it gives me a break."

"So, your husband's a fisherman, huh?"

"Yes, he's done it since he was a teenager."

"What do you think about it?"

"I respect him, he works harder than anybody I know and makes his living from the natural world, like a farmer, not pushing anybody around, just…"

"Wresting a living with his bare hands huh?" Nick interrupted, but his teasing eyes held mine in a warm, friendly look. "And you keep the home fires burning?"

"Well, yes, I guess I do."

"Well, I don't know who's prettier, the mama or the little baby." He winked at me and walked away.

After the bazaar, we divvied up our profits, excited by the piles of money on the table in front of us. We made big plans for the next year's bazaar. Neil and Scott came in to pick up Robin and Karen. Robin sat next to Neil and snuggled up to him. "Hey Nora, would you and Chelsea like to come with us to Port Lions for Thanksgiving? We're going to have dinner with the Larsons."

"I don't know if Matt will make it home by then or not."

Neil kissed Robin's ear and neck and she wriggled in his arms. I looked away, choking back the angry words rising to my lips. *Don't you know how smug you look, basking in your intimacy?* I felt like a child waiting for their attention. It seemed like forever before Robin looked at me again.

"Come on anyway, you don't want to spend Thanksgiving alone."

Karen said, "Yeah, Nora, come with Chelsea. The Larsons have two little boys and they live in a huge log cabin.…"

Scott broke in and began talking, "Yeah, he picked those logs himself, but the dumb fucker didn't realize you have to age them and now they've got sap-saturated carpets," he snickered. Karen hadn't stopped talking and the little room was echoing with both their voices at top pitch.

"So we can all go in the skiff and spend the night," she concluded with finality.

I was torn. I didn't want to be around all these happy couples, but with all the holiday preparations, it would be hard to ignore Thanksgiving as I had the year before.

It's 2 a.m. and I just can't stand any more of this "nothing I can do about it" feeling. It's so frustrating, it makes me cry even when I've been able to hack the loneliness and the longing. Half the year—more than half the year—our marriage is just a word. All Matt does is support me financially like some blackmailing mistress. I want to talk to him and hold him and make love and be loved and care for him, or I'll go crazy. I just ache and there is nothing I can do about it. God, how am I going to hold up?

Matt got home the day before Thanksgiving. After waiting for weeks, he just called one afternoon by radio from the boat and said he was bringing the *Sea Lion* home and would be in town in a few hours.

So I buzzed through the house straightening things up, and ran to the grocery store to buy some of Matt's favorite foods.

When Matt came, the moment was low-key. It was the middle of the afternoon. Chelsea, wide-eyed, silently watched us hug. She left the room and brought Matt her toothbrush. Finally we were just a normal little family doing unimportant things.

As I told Matt what I'd been up to he said, "I'm glad you're making friends."

"I hope they can be your friends too, Matt. It would be nice to be in Port Lions having Turkey Day with friends.…"

"No, Mama, I want you all to myself."

And it was better having Matt home than going to Port Lions by myself and Chelsea—the relief of at last being a couple.

The house was small enough that it was easy to rub up against Matt's shoulders or back into him, and he'd put his arms around me and I'd close my eyes and feel so right.

Matt had grown a beard and was so dark-looking and forbidding, with his golden eyes and white teeth the only bright spots in a head of black hair. I told him, "You kind of scare me with that beard."

"I don't mean to scare you."

"I want to feel you when you kiss me and not some little animal you keep under your lips."

"You're the only little animal I want to feel under my lips," Matt said and he pulled my hair back from my neck and started kissing my throat and under my ears. He pulled back and looked at me. "I'm scratching your skin, aren't I?"

I nodded, so he went into the bathroom to trim and shave his beard and then turned on the shower.

When he got out, he inspected my paint job and seemed a little disappointed not to find a blatant goof. "You did it all yourself?"

"Doesn't it look great, Matt? I'm so proud of the house." I'd gotten a braid rug that fit in the living room, so I rolled up the Oriental carpet and stuffed it behind the clothes in our bedroom closet. The brown-and-red Peruvian wall hangings decorated the beige walls, the plants sat in the window beneath the gold curtains I'd made, and red velvet material covered the sofa.

The next morning after breakfast, Matt started going out the front door.

"Where are you going?" I asked.

"Oh, I've got to do some things. You stay here."

"Can't I come too?" I wanted to say, but I didn't want to start a fight the day after he got home.

Matt returned four hours later with a huge box under his arm. He paced back and forth in the tiny living room, puffing on a cigarette. "C'mon, Nora, the suspense is killing me, don't you want to open your Christmas present?"

From the size of the box, I thought it would be much-needed pots and pans. As I opened it, I felt a satiny rustle and pulled out the lining of a fur coat of red fox, with the mottled colors of brown and red and gold.

I'd been wearing the brown-checked lumberman jacket Gramma Hunter sent us last Christmas, or the black velvet jacket for fancy times. A fur coat was the status symbol of the wife of a successful fisherman. Matt glowed with pride as I tried it on in bewilderment. The sleeves came down past my fingertips, the weight dragged on my shoulders and the front of the coat wrapped around me. I thought of movie stars and I thought of fur traders but I hardly thought of me. Matt had a smug grin as he looked at me. I couldn't tell him it wasn't worth it. I hugged him, but I couldn't feel him through the thickness of the fur coat. "You are so good to me."

"And I want a gold watch," he said. So we went out, me wearing a fur coat that would fit two of me, and compared all the gold watches in town before buying one with nuggets and jade stones in the watchband.

I wore my new fur coat over my blue jeans to a bridal shower that Robin had for Karen. Robin hooted at me when I walked in the front door. "Blue jeans and a fur coat! I suppose you wear your pearls to take out the trash."

"It's cold out, Robin—isn't that why you wear fur coats?" I was sweating underneath the heavy jacket. I felt like an underfed ox in a heavy yoke.

Afterwards the men came in to join us. Matt came to pick me up after working on the *Sea Lion*. He walked in with a distracted air and absent-mindedly took a glass of wine. He refused to be drawn into the gaiety, but waited impatiently, making hints to go, until I gave in and went home with him.

"You've been gone three months, you did fantastic. Why can't you enjoy yourself? You sit there worrying about who'll be on your crew and you can't enter into anything," I complained.

"You're too perceptive," he said dolefully, reminding me of my mother's comment, "He's a man who takes his pleasures seriously."

Then Matt left again. The season for larger king crab around Kodiak Island opened early in December and Robbie turned the *Sea Lion* over to Matt to run— the reward for being such a good crewmember in the Bering Sea.

The "brown paper packages tied up with string" began to arrive at the post office, and I made gingerbread cookie decorations to flesh out the ornament collection for our tree. I finished knitting Matt a heavy sweater with a Kodiak grizzly bear knit into the pattern on the back and sides.

I sent our cards out and put the manger scene up. Matt made weeklong trips, coming in at midnight and leaving before noon the next day. I'd always valued his determination, my "rock," but I was beginning to see a driven slavery to it.

Two days before Christmas I had myself a hissy fit and opened our presents while Chelsea napped. I knew Matt would not be home for Christmas, and I refused to be suckered into another waiting game. So I unwrapped everything, had a good cry, and wrapped the presents up again before Chelsea woke up. Matt got home at noon on Christmas Eve.

We celebrated at a party at Neil and Robin's trailer. When we arrived home, close to midnight, the snow was falling. I felt so unclaimed. As Matt carried Chelsea inside, I said, "I think I'll go to midnight Mass, okay?"

"Okay, you do what you want."

The church was warm and crowded. I stood at the back, just inside the door. After Mass began, a young couple squeezed in behind me. The smell of alcohol floated around them. He stood behind her and put both arms around her, hugging her passionately.

Then Dr. Copstead straggled in, and we shuffled to make room where there was none. Looking down, I saw dried bloodstains on his shoes.

Good old Kodiak, where you can do what you want without worrying about how you look. We're all just crummy humans. No angels here.

On Christmas Day, we celebrated with the gift-opening, turkey-stuffing, and naps. I put Chelsea down after getting the turkey in the oven and then sat on Matt's lap. "Did you have a good time at church last night?" Matt asked me, and ran his fingers around my neckline.

"Matt, that's a big part of Christmas to me, going to church. And going at other times, too. It's the only place I meet people who have kids. I wish you'd go with me and then people would know who my family is, where I belong."

"Nah, I used to go with my mother when she sang in the choir, but soon enough I realized that was bullshit."

"But I don't think it's bullshit to be thankful to be alive, with good health, or to think maybe there's something more than what you can see and touch. I like the idea that God sent a baby to make a bad old world good again."

"Don't get religious on me." Matt kissed me and then stood up, holding me close while pushing me off his lap. "C'mon, we could use a nap too."

Sloopy Don knocked at the door. "Hey, Eleanor, you having a good Christmas? Santa good to you?"

I liked this. Here was someone dropping in on us to celebrate the holiday. While Matt made Sloop a drink, I grabbed a present I'd given Matt from under the tree and quickly taped it up again. I handed it to Sloop when he sat down with his drink.

"Eleanor, here, you nice lady, giving me a present, I don't have nothing for you," he muttered and I was touched to see him struggle to unknot the ribbon.

"Just tear it open, Don," I said. He opened the book of Robert Service poetry and laughed, shaking his scraggly hair. "Hey lady, this is nice, but I can't read, except my name."

I was so embarrassed, how stupid and schoolmarmish of me to think he'd like a book. Matt saved the day, though. He handed Sloop a pair of wool socks and said, "Well here, this'll do you. Keep your feet warm."

"Oh yeah, now this is great. Thanks, you're good people."

Then he and Matt started talking fishing and gear and quotas and Chelsea woke up so I was occupied with her until Don left. Then we took a drive to see the Christmas lights, and when we got home the turkey still wasn't done, so we had more drinks. I'd miscalculated the turkey's size, mixing up the number of pounds with the number of dollars. It was finally done at nine o'clock, and by then we were almost incoherent from our cocktails. We nibbled at the turkey, and then collapsed in bed.

The next morning I was floored to discover Matt planned to go out fishing. I looked out the window with tears running down my face as he bustled around, getting himself ready.

"I hate to see you cry," he said.

"Then don't go. Christmas isn't just throwing presents at each other. It's a season to kick back and enjoy whatever your year has brought you."

He shrugged his shoulders and left.

CHAPTER FIVE

HOMEFRONT
In which we spend the winter with Matt at home;
we enter Kodiak's social scene of television, bars, and dances;
I become pregnant

I wanted Matt home for New Year's Eve. I wanted to have what I wanted, not to be called upon once again to be noble or indifferent, to sacrifice another holiday to the god of fishing. I stayed up until midnight, afraid to hope, afraid to accept disappointment, reserving until the last minute the expectation that Matt might barge in with a bottle of champagne to sing "Auld Lang Syne."

As midnight passed, I prayed out loud. "What's it to You if he does or doesn't come home? What's the big deal if I get what I want occasionally? Why can't I be spoiled just once?"

A few days after New Year's, Matt came in from fishing. Robin called and asked if Matt would escort her, Neil's sister Tina, and me to a dance at the Harvester. "I wouldn't mind having a harem for one night," he chuckled into the phone.

We met at the barn-like Harvester Inn on Mill Bay Road. After a few strong drinks, Matt pulled me up from my chair and let me push him around the dance floor, spinning and grabbing me till I was laughing. "You got that shit-eating grin on your face again, Mama," he growled into my ear and kissed me.

After we sat down again, Matt asked Robin and then Tina to dance.

"Good for Matt," Robin approved, as he led pale, bespectacled Tina to the dance floor.

I was pleased that Robin and Matt got along so well. She wasn't intimidated by his gruff, wordless manner, but teased and laughed at him till he'd have to respond. His killer comebacks didn't insult or shock her, and she'd laugh back even harder. I loved her mixture of common sense and high standards. It was a relief to have one of my friends who could break through Matt's tough reserve and not be horrified at what he said.

The band blared on, while we shouted at each other across the table, our heads practically touching. The darkness and smoke would have been intolerable if we hadn't been drinking and smoking ourselves. A crowd of Matt's fishing friends came in and hunkered over our table.

Here I am and I belong. I'm Matt's wife. This time I'm not going to get drunk and get Matt mad at me. His friends are going to think he's so lucky.

I listened to their gossip.

"Gloria's a great lady—nice looking, four kids, keeps the house together, has fun."

"Gloria's a fool—to put up with Robbie's chippy shit."

"Oh, come on, she knows about it—they must have some kind of deal going on between them, some kind of understanding."

"Yeah, well, they better, or she *is* a fool."

"What about him? Jan jumps out of his truck, and he jumps out after her. Scrapes the shit out of his arm. Jeez."

The waitress came to our table. "They sent ya a six-pack, rum and coke okay?" She set six drinks in front of Matt and jerked her head over towards a table of fishermen across the room. Matt grabbed the first glass, saluted the crowd opposite us, and took a hearty swig.

"How are you going to finish all these and drive home?" I asked.

"Ah, car knows its way home. I can drive it with my eyes closed. Drink up." He set a glass in front of me and I sipped at it, tasting the sweetly heavy rum on my lips. I remembered my dad's breath at his worst moments.

Robin was talking earnestly to a skinny young guy with glasses. Matt glowered at them. "I wonder what Neil would do if he saw this," he muttered.

I couldn't believe he was serious. "They're just talking," I said.

"That's how they want it to look," he said. "Here Neil's out fishing, busting his butt, and his wife is hustling and I'm supposed to be looking out for her."

I wondered if he ever worried about me when he was out fishing, if he was proud that I didn't flirt with other guys.

Matt leaned over to the table where Robin was sitting. "What the hell you think you're doing, buddy?" he snarled.

"Matt, he's the dogcatcher—you know, animal control?" Robin told Matt and laughed.

Sloopy Don poked me, and I turned around to talk to him, but then I heard chairs falling to the floor. When I turned my head, Robin, Matt, and the dogcatcher were all standing.

"Hey, buddy, you're way out of line!" Matt yelled at the skinny man and slammed a fist into his face. As the dogcatcher reeled back, Robin threw herself on Matt.

"Oh Matt, I love you! I love you!" she babbled, putting herself between Matt and the dogcatcher. I thought she was trying to distract Matt from the other guy, to stop the fighting. She was pretty drunk, though.

I could envision blood and bruises and the police coming after us. I grabbed Matt's arm and pulled him out of the mayhem. If he'd shaken me off, I couldn't have forced him to leave, but he let me shove him through the crowd till we were inside the truck. We silently drove home, seething like two festering volcanoes.

Robin somehow was already at our house and as we walked in, she broke off whatever she was saying to Tina, who looked even more bewildered than usual. "I wanted to make sure Matt didn't hurt you, Nora. Are you afraid of him hitting you?"

"Robin, I brought Matt home. He's not going to hurt me."

After Robin and Tina rushed out the door, Matt growled, "Robin better watch herself. That guy had ideas."

"Oh, come on, Matt. Robin can handle herself. They were just talking."

"Yeah, well, the reason that's all they did is because I stepped in."

"Yeah. The big strong bully has to muscle some skinny little wimp. Real big man," I sneered, "takes the law into his own hands."

"Damn straight, and it's a good thing I did, too."

"Yeah, well, I would much rather have had some loving, concerned wimp come home to me than a selfish oaf stay away from me."

"Right, Eleanor." He threw himself onto the bed, fully dressed, reeking of smoke and alcohol, his legs falling over the side.

"You big bully...." I kicked his foot.

He charged up from the bed and put his hands around my neck and held me up against the wall. Then he dropped me and flung himself back on the bed.

I crumpled up on the rug and Chelsea woke up crying in the next room.

I've thrown my heart away to a monster.

Matt passed out immediately. I got Chelsea up and dressed the frightened little creature. I cried as I packed a suitcase with clothes for Chelsea and me. With the baby on one shoulder and my suitcase in hand, I left the house. I strapped Chelsea in her car seat, all the while wondering where we would go.

Not to a friend's—I can't let them know how bad we fought. I don't have the money or the guts to go to the hotel and check into a room. I can't even drive all night, there's not enough roads.

I unbuckled the baby and came back inside.

I made her a bottle of warm milk and rocked her to sleep and then lay down on the sofa.

In the morning Matt came out of the bedroom and put his hand on my shoulder.

"You throttled me," I said.

"Well, what about you? You kicked me."

Yeah, I guess I asked for it. This is too scary.

Matt went back to work for Robbie, fixing and painting the *Sea Lion* after its tough season in the Bering Sea. One morning, I went to wash clothes at the laundromat. Before I could stop her, Chelsea toddled up to this forbidding-looking guy with his foot crossed over his knee. She touched his muddy boot and started putting her mouth on the boot. "Chelsea, baby, no!" I pulled her away and recognized Eric, the stuttering horseshoer.

"Eric! How're you doing?"

"W-well, I tried the fishing but just c-c-c-ouldn't take the sea, throwing up all d-d-day long."

"Your wife must like having you home." When I saw his face fall I could have bitten my stupid tongue off.

"Sh-she's…working at a fisheries p-p-project on Afognak Island. Well, we're s-s-s-splitting up." He looked sad and wistful.

"Oh Eric, I'm so sorry."

"Yeah, well, I w-w-w-w-ant to have k-k-kids someday, and she just d-d-d-d-doesn't w-w-w-ant to."

I should match her up with Matt and me with Eric.

Tricia sent me a letter with newspaper clippings about Jamie and Fitz and Doug being busted for dealing cocaine.

"Look, Matt, Jamie and those guys got arrested. I always thought this would happen."

"Yeah, there's been busts all around them for over a year and none of the characters they rounded up can keep their mouths shut." Matt was trying to dress Chelsea, and she wriggled around, making her big burly dad sweat.

"Poor Gail, she was always so worried and disapproving and careful and now she has another mess to deal with."

"Those guys were idiots, thinking they could get away with it. It was too good to be true."

"I feel sort of guilty. We all enjoyed the scene—the glory, the rebellion, the parties, the thrills, but I guess they had the biggest share of all, especially the adventure."

"Oh, so you miss the great adventures you had with Sam?"

"No, Matt, he always cut me out of it. Now I'm glad he did, especially since Fitz's girlfriend was indicted for the time she made a trip to Colombia with him. I remember telling her it sounded like fun, and she said, 'Oh yeah, sitting in a hotel room, blowing up rubbers and bouncing them off the walls. That's real exciting.'"

"Yeah, they dreamed up a plane-flying scheme to involve me when I was going to aviation school, but I never bit. They were half-assed." Chelsea squirmed away from him, but I tackled her and started brushing her hair. She squealed like I was pulling it out.

"Oh, let her go, it looks good enough." Matt lit a cigarette, obviously relieved that his ordeal was over. I came up behind his chair and put my arms around his neck.

"Matt, you saved my life. Those guys were crazy. Don't ever think I wish I were back with them. You're real and you're here."

He patted my hand and grunted. "So you want your piano sent up here?"

"Oh yes, Matt, that would make me so happy!"

He stood up. "Okay, we'll get it shipped up here. Call your mother, why don't you, and tell her to get somebody to crate it up and get it to a freight company?"

I hugged him close and then he pulled away, holding me at arm's length. "Look, Nora, I don't think now's a good time to take a vacation. I'm finally getting known and it wouldn't be a good time to skip town."

"Yeah, and besides a trip to Bali would be over in a month. I'd rather have you here at home if you don't have to be out fishing. You can take a vacation from fishing and stay home and let me take care of you."

"I don't need anyone to take care of me."

I didn't know what to say and he put his parka on and walked out the door, growling, "Be back later."

The rest of that winter, Mat would leave early in the morning and usually be home for dinner. I could chatter at him while I cooked, and fold clothes next to him on the sofa. On Saturdays I'd clean up the house, listening to "America's Top Forty" on the radio while Chelsea napped, waiting for Matt to come home. He'd stay up late watching "Saturday Night Live," and I'd fall asleep with my head in his lap.

One Sunday he said he'd paint the bedroom, and we picked a warm butterscotch color. We moved the furniture around and I took Chelsea out of the house so he could get the work finished that day.

That night I got into bed after Matt and crowded into him, rubbing his legs. He had his back to me and said, "Ah no, Mama, I'm too tired."

I was stopped cold at first, so embarrassed, and then I said, "Shut up and roll over."

He chuckled and obeyed. With the gold quilt on the bed and the red rug on the floor and the walls now a warm glow, I felt like a caramel candy melting in Matt's mouth, just warmth and goldenness and no danger of frostbite, like blood under my skin warming out from me, rich and alive and reaching to Matt.

The next morning I sat next to Matt on the bed as he was putting on his socks. "Hey Matt, if I got pregnant now, the baby would be born in November...."

"I thought you were using birth control."

"I am, it's called fishing." Matt's brows knit in incomprehension. "It's a joke, Matt. I want another baby; Chelsea's almost two now."

"You like being pregnant?"

"Yeah, I do. I like feeling real big and full of your love and holding our baby under my heart until he's ready to be alive."

"He?"

"Or she; does it matter to you?" I plunked myself in his lap.

"No, just as long as it's healthy." He kissed me and we smiled at each other. "Well, yeah, I want a boy."

"I know, Matt, I do too. Would you be with me if I had the baby at the end of king crab season?"

"Yeah, that should be over by Christmas."

"And I can have the baby in Seattle with the same doctor and hospital and everything?"

Matt squeezed me and then stood up. "Yes, Mama, anything your little heart desires."

Still feels like winter in Kodiak. Sundays are quiet and restful, and with Matt working in town, I don't feel that abandoned Sunday feeling. I love to read, knit, bake, but Matt gets edgy if he's not working.

As long as he is working, Matt's happy—he doesn't know how to play. He doesn't care if I don't work as hard as he does, but our roles are clearly divided in his mind. He can't respect himself if he has fun with me.

One Sunday afternoon, after I'd taken Chelsea to church and Matt came home from the boat harbor, I put a roast in the oven for Sunday dinner and talked Matt into driving up to Baranof Park.

It was cold and windy and the gravel in the play area was frozen, but Chelsea could still swing on the swings. I jumped out of the Jeep and lifted

Chelsea from her car seat. Matt reached up to the dashboard and grabbed a magazine.

"Well, come on," I said. "Come with us and see."

"No, I'll stay here. You go ahead."

"Matt, I want you to come. You should see how cute Chelsea is, how much she loves to swing."

He gave me one of his snorting, derisive laughs. "I don't want to push swings."

"Is there anything you want to do besides fish? Is there anything that means as much to you?" I slammed the door.

The piano arrived at the port dock. We drove down to the freight warehouse and put it on Robbie's truck. It was so heavy, I was afraid the wood stairs would collapse under its weight, moving it into the house.

When we got home, Robbie and Matt and Leo Davidoff got the piano off the truck and unloaded it from the crate. Robbie was a skinny, wiry kind of guy, but Leo was like Matt, as strong as an ox, and if it weren't for the awkwardness of getting it down the wood stairs, Matt could almost have moved it himself.

So they just walked down the steps with the piano between them and set it on the floor. They put it against the window in the middle of the living room and then took a smoke break. Matt looked out the front door at the crate at the top of the stairs. "I'll make a garbage can stand out of it," he said. "It's as big as half the living room and sturdy as the house."

Robbie looked right at me. "Now play something. C'mon, Eleanor, play us some music."

I rarely played in front of people; whenever someone was listening I choked and got embarrassed, felt like I was performing for a recital. But I had to play for them.

All I could play was the first song I ever learned—an easy Mozart sonata. The men looked like I'd handed them finger sandwiches and bone China teacups.

Robbie said, "Yeah, now how about some boogie-woogie, some honky-tonk?"

"I don't know much by heart," I muttered, knowing my recital pieces would sound like some strangled Teutonic opera to them. But thank God, just then Chelsea got into something, so I ran after her and the men took off.

Matt and I decided the piano would look better against the wall, after we'd moved the bureau into Chelsea's room. Matt pushed one end of the piano and I placed my hand on the other and put my shoulder to the end of the upright. We grunted, and I said I had to rest. Matt shoved the piano into place and came up to me with a big smile on his face and said, "You know, you're just about worthless. But I think I like you that way."

Then Sloopy Don came to the door and took Matt off drinking downtown, and I sat down to play "The Minstrel Boy."

I'm being good-natured and reasonable. Someone has to stay with the baby.

It took forever to get through the song, because I insisted on playing by ear and refused to look at the notes on the page. I played it over and over till I got it right, remembering all the dreary classical music I'd had to memorize for lessons. *I can do this.*

Then I went to bed. When Matt came in, I snuggled next to him and he put his arm around me and passed out. With him breathing next to me in bed and our baby in the next room and the music from the piano faintly echoing, still warming the house, I thought, *I have everything.*

The next morning the phone rang and when Matt hung up, he said, "Davidoff took the *Maggie J* out last night after we were out drinking."

"What happened?"

"He hit a rock in Whale Pass—it's got a big hole in it now. They're back in town, but he won't be fishing again till he gets that fixed. He'll lose a week."

"Doesn't he know not to drink and drive?"

"Oh, they all think the road's so wide, the sea's so big they can avoid any rock. Davidoff's got a problem, but you can't tell him what to do with his boat."

One night Matt and I threw a dinner party, inviting Robin and Neil and Karen and Scott. I envied Robin and Karen. Neil and Scott worked together on Scott's boat, the *Wolverine*, and it seemed like they had time for parties and hunting and exploring the wilderness, visiting people and making new friends.

"Neil's got such an inquisitive mind," Robin said. "He has a scientific approach to everything. The rest of the crew couldn't believe it when they hauled a huge boulder in the trawl and wanted to examine it!" she hooted.

"What did they think they would find?" Matt snorted.

Karen had just gone out on a trip with Scott. "It was rough and I was really scared and I kept telling Scott, 'You've got to call the Coast Guard, we're not going to make it!' But we did." She shrugged. "I don't really like going out on the boat. It's cramped and I get so seasick."

"I just know I have this affinity for the sea and wouldn't get seasick, like I'm just sitting in a big rocking chair," I said.

Robin said, "It's all in your mind. If you work hard and get out in the fresh air, it's not so bad."

After dinner, we all left the crowded table and walked two steps to the chairs and sofa at the other end of the room. Six people and a baby packed the house.

Matt put on his Waylon Jennings album and Karen stopped to listen. "I love this! Listen to the strong beat!" She rocked to the beat as she sat on the sofa. Scott laughed at her, but Matt was pleased.

"You like country western, huh? So do I."

I sat down on the sofa next to Karen. "I like country western, too." I sat on Karen's skirt, and she raised herself to free it.

"Well, you put up with it, but don't you really like more traditional stuff, like classical music?" She sat down on my skirt, pinning me to the sofa.

"I just like all kinds of music, like all kinds of religions." I tugged my skirt from under her and as she started to get up again, we stopped and looked at each other and everyone started laughing.

"Well, don't stop now, " Scott said, "You two are just getting into it."

Everyone laughed and I felt so happy and proud. *Everyone has fun at my house.*

Afterwards, when everyone left, Matt and I played Scrabble, but I got a 50-point word with my first seven letters. Matt flipped the board over and said, "What a stupid game."

I raised holy hell over the TV. There was a sick show about a priest who practiced devil worship and killed kids. It was bad enough that Matt watched it at all, but it was late at night and Chelsea had been put down for the evening so I busied myself in the kitchen cleaning up.

But, like most of the evening shows, the station showed it a second time the next Saturday afternoon.

"Matt, it's sunny outside, let's go for a walk. You already saw that the other night. Remember?"

"No, I'm just gonna sit."

I felt disgust and rage overtaking me. I dressed Chelsea in her snowsuit and went outside, but instead of blowing off steam, I got madder and more righteous. I came back in, and Matt was still watching.

"How can you sit in front of that? Don't you have any respect for your mind?"

"I'm relaxing, okay?"

"What kind of an impression do you think that makes on Chelsea?"

"She's not even watching it, Eleanor. It's not making any impression at all."

"Don't you think she can pick up the feeling, the scrounginess of that show?"

"Look, this is my home! I work hard, I come home to eat and sleep and relax, and I don't want to get my ass chewed for watching TV!"

I went wild. "This is my home too, and it's not a pit stop for your creature comforts. I don't want the TV blaring low life and sleaziness at me!" I ripped the cable out of the wall. "And I'm sick of cooking your meals and being your mommy and being left to deal with everything by myself when you're gone and being walked all over when you're home!" I tore open the refrigerator door and grabbed an armful of jars and threw them out the front door onto the steps. Matt didn't stop me as I made several more trips, throwing the entire contents of the fridge out the front door, but when I was finished, he had his parka on and was out the front door and roaring down the road in the Jeep and gone before I could stop him. I was all worn out.

I didn't start crying till after I put Chelsea to bed, and Matt still hadn't returned. I called Tricia in Seattle and told her I was afraid he'd never come back. "He will, Nora, and when he does, just put your arms around him and tell him you love him. He'll be back."

The next morning, Chelsea and I were up early when the Jeep roared up and I heard Matt outside cleaning up the front steps. He finally came in with an undamaged ketchup bottle and put it in the fridge.

I put my arms around him. "Matt, I'm sorry."

"No, you were right. It's okay."

"Are you hungry? Do you want some breakfast?"

He drew back, feigning horror. "Heaven forbid I should ask you to make me breakfast. C'mon, I'll take you out to the Mecca."

So we had breakfast at the Mecca with its mirrored ball revolving above our heads, and the early-morning drinkers staggering in to get their first round of the day.

We ate in silence, Chelsea in her high chair. Matt started chuckling to himself.

"What's so funny?"

"You are, Nora. You get so excited. My sweet little thing detonating like that...."

"Hey Matt, I'm going to take a test at the doctor's today."

"Are you pregnant?"

"I know I am, I'm just getting confirmation. Are you glad?"

"Oh yeah, I want a boy! I'll buy you a diamond ring if it's a boy!"

"You'll reward me with a diamond ring for a boy?"

"C'mon now, Mama, don't get mad. I'm happy. You're just too sensitive."

After Allison's piano lesson, I was visiting with Gloria, folding laundry.

"I've got to get Robbie more heavy socks before he heads out to Bristol Bay. Does Matt go through socks like they were Kleenex? Robbie does."

"When's Robbie going out to Bristol Bay?"

"Herring's due to start in May. They may strike for prices, but he'll probably leave anyway end of next week. Then he'll be back for the salmon season around the island in June."

"After Matt being gone for three months last fall, I don't think he's planning to go too." It sounded like a prayer.

Gloria rolled her eyes. "I think you better have a talk with your husband."

"Matt, you're not doing herring, are you?"

"Why do you want to know?"

"Because I live with you, this is our home, we share a life."

"Yeah, I'm going with the *Sea Lion*."

"But...."

"I'm a fisherman. I'm with the *Sea Lion*. Herring is a fishing season. I'm not lazy Eleanor."

"And I'm not single. We belong to you. You and I are having another baby."

"Ah Mama, it will be OK." His eyes softened and he pulled me to him.

"I'm lonely without you."

"Why don't you go to Seattle, visit your Mom and Tricia and check in with your doctor?"

"Don't you want to come too? Don't you want to have some good times?"

"Look—you go to Seattle. I'll go to Bristol Bay and come down to see you when the season's over. Then we'll come back and I'll tender salmon around the island this summer and I'll be in town every couple of days."

Robin stopped by later that day while she was out walking Monster, Neil's huge dog. Robin gets to the nitty-gritty so quick. I told her about my fight over the TV with Matt, and she said, "It's so funny. Before you're married, you think, 'Well, if we have a disagreement, we'll just work it out, nothing's insurmountable.' And then afterwards you think, 'Oh no, I just can't stand this, I can't live with this, what have I done?'"

"Yeah, it doesn't take long to find out how irreconcilable your differences are."

Robin stood at the front door, looking up and down the street for Monster. "Darn it, where is he? Neil has this special whistle for him, it sounds like a shriek—how does he do it?" She put her fingers in her mouth, but couldn't produce a whistle. I called and whistled, but we sounded so puny and thin and stupid with the trucks roaring on the roadway above us.

CHAPTER SIX

SUMMER IN SEATTLE
In which I ripen in Seattle while Matt fishes the Bering Sea;
we go on a fishing trip

On one of those fresh spring days, when Kodiak felt like a freshly washed sheet snapping in the wind, Matt left for the herring season in Bristol Bay. Before I had one night to miss him, I boarded a plane and took Chelsea down to Seattle. I wore a new skirt and blouse I'd made, and thought I didn't look too pregnant yet.

On the plane, I sat next to a burly man in his 30s who offered to buy me a drink. As I described my life to him, he shook his head. "I couldn't live like that. I couldn't be faithful," he said flatly. "After three weeks, at the most, I need to have someone. I couldn't do it."

"What if you had to?" I asked.

He shook his head. "Couldn't do it."

How did he find someone to sleep with, just because it was time for him? Did he mean he paid prostitutes, or did he have no problem finding willing women? All a man has to do is reach out his hand, any woman will do. What would it be like to sleep with someone you didn't really know? I don't want another man, I want Matt.

I loved being in Seattle with Chelsea getting lots of attention for all her cute two-year-old tricks, with Mom and Tricia and even Lou laughing at how funny and dear Chelsea was. We just sat around sunning ourselves, drinking tea and watching the days pass by in the back yard.

Peggy was pregnant too. Her baby was due a month before me, around Thanksgiving. "Couldn't stand having me center stage, could you?" she said with a big smile.

Is she being mean or just teasing me?

Toward the end of June, Matt called from Kodiak. "Well, I'm back in town," he sighed. "When are you coming home?"

"Are you all through for the summer now?"

"Nah, I'm going out with Robbie on his salmon charter the first of July."

"Around the island?"

"He's chartered for Bristol Bay. It'll take us about a week to get out there from town."

"Matt, last fall when you were gone to the Bering Sea for three months, I thought I'd die from missing you. And then you went herring fishing and now you're talking about being gone from home until…?"

"I'll be back the middle of August and then I'll be fishing king crab around Kodiak."

"Matt, I don't want to come back to Kodiak for two days if you're just going to go again for another month. Why don't you come down before salmon season starts? Besides, the doctor wants me to take an ultrasound test to see if everything's okay with the baby.…"

"Why, what's wrong with the baby?"

"I don't think anything is—just to make sure, I guess. I just feel like an unwed mother going through all this without you to talk to and be with."

Matt grunted.

"Couldn't you come down and we could play a little before you have to go fishing? It's not like home when you're always gone. This way we could at least have some time together before you go out fishing for another six weeks."

"Well, I'll think about it and talk to Robbie," he sighed.

After he hung up I called the airlines and all the regular seats were filled but there were a few first-class seats available, so I arranged a ticket for him.

Matt called back. "I checked with the airlines and there's no seats available."

"There is in first class, Matt, so I got you a ticket."

"First class? Hey, I'm not made of money, you know."

"But it's worth it to me to be together."

He sighed. "Okay, so when's the flight?"

After talking to Matt, I sat in the garden, sunning myself and feeling contented, looking forward to him coming down and being carefree together in Seattle.

When Matt got off the plane at the Seattle airport, he put his arms around me, and glanced down. "You've grown a lot bigger the last two months. Your round little belly looks cute."

The weather was beautiful and I felt like a sun-warmed peach, bursting with love and life. At Shine, Matt stood behind me and rubbed my shoulders. He loosened the shoulder straps of my blouse and we went inside. I fantasized about steam heat as we made love.

We stayed with Tricia and Lou, and it felt like we were a bunch of teenagers with our parents out of town as we partied through the next week. Peggy lent us her VW bug to use while she and Glenn went on vacation. We drove to the airport to see them off. Matt told them he'd had a beard when he came back from the Bering Sea, but shaved it off. Peggy said to me, "Did you tell Matt he had to get rid of his beard?"

Before I could answer, Matt said, "She didn't like the way it scratched her tender thighs."

Everyone was stark silent and I could have died. Matt just grinned.

On the way home we stopped at an Italian restaurant just off the highway with a phony grape arbor in the ceiling, latticework with plastic leaves and grapes twined in it. I thought of *The Godfather* and how the mother said to Al Pacino just before he killed his brother, "You always have your family." I envisioned having Chelsea's wedding reception or our 50th wedding anniversary there.

Will we be a devoted couple then, beaming with pride among our friends and progeny?

We went out for dinner with Matt's old friends, most of them under indictment for drug dealing. "Gail says they're coming down hardest on Jamie," I said to Matt as we drove downtown.

"Probably because he's the most arrogant about it," Matt said.

We sat in a private booth in a Japanese restaurant, eight around the table. Shoji screens secluded us from the rest of the diners. The dinner was served one small, neat course at a time. We drank sake continuously.

Jamie was performing the story of his arrest. "Yeah, so they bust in the house and this agent looks at the fireplace made out of Harley bumpers welded together and says. 'So this is where Jamie Campbell lives'...."

"And Jamie's little brother Mike, you know the one that's almost deaf, is yelling 'What? What?' the whole time they're reading him his rights," Gail added, laughing.

"So now what happens?" Matt asked.

"Well, I got a pretty good defense lawyer...."

"That my mom's pension is paying for," Gail muttered.

Jamie flashed an irritated look at her. "I don't know how this will turn out, they're bringing up people from South America to finger us."

"It's so unfair. It's all recreational drugs! Everybody does it!" Rita said.

"Oh, not anymore," Gail said. "Now everybody's into making money and dressing for success."

"Conformity is back," I put in.

Rita said, "Meanwhile these guys where I'm working—Microsoft—wander around barefoot with stringy hair making computers...."

"That's dressing for success?"

Gail finished, "Well, you know, they're a breed apart, real goofballs, but the days of smoking dope and making music on every street corner and turning the world green are over."

We cruised town that night, going from place to place till finally just Doug and Rita, Matt and I were at a restaurant at Shilshole Marina. I was beginning to get the urge to lay my head down on the table when Matt said, "Let's call it a night. I'll go get the car and bring it to the front."

Rita and I stood at the restaurant door for the longest time, when finally Doug and Matt roared up, the front bumper of Peggy's Volkswagen dragging and dented. "How'd that happen?" I asked.

"Oh, somebody must have rammed it while we were inside," Matt explained. "I think I can fix it."

We spent the last days of our vacation cruising auto body shops, finding a replacement fender, pounding out the dents, and taking the car for a new paint job, so we could return it to Peggy without explanation. Tricia and Lou invited some friends over for a dinner party, and Matt excused himself early and went out to the garage, hammering away at the car.

Before Matt flew back to tender salmon in Bristol Bay, we made plans to explore the Kenai Peninsula in August, when I was back home and Matt finished tendering. His mom wasted no time in calling me to say that I should be going back to Alaska with him. "I just think wives should be with their husbands."

"But I can't be with him out on the boat. That's where he'll be."

"You knew what to expect. He was a fisherman when you married him."

But I just said, "I need to make sure the baby's okay."

Peggy, too, chastised me for staying in Seattle when Matt went back fishing. "Don't you feel guilty, partying down here while he's working on the boat?"

"I'm not partying, I'm looking after Chelsea and if her dad can't be with us, then the next best thing for me to do is surround her with people who care about her—and me."

"But that's so selfish, with Matt up there all by himself."

I swallowed hard, so afraid to say too much, afraid that my heart would start pounding blood into my brains and tongue, but so fed up with sly little digs. "I know, I wish he could be home more with us, but he's a fisherman. We're home by ourselves most of the time, but now that I'm down here, I should take the tests for the baby."

"Couldn't you have those tests in Kodiak?"

"No. Besides, I want to go to the same doctor who'll be delivering the baby down here. Would you want to have your baby in Kodiak if there were complications?"

"Oh, no way! Glenn would never let me, even if I wanted to!"

Matt's mom and dad drove us to the airport to see Matt off. We were sitting, waiting at the gate when Gail and Jamie strolled up to us.

"Well, hi there," Jamie greeted Matt's dad, who picked up Chelsea and walked away from us all without acknowledging Jamie or Gail.

"We'll take Chelsea for an ice cream cone—you go have a drink," Matt's mom said and they bustled off like we were going to offer them a joint or hand them a subpoena.

When Matt and I were walking towards his plane, I asked him, "Why do your folks always isolate themselves from everyone? Do they really think we're all so pure?"

"Well, Eleanor, Jamie was a drug dealer."

"Yes, and he dealt the drugs—or rather gave the drugs—to us. Would they snub us if they knew we were in on it, too?"

"Probably."

After Matt flew back to Alaska, Chelsea and I went to stay with Gail. She walked in the door of their riverfront cabin with a stack of frozen pizza crusts up to her chin, two five-pound bricks of mozzarella cheese, and a ten-gallon tub of tomato sauce. We made pizzas all weekend and Gail waded through the legal files regarding Jamie's upcoming trial.

"Are Doug and Rita going through all this, too?" I asked.

"Oh, Jamie thinks they don't have any solid proof on Doug. He never went to South America. But I think his dad hired the most expensive lawyer on the Eastside and he got Doug to cooperate for lesser charges."

"Doug always seems to make out okay, doesn't he?"

"Yeah. But Rita's coming over, so, you know...."

"Oh yeah, shut up."

Gail described her hike in to a mountain hot springs. "It was magical! The moon was full, this big orange globe, and we were singing Kris Kristofferson songs and then later it started to rain, and we'd get out of the pool, standing around in the driving rain till we were shivering and then hop back into the hot water. I felt like I was melting."

"I wish I could do something like that."

"Don't you and Matt do stuff like that up in Alaska? I thought that was what it was all about, the Great Outdoors and getting into nature. Why don't you take advantage of it?"

"Matt's rarely home for a full day, and we never can plan to do something like that, it's just laundry and dinner and maybe a run to the bank for excitement."

Rita arrived and showed me a bill for car repair. "That's from when the guys smashed the cars in the parking lot."

"Your car got wrecked too? I thought it was just Peggy's VW that got hit."

Gail rolled her eyes and said with a knowing smile, "Nora, Doug and Matt were playing bumper cars out in the parking lot. Doug hit Matt's sister's car deliberately and ripped the bumper off it."

"That makes me so mad, that he lied to me!"

"Well, Nora, look how angry and judgmental you get when you know the truth," Rita said.

"What am I supposed to be—pleased? And then to lie about it!"

"Yeah, Rita, it makes Matt and Doug partners in keeping the truth from Nora, you know, hide the truth from the little woman, patronize her," Gail added.

"I just wish Matt didn't have to have such reckless fun, that he could loosen up with me and Chelsea. I guess we're not enough of an adventure for him, but playing bumper cars in the parking lot is."

The return trip home involved another hairy landing. The pilot had trouble seeing the runway in Kodiak, and he tried repeatedly to land the plane. After circling the runway for what seemed like hours, we managed to land on the third approach. The weather in Kodiak was as dismal and blustery as February, but I was so glad to see Matt at the airport.

When we walked into the house, I remembered when we first moved in, nearly two years before, and thought, "This really looks like our home." It was modestly beautiful, the shiny red-brick linoleum, the tidy little living and kitchen areas, the pale green glow from the grassy bank outside the front windows.

Karen and Scott were getting married, and later that week, her family flew in to Kodiak for the wedding. As the salmon season around the island ended, the fishermen and schoolteachers who fished at camping sites during the summer headed back to town. Kodiak was bustling with anticipation and shortened days.

Robin's younger sister Sarah was coming to live with Robin and Neil for a while, too. I drove out to the airport with Robin to pick Sarah up. She strode off the plane, looking totally different from Robin's button-eyed pertness. Sarah fit the image of a lumberjack woman, tall and stocky with everything about her saying "big"—big blue eyes, lush bond hair, big wide lips in a ready smile.

The next day we climbed Pillar Mountain to pick Alaska cranberries from the low bushy plants that straggled up the wind-swept slopes. At the top we could look out over the town and boat harbor. We scrambled around, crouching low to pick the hard little crimson berries.

"They almost taste like poison—bitter and pithy," Sarah said, spitting a berry out.

"How do you know what poison tastes like?" Robin chirped in, and Sarah cast her eyes sideways in exasperation.

"'Tis pity they're pithy," I remarked and Chelsea, squirreled away in a back carrier, picked up the singsong.

"Pitty, pitty, pitty."

"Itty bitty berries are pitty, my pretty," I chanted to her.

Sarah chimed in then with a Wicked Witch imitation from the *Wizard of Oz*: "…My pretty…and your little dog, too!" She came up to Chelsea, who was squirming and giggling, and made a face at her. "We're nuts, huh, little snickerdoodle?"

"Let's head down and soak these and make cranberry jam," Robin said.

But when I got home, I mashed some of the berries and smeared them like rouge on my cheeks. "See Matt? Now I don't have to buy blusher."

"Really living off the land, aren't you Mama? You're beautiful without any of that shit."

"I love you, Matt."

"I love you, too."

A few days later Matt and I looked at Larson's trailer, located further out on Mission Road, past the Beachcombers. The trailer sat parallel to the road, beneath the hill where the Baptist mission housed kids from the villages and kids who needed foster care. The trailer had a huge front yard, a built-in fireplace and a view across Mission Road of the channel and Long Island. Next to the trailer was a pasture where the mission kids raised some cows.

Looking inside the trailer was a little dismaying. The kitchen was tiny, though it had carved woodwork. The living room was enormous for a trailer, ten feet wide by twenty feet long, but furnished with a pea-green rug and dismal gold sofas with flowered cushions. At least the cushions could be turned over to the backside, which was solid gold material.

Although the three bedrooms were small, they had built-in drawers with lots of storage space. The two bathrooms were dank and moldy-looking. But of all the houses or trailers we'd looked at since coming to Kodiak, it was the only one that I could envision myself living in. Back at the rabbit hutch, we called up the Larsons, but they didn't call back.

I put Chelsea down for her nap and went back out to the living room. Matt was standing in the front door smoking. I went up to him and put my arms around him and he gently pulled them away and drew back to look at me. "Look, I hate making promises to you that I can't keep, but I decided, instead of fishing around the island, to head out to the Bering Sea with Robbie again this year for king crab."

"No, Matt, I don't want to be pregnant and alone. You went herring and salmon fishing and you said you'd fish king crab around Kodiak so you could be close to home this fall. We talked about it and that's what you said. Please, Matt."

"I need to make more money. I want to get out of this little Hobbit hole. I can do that with Robbie."

"Matt, there's more to life than making money. Please don't go now."

"It's not just the money, Eleanor. What other job do I have? Or am I just supposed to twiddle my thumbs and go on welfare?"

I knew I'd lost when he called me Eleanor. Now I was the enemy and he had to win. "What kind of wife would I be if I didn't want you around? Don't you care about that?"

"Oh, Mama, come here." He tossed his cigarette butt outside and held his arms out to me. "I hate leaving you too. I just wish I had a choice. The time will go by fast. Just keep busy."

One night Karen invited Robin and Sarah and me over to make table decorations for her wedding. I invited Donna and she came too.

I introduced her to Sarah and said, "Sarah just came out from New York after graduating from high school."

"Yeah, I never finished high school. Well, I got my GED, but I wish I'd done it the regular way."

"What are you doing now?" Sarah asked her.

"I'm back working at the canneries—not real glamorous, but it pays."

"Are they hiring now?" Sarah asked.

"Yeah, maybe I can help you get a job on the same line as me, if you want."

"That'd be fun!"

"You want to? Really?"

"Sure!"

Donna was rummaging through her purse to find a scrap of paper to write down her phone number when Robin burst in the door, her arms full of boxes of fabric scraps and trims. "Hey, you guys, I was telling Sarah about the Christmas bazaar last year. Want to do it again?"

"Well, yeah, we won't have the printer trays, but I can weave some stuff like table mats," Karen mused.

"And I can sew some aprons and potholders and kitchen stuff," Sarah added.

"But I won't be here for the bazaar, and probably Christmas, with the new baby," I put in.

"Yeah, but we can still get together and make stuff while the guys are out fishing," Karen said.

"Don't you hate it when they're gone? Don't you worry?" Sarah asked

"I don't worry, 'cause I figure Matt knows what he's doing and he's been doing it for awhile, but I sure miss him."

Robin said, "Dr. Copstead's wife is looking after two little boys whose mother had a nervous breakdown. She's in the hospital after attempting suicide. Do you ever take Chelsea to Shine Bright, Nora? The daycare center? She worked there."

"Which one was she?"

"Linda—the tall skinny blonde."

"Oh, she's beautiful, she looks like an angel, and so gentle with the kids! What happened?"

"Nobody really knows—guess she just couldn't take it. She sits and stares and won't connect with anybody."

"She seemed so together and calm," I dropped my glass of wine and Robin laughed.

"Not like you, huh? Some people just do a better job of keeping it all inside. But it turns out to be not that great."

"Yeah, but it can all be so overwhelming sometimes, and you feel like nothing you try to do works and you're never going to win, that you're just a big loser that everybody wishes would go away...."

"Nora, you sound desperate!"

"Well, it scares me that someone who seems to be maintaining, to be in a responsible position, could crack so bad. What's keeping me in the swim and drowning somebody else? I know how bad you can feel, and it's scary to me, like what can you do to be okay when hard times come?'

Karen said, "But you just can't let it get to you, you've got to take care of yourself."

We had all the ribbons and baskets and paper flowers on the floor, when in came Pete, Karen's older brother, and a friend. We all stopped our work and sat around drinking wine and talking. I felt a charge in the air between Pete and Sarah, and his friend and Donna, and the total lack of any excitement when either of the men spoke to me.

They're not even looking at me at all. I'm the invisible one. Of course I am six months' pregnant. Now I know how a matron of honor feels.

I was telling Matt about the evening. "Boy, I've sure turned into an old lady. Donna and Sarah are almost the same age, and maybe they can be friends."

Matt said, "Your little friend Donna's been dancing topless at Tony's, but they fired her ass when they learned how young she is."

"How do you know that?" I caught Matt's eye and held it. Finally he looked away.

"Oh Jeez—yeah, I was in there."

"Matt."

"It's just entertainment, Nora, it's no big deal."

"It's a big deal to me. Plus, Donna's my friend, I hate the idea that you've seen her naked."

"Well, I didn't see her naked, she was walking out of the office and I heard about it."

"So how often do you go there? I thought you were glad to come home when you got back to town." I felt like I'd eaten dirt.

Matt got up and stroked my arm. "I am glad you're home waiting for me. You shouldn't feel bad. Don't feel bad."

"But I do." I sat down heavily and wiped the tears off my cheeks but what I wanted to do was lay my head on the table and cry and cry.

Matt walked out the door without another word between us and then I did cry. I cringed to imagine Donna in the dark, damp bar with slobbering men leering at her. Sometimes when I'd walk past Tony's at the corner of the plaza, I'd catch a glimpse inside as the doors swung open. Once I snuck a peek at this naked skinny girl, totally self-conscious and awkward, dancing in front of these loud creepy guys. How could Donna do that?

An hour later Matt came back with a small bag of groceries and a bottle of Southern Comfort. I was putting the groceries away and there was a little box in the bag. I opened the box and it was a diamond ring, the diamond set so delicately in a curving gold band.

Matt had come up right behind me. "Put it on."

"Oh Matt, it's beautiful. Thank you." I put it on and hugged him and cried a little more.

Even though a ring is just a material thing, I was proud to gesture gracefully with my hands as Matt and I attended Karen and Scott's wedding. Karen was dressed in an elegant satin brocade gown and Scott wore a black velvet jacket with satin edging. "You two look beautiful, and so happy," I said.

Scott preened. "Yeah, now I've got a bride and a smoking jacket. All I need is cigars."

"You have to wait for a baby for that," Matt shook Scott's hand.

"Well then, for now I guess I'll just stick to reefer," Scott said

Matt drifted off to the deck with Scott, and Donna and Sarah came up to me, standing aside with Chelsea on my hip. "Hey Nora, do you know how to get into a locked car? Donna locked her keys inside her car by mistake."

"Oh, don't you just use a coat hanger and jimmy it inside the window? Let's go get one out of the closet."

We got a wire hanger and twisted it into a hook-like jimmy and went out to the parking lot. The twilight was deep blue and we maneuvered the wire hanger inside the window and managed to lift the lock. I felt like part of a gang, and it felt good.

"All right!" Donna and Sarah and I charged back into the hall, flushed with streetwise success, just as dinner was being served. We sat down at the table, Chelsea on my lap and Sarah looking around for someplace to toss the hanger.

"Wait a sec. We can't just dump him after he rescued us," I said. I reached out for the hanger, now back in its standard shape, and bent it in the middle and forced the curved hook into a full circle. It looked like the shoulders and head of a wire man. I placed him on the empty chair at the table. "That's Jimmy. He would like some dinner, too."

Sarah and Donna convulsed with laughter as we served Jimmy and solicited his comments. "He's very shy," I said and Sarah and Donna cracked up again. Tears were running down our cheeks and everyone looked at us to see how we were having so much fun.

After Karen and Scott's wedding, and before Matt went out to the king crab season in the Bering Sea, we went on our fishing trip to the Kenai Peninsula.

After driving most of the first day, we stopped at a motel. Matt turned on the TV and I began to fuss. "I don't want to spend our precious family vacation time in cars and motels."

"What do you want to do?"

"I want to hike and make campfires and go fishing and canoeing."

"You're six months' pregnant and look like a blimp."

"Yeah, but I feel like Mother Earth and I want to commune with nature, get out in the wilderness."

The next day the weather turned ugly with low clouds and rain, but we dressed in sweaters and ponchos and boots and hiked, fighting knee-deep undergrowth, around a lake. At noon we stopped at the opposite side of the lake. Matt tried to make a campfire, but all the wood available was green and wet, so I sat heavily on a log and watched thin grey tendrils of smoke rise from the puny fire, while Matt cast again and again for fish.

On the way back to the motel, fishless, Chelsea grew tired so Matt carried her in the backpack. The weather began to lift, and we saw canoe streams with signs indicating they were part of a portage system.

Outside of Kenai we rented a boat and Matt rowed us up and down the river, seeing all the big homes and little planes occupying the riverbanks. I took pictures of a mama moose and two calves before we got back into the Jeep and drove back to our cabin.

"I never really thought about a female moose—just the male with the antlers as big as a sofa."

"A rack—yeah, I wouldn't mind bagging one of those daddies," Matt said. Then we saw a black bear on the edge of some woods and another moose in the grasses.

"I'd hate to shoot an animal, especially on their home ground, where they think they're safe."

"Chain of survival, Mama, it's a fact of life."

"My home is my castle, Dad; that's a fact of life too."

"No, that's pretty sentiment."

"You've got to stop the Jeep, Matt, I'm starting to hurt." He pulled the Jeep to the side of the road and I wondered what would come after the aching, if it would get worse, if I was in danger, and the baby too.

"Are you going to have your baby now? Is this going to be a birth in the wilderness?" Matt smiled teasingly at me, but I wanted him to wrap me in his arms and treat me like he would take care of me. I couldn't tell him what I wanted, not if he made fun of me. We sat by the side of the road and when the pains eased I wandered into the grass, picking wildflowers. When I came back to where Matt and Chelsea sat, he was letting Chelsea put his hair in stubby little ponytails. He looked like a big gruff pickanniny and I loved him for letting Chelsea make him look so foolish.

We drove down an unpaved road where we saw a huge sign, "Moonwine." We followed the signs to a building where two brothers, both former priests, made wine in plastic milk jugs from reconstituted powdered milk, using a Slavic recipe.

"We get this powdered milk free from the government," the wizened old man explained.

"Gives you immunity from the bubonic plague!" the older brother boasted, his pale blue eyes streaming.

"There's two kinds, the sweet and the dry," the elf-like priest explained, "Now the colored people—they like the sweet. They always do. And the Indians—they like the sweet, though not very. Just a little bit."

The other brother, with his scarily intense eyes, lifted his glass and saluted us. "No hangover, no bangover. Just moonover."

"For fourteen years!" Father Elf added.

We bought a plastic milk jug of each kind. Both flavors tasted like vomit.

We were just a short way from Talkeetna when the Jeep overheated and broke down. We spent a couple of hours by the side of the road while Matt tinkered with the engine. A trucker stopped and gave us a ride in to the garage in Talkeetna, where Chelsea and I rambled around town while Matt went back with parts to fix the truck.

I was struck once again by how a whole town can seem to possess a personality. Talkeetna was like Homer, with a frontier-hippie feeling. But whereas Homer was a port town, and seemed to snake out along the spit to the Salty Dawg tavern and ferry terminal, Talkeetna was more foursquare and self-contained. It had beautiful artsy little craft shops, and rustic log cabins with green-painted trim and flowers blooming in window boxes, and somehow I never saw the piles of junk cars and rusting litter that surrounded Kodiak

Kodiak seemed driven by a 50's modernization ethic where the supermarket and hardware store and Sears promised the latest conforming convenience, but Homer and Talkeetna seemed more liberal and soulful, where the hip just moved in and funkified the place.

After the truck got fixed we drove towards Mount McKinley and camped in small cabins on Carlo Creek. The cabins were right on the water across a lopsided footbridge. Our cabin had a wood stove and running water, and was clean too, not about to fall down on our heads. We ate by candlelight late in the evening when even the midnight sun left the sky.

It started to rain when we went to bed and I felt so good and healthy and big next to Matt, holding him close, being held by him. In the middle of the night, Matt sat straight up in bed and said, "I got him. I got the big one."

"What big one?"

"Salmon. He was a fighter, but I got him. We gotta stay here till I catch him. Okay, Mama?"

"Okay, Matt."

I love this place. There's a supply of firewood and everything feels like home. I feel free, unburdened, at last in comfort. It's so undemanding, no make-up, my hair in braids, barefoot, just wearing Matt's T-shirt and shorts. Unrushed, we sit at the window, drinking coffee, watching Chelsea climb up and down the steps to play with the chickens and roosters roaming about. Just natural, reading, talking, unscheduled. I must have been a hillbilly in a previous incarnation. This is the life I was meant to live; this is the mood I want to float through.

I'm enjoying our trip, too, the doing-nothingness of it, feeling like a wanderer and just singing, talking, and looking to concentrate on. Always on a trip I plan what my regular life will be like when I get back, and it's always much more regular to plan than it turns out to be. I just want to knit and sew, maybe take a photography class and pickle some salmon this fall. Read, play piano, and write songs. Whew, already sounds busy! I know I'll miss Matt as I grow bigger each day, and hope things all fall in place and that he can quit fishing at Thanksgiving.

I'm hoping to get that trailer. I want the room, the cozy kitchen, the fireplace, the yard, the cows next door, the two bathrooms. I can make it clean and warm and we could live there for a while.

Then if we could build a log house, and move in when Chelsea's around six or seven....We've seen lots of log cabins on this trip—so solid and warm-looking.

When we got back to town Matt and Robbie were busy getting the *Sea Lion* ready for the trip out west to the Bering Sea. I loved having Matt home, but I dreaded the day when he would leave me, knowing he'd be gone until our new baby was born.

CHAPTER SEVEN

A CHILD IS BORN
Matt leaves again for the Bering Sea; he defends the honor of womanhood;
I give birth and celebrate Christmas at Shine

Matt was almost ready to leave on the *Sea Lion* when we got a call from Larson, the man in Port Lions whose trailer was for sale, who said we could rent the trailer immediately with an option to buy. We just decided to go for it and wham! The rabbit hutch house was turned upside down and we moved everything over to the trailer court. Two days of moving and Matt was gone.

Robin invited Chelsea and me over for dinner one night, and when we walked in the door, Donna and Sarah and Karen were there, too—it was a surprise baby shower for me! Karen made me a beautiful baby quilt of white satin material left over from her wedding dress and delicately patterned blue butterfly material.

Robin said, "I just wish I knew if I want to have children. My mom had five, and I can remember when we were little and Sarah was just a baby and she threw her cereal on the floor, and mom just crying frantically, and I was just a little kid and trying to comfort her...." She broke off and shook her head grimly.

"I'm glad it was a foregone conclusion for me. I always knew I'd be a mother, and my pride motivated me. I'm going to raise my kids the way I wish I'd been raised," I said.

When Chelsea and I got home at eleven, I discovered I'd locked myself out, so I knocked at the neighbor's door. I introduced myself, and the lady, Tuffy, invited me in while her husband Jake, went to see if he could get in. It didn't take him long, and Tuffy invited me to come back over the next day.

Outside in the dark as we were walking back across the yard, Chelsea looked up and said, "Oh Mom, look at the 'tars." I looked up at the blue-black velvet sky, the diamonds sparkling through. My heart swelled with the beauty of it. I longed to share the beautiful night, my kind new neighbors and sweet little girl and full pregnancy with Matt. He was why we were here.

The next day, we went over to Tuffy's for coffee. She lived in a narrow single-wide trailer, with everything stored tidily, like on a little boat. She had short straight red hair, cut like a boy's, and a no-nonsense manner of talking.

"I used to work at the bank before I had Christie—she's three now. I'm still reeling from motherhood, though. I didn't even realize I was pregnant at first and I sure didn't feel motherly. Right after she was born, here was this little baby and I didn't know what to do with her or how to feel."

She set a plate of salmon sandwiches in front of me. "Now we can do everything we used to, just take her with us. We fish at a set net site in the summers, on Olga Bay down at the south end of the Island. We take the Boston Whaler out fishing whenever the weather's nice. Jake smoked the salmon in these sandwiches."

"What does Jake do?"

"He's an enforcement officer with Fish & Game, so he usually gets weekends off and we just get gas and supplies and get the boat out in the water and enjoy ourselves. You probably do that when you're husband's home from fishing, too."

Tuffy lent me some of her maternity clothes before I left for Seattle, where Chelsea and I would stay at Mom's in Shine until Matt would come down around Thanksgiving, a month before the baby was due.

I went to my high-school reunion wearing my fur coat that, with my fifty extra pregnant pounds, didn't bury me in its fur. I talked mostly to the old crowd. Maureen made sure everyone knew that though she was now six months' married, everyone's husband had at one time or another been her boyfriend and was still pining for her.

But not Matt.

Several of the women who'd dragged their husbands along said to me, when I told them I lived in Alaska, "Oh, don't tell my husband; he's always dreamed of moving to Alaska." Men are so entranced with dreams of the last frontier and a lawless land.

I made Chelsea a pink bunny suit for Halloween and took her on the ferry to Tricia's home, and she went trick-or-treating with Adam and Elizabeth. Tricia and I shadowed them.

We passed a cluster of little gargoyles and a man behind them, his jacket buttoned over his head so he looked headless. Chelsea stared, awestruck, at him. "I love it when people get into the spirit of it and do scary, ghostly things for Halloween," Tricia murmured.

"And then contrasted with the little kids running through the dark with their kitty and bunny suits on," I said.

We were relaxing back at Mom's house in Shine when the phone rang.

"What's going on?" Matt said, but I couldn't read his voice.

"We're fine, we went trick-or-treating in Seattle yesterday, I made Chelsea a bunny suit. How are you? How's fishing?"

"I'm flying down this afternoon."

"Did the crab season end early?" To have Matt with us until Christmas and the new baby was born, that would be great!

"Well,…uh, no…well, I had a little accident."

My heart lurched. "What happened?"

"Well… there was a little incident at Dutch Harbor, and they want to do surgery on my eye up here, but I think I'd better have someone look at it in Seattle."

Instantly I felt cold and twisted with fear. He tried to make it sound so casual. "Are you in the hospital up there?"

"No, no, I'm at the hotel, but I've got reservations on this afternoon's flight. Can you meet me?"

"Of course! When? Oh Matt, are you okay?"

"Don't make such a big deal out of it. I should be in at three. I'm flying Western."

"Okay, Matt, I'll be there."

I spent the afternoon on the phone with the doctors and the hospital, trying to weed through their bureaucracy to make arrangements for a specialist to see Matt. It was frustrating, but staying calm and persistent kept my mind from worrying about Matt. Would he be horribly disfigured? Would he lose his eye and wear a patch? Thoughts of fishing and the new baby were just about gone.

As Matt got off the plane, I saw the whole right side of his face was black and swollen with bruises. He smiled at me and his bravado broke my heart. When I asked him what happened, I was assuming he'd say that a huge crab pot had come loose from the winch and swung into his face.

"We'd delivered crab in Akutan and were up at the Roadhouse having a few drinks. Some Samoans off the *Alaska Shell* were hassling this woman, so I told them to back off and they jumped me, pulled me by the hair to the ground, held me down while they stomped on my face. Fucking savages. Robbie and Sloop got me out of there and tried to clean me up before I got on the plane to Cold Bay." He snorted, "Then in Cold Bay the plane had to fly in circles for an hour to dump some fuel."

I wanted to wrap him in a blanket and hold him close and never let anyone hurt him again. I wondered how he stood it, not knowing if he'd lose his eye, the weather so vicious out there, the plane flying around in circles.

"When I got to Anchorage, I couldn't get a room at the first two hotels. I guess they didn't like my T-shirt." Then I noticed that he was wearing the black

"Eat Shit and Die" T-shirt we'd gleefully ordered from *Rolling Stone*. "The cab driver asked me if I wanted some company at the Plaza B hotel."

"Company?"

"He meant a hooker." Matt chuckled, proud of the hard-living impression he must have made. I saw a big hurting man brutalized by bullies, abandoned by his friends, alone in the big city.

"Anyway, the doctor that I saw there said I needed surgery immediately because the bone below my eye is broken, and he says my eye will fall down into the socket, behind my cheek."

My beautiful Greek god made into a hideous freak.

At the hospital, they determined that whatever permanent damage was done, the condition of Matt's eye was stable and the ophthalmologist would look at it more extensively the next day when the swelling went down.

Poor stupid brawler. I relaxed a bit and began to feel the first twinges of resentment. *What was he doing anyway, risking his life in defense of some stupid woman in no-man's land when he should be hovering tenderly at my side as we awaited the birth of our child? But here he is, almost blinded and I'm thinking of myself again.*

On the ferry ride back to Shine, Matt showed me a scrap of paper. Handwritten on it was "I hereby sell Matt Hunter my set net site for $5000," signed by someone I'd never heard of.

"Is that good? Where'd you get $5000?"

"Oh, we were playing poker. Yeah, it's good. The set netters are the guys who make all the money."

Drift net, set net, purse seiner, trawler, trolling, blocks, winches, lazerette, layette, epidural, spinal block—where do I fit in?

The blackness and swelling in Matt's face subsided a little each day, but his angry attitude troubled me. He seemed itching for a fight, so different from the usual mellow facade. When we went out to lunch after seeing the doctors, Matt almost bit the waiter's head off because he sat us by the back door.

But he wouldn't talk to me, admit fear or anger, or let me take care of him. When we went over to his folks' his dad said, "Oh, I thought you'd look a lot worse." I was furious at the casual tone of his concern.

Is stoicism such a great value? Does strong and silent really mean untouchable and uncaring?

I'm getting more and more hyper. With Chelsea, I'd had the nesting instinct bad; with this baby, it's just the opposite. I want to live it up, to go dancing. I'm getting more and more restless. Besides, Matt's with me every day without a boat for the first time since we got married.

"Let's do something," I said to Matt.

"Like what?"

"Like dancing?" I suggested.

Matt snorted.

"I know, I do look rather like a dinosaur, but I want to kick out the jams a little."

Matt felt we had to have a car. "I don't want to be stuck in Shine, or bum rides whenever I need to go somewhere," he said. "Glenn bought a BMW sedan for Peg, so I'm going to buy her old Volkswagen bug."

At Peggy and Glenn's house, we signed the papers and Matt said, "I think I'll go out to Campbell's tavern."

"Aren't you going to come home with us for dinner?" I said, but Peggy broke in.

"Can't the poor guy have a night out with the boys anymore?"

I was so stunned and mad I couldn't say anything. I was afraid I'd pop. Outside, Matt said, "Okay, so I'll meet you at the ferry dock."

"You mad at me, Matt?"

"No, I'm okay. I'll see you in a bit."

Chelsea and I left for the ferry in Mom's car, which we'd borrowed to get to Peggy's house, and Matt followed in our new car.

It began to snow. "Oh boy, Chels, we can go home and have hot chocolate in front of Gram's fire and be cozy and warm like real live teddy bears."

When we arrived at the ferry dock, I waited for Matt to putter up behind us. But he didn't show up by the time the ferry left.

At Mom's, I made dinner and a fire and got Chelsea and myself into our flannel nightgowns and rocked her and read to her with a growing anxiety. I held myself patient and waited and hoped.

I slept lightly, even though I realized it was too late for any more ferries to arrive, bringing Matt home.

I'm the one who stood by him and this is his response. The only good thing is that Mom's gone to Canada and isn't here. The last thing I want is her pity. I feel sorry enough for myself.

The next day I called Jamie Campbell's tavern. Doug Bradley answered the phone. "Doug, this is Nora. Is Matt there?"

"Just a sec. Oh Mattie, the little wife wants to talk to you...."

I could hear the snickers in the background.

"Yeah?" Matt barked into the phone.

I sputtered with anger. "Don't you have the basic courtesy to let me know what's going on?"

"Nope," he laughed me off.

92

"I don't think I like you any more!" I yelled, and hung up.

Chelsea came running down the stairs. "What's the matter, Mama?"

"Your dad never thinks of anybody but himself. His accident, his boat, his pride, his life! Why'd he have to drag us into it if he can't be bothered?" I was frightening Chelsea, and I took a deep breath, reached out to hold her as I cried.

I couldn't stay there, poisoning her with my anger and hurt. We went over to Tricia's, where Chelsea's cousins distracted her.

The next morning, Mom called. "When I came home to Shine and Nora wasn't there, I figured that they'd all left suddenly for the hospital, that the baby was on its way."

"Well, Matt's gone off with Campbell and Bradley, so Nora decided to come here for awhile," Tricia said to Mom lightheartedly. Tricia understood that if Mom knew how I felt, she'd never forgive Matt.

"Oh, my poor baby," Mom moaned. "She spends her whole life waiting."

I'm almost okay, except I feel so publicly rejected. I'm not the one who beat his face in, I'm not the one who pushed him out of town or discounted his brutalized face. I'm the one who cares what happens to him, who wants him safe at home. I'm the one who has his babies. He promised to cherish me. Why did he say it, make a holy vow, if he didn't mean it? Where is his honor? Aren't I his crowning glory? Does he have to announce to the whole world that I mean so little to him?

But he has a party to go to. Fitz and Lisa are getting married. Everyone will be there from the old crowd, except for me. Matt and I are fighting, estranged.

Damn Bradley. Matt makes such an issue about how easily influenced Doug is, what about Matt?

Rita Bradley called me to say that Matt was staying with them. "You should hear Matt talk. He really has a bad attitude about women. I don't see how he could joke and act like everything's hunky-dory at Fitz and Lisa's wedding."

That night the phone rang and I took a walk around the block, not ready to talk to Matt, wanting to make him worry. When I came back, Tricia said, "Your mother-in-law just called. She said, 'What's going on with Matt and Nora? They're supposed to come here for Thanksgiving.' I told her that Matt had bolted with Bradley again and you were staying here with us. She said she tried to stay out of family squabbles."

"Yeah, just like Pontius Pilate."

Matt came to the door and everyone scattered, leaving us alone, sitting at opposite ends of the dining table. It seemed like he'd come to take his punishment, get it over with and pretend it never happened. "I just wanted a little freedom, a night out with the boys."

"Do you ever think I might want a little freedom, or a little fun? Wouldn't you be concerned if I took off, especially knowing you were spoiling for a fight? Do you ever think of how it feels for me?"

I knew he didn't. I knew his deepest concern was protecting himself. My rock. He was so secure because he was single-minded in his concern for himself. "With you and Bradley, how do I know you're even safe and not smeared over some highway?" My hands shook as I watched them in front of me on the table.

"Where is this going, Eleanor? If all you want to do is chew my butt, I'm ready to go back and fish the seven-inch season around Kodiak."

I folded my hands. I had a baby coming. I had a family to patch back together. I had Christmas coming.

What kind of future do I have if Matt leaves us to go fishing now? What kind of mother am I if I have my baby without its father? I feel so unsettled and frustrated. There's a million things that I can't organize into something whole. How can I change my life? I don't know. I think I would like to just go off on some kind of a binge, but I can't leave Chelsea. I want to bask in having my little girl, having my man, having our time together. Instead I feel like Matt wishes he could dump me and do something reckless.

I guess the thought of this new baby is scaring me, too. When it kicks and my stomach's upset and I feel like I'm dragging a bomb around, I just don't want to physically exist anymore. I'm so tired, and I feel scared. I'm so worn out from worrying if and when Matt will be here. For the baby? For Christmas? Why do I care? How can I not care? Can I do it without him? What if I have to? Is he going to buy a set net site? What is a set net site? Is he going to buy a boat? Should we buy any boat even if we can't afford it? Can we make it in Kodiak with everything so expensive? I just want to cry and not think anymore.

I just want some time off with peace and fun and security without Mother yakking in my ear, without Matt bringing up some scheme, fishing or otherwise, that scares the wits out of me. But if he's not going to take care of us, and if he doesn't want to blow his money on us having fun, if he doesn't want to spend time with us and have a home, then what can I do?

We all trekked to the hospital, Matt to check his eye, and me to monitor the baby's development and schedule the Cesaerean. The ophthalmologist advised against surgery. "We should wait and see, until the swelling in Matt's cheek subsides more. The delicacy of facial nerves and muscles makes surgery inadvisable unless absolutely necessary."

I had an amniocentesis test to determine if the baby's lungs were fully developed, if he was ready to be born.

After the test, Matt and Chelsea and I went to the zoo. As we walked through Woodland Park, I was sure I could smell the sap in the leaves warming them into gold. The air was pure and clear and the wind freshened me almost to shivering. All we had to do was keep up with Chelsea getting lost in the wonderment of exotic animals. I felt so full and tuned-in as we wandered about the nearly deserted park. After three hours, I couldn't lift my knees to move my feet, so I just shuffled them in front of me.

Back in Shine, I gratefully stretched out on the new golden carpet, the floor supporting my enormous belly.

I woke in the middle of the night and sat up on the edge of the bed. "Matt, the baby's coming. My water broke, Matt."

Matt stirred. I crawled back under the covers, it was too cold to be up. But he hustled us into some clothes and out the door, leaving Chelsea with Gramma. We caught the first ferry of the morning.

At the hospital, Dr. Gentler turned to Matt after examining me. "Does she always open her Christmas presents early?"

Matt looked confused at first and then smiled. "Yeah, we thought we had about two more weeks."

Gentler said, "The amniocentesis we did yesterday show that the baby's lungs are ready, so we'll go ahead and get her in there."

Inside the operating room, they gave me a spinal block so my body was numb from the waist down. But the way they were tugging at my numb insides made me feel like a pizza oven, with a huge wooden paddle trying to slide the pizza out. I grunted with the force of their tugging, but I wasn't really in pain when I heard the little kitten mew of my son.

Then the nurse held him up to me, already wrapped in a receiving blanket. My baby boy looked like a grocery-store chicken with a big head, long fingers and scrawny, loose-folded skin. "What's wrong with him?" I asked.

The nurse said, "Nothing's wrong with him; he was just born," and whipped him away from me.

I struggled to stay conscious, as I wanted badly to see the baby again, to see Matt's face and his reaction to our baby boy. But I couldn't stay awake with the anesthesia I'd been given. All that first day, remembering Matt's tenderness when Chelsea was born, I was trying to be fully aware, but I drifted in and out of consciousness.

Finally, late that evening Matt came in. "I don't think much of this hospital."

"What happened?"

"Well, right after they took the baby out of the delivery room, a nurse was trying to clean him up. The baby was struggling to breathe or something and I told her 'He's turning blue,' and she said 'Oh, that's nothing.' But another nurse spun right around and sort of shoved the first nurse out of the way and began suctioning some mucus out of the baby's throat."

"Matt, what if you hadn't been there?"

"Yeah, I know. He could have suffocated."

"And the baby was in danger and I didn't even know it."

The days in the hospital were a nightmare. I was unprepared for the painful cramps that followed the first day's oblivion, and it seemed that the nurses were willfully confused about me. I called for a pain shot, and was told it was too soon after the last one. Twenty minutes later, I was sobbing and gasping when I again rang for help. Another nurse came with a beautiful syringe in hand, and as she administered the shot, she said, "You shouldn't wait so long before calling for something for the pain. That's what it's for." I was too exhausted to answer her.

Mom brought me a plush, honey-colored robe. I was buried in it, but I felt like a lovely golden bear, protected by my fur. "Has Matt been in yet today?" she asked. I shook my head. "Well, he brought that Don fellow home last night."

Later, Matt came in, flustered. "I've been driving all up and down the country today. I planned to take Chelsea pony-riding at Gail's place, but then I had to drive Don to where he's staying in Tacoma, so I left Chelsea with Peggy."

"How come Don's in Seattle?" I asked Matt.

"Oh, Leo Davidoff's seiner's in town for an overhaul. I'm going to work on that."

Who means more to you, Sloopy Don or your own daughter? Why can't Don find his own way home? Matt always has to be Mr. Mellow Nice Guy until it comes to us. He has no problem turning us down.

We named the baby Liam Daniel. He was jaundiced, so they put him under bilirubin lights. The next morning I woke to a loud metallic bang as the nurse's aide dropped the side of the bed. Then the doctors came on rounds. "Mrs. Hunter is doing well after having her baby yesterday."

"He was born on Wednesday," I said.

"No, Mrs. Hunter, you're confused. It was yesterday—oh, I see you're right—Wednesday."

Right after they left, the aide again dropped the metal railing of the bed. I crawled out of bed and put my bear robe on and went to the nursery to rock and comfort Liam and me. "Let's go home, little boy of mine," I whispered to him. I called Matt at Peggy's and told him I wanted to go home. I put Liam in a soft yellow bunting and he looked like a tender little delicacy in a pastry puff. Then we went home to Shine.

Matt started working at the shipyard on Davidoff's boat, catching an early ferry to Seattle each morning. Liam was still jaundiced and I had to take him back to the hospital clinic every other day for bilirubin tests. I'd dress Chelsea and myself and the baby. We put on lots of warm clothes for the weather, and I felt stuffed into my clothes, but once we got to the clinic, after the ferry ride, I'd be sweating and anxious, chasing Chelsea and soothing Liam's cries when they pricked his toes for blood. Then the long drive and the ferry ride back home.

One night Matt told me, "The *Maggie J* is almost ready. Davidoff wants to get home to Kodiak by Christmas so we'll be set in place for the tanner season in January. You better make reservations to fly back with the kids."

I'm supposed to be the beloved Blessed Mother, and celebrate Christmas with family and holiness and Christmas carols and goodies and cozy fires and a baby coming in its innocence to save the world and the blessed stillness. My whole rosy scenario is shot to hell.

"I understand, Nora," my mom said when I complained to her, "but you have your own family now. If you have to go back, you can't try to recreate our old Christmases here."

So I bought the piano score to the "Nutcracker Suite" and began picking it out on Mom's piano.

Matt stayed out all night again. "I missed the last ferry last night," he said when he walked in at eight the next morning.

I said, "I guess the only thing I can count on with you is your unreliability, Mr. Playboy." I knew that it was a cheap shot, but I wanted to make him as mad as he made me.

"I am not a playboy!" he retorted.

"Well, next time it's my turn to go out all night with my friends."

"Then you'd better make it quick, because I can't say when I might stay out all night with the boys again." He changed into his work clothes and turned around and left.

"Oh great," I said, jostling a fussy Liam against my shoulder.

"Well, what did you expect him to say?" Mom asked. "He's not the type to bow his head and say 'Oh please, don't be upset darling.'"

Through clenched teeth, I spat out, "I'm so tired of figuring out what makes him tick, of protecting his precious ego. Why doesn't anyone care how I feel, what makes me hurt and angry?"

Another stony silence lasted until a week before Christmas, when Matt came home and said, "Davidoff doesn't need me to take the boat up. You get your way after all. We'll fly up to Kodiak the day after Christmas."

So the morning of December 26 found us with clothes and suitcases, duffel bags, and the dog kennel spread from one end of the living room to the other. We stuffed everything in unsystematically and flew to Anchorage to find that the flight to Kodiak had been canceled due to bad weather. We luxuriated in our hotel room with a hot quiet bath, room service dinners, and huge roomy beds with immaculate sheets.

It's funny—I had such close, cozy expectations for Christmas, our first with all the family since moving up to Kodiak, and a new baby to boot. But it was so unpleasant. I almost feel disloyal to our Seattle relatives. And now it's such a relief to be heading home, just my baby family, warts and all.

CHAPTER EIGHT

KODIAK SOCIETY
In which Matt glories as a fisherman and I glory as the crown of the home

Liam was a fussy baby, and I didn't bounce back as quickly as I had with Chelsea. But Matt was there for me. One night I was pacing the living room with Liam wailing. I didn't know what to do for him, just walk him and croon to him. Finally, after midnight, Matt got out of bed and came into the living room, saw me in tears, and just held his arms out for the baby. He finally got Liam settled down and came back to bed. I felt such gratitude for him. Maybe in Seattle he felt forced to resist all the demands he'd felt while we were staying at my mother's house—maybe the benign pressure of staying there was too much for us all.

With the new year's crab season, Matt would often come home from a fishing trip after midnight with a huge purple-brown king crab dangling from each hand, then we'd cook the crab until it was bright red, crack it and eat it, drink beer, and cut up halibut before crashing into bed. Liam would wake before dawn, Matt would leave about seven for the boat harbor, I'd put Liam back down, then soon after Chelsea would wake up, then Liam up again by midmorning and stay awake all day, unless I was lucky and could get both Liam and Chelsea to take afternoon naps. Many days I'd doze on the sofa, watching "Sesame Street" with them at ten in the morning and then again at four in the afternoon.

When Matt and the other fishermen were out, my friends would get together for our crafts circle, or terrorist society, as we liked to call it.

Robin was the first to stop by. As she pulled out her project, sewing suede patches on a sweater for Neil, she blurted out, "Neil's friend from college is coming to stay with us for awhile and I'm kind of nervous about when Neil goes out fishing—I'm really attracted to his friend. Do you ever feel that?"

I laughed. "I'm never around men and I spend all my mating energy just fighting for Matt to stay home."

Robin said, "What about swimming at the pool? Don't you think the lifeguard's attractive? And everyone's wandering around with next to nothing on."

"Yeah, but the pool's all wet and damp unless you're in the water, and I don't have my contacts in so I can't see anything, and I just feel the freedom of gliding invisibly through water…. No, I don't think about any of the guys around."

"Maybe I'd be less interested in guys if I had kids. What are you making now?"

"I'm putting together a baby quilt for Liam. This soft yellow flannel is the backing and the squares on front will be an embroidered sun, a satin moon, and a rainbow out of these ribbons and billowy clouds out of white flannel."

"You know about Sarah and Karen's brother Pete, don't you?"

"What, are they getting together?"

"Oh yeah, Pete told her, 'I'm coming over with love in my heart and danger in my pants.'"

"Oh God!" I laughed. "But Pete and Sarah are such a good match, both big and strong with good hearts."

"Damn it!" Robin jerked her hand out from inside the sweater where she'd stabbed a finger with the needle. She stuck her finger in her mouth and sucked it and then waved it in the air. "But Sarah's only 19 and they're talking about living together already!"

"Yeah, but she's full of love and confidence and eager to learn and aware of how she's learning.…"

Just then, Sarah and Karen stomped snow off their boots on the back porch and came in.

"Don't get too close to me, I have the Egyptian flu," Karen laughed, her eyes sparkling.

"The Egyptian flu?" I put the kettle on and turned around to look at her.

"Yeah, I'm going to be a mummy!" Karen was triumphant.

"Oh Karen, I'm really happy for you." I gave her a hug.

"Nora, you're a great mother—you're part of the reason I think having kids will be okay. Will you teach me to knit so I can make some baby sweaters?"

"That's wonderful! What does Scott say about it?" Robin asked.

"Oh, Scott—he thinks it was all his doing and only his doing!" Karen said. "He's thrilled, though."

Robin said, "Well, I've got news too. Neil and I are going to buy that old house on Mission Road overlooking the channel and tear it down and build a new house."

"Oh, yay! So that means you're going to stay in Kodiak, right? What about Neil's plans to go to medical school?" I asked.

"He still wants to do that someday, but first he wants to make some money up here and we figure if we build now, we'll be able to sell it for a good profit in a few years and pay for medical school without having to take out huge loans."

"Wow, Robin, what kind of a house are you going to build? You're going to have to get plans and everything," Sarah said.

"Yeah, it's going to be three stories, because the lot is pretty narrow."

"Can you put three stories on that piece of property without it sliding into the ocean?" Karen asked.

"We'll apply for a variance to build it right over the same foundation as the old house," Robin said. "It sits on bedrock."

"How exciting!" I said.

But it would give me the creeps to be perched on a cliff overlooking the ocean. What if there's another earthquake?

Donna came in with Andy toddling behind her. He and Chelsea played together as we cut out patterns and sewed on buttons and knit and quilted while we chattered away. Donna announced she was moving out to Larsen Bay, one of the villages. "My sister Laurie lives there with her husband and little boys and I'm tired of getting nowhere in town."

"Wow, everybody's changing. Sometimes I ache for the unattached footloose days, but these days I like hibernating, being enclosed by my family." I said. "It makes all the difference if Matt's here."

Later that month, Pam and Fred Nelson, the trailer court managers, came by to collect the space rent we paid for the land the trailer occupied—$175 a month on top of the mortgage. While Fred, a tall skinny guy with black glasses and a cowboy hat, moved some of Larson's gear from the shed, Pam's kids flitted round her, running away, coming back. I came outside while Liam napped, Chelsea fussing as I struggled with the zipper on her jacket. "There!" I said, "Done! Now you can run and play your little heart out!"

Pam brushed her long straight hair away from her pudgy innocent face and said, "Fred and I had two little boys and then we prayed and prayed about another baby, and the Lord answered our prayers with Amy. We used to live in this trailer, before the Larsons. Now we live out towards Monashka Bay, in a log house we built ourselves."

"Oh, I hope someday we'll be able to do something like that."

"Fred takes hunting parties out, showing them the best spots to get deer and we freeze the meat and I keep a bowl of sourdough in the corner of the kitchen always ready and I can always get meat out of the freezer or add flour to the sourdough and invite as many people as we want to stay for a meal."

Chelsea came up to me and was whining about something, and I said to Pam, "It seems like I say no all the time to Chelsea these days. I told myself this morning. 'Today, whatever she asks for, I'm going to say yes.'"

Pam smiled. "You know, I say, 'You can't have the chainsaw, honey, but you can have an apple.'"

It seemed like they had it all figured out—a family man, a spiritual life, respect, stable home, self-sufficiency, living within their means—everyday, solid accomplishments.

Matt came in from fishing unexpectedly. When I hugged him, he pulled back just a little. Then I noticed how tenderly he was holding his hand. "What happened?"

"My thumb got caught in the block," he said impassively. "I've been up to the clinic. Copstead took the nail off."

"Is it going to be okay?"

"Yeah. I have to go up to the pharmacy to get some stuff though. Give me the checkbook."

When he got back home, his mood demanded silence and he moved so testily that I knew his thumb must be killing him.

Later, Sloopy Don came for dinner. He and Matt sat down at the table smoking cigarettes while I cooked dinner.

"Yeah, Nora, it was ugly. Liz ran Matt's thumb through the power block."

"Ow, ow, ow!" I responded.

Don laughed. "Yeah, her big tits always get in the way. Women on boats are always trouble. They always turn out to be the captain's playthings."

"Davidoff will kill you if he hears that," Matt said.

"Oh, Davidoff, he's got so many problems. Ever since he got kicked out of that house on Spruce Cape. He's got woman problems."

Matt set a couple of beers on the table. "What kind of woman problems?"

"Oh God, it was hilarious. Him and his wife and Lizzie were all fighting one night and wound up downtown and the police chief says, 'Well, Lizzie, what's going on?' She says 'Oh, Dad's just teaching me positions.'"

"'Positions? Whaddymean positions?' he says."

"'You know—sex positions!' God!" Sloop slammed his beer bottle on the table and laughed.

"Davidoff's her father?" Matt gulped out.

"Her stepfather! God! 'Positions!'"

After Sloop left and the babies were in bed, I said to Matt, "So are you going to keep working with Davidoff?"

"Oh yeah, this thumb is nothing, just a couple days' grief."

"I thought Davidoff was a nice guy, but he sounds kinda raunchy."

"Well, yeah, but I'm glad to be off the *Sea Lion*, we're having fantastic fishing, what with the weather being so mild. You hear Robbie's daughter's pregnant?"

"Allison? Gee, Matt, she's only sixteen."

"Well, she's sixteen and five months' pregnant."

"That's sad."

"Yeah, but I guess she wanted to be," he said.

"As much as any sixteen-year-old can know what they want. When I think of where I was ten years ago, before college and Vietnam and radicals and hippies and life at the Hotel Universe until you came along...."

"Never thought you'd make out so good, did you?" Matt teased.

I am becoming frazzled. My hair and skin look so lifeless and my body is a dumping ground. My eyes itch and I smudge my mascara continually, but mostly I just think I need a solid eight hours of sleep. Bed is where I should be right now.

Liam is demanding more of my attention—wish I had limitless time to devote to him. Last night I kept flitting about doing this and that while feeding him. I was thinking I had to strip and make the bed, take out my contacts, put my hair up so it wouldn't get wet and jump in the shower to wash Matt's hair so he doesn't get his thumb wet.

Boy, is my time gone. I have to consciously give up or I run around trying to accomplish everything. I made a schedule to follow. Wouldn't it be great if I could? Ah, fuck it, Liam just woke up, so I stuck his sucker back in his mouth, put the kettle on, and now I'm lighting up a joint. Though perhaps I should just try to cut down in all things.

It snowed again while Matt was home and the snow stayed around for a week, making things wintry and beautiful. Finally it rained and stormed continuously all one day and night, like a winter apocalypse, with the wind blowing the curved roof of the trailer in like a giant flapping a thunderous metal sheet.

Matt returned to work, fishing with his smashed thumb. He came in late one night, saying the storm was too strong for them to get to their crab pots. He left early the next morning, but when I returned home from doing errands, he was lying on the sofa. "Blowing too hard to be out."

"Oh, that's good, you can be home with us again. I like this season."

"Yeah, and we're still doing pretty good. Davidoff says if we bring in half a million pounds like I've been pushing for, he'll buy us tickets for Hawaii."

"Really, Matt?"

"Yeah, it's working out that way."

The afternoon grew very calm and still and we could hear lots of little boats going in and out of the channel in front of the house.

The winter tanner season went by and it seemed like things were finally going our way.

I'm just sitting here with my cup of coffee watching the sun break through the clouds. The fern is so beautiful with the sun shining on it. We've had some beautiful weather lately and I'm so glad to have windows and a front yard to enjoy.

Chelsea and I both have our hair in buns today. I tried tendrils a la Anna Karenina and wound up looking like a geek with frizz around my face.

Up the hill behind our trailer, the Baptist mission spread out over five acres of land—three large white frame houses where the orphanage kids lived, and a little building where they had a rummage sale every Saturday, plus a huge two-story garage for farm machinery with a wood floor running the length of the whole room on the second story. I signed Chelsea up for a ballet class that met there. It was perfect for ballet, with a whole wall of paned windows that look out to the channel.

Behind the garage was a row of real rabbit hutches, complete with bunny families. The Mission was a great place to take the kids for an outing, plus there was a swing made from a fishing buoy hanging from a tree, and a playground merry-go-round. Further on, a dirt path through the spruce woods led to the log cabin where the head of the Baptist mission and his family lived. The whole scene reminded me of *Dr. Zhivago*.

Chelsea came into my bed about six and said, "Mom, cover me up." She rolled out of bed a little while later, and I put her back in her bed after giving her a glass of milk. Then I went back to lay down and Matt made an attempt to get up, but I pulled him back to kiss him. Don knocked at the door to take Matt to the boat. I packed all but six of the cookies I'd made the night before after Liam went to sleep, and Matt left with a cup of coffee in his hand.

When I got Chelsea to preschool, she happily left me to play and I went straight home, put Liam down for a nap, made another cup of coffee, and wrote letters. Liam woke up and I fed him some more juice and played the piano.

Then I picked Chelsea up, and she was so happy, and I was too, so we went to the delicatessen for magazines and doughnuts before going back home. Inside the trailer, I turned the radio on and listened to the hourly marine forecast on the radio and heard the Coast Guard report that a Larsen Bay man was missing and I wondered if it was Donna's brother-in-law.

The phone rang and Sarah asked me if I'd heard the Coast Guard announcement. "You know, Donna's brother-in-law Mack is the only man I know who lives in Larsen Bay, but I have this creepy feeling it's him," I said to Sarah.

No sooner had we hung up than Karen and then Robin called me and we were calling each other back and forth all afternoon, waiting at home by our radios for further information. Finally, late in the afternoon, the Coast Guard announced that the Larsen Bay man had been found dead in his skiff, name withheld pending notification of next of kin. A few hours later, they announced his name and it was Donna's brother-in-law.

The next day it was written up in the newspaper, and I read it over and over, so surprised that it was Mack's name in black and white, even though I already knew it was him. I wondered what it was like for Donna, with her sister's husband dead, staying in a little village, having to comfort her sister and facing Death's inarguable decision. No choices left.

When Matt came in from his next trip he said, "Davidoff hit another rock in Whale Pass last night. He fell asleep at the wheel about twelve hours out of town."

"Oh my God, Matt! But everybody's okay?"

"Oh, yeah. I was asleep in my bunk when I heard a crashing scrape. I jumped up and looked out the galley window and saw trees so I calmed down a little and went up to the wheelhouse. Leo was really shook and I asked him if he wanted me to take over so he could get some sleep. I was kind of surprised when he said yeah, but I guess he knew he was in no shape to continue."

"He'd been drinking in town before he left, right?"

"Oh yeah, but the boat's okay, it's a tough little slab. I went down below and there was no hole. It's up on the ways now just to check everything out. We've only got a few weeks left to make our half-million goal, and then we go to Hawaii."

"Davidoff's really going to buy us plane tickets?"

"Yeah, we filled our part of the deal, and it's just pennies to him considering what we made this season."

"And this was going to be our do-nothing-but-work year!"

"See what happens when you're a Highliner?" Matt grinned, so happy.

Can't believe what I just did—picked some oatmeal cookie crumbs off the floor and ate them.

A storm picked up last night and it kept me awake most of the night. It was still going strong this morning, really shaking the trailer. It blows so strong, it makes everything rumble and the spruce trees bend way over.

Matt is being so good to me, taking charge around the house so I can just sleep or read or play the piano. Sunday he made coffee and sent Chelsea to bring me a cup in bed. Then he made breakfast again today. Sunday night Robin babysat while Matt and Chelsea and I went to the movies, The Mouse and His Child. *Matt rode Chelsea around on his back, fed, changed and rocked Liam, scratched my back, and even played ball in the front yard with us.*

When he's happy with fishing, we're all happy. I only wish for more calm, so I could be more patient, and for complete confidence about Liam's health. He cries so much and is a fussy eater. I'm really tired today but still feel pretty good. The whitecaps outside are really ferocious, though the sky has breaks in the grey. Liam's waking.

Tuffy called and asked me if I wanted to go to Buskin Beach and take the kids. Even though the sun was shining, it was bitterly cold and windy as we peeled oranges and watched a Coast Guard plane practice approaches to the airport runway. "So how you like the old trailer court?" Tuffy asked me as we sat on a log.

"Well, I really like the big front yard and looking out the Channel and our trailer, but all the other trailers are kind of crowded in, and it looks sort of bleak. But I don't know, it's nice having other little kids around. Chelsea plays with the Browning twins, they love to scream even more than she does."

"You know about their family, don't you?"

"What?"

"Their mom lives in that tiny trailer with four kids and her husband was shot at a robbery in a cannery store on the Alaska Peninsula a few years ago. She drinks a lot."

"God, I remember hearing about that then, and now they're my neighbors."

"Well, it's not her fault that her husband got shot and all, but she's got men coming at all hours, and can't get up in the morning to look after those kids...."

"How do you know?"

"I watch. I see things."

Something about the way Tuffy said that made me feel creepy, like when teenage kids make prank calls on the phone and say, "I saw what you did and I know who you are." More than what she said was the way she said it, kind of in a gloating tone of voice, and the look on her face, like excited at somebody else's lowlife. Like enjoying bad news.

I caught the beginning of the worst cold. My throat and head ached and I sat through the afternoon, willing Matt to come home, wishing I could call him at the office and tell him he *has* to come home. I could imagine him chasing the kids away from my bedside, saying, "Let your mother sleep now. She needs her rest."

That night Matt knocked on the back door after midnight when I'd been in bed a few hours. I put my arms around him and I know he felt my relief when I said, "I'm so glad you're home."

"What's the matter, Mama?"

"I'm getting sick and I can't take care of anything." I went to bed and spent almost two days there, and how luxurious that was! Chelsea would still charge in to talk to me, but Matt came after her once and said, "Let Mama sleep now, she needs her rest"—just like I'd dreamed.

One Sunday morning, after we'd ventured to church and back home, Matt called for me to pick him up at the boat harbor, so we all packed into the Jeep again and drove down to the New England cannery where they were unloading crab off the *Maggie J.* It was a beautiful day and I took some pictures of the boats and the harbor and the mountain.

Matt said to Davidoff, "Now, you agreed to first class plane tickets, right?"

Davidoff laughed and came over to me and said, "You'd better get your grass skirt ready. You gonna take those little varmints with you?"

"Of course, it wouldn't be a vacation without them."

When we got home, Matt said, "What are we going to do in Hawaii with a four-month-old baby?"

"Well, we'll just do the same things we'd do without a four-month-old baby, only carry him with us—go to the beach, check out the tourist attractions, go out to dinner. What are you worried about?"

"I don't want to eat in nice places with the kids—that would be a disaster. And how will we get to the beach?"

"Matt, don't worry, we can work it out, but don't make me feel irresponsible and guilty for wanting to have fun. If you don't want to go, let's just bag it, but if you do want to go, then we'll figure out our plans."

I made a fancy sausage quiche and then put the kids down for naps. Matt made drinks for us and we sat down and watched *Anna Karenina* on TV. I started crawling on Matt and he said, "You're not going to win me over so easily, you have to try harder than that."

I backed away from him and started unbuttoning my sweater and then pretended to be totally absorbed in the television while he ran his finger around the neck of my sweater. "Leave me alone," I said, moving so his hand went even deeper into my sweater.

"Yeah, I'll leave you alone all right," and he got up and dragged me by the arm down the hall to the bedroom.

Just as we got into bed, Chelsea woke up groggy and crying. She came in our room and I asked her, "Are you awake, honey?"

No response.

"Do you want me to tuck you back into your bed?"

Shake head no.

"Are you awake?"

Nod head.

"Did you have a nice nap?"

Nod head.

"Did you dream?"

Nod head.

"While I have my nap, do you want to make some pies? There's some dough and the rolling pin, and bring me the knife, OK? Real careful?"

So off she went and we were just getting hot when Chelsea called, "Mommy, I can't find it!" and I jumped naked from bed, showed her the counter and pie-makings, threw the knife in the sink and ran back to the bedroom as I heard Liam rousing from his nap.

I jumped back into bed, Matt grabbed me and we had another wonderful time. When I finally got up, there was Chelsea with some filthy pie scraps, flour all over her face, a roll of lifesavers all out of the wrapper, having a ball. When Matt got up, she told him, "Dad, I'm makin' chicken pie. I'm makin' lifesaver pie."

"You're a good cook, Chelsea," he said. "Just like your Mama."

The Saturday before Easter, Sarah came over and we spent the whole day making Easter breads—kulich, semlova. She said, "Aren't mornings beautiful?" and pulled Chelsea on her lap and snuggled her nose into Chelsea's hair and said, "Mmmm, what a sweet-smelling little honey bunch you are!"

"Pete and I are talking about getting married."

"Really, Sarah, that's wonderful! He's a nice guy."

"Yeah, he's my Buddha, such a big peaceful guy. I can't let him get away."

On Easter morning, Matt was out fishing, but Sarah and Pete and Karen came over for brunch after church. The house was beautiful and decorated for spring. Chelsea looked like a sugary confection in a pastel dress with a white lace pinafore, and she was childhood innocence personified. We went to Karen's for a dinner party. The music was so loud, Liam stayed awake the whole time, but he was good. We played pass the baby and he charmed all the baby-shy men. We had such a good day. I felt so good and was so proud of the kids.

I just wish Matt wasn't out fishing. Feel so badly the need for deep sentiment, romance, dancing close, partying together, sharing experiences, respect. Things moving so slow and routine.

Best songs are so simple. Hank Williams, Bob Dylan, writing before dawn—don't they ever get tired?

Have felt the luxury of time since yesterday. If I can just hold on to my resolve not to start any more projects, I might get somewhere. Less is more—simplify, simplify. Am using things up, not buying new presents, remembering my hoard of treasure when I need to send a gift.

I called Tricia late Thursday night after Matt left and felt strangely unrewarded. Of course, she'd been deep in sleep. Now I wonder at the lengths I'll go to distract myself. I feel thirty coming hot and heavy as a roadmark that I've done nothing and am nobody special.

My whole life is such a contrast to my glorious dreams. Is this what I can expect from now on?

Chelsea came in and climbed on my lap, drowsy. She said, "Where's my party gone?" Good song title.

While we were at Mill Bay Pharmacy to pick up Liam's formula, Allison Wade came right up to me, seven months' pregnant. "So what's new?" she asked.

I was ashamed of the way I treated her. I should have said, "When's your baby due?" "Have you felt it move yet?" "I bet you have a boy." "Are you still going to school?" or something. Instead, I ignored her pregnancy and made some lame remark about Matt being out fishing or Liam growing up. The trouble is that I feel ashamed for her.

Donna came to town from Larsen Bay. "Laurie, my sister, she's the health aide now, and I'm her wife!"

"You mean you stay home and watch the kids?"

"Yeah. It's working out pretty okay. Already we've put a new engine in the skiff, dug a sewer line, put out a grass fire, and shot and butchered a deer on the beach."

"Wow, I'm impressed."

"Well, Laurie's kind of driven. She acts like if she works herself hard enough, she won't hurt about Mack dying."

"What happened—on Valentine's Day, I mean?"

"Mack couldn't get the kicker—you know, the engine—on the boat started and it swamped and he died of exposure before they found him. Everybody said he'd been drinking, but he wasn't."

"Poor Laurie."

"Yeah, and his little boys too. They're so cute, and Mack was so good to Andy. Mack told me that although Andy wasn't his son and he had two little boys of his own, he tried to be fair to Andy and include him in."

"God, that's so honest and fair of him to know that about himself and to tell you. It makes me feel better, like there's some point to death, if I feel I can learn something from someone's dying, a lesson to live by. It makes me think of my Dad and Granny and my old boyfriend Sam all up in heaven, perfectly happy, friends, and caring for me...."

Donna burst out, almost crying, "Yeah, but see, you know all these people who have died, but for me it's the first one!" and she started crying and I felt so bad and shopworn and cold and world-weary.

Karen came over after church. I was doing wash and said to her, "I feel guilty about always doing laundry, using up so much water."

"Don't feel guilty about that! There's so many other ways to conserve, like wouldn't it be neat if people all rode horses in Kodiak—all these old nags hitched up in front of Solly's and the Mecca? Like the Old West. One night last year when we took the boat to Ketchikan, we were at some nude dancing place with sawdust on the floor. Whoa, talk about the Wild West! Actually I felt kind of funny there with all these nude women flippin' and flashin' away."

"Matt used to have wild old days when he fished out of Ketchikan. Sometimes I wish my life wasn't so well-modulated and responsible. I wouldn't mind being bad for Matt and him singing the blues for his wicked woman. I'm always so respectable now."

Then Robin called and said, "My Girl Scout troop is coming over this afternoon and we're going to sing songs. I was thinking—you're so good at singing, but I can't carry a tune, much less teach songs. Would you want to come over to help?"

My heart sank. From visions of flashy decadence to goody two-shoes Girl Scouts. "Sure I will, Robin."

Karen said, "Well, that takes care of your public."

The kids were good on the plane trip to Hawaii, and Matt and I took turns with Liam on our laps. The moon was just outside my window for the whole flight Then we put Chelsea to sleep on a bed we made for her on the floor and Liam slept in the middle seat while Matt and I had dinner and watched a good sad movie where I could bawl my eyes out.

We landed in Maui soon after sunrise and drove to the hotel, stopping first at a supermarket where we got coffee and doughnuts for breakfast and bubbles to blow for Chelsea. We just slouched around the first day, sqinting like moles in the bright sunshine.

The next day was cloudy, so we decided to drive to Haleakala Crater. A long winding road led uphill, and Chelsea fell asleep. We climbed higher, above the clouds. It was eerie and the crater was immense. On the way back down I sat in the back seat with the kids and sang to them until Liam and Chelsea fell asleep. At the hotel, Matt and Liam napped while Chelsea and I went swimming in the pool. Chelsea was in high spirits, calling me Chickie and Muffin, and going up to the 3-foot mark on the side of the pool "Hi, Number 3—we're Charlie's angels."

We attended a community luau at Lahainaluna High School, halfway up the mountain on the windward side of Maui. It was a boarding school like Kodiak High School, housing students from the nearby islands—Molokai, Lanai, and others. We wandered around among native Hawaiians and other big families ranging from babies to grammas. Some of the guys looked kind of hostile towards Matt and me, but then they'd notice the kids and relax. Later, Matt was talking to some of the men, and bragging about how he came to Hawaii because he did so great fishing. "Yeah, it can be dangerous, all right, but it pays off if you're willing to do what it takes," I overheard him say.

It made me feel like Bianca Jagger, a real jet-setter.

The morning of the day we were to leave I woke up to hear it raining. Chelsea got up with me and she stood on the porch with her pink blanket and her bright chartreuse pajamas, her droopy ponytails framing her little poppet head as we gazed out in the tropical drizzle.

On the trip back in Kodiak we had a frightening landing where tailwinds forced the pilot to make a circular approach over Pillar Mountain, and then throw the engines into a screaming reverse—this after overshooting the runway twice. I was a wreck.

The rest of that spring, Matt became a "man about the house." First he put in a new front door. The old one looked like it had been pawed to death by dogs. The new door had nine panes of glass, about half the door, and it let more light into the living room, although when the wind blew really strong, it would blow the door open, because the doorjamb was a little cockeyed and the latch wouldn't hold. Then Matt painted the outside of the trailer and put new plywood skirting around the bottom, fixed all the plumbing for the sink taps, laid a new bathroom floor in our bathroom, glued Liam's high chair together again, and screwed new hinges into the woodshed door. For a grand finale, he mowed the lawn in front of the trailer court and it looked like a country club.

I hung a wooden baby swing from a tree limb for Liam and the neighborhood kids built a fort in the trees. Rhubarb and strawberries sprouted up in the garden and I planted flowers and pumpkins seeds.

I worked on making our surroundings beautiful too. The living room was large and open with twenty feet of windows on one side overlooking Mission Road and Spruce Haven, the secluded compound of log cabins where the town's first doctor lived. We laid the old Oriental carpet over the moss-green rug, with the piano at the end of the living room with ferns on top of it. The piano was black and ornately carved and picked up the black border of the Oriental rug. The sofa and loveseat were gold, and all the greens and golds and dusty blues of the carpet harmonized with the plants and the grass and pale blue-grey skies outside.

The walls of the trailer were fake wood paneling, but light-colored like birch, not the oppressive dark cedar paneling that made you feel closed in your little hole. In the dining room, four white-painted chairs matched the carved kitchen cupboards and looked rustic and Scandinavian, fitting in with the Carl Larsson poster on the wall. I painted the moss-green colored wall behind the table white, and covered a kitchen wall with yellow check wallpaper and hung my copper and tin molds on them. The best thing about the trailer was all the built-in drawers and closet space so I could clear the clutter out of sight. The three-foot square counter space above the dishwasher was "my space" that I guarded as my only un-invaded territory.

One afternoon after all this was accomplished, Chelsea and Tuffy's daughter Christie were drawing on the back door and shed with chalk, just after Matt had painted the trailer. I was working in the kitchen and I heard him pull into the driveway and come up the back stairs and say, "What a nice picture, girls," instead of throwing a fit about how they'd drawn over the new paint job.

I asked Matt if he'd ever be content to do some business, indoors-type job and he said, "What? And be a flannel dwarf?"

There are some beautiful things about Kodiak—the lengthening days till midnight sun for one. The kids flocking over here to play outside till it gets dark—it's even better when I get out there myself. I want Chelsea and Liam to grow up in a neighborhood.

The sun rose now and is giving such a beautiful glow. I'm really happy here with my three prerequisites—a fireplace, a yard, and a view—even if it is a trailer. The new door Matt put in is making me house-hungry, except instead of a dream house I'll have a dream door. I don't think I'll find a prettier spot than this, so I'll be content for a good while, savoring these beautiful days with the boats going in and out. I'm proud of our stamina and stubbornness, and grateful for our luck in living such a real life.

I finally figured out what the appeal of the radicals and flower children of the late 60s was for me. They were the ones who gave me the idea that romantic dreams could be realized. They pictured dreams as reality. Professor Lerner said, "After the revolution, I want to sit in

Sproul Plaza discussing philosophy," and Sam said, "One day we'll be able to go down the street for miles, and see neighborhood rock concerts every few blocks, and greenhouses and playgrounds everywhere." And my dream was a garden farm on the sea, kids, cats and dogs running around, a home of good feeling, stimulating conversations, wild dances. It's so clear and gorgeous out, still nobody up, just Goldie and me. Yesterday I hung Chelsea's wooden clock and it makes such a homey sound, ticking in the quiet.

On my birthday, I opened my birthday presents after church and then Sloopy Don came over as I was bathing Chelsea, then Pete and Sarah and Donna and Andy in from Larsen Bay.

Tuffy and Jake came over too, a leisurely rainy-day afternoon, although both Tuffy and Jake had been drinking and Tuffy was having a hard time holding on to reality. "I think I'm gonna move to LA—take up modeling again. Ya know, I used to be a model in high school. Was on fashion board."

She stumbled as she walked toward the door. Jake caught her and mumbled, "Let's go home now, Tuffy."

"Yeah, gotta work a little on that runway walk if I'm gonna be model 'gain."

"Better work on a lot more than that," Sloopy Don said when the door closed behind them. But nobody laughed.

After everyone left and the kids went down for naps, Matt and I smoked dope and watched "How to Marry a Millionaire," and then Matt said, "I'm going to go into town for a little bit to look for Animal."

"Who's Animal?"

"Oh, he's a guy working on Robbie's boat now. I lent him some money."

A little while later Matt called. "I tracked Animal down and he paid me back. Why don't you get a sitter for the kids and meet me downtown for dinner?"

I walked into the bar to find Matt sitting next to a huge guy with long curly hair, wearing a sleeveless undershirt and leather cuffs around his wrists. I sat down next to Matt, and Animal said to me, "Don't ever cut your hair."

Sloopy Don was there too and they started making their dumb ugly comments about Chelsea. "That little girl of yours is going to be a killer when she grow up. Think I'll wait for her."

But instead of getting mad or uppity, I said, "I wouldn't want you to go to waste for the twenty-five years it would take for Chelsea to realize all your charms." The guys all grinned and it felt so good to have a comeback that wasn't nuclear, just snotty.

After two watery drinks, we went to the Village for lobster dinner and then to the Harvester for dancing and a snort of cocaine. Oh, I was so happy and wild and beautiful! Matt was tossing me around and I didn't even slip. We even had the foresight to leave earlyish, around two, so we could get up to go clam-digging as we'd promised Sarah and Pete.

The next morning, on the way out to the beach to dig clams, I threw up on the side of the Jeep. I carried Liam in a backpack and felt hungover. As the guys were digging in the sand with shovels, Sarah came up to me and asked, "Nora, the King Crab Festival is coming up. The record store is sponsoring the first annual Kodiak Music Festival and they want everyone who can do something musical to perform. You should play the piano for it."

"Yikes, you mean play for everybody?"

"Yeah, and it will be broadcast over the radio and everything."

"It'd be cool, Sarah, but I think I'd get stage fright. I'm not very good at winging it, I have to read and memorize all the music… "

"Oh Nora, don't be silly, it's a gift I wish I had. If I could play the piano, boy, I'd be up there—it'd be fun. You should do it."

"You think I can do it?"

"You'll sound great! It'll be fun!"

The next week, Sarah was over when someone called from the music festival for me to play. "Yeah, we need somebody right now. Can you get down here fast?"

"Okay, but…"

"Great! As soon as you can!" He hung up.

"Oh, Sarah, I can't do this."

"Sure you can, c'mon. Let's go."

"But I need someone to turn the pages."

"Oh, I'll do it!"

So I did…scared to death. I did okay.

The next day, when Matt was home, we went to the Crab Festival parade and to the carnival rides and booths and art show. I carried Liam in the backpack and Matt had to pack Chelsea around for the end of it, but we finally got both monsters in bed and were smoking dope when Sloopy Don and his girlfriend Jessie came by to congratulate me for playing in the music festival—they'd heard me on the radio. Don said, "'Hey, that's Ahab's wife!' I told Jessie."

"Ahab?"

"Yeah, don't you know that's what they call your old man?"

Matt was messing around with the tape recorder, and then I heard me playing the piano at the music festival, and then I could hear Matt's voice in the background, telling the kids, "Listen to your Mom play."

Matt picked up some beer bottles and took them into the kitchen. I followed him and put my arms around him as he pulled more beer out of the fridge. He turned around and I said, "Thanks, Ahab."

Pam and Fred stopped by to pick up some of the fishing gear that they'd left in the trailer courtyard. They were preparing for their summer fishing site.

"So what's a fishing site like?" I asked Pam.

"Oh, it's basically camping in shacks and then fishing from skiffs on the shore with a drift net," Pam said, "It's heavy, exhausting work and Fred yells at me if I can't pull and haul and keep up with him."

"Mmmm, the camping part sounds like fun, but that work sounds backbreaking."

Fred said, "Well, the part that galls me is the Nates, just cause they're Indian, they think they're entitled to more than their share."

Pam chimed in, "All they can talk about is how screwed over they are."

I said, "Matt's mother's a Native," just to shut them up and see them squirm, and Matt played along as they stammered all over themselves, trying to take back what they'd said.

We had a wild night after everyone went to bed. Chelsea woke up about two, hollering and screaming and pointing to a corner of her bed where a "big cat" was. She came in with us for a while. Then Liam woke at five, probably because he was so wet, and I changed and fed and patted him and went back to bed and prayed Hail Marys furiously till it was quiet. We slept in till eight and then I had a shower.

It was really foggy this morning, with the boats blowing their horns in the channel, and it sounded eerie. Matt made a pot of coffee and went to the boat harbor to check if the Maggie J*'s in. The sky's still grey, but the sun is shining and trying to break through. Now it's the afternoon and both darlings are napping, the house is all clean, the dishes are done, "Scheherezade" is on the radio, my hair's fixed, and a rhubarb pie is cooling. The clock's ticking. Matt's bringing home some fish and I'm watching the waves in my peace and quiet— my Apollonian moments. I feel so good.*

Next week will be the old grind with Matt fishing salmon on the Maggie J *when it gets back in town.*

Salmon fishing started and Matt was actually fishing salmon for the first time, not tendering, on the *Maggie J*. But as soon as it was supposed to start, the fishermen struck for a higher price. It was hold-your-breath for the next few days before the canneries gave in to the fishermen's price demands.

We had a party on the Fourth of July and Sloopy Don brought his mother Belle over. She was a tough old bird and neither of them pulled any punches when they talked. Sloop got pompous and said how only scum would break the strike when the fishermen are holding out for a fair price, and Belle said, "You can't say you wouldn't violate a picket line if you had a family to feed. You couldn't come home empty-handed and tell your kids that you have principles!"

I loved it. She answered the thoughtless macho clichés Sloop and Matt and so many other fishermen are so fond of spouting.

Matt picked up the half-gone bottle of Crown Royal and said, "Sloop, how about some whiskey?" and poured half of it into Slip's glass and the remaining booze into his, without even looking around or offering any to anyone else.

"Hey, did you hear the mayor got shot in the Village Bar last night?" Matt said. "He's been carrying on with some married woman, and her husband was in the bar and came up to the mayor and said, 'If I had a gun I'd shoot you,' and the guy on the next bar stool, says, 'Well, I have a gun—here!'" and gives it to the guy, the husband, and he unloads it at the mayor."

"Wow, was he badly hurt?" I asked.

"No, the guy was so fucked up, he only hit the mayor with a flesh wound in his shoulder."

"The mayor was messing around with some married woman?"

Belle growled at me, "Honey, don't think he's above it. In this town it's like the bumper sticker says, 'There is no town drunk, we all take turns.'"

"That's one of the things I like best about Kodiak, there's no virtuous elite. Like on the dance floors, if you want to dance you get out there—scroungy or dressed-up, hip or square—it's not like you have to be cool to have a good time."

"Yeah, but I'm cool and it helps," Don saluted me with his glass and everybody laughed.

It never did get really dark, but around eleven we went outside and lit off some fireworks, Matt acting blasé as always and me screaming and jumping up and down. When everyone left, Matt said, "Well, you and Sloop certainly seemed to enjoy making goo-goo eyes at each other all night."

I was so disheartened. "Other people can throw parties and have a good time after everyone's left, talking over the evening, but if any man talks to me directly about something outside of fishing, you call me on the carpet for it."

"What do you think it looks like, my own wife flirting in front of me?"

"You don't seriously believe this jealousy crap. It's just an opportunity to make me feel bad. Some love."

And with that Matt walked wordlessly out the door, leaving me with the party clean-up and the now-dead celebration.

The circus came to town, just like in the olden days. They arrived on a boat in the Channel, and we went down to watch them unload. The animals paraded off the boat and up the street to the school gym—strange to see wild animals in the street, although they were pretty pathetic to my eyes, slow baggy elephant, dingy zebra, hyper little monkey, all on chains. The bears on Kodiak Island are the last great monsters, but of course there weren't any Kodiak bears in the show.

I asked Tuffy if she wanted to go with me and take Christie. "Nah," she slurred her words. "You go, I'll watch the little guy." I was kind of worried about leaving Liam with her, but I couldn't very well say I decided not to go, or that I didn't want to leave the baby with her. She didn't seem that drunk, just a little bleary-eyed and unfocused—in the middle of the day in the summer.

I took Chelsea and Christie to the performance. What a shlocky show. They led the pitiful zebra in a circle on a leash, forced the old wild-eyed pony to jump over a hand-held pole, and brought a broken-down cowhorse to its knees.

When I brought the kids back, Tuffy asked me to stay for a drink, but I said I had to get dinner started. Tuffy waved me out the door, yelling, "Yeah, get those three square meals in the little bastards, that's a super Mom!"

One summer night while Matt was still out fishing, we celebrated Pete's birthday at a party in their watchman's cabin at Fort Abercrombie. Pete had built a banya out there for steam baths like the Russians and the Natives had. I knew from Karen and Sarah that they had banyas all the time, but it was the first time I'd been invited. I left Liam with a babysitter, but I brought Chelsea to the party with me. When I showed her the banya, she was afraid of the hissing and the darkness and the steam. I left her with the guys watching her and feeding her potato chips and pop, while all the girls took a banya together.

We were like a bunch of naked birds on telephone wires as we perched on the benches and talked and sprinkled cold water on the steaming rocks and added cedar logs to the fire underneath the rocks.

Karen showed us a huge, old-fashioned merry widow that she'd bought for Sarah as a joke.

"Yeah, if you go to bed wearing an underwire bra, you wake up strangled in the morning. You should have seen Pete's eyes when Sarah came into the banya for the first time last winter."

Everyone cackled and I said, "What?"

Karen said, "Oh, Pete's mouth just dropped and he said, 'I think I'm in love.'"

Even in the steam heat, Sarah blushed. "Oh, you guys!"

117

When we trooped back into the cabin, Chelsea was under the covers in bed, but her brown eyes were wide open. After the guys had their banya, Neil brought out his banjo, and Pete had his guitar, and we sang while they played.

We left around one and it was so beautiful outside with the spruce trees towering overhead until they poked into the deep violet sky pierced by the stars' brilliant twinkling.

"Oh, Chelsea, isn't it a pretty night? I wish your old Daddy was here with us."

CHAPTER NINE

LIKE A PREGNANT TEENAGER
In which Matt is injured and is confined to the sofa; I suffer the consequences

Matt called me through the marine operator the next morning and asked me to pick him up at the oil dock in an hour. I didn't think anything of it and asked Tuffy to come over for a little while to watch the kids.

When the *Maggie J* pulled in, Matt hobbled up the ramp, pain distorting his face, and I went down to help him.

"What did you do?"

"I think I might have broken my ankle."

"Oh Matt, how?"

"We were just finishing the last set and I jumped from the pile of corks onto the deck. I slipped on something and my ankle gave way under me."

He heaved himself up into the Jeep, sweat trickling down his pasty-white face.

At the hospital, Dr. Copstead looked at Matt's ankle and said, "It doesn't really look like you broke your ankle, but you've strained the tendons, which is probably more painful than a broken ankle. We'll have the radiologist look at the X-rays when he comes in from Anchorage this week, and for now, we'll send you home with some painkillers. You'll probably be laid up for awhile. You'll have to stay off it for a month or two."

"Oh, Jeez," Matt groaned. "Well, it's got to be back to normal by king crab."

"You'll just have to see about the king crab season. Hopefully, it will be okay by then," Dr. Copstead said.

Matt camped out on the sofa, and for all his worries, we didn't have to go on welfare. The summer days were long and peaceful. Matt and Liam took naps together, with Liam nestled in Matt's arms, or between his legs, on the sofa—my Fisherman Madonna. Chelsea and I could just wait for Matt to wake up to be with him. I wasn't worried about Matt's recovery, and I felt entirely safe with everybody home.

The radiologist reported that Matt had fractured his heel bone, the very bottom of his foot, but it was the tendons around his ankle that really hurt. Matt started going to physical therapy.

"After your physical therapy, I'll take you home for some occupational therapy," I said. I thought I'd teach Matt to play the zither. After a few minutes he stopped for a cigarette break, and then he taught me to play pinochle. I beat him twice.

"Beginner's luck."

"Wanna play another hand?"

But he hobbled over to the sofa. "C'mere."

He lay down and I lay down on top of him.

"No, pull the curtains."

So I got up and pulled the curtains and it was so lovely and decadent to be lying there in the middle of the day, with the screen door singing in the ocean breeze, kissing him and getting naked.

We heard Chelsea stirring from her nap. Matt threw the sofa blanket over me as Chelsea appeared in the hallway.

"Want Mama to take you for an ice cream cone?" Matt called to her. She nodded eagerly. "You go get your pretty skirt on and Mama will take you."

She went back into her room and I jumped off Matt and into my clothes as he pulled his jeans up.

"Matt, my heart's pounding."

"Yeah, well, we've both got things pounding, but it'll have to wait."

"Hey, Matt, we better be careful."

"Whaddya mean?"

"Like birth control...."

"Well, what are you going to do?"

"Oh, I don't know. It's all such a hassle, but I don't know if I trust Mother Nature to wait until Liam's older."

Matt grunted.

"So Matt, do you think I should get a job and try to bring in a little money just so we don't dip too deep into our savings?"

"Well yeah, maybe that's a good idea. I can hobble around a little bit now. What do you think you could do?"

"Well, you'd be going back fishing in the fall, right?"

"Oh yeah, of course. But I could look after the kids and the house by myself now, if you wanted to make some money. I'll probably go out with Glenn in the fall on his new boat."

"Out in the Bering Sea?"

"Yeah, that's where he'd be going."

We looked at each other and I knew he really did have to fish the Bering Sea season this year. "We do need the money this year, don't we?" I came up to Matt and put my arms around him. "I always miss you so much. I'm glad you got hurt and had to stay home."

"Yeah, well, it can't get to be a habit."

"So if I got a job, it'd have to be temporary so that I could quit when king crab starts in September. Maybe I could get a job fixing up a boat, getting gear ready for the season?"

Chelsea came skipping back into the room. "Okay, let's get some ice cream. C'mon, Mama."

Robin and Neil came over to visit. Liam was still up and I gave him a bottle and rocked him until he fell asleep, and Robin said, "Good little mother, Nora."

I don't need your pats on the back, your pronouncements. I know I'm a good mother.

Robin went on. "I get so frustrated in my job. It's just pathological, all the teenage mothers that come into the clinic, without the slightest idea of how much responsibility a baby really is, still thinking they can go out and party and drink and sleep with anybody they want, without taking any birth control measures."

Neil chimed in, "And in just a few more years we'll all be in the position Africa and India are in today—too many people and not enough food. We've simply got to control population at a zero-growth rate. Robin and I decided we just don't want to have kids—our lives are complete with the love we feel for each other."

"But people have a right to choose to have children. You can't legally regulate that. What if they want to have more than one or two children? What if they want to pass on their heritage?" I said.

"Yeah, but Nora," Robin said, "these teenage mothers are having babies because it's a status symbol—they have a baby, they're grown up, nobody can tell them what to do. And these kids that nobody wants to raise or knows how to care for become the responsibility of society, and of the government."

"I know that's true and that it's a terrible problem, but you can't just impose your morality—even if it's for the better. People who want families, who want to raise and nurture their children, can't be discriminated against just because they're a minority in a world where most pregnancies are accidents."

Matt said, "I know what you mean, though, Neil, about overpopulation in India. When I was there, those cripples and beggars—I wanted to kick them."

I felt like crying, he sounded so mean and stupid, but Neil finessed it by talking about his experiences as a medical worker in India. I could see it made Matt feel like he and Neil were the experts.

"I don't know what the solution is, but I know you can't make babies illegal," I said.

I wonder if and when Matt will be able to go back fishing and what's going to happen to me. He's still planning on going out to the Bering Sea for king crab with Glenn Mayhew. I feel so busy at home.

Tomorrow I'm going job hunting and Matt will be the Mama. I'll either work temporary at the canneries or a bank, or maybe something really high-paying. I'm kind of excited to get out in the workaday world, but don't want to do it forever. Maybe till Christmas, maybe not that long.

I'm sitting here in the front yard in Tricia's old jumper that she calls her insane-asylum uniform, trying to get Liam to crawl forwards. It's a beautiful peaceful afternoon, Chelsea's napping, and Matt's at the hospital for physical therapy. There's nothing really to be done for Matt's foot except giving it time.

Karen asked me if I wanted to work readying the *Wolverine*, Scott's boat. She joined me out on deck, dremmelling holes in plastic bait jars, painting buoys, cutting plastic collars and bridles for them, and painting the boat. A lot of it was just repetitive, boring work. "Hey, Karen, I'm getting muscles in my neck and arms from hauling rope off the spools."

"Hurts, doesn't it?"

"Yeah, but it feels kind of good, too."

Robin stopped by the boat and I felt such role-reversal, like I was living Matt's life where the guys schmooze around on the docks all day.

"Hey Karen, you really shouldn't be painting, those fumes aren't good for the baby," Robin said.

"Yeah, but I figured it's out in the open air, and I'm not doing very much of it."

"Still, I wouldn't take any chances. It's easy enough to avoid. Hey Nora, were you mad at us the other night? Neil said to me, 'You know, I think we insulted Nora, here she's got two kids already and we're talking overpopulation.'"

I said, "No, I wasn't insulted, I just don't feel the same way you do. I want kids in my life. I'm glad I have two kids. Someday maybe we'll have another baby."

"Matt seems to be enjoying himself playing house." Robin said. "I stopped by and he was doing laundry, folding clothes on the sofa."

"The first day was real hard for him—Liam was fussy and I was gone all day. He picked me up at seven, mad about something."

Karen laughed. "I'd just run into him and teased him about his day, laying on the sofa reading romance novels and eating bon-bons!"

"Oh, so that's why. But the next day, he made an apple pie and had a lot of company, smoked some dope, talked to his brother-in-law Glenn about fishing out in the Bering Sea in the fall."

Robin said, "Maybe he's going to like being a house husband."

"Oh, he knows he'll be back fishing. It's not like he'd ever be the one who always stays at home, cleaning a house that just gets messy again, cooking meals and clearing up and starting over again. It doesn't seem like you're achieving anything, just running to stay in place. It takes a lot of self-esteem to be a stay-at-home parent."

Scott came on board with a tall guy wearing a baseball cap and a beard. "Well hey, it's the ladies from the Christmas Bazaar, all together again!" he said.

"Hi, Nick," Karen said, "So you remember all that long way back, huh? Yeah, this is Robin O'Hara and Eleanor Hunter. Robin's taking a lunch break from working up at the clinic and Nora's helping us get the boat ready."

"You going to fish king crab?" Nick asked me with a frown, and then I recognized it was Nick McAllister from the Christmas Bazaar two years ago.

"Oh no, I'm just doing a little work while my husband's laid up with a twisted ankle."

"Oh good, that king crab season, that can be wicked. You wouldn't want to be out there."

"No, I don't think I would. Do you ever go fishing?"

"Oh, maybe sometimes I help out in the summer, but mostly I work with my dad at his chicken ranch, and then I fly with the local air taxi company—just brought Scott in from Karluk. So Karen, you gonna be ready for a little Scottlet or Karenina this winter?"

"We're moving right along, here," and Karen stretched her shirt over her stomach and patted it lovingly. "Feels like a little football game going on most nights."

"That's great, that's great, Scott's a lucky man."

Summer ended with a thud the day before yesterday and now it's pouring-down rain. It makes me feel nice and cozy inside and for once my timing is perfect—clean house, kids in bed, curled up on the sofa reading with chocolate cookies and milk. Oh, how I'd hate to be out on the streets tonight.

I've been feeling I should change but I don't know how. Tonight I thought again the answer is give up, let it be. Being ambitious causes too much pressure.

"Leo Davidoff came by today to give me a check for my salmon season pay before I hurt my foot. He made an offer to fish with him during king crab."

"What kind of offer?"

"I'd run the *Maggie J* for three times the percentage Glenn's offering me on his boat. Even though Leo's boat is little and fishing around Kodiak isn't supposed to be as good as out in the Bering Sea, I'd rather be running it than working crew, and Davidoff wants some time off."

"So you'll be here and won't have to go the Bering Sea?"

"Yeah, and I won't have to work on deck, which will be easier on my foot. It will be a bigger gamble money-wise, though...."

"Yeah, but Matt, you can do it and you'll be home regularly. I'm so glad! I figured out the equation around here—you make money and I spend it, but you waste money and I save it."

"Right, Mama, you got it figured out all right."

I would love to have a little touch of pregnancy that would go away with two aspirin and chicken soup. But I wake up in the mornings and know I'm still pregnant.

It could be okay. I'll have to run a tighter ship and be more disciplined and steel myself for all the times when Matt is gone, but it will work out. It's not as if you choose everything that happens to you in life.

Last night was a beautiful starry night and Matt and I went down to the Maggie J. *I made coffee and cleaned up the galley a little. It made me feel like a couple to be around a boat with Matt.*

Chelsea has abandoned her blanket and now carries her baby doll around with her. She wakes the doll up by slapping its cheeks from side to side. Well, there goes Liam crawling down the hall towards his favorite place—the bathroom. He loves to stare into the tub and meditate. Picking up orange peels off the floor makes me feel like a zookeeper.

Later that week I went to the public health department to have a pregnancy test. It came out positive. The nurse said, "You've got a three-year old and a nine-month old and you're pregnant. What are you going to do?"

I'll go crazy.

"Well, I guess I'll cut my hair." She looked at me like she was sizing me up for a straight jacket.

I came home to Matt and lit one of his cigarettes and strutted around the living room as elegantly as I could before standing in front of him and said, "Congratulations, darling, you're about to be a father again."

He looked at me and waited for me to start laughing like it was a joke and then he smiled his big proprietary smile that I just love and said, "Life with you is one big surprise after another. I didn't even know you were thinking like that."

"It wasn't thinking that got me pregnant," I laughed. "I didn't want to worry you if I was wrong."

"No, Mama, that's fine by me—you gonna be okay?"

I was so glad it was all right with him and I was so relieved, even though my worries had just begun.

Aside from being pregnant, I'm scared of having this baby, of going through that operating room again and the pain—and will Matt be there? And even if he's there, will he be mad at me or love me, and I just feel scared and I try to hold my head up high and have confidence that it will work out, that I can handle it, that three kids isn't a litter of piglets and I won't turn into a sow or a crab that doesn't love her kids.

Liam was fussy around dinnertime. But I'm pretty sure I made it through the day without yelling, didn't I?

I took Liam for his well-baby check up—nine months. I got him all dressed up clean in red overalls and white sweater set and a hat. He looked so cared-for. Afterwards I got the birth-control pills Donna asked me to send her and went right to the post office to mail them.

I ran into Leanne Hartwell, another mom from Chelsea's preschool and she and I talked for a good twenty minutes, me sweating in a turtleneck with Liam squirming in my arms.

"So how do you like living in the Larsons' old trailer?"

"Oh, it's fine. I always thought I wanted a sturdy little house, and trailers seemed so transient to me, but we have a huge front yard looking out to the Channel, and a big spacious living room and all, so it's okay."

Leanne had always seemed so establishment-perfect—tidy-looking blonde, taught school until she had her perfect little girl whose curly long hair was always brushed.

"What a hassle it was moving into the trailer we lived at near Mill Bay—two dogs had been abandoned there, one room was locked up with the previous owner's junk, the pipes were frozen, the septic tank was overflowing, the well was dried up, the windows were warped and then one night this big rat crawls in and I jumped up on the bed wearing Chuck's boots and started flailing around with a tennis racket."

"Oh my god, I would have died! How could you stay?"

"Yeah, and to top it all off, I find out the woman who lived there before had been raped!"

"And you still lived there!"

"Well, you know how hard it is to find a place to live."

"And even if you do find something, well—like Matt wants to buy his own boat and our trailer's pretty good, and fishing's why we came up here, so a house isn't the priority."

"And every man needs a hole to throw his money into." Then she asked me if I wanted to join a group of moms in a babysitting co-op where we look after each other's kids and barter our time.

I took Liam to the clinic later that month. He'd been running a fever and had spots on his throat. They didn't know what it is, but they weren't too bothered about it.

Robin said, "It's not real serious, maybe roseola, or thrush or German measles."

"Well, how can you tell which one it is?"

"You shouldn't be too concerned. Liam isn't threatened by whatever this illness may be. The only problem would be if it was rubella—you know, German measles—and you were pregnant, and even in that case, you were probably inoculated for it when you were younger."

"Oh yeah, right." *I don't want the whole town knowing I'm pregnant yet.*

But I went straight home and read Dr. Spock, who emphasized how hard German measles is to diagnose, that symptoms could even be non-existent. Then Spock described how threatening the infection is to a fetus—blindness, deafness, retardation, deformities.

Did I get a shot for rubella when I was younger? I remember lining up in the school dining room for some shot, but was that for rubella or polio boosters or what?

What if Liam does have a mild case of German measles? Will the baby be blind or deaf or have a cleft palate or brain damage? God helps those who help themselves. Dear God, I just can't handle a crippled baby on top of everything else. It's not just an excuse to justify not wanting this baby; it's a question of my family's survival. I can't handle not knowing if my baby's damaged for seven more months, and I can't cope with the fatigue and heartache of caring for a deformed child. I know it can be for the best for some people, but I'm me—crazy, nervous me. I'll drown and I'll take everybody down with me.

Finally I called Robin at home to ask if they could test me to see if I had been inoculated for rubella and she said, "Oh, Nora, Karen and I were just talking and I said, 'Why would Nora be so worried unless she's pregnant?' Is that what's going on?"

"Yeah, Robin, I'm worried sick. When I found out I was pregnant about a month ago, I felt blindsided, but I thought it over and decided it would be okay. I'll handle it. But Robin, I can't handle a baby with birth defects, too."

"I know, Nora, you've got your two kids now to answer for."

"Yeah, and I can't just say 'God will find a way,' because I'm the one who's got to deal with whatever way I choose."

"Nora, I wouldn't feel bad about an abortion at all. To me, it's just a group of cells and whether they grow or not is my decision."

"But it's not just a group of cells to me, it's my child, and Matt's child, because we love each other. I have to decide how I'm going to be responsible for it. I mean, would the best thing I could do for a crippled child be to prevent its suffering for a lifetime? Would that be the most loving thing to do?"

"No one can judge you."

"I'm not worried about anyone else judging me; I'm the one who will judge me and I have to make the right decision to live with myself for the rest of my life."

Matt came in early the next morning, unexpected. "Oh, I got a hassle on my hands—I was fishing around Two-Headed Island before the season opened, and Fish and Game busted me."

"So what does that mean?"

"Oh, I'll have to go to court and they'll probably just slap my hands."

"Matt, I've got scary news too. Liam was sick last week and I think it might have been German measles. He's okay now, but if I was exposed to German measles and passed it on to the baby, he could be blind, or deaf, or retarded. Matt, I'm so worried. My cousin had German measles when she was pregnant and her little boy was born deaf, and they had to take such special care of him, and schools and operations and all, and I just don't know what to do."

"Have you been to the clinic? What do they say?"

"Oh, they don't know, and I read in Dr. Spock that what Liam had could have been nothing or it could have been serious, and not even doctors know, and I told Robin, and she thinks 'Oh, just have an abortion, no big deal,' and I'm scared anyway about having three little kids to take care of, but I can't have an abortion, I'd hate myself. I want to have this little baby now, even if he…she…is an accident."

Matt sat there, smoking, not saying anything. "Goddammit," he finally said. "Well, how are you going to find out?"

"Well, I better make an appointment to see Copstead, right?"

"Yeah, you do that. Maybe it'll be okay. See what he says. I gotta go see a lawyer now."

In the midst of all my uncertainty about the new baby, Karen delivered her own newborn. Robin was Karen's coach, and she came to me with her account of the birth.

Robin said, "I'm helping Karen with her timing, and Scott's weaving back and forth over her. Finally the baby's really coming and its head emerges and Scott says, 'I gotta get out of here.' Then the baby was born and the first thing Karen said to me is, 'Robin, go check on Scott, I'm worried about him.' Dr. Copstead looks at me like 'Who are these people?' so I go outside and say to Scott, 'You have a little boy.' He said, 'Oooh, I'm gonna have to rethink all this,' and passed out on the sofa."

I said, "Gee, Robin, Scott's only kidding, isn't he? He can't be serious."

"But Nora, he is! I used to think that too, that he can't really feel that way, but he really does. And Karen does too."

Later, I went over to Karen's with the kids to see the new baby. Karen looked exhausted and bedraggled, still in her dressing gown. She bounced the screaming little red-faced newborn up and down her shoulder. I took the baby from her and paced up and down the hall so Karen could at least get dressed, but when I handed the baby back to her, I hadn't been able to work any magic. He was still crying and scrunching up his body, refusing to be comforted. "Looks like you got a live one," I tried to joke.

Finally he settled down. I told Karen and Scott that Matt had been fishing early.

Scott winced and said, "He got caught, huh? You know where Two-Headed Island is?"

I said no and Scott showed me Two-Headed Island on the map, halfway down the east side of the island, by Old Harbor.

Afterwards, Matt arrived back home and said, "They fined me $500. They just had to prove they've been out patrolling. Everybody fishes early, but they can't bring in the Native fishermen who go out early."

"So is that all that's going to happen?"

"Yeah. I'll just have to bring in $500 worth of extra crab."

"So are you going out again?"

"Yeah, tomorrow afternoon."

"Because Matt, I made an appointment for tomorrow morning to see Dr. Copstead and talk to him about the new baby...."

"Oh, the good doctor, the town savior, he's back in the healing business?" A look of disgust flashed across Matt's face as he lit a cigarette.

"Why are you mad at him?"

"It's not enough that he has his cushy doctor life in town, raking in the bucks. No. He has to have his fun out fishing salmon in the summer, too, so there's no doctor in town because he's out playing at being working class on the fishing grounds. Make up your mind, man!"

"Yeah, but Matt, he's the most experienced person around that I can go to for advice, and he's not a bad man, and I need some help figuring this out."

"What do you have to figure out?"

Shoot Matt, could you just try to help me out with this?

I took a deep breath. "If our new baby's going to be deformed, if Liam had German measles—rubella—if I've been exposed to rubella before so it wouldn't matter even if Liam did have it, if the baby's going to come out twisted, if I'm going to be able to handle this."

"Okay, you go. I'll stay home with the kids and wait till you get back."

I started to cry and said, "I can't deal with the possibility that after nine months, my baby may be born blind or deaf or worse. There'd be no turning back then, and I just can't do it."

Matt will just go along with whatever I decide, whatever I feel I can handle, because we both know I'm the one who'll be involved. Might as well face it.

Before I left I said, "I think I'll tell him to schedule an abortion. I just can't invite disaster into our lives." Matt nodded.

That struck me as kind of ironic. It seems like if disaster comes without warning I'd have no choice, but if disaster says it's coming, I'd be an irresponsible ninny to sit there, wringing my hands and letting it in. Once it's in, though, I can't ignore it. So I'm strong because I don't collapse? I wish sometimes I would be weak. But I don't know what I am now, strong or weak, right or wrong. And I may ruin my life and others' if I make the wrong choice. Who is this baby inside me?

I don't believe there's a judgment day where God says you broke the fourth and sixth commandments and so you're going to hell, because I would go to hell many times over if God is as officious and nit-picking as that. But I do see a judgment day where I'm asked how I took care—how I took charge—of the situations I got myself into. Did I multiply my talents seven-fold, or did I throw them into the gutter, sit down on the curb, and cry?

Oh God, I wish I could get some peace from all these questions just for a little while, but they haunt me. I'll be going along doing something totally mundane and then all of a sudden visualize a little cripple with artificial ears at my side and start crying.

Dr. Copstead came into the exam room and asked me how far along I was. *He has such kind eyes. Maybe he does get off on the philanthropic doctor-wild adventurer reputation, but doesn't he deserve it?*

I said, "I think about eight weeks. This baby wasn't planned, but my husband and I have made up our minds that it would be okay. But now, if the baby will have birth defects...."

He said, "Well, since we're not sure you were exposed to German measles while you were pregnant and since Liam wasn't terribly ill, the odds by no means favor the outcome that your baby would be deformed. We can give you a titer test to determine if rubella antibodies are in your blood. But if you'd been exposed to rubella before or even if Liam has had German measles this fall, the chances of it affecting the baby are just about nil after the first trimester. Let's take a look at you."

After he examined me, he said, "Nora, you're a lot more pregnant than you thought. The size of your uterus indicates at least three months. At least. This baby probably wasn't affected, even if you were exposed to rubella during Liam's illness."

Percentages were racing up and down my brain, but I wanted a sure thing. "Dr. Copstead, if I was your wife or your daughter, could you tell me that my baby's going to be healthy?"

"As far as any doctor can tell in any pregnancy, there are no signs to indicate that you'll have problems with this baby."

So I felt almost at ease, though I found it hard to believe I might be as far along as he thought, but I decided to wait for the results of the titer test and not think about rubella any more until the results were back.

"If I have been exposed, I'll have to weigh the odds again—when was I exposed? If it was this last month with Liam, will I gamble on the health of this new baby? When will the results be back?"

"In about a month. The test will show the antibodies if you've been exposed to German measles, ever."

"I've come to want this little baby. I hope—I know—the results will be okay. I think."

I came home and told Matt. He grunted, and put out his cigarette and opened his arms. I went to him and we just held each other.

Donna came to town from the village with Andy. She said she had a doctor's appointment, and I said, "Oh, are you sick or are you pregnant?"

And she said "Yeah."

Andy had impetigo sores on his face. Donna was all bummed out.

"It's like I take one step forward and two steps back. And now an abortion."

So of course I didn't tell her that I was pregnant again. I couldn't tell her I was facing, or rather avoiding, the same decision. I didn't know if my situation was going to be just tough, or impossible.

"Oh, Donna, I don't think you can be both the homemaker and the breadwinner, and that's what a baby needs. It's seems to me the only choice you have is how to make your life better from now on."

"Yeah, I know, the father's married, and he's a drunk."

"Maybe you should move back to town."

"No, I think Laurie needs me to stay there. She's all wrapped up in this Worldwide Church of God. Maybe I should join, too."

"If it helps you, why not?"

I want two things—I want to be busy, I want nothing to do. I want to go to two meetings tonight—the babysitting co-op and the Kodiak Artists' Guild. I want to stay home and be Mommy, and I want nothing, no yearning. I want to talk to Matt, but even though he's home, he keeps me at a distance.

I feel like I'm ready to have the baby now. I want a new working washer and dryer and a laundry maid. I want someone to come visit me, talk in a way that will make me feel mellow.

It's sad that Kodiak can't take people to its bosom and make them feel like they're home, that people have such a need to get away from Kodiak, but it's definitely a real feeling.

Leo Davidoff's 16-year-old son Ryan came to the house while I was doing dishes. I opened the door and invited him in, and then called to Matt.

Ryan was outstandingly good-looking, like a young James Bond, but he was so gawky. "Um, yeah…um…Matt, I, you know, left some tapes on the boat, you know, Metallica and Led Zeppelin and all, and I, you know, was…well, I wanted to go down and get them back, you know, if that's okay."

"Yeah, well, you can come down tomorrow morning and I'll let you get them." Matt stood by the door like he was ushering Ryan out and his tone of voice was cold as ice.

When Ryan left, I said, "How come you were so mean to him?"

"Hey, I saw his eyes pop when he saw I was home. He sure didn't expect to see me when he came visiting you."

"Matt, he just came to get his tapes! He probably saw his dad's boat in the harbor and figured he could catch you at home and get his stupid tapes back."

"Yeah, well, that's what he *would* say if he came to see you and I was home."

"Right, Matt, here I am, stuck at home with two babies, four months pregnant and looking like a refugee, and the high school hunk comes looking after me. If it weren't so ridiculous, it would be demeaning. Where's your trust?"

I asked Leanne to babysit one day, but she said she had a bad cold. Turned out she had pneumonia. Robin said, "I was helping Leanne out with her baby and some meals, but now she's found someone to come in every day to help till she's better. I ran into Chuck by the hardware store and he said, 'Look after Leanne while I'm out fishing, will you?'"

"That was nice of him."

"Nice? It just kills me how off-hand these guys can be about their wives and families when it's fishing season, leaving her to find some help while she's so sick and Chuck tossing off a casual comment to a friend. And Chuck isn't even your stupid redneck chauvinist, he's like this jock-businessman that assumes everybody's out to help him make it big time."

"Well, I'm taking a casserole out to them tonight, and the babysitting co-op's got it lined up to help out with meals and babysitting, so she can just concentrate on getting better."

"I look at you, Nora, and think, why are you rushing around, why don't you settle down?"

"But if I settle down, I worry about everything, about this new baby, whether it's okay, and what I'll have to think about if it isn't, and just waiting, waiting, waiting for answers. I feel really pregnant emotionally, ready to break and explode."

Finally at the end of October I learned that I hadn't ever been exposed to rubella, meaning Liam hadn't had rubella when he was sick.

Robin called me from Dr. Copstead's office to tell me.

"Oh, I'm so glad, I'm so glad!"

"Right, Nora, now you can just worry about the normal things every pregnant woman worries about."

"Oh, I feel so good, I'll never worry again! I'll give up dope and coffee, and I can just be pregnant and get huge and have a big fat baby!"

It's beginning to snow and is so beautiful in an Alaskan way—stark, snow-covered grandeur. Come on, keep snowing. As the sun rises, the sky is beginning to clear. Will I make it through the operation again, will the baby be good, will Matt be there?

Peggy called that weekend to say she was flying in to Kodiak to visit Glenn, who was bringing his boat into town from the Bering Sea. Matt and I planned to tell her about the new baby Sunday night, after we'd called his folks and told them. We rehearsed a little routine, where he'd tell them the doctors discovered a growth from his foot accident, except the growth wasn't on his leg, it was in my belly.

We picked Peggy up at the airport. She had a radically short haircut. Chelsea and I both wore sweater dresses. Mine made me look bulky all over so Peggy wouldn't notice my stomach.

Peggy said, "You didn't need to dress up for me."

I was kind of taken aback, but I said, "Well, it's Sunday; I like to dress up at least once a week."

Peggy said to Matt, "Remember how Mom used to make us dress up for church on Sunday?"

Matt replied, "Yeah, it didn't take long to see the bullshit in that one."

I felt like the Hunters' "It's us against the intruders" routine was starting up again.

"So Matt, when are you going to get your own boat?" Peggy asked him at home. "Why don't you do what Glenn did, get together a group of rich Anchorage businessmen—lawyers and accountants and a congressman who want to invest in a fishing boat? You can be skipper and part owner, like Glenn."

Matt snorted, "Well, I'm not a politician. Guess we'll have to sell something first."

I laughed from the kitchen where I was putting the meat pie in the oven. "No, Matt, you're not selling me, or the kids either!"

Peggy said, "Glenn said things are really cheap in Dutch Harbor. You could move out there and really put some money aside."

I answered, "And really be at the end of the world. No, Kodiak's as far as I'm moving."

Gee, I sound like a real bitch. Where do I think I can get off dictating where we'll live?

I pulled the oven door open to see if the pie was done just as Matt was calling his folks long distance. The damn pilot light had gone off again and the oven was cold. "Whenever I cook something for more than a half-hour or so, the oven goes out," I said to Peggy.

"The propane line must get clogged," she said.

"Yeah, maybe someday we'll explode."

I wanted to hear Matt talking to his folks on the phone, but I had to get my coat on and run over with the pie to Tuffy's and ask if I could use her oven for a while. It was snowing and the pallet boards to Tuffy's trailer were slippery. Tuffy seemed distracted and bleary-eyed.

"Where's Christie?" I asked.

"Oh, she's in her bedroom, watching TV." It was dark and sad inside the trailer, but I was anxious to get back home.

When I got back in, Matt was still on the phone. "Did he tell them anything?" I asked. Peggy shook her head no. We both stood at the dining room table listening to him talk. He repeated the lines we'd rehearsed over and over.

"Yeah, I got a side effect from my ankle."

"Yeah, I've got a good doctor."

"No, no, I'm fishing now. Yeah, Davidoff's boat. No, it's something else. It's Eleanor. Yeah, yeah—she's gonna have another baby here. Yeah. No, I'm not kidding."

Peggy looked down at the table, her eyes open wide as she tried to understand what he was saying. "She's going to have a baby?" She murmured to herself. She looked at me and smiled, disbelief written all over her face.

"No, no, I'm not kidding," Matt said over and over. "Yeah, it is great, yeah. No, I'm not kidding. In April. No, I'm not kidding." Then he said, "Eleanor! Here, get the phone."

I moved into the living room and picked up the phone. "Hi. Yes, it's me," I said.

"You're going to have a baby!" his mom bellowed.

"Yeah," I was grinning.

"I said to Matt, 'You're kidding me!' and he kept saying 'No, no, I'm not kidding!'"

"Yeah, I guess so."

"Now no more!" she said sternly and then laughed. "Three's enough! No more! Are you okay?"

"Yeah, I'm fine."

"Are you feeling okay?"

"Yeah, I'm okay."

"Now no more! You tell Matt no more!"

"Okay!" I said, laughing, and handed the phone back to Matt.

After Matt talked some more and hung up, Peggy said, "You really should have called earlier. They drink all weekend, and by this time Sunday night they're pretty gone."

Late that night after we all went to bed, Glenn knocked on the door and he and Peggy went down to his boat.

The next night was Halloween and they babysat Liam while Matt and I took Chelsea out trick-or-treating. She was the pink bunny again.

Matt left the next morning, and Glenn and Peggy went to the school carnival with the kids and me. They were raffling off a choice of a side of beef or the quilt I'd helped make for first prize.

"Why would anyone choose a quilt over a side of beef?" Glenn wondered.

"Lots of guys hunt deer around here and don't need to buy meat for the freezer," I said.

The *Odyssey* went down, one survivor picked up by the Coast Guard.

Matt called from Larsen Bay. He was holed in because of weather. My heart lurched when he called for fear there was another accident, but he was just near a phone and thought to call. "We all went hunting and got deer. I'll be back in as soon as we put the gear away."

"Did you hear about the *Odyssey* going down?"

"Yeah, they called a mayday over the radio just after the weather call the night before. They sounded really scared, only had time to say 'Mayday, we're going over.'"

"Oh man, so sudden."

"They had too damn many pots on deck, makes it unstable."

It's so sad and scary. Somehow you think you should have a warning or a little bit of fussing around or hope and not just be there one moment and gone the next. I remember seeing the Odyssey *in the harbor when I was working on Scott's boat, and telling Matt what a beautiful, neat-looking boat it was. It looked so well taken-care-of.*

Getting into Thanksgiving baking. I've been reading to Chelsea an illustrated version of "Over the River and Through the Woods." Makes me so homesick, but for an idealized version, not real life. I wish Mom had a grandpa to bring in wood for her and jolly her up. I wish I had someone to bring in wood for me and jolly me up.

Tomorrow I want to mop the floor and bake apple and pumpkin pies.

Liam started walking before Thanksgiving. Donna called from Larsen Bay and asked me to pick up her sister Marnie and her baby at the airport and get them on their way to Larsen Bay. "If they need to stay in town overnight, would it be okay if they stayed with you?"

"Sure, that would be fine."

We picked Marnie up at the airport with her baby, painfully small for nine months, with haunting black eyes in a tiny face. Leanne was at the airport meeting someone and she said, "Let me see the newborn" when I was holding Marnie's baby.

Leanne had a hard time disguising her shock when I said, "She's nine months old."

Marnie was a lot like Donna, friendly and open and endlessly patient with her little girl. She got up constantly during the night, cooing to the fussy baby.

The next day, getting them on the plane to Larsen Bay was a hassle. First there was no room on the planes. I was growing used to the idea that they might be our guests for Thanksgiving. We went back home and later Marnie called the air service and they said they had a place for her on a chartered plane to Wide Bay, but when we got to the air service offices the plane had left without them.

I was steamed, but Marnie just sat down and waited in the office in hopes that another flight would be put together so that they could get on it and out to Larsen Bay.

Finally, just as Liam became unbearably fussy, things clicked in place. Nick McAllister strode up to us and said, "I hear the plane you were supposed to be on left without you."

"Yes," Marnie said, worry and fatigue making her look old.

"Well, I'm flying down to Karluk in about twenty minutes. I can swing by Larsen Bay and drop you off. Will that help?"

"Oh, that would be so great," Marnie jumped up in excitement, gathering her things.

"Nick, thank you," I said.

He winked at me and said to Marnie, "Okay, don't rush now, I'll make sure you know when we leave."

Marnie sat back down again, cooing to her whimpering baby. I ran out to the truck and gave Marnie our frozen turkey. She waved to me from the window of Nick's plane as it took off. Then I got another turkey at the store and went down to the boat to see if Matt wanted lunch or a ride home, but he was still puzzling with the engine, so I took the kids home for naps.

Thanksgiving Day was peaceful, snowy and cold. We had oatmeal porridge for breakfast and then I popped the pumpkin custard into the oven. Matt stuffed the turkey. I'd just curled my hair and Matt was making lunch when Sloopy Don drove up with a double whammy: he was quitting Matt to work on another boat, and then he told Matt about a poker party that night. So we had a little tempest.

"Are you going to go?"

"Maybe."

"This is Thanksgiving!"

"Okay, okay, I won't go!" He turned his back on me, shrugging and mumbling.

After dinner, Karen and Scott called and asked us to come over for dessert. They'd just had their family dinner and now a lot of people were coming over. I was so glad when Matt said yes.

Robin and Neil had gotten friendly with two guys and a girl who they found camping out in the framework of their new house, so they came over, too. They had spent the summer rafting down the Yukon and showed us slides of their trip.

Back home I said to Matt, "Sometimes I wish I were free to go rafting down rivers, or tramping around the countryside."

Matt said, "Well, why don't you ask those guys if you can go with them? It looks like they need another woman. Why don't you go with them if you're so unhappy here?"

"Matt, it's just a fantasy! Why can't we just talk to each other like friends and tell each other how we feel without it always ending up a big fight? Do you think we'll ever raft down the Amazon or have any adventures together?"

He went down the hall to the bedroom, and a minute later I heard the mattress springs creak. After a while I went to bed. And that was the end of Thanksgiving.

We're having the most beautiful pink-magenta sunrise today, and I'm making my fruitcakes. It snowed last night. I hope Matt has fantastic and fast fishing. My tea tastes like fish, sour milk, and weak tea bags. Start again.

Jake came over and asked me to watch his house. "Yeah, I've got to take Tuffy Outside. She's not doing so good."

"What's wrong?"

"Well, we haven't been getting along for some time now, and—well, she swallowed a bunch of pills the other night, and thank god we got her stomach pumped in time, but she's just gone round the bend, won't talk sense, just cries and comes swinging at me—just out of control."

"Wow, Jake, I wish I could have helped her."

"Oh, nobody can help her. Her dad was a real Bible-thumping child beater and she's just not strong enough to be by herself up here, and I don't think there's anything anybody can do now."

I wonder if it's the aloneness that gets to people. I'm in a mixture of responsibility and powerlessness. I'm responsible for answering Chelsea's needs, Liam's needs, Matt's needs, but who's responding to my needs? I feel like I'm all alone in caring for the kids, all alone in my desire to have some fun, all alone in my concern for the new baby, all alone in my worries. It's up to me to work them out, to find a better way, to avoid the yelling and unhappy scenes, and I don't know how.

I don't know how to feel calm and giving when Liam cries and Chelsea whines, to feel interested when Matt talks about buying a boat that may threaten my whole lifestyle, to pursue my interests when the house and kids are so demanding.

I want to be competent and successful, but I don't know the formula. I feel so overwhelmed and lost. Nobody knows how I feel.

What's the matter with me? I feel tired. I want to lie in bed and do nothing. I feel heavy. I want to eat right and not be hungry. I feel crowded. I want to relax and read a book or have a cup of tea and do nothing. I feel uncertain. Oh God, for once in our lives I want to know definitely we will be doing something. I want to feel like I matter to somebody.

The wind is really blowing. I wonder if Matt's even made it out to the fishing grounds.

I got home from a class and the babysitter said, "Matt just called from the Mecca and said for you to go down there. Don't worry, I can stay. You go." So I skipped out the door.

Robin had tried to get out to see Neil, who was fishing king crab, by hitching a ride on the boat with Matt, so when I came into the Mecca, she and Matt and four guys were sitting there in the crowded dark and smoke with the band blaring out.

Later, when we went into the bathroom, Robin said Matt had been telling some of the people in the bar about our baby and I said, "I feel sort of embarrassed, like all the baby books say you should wait so the older child is at least two or three years old, and then there's people that think you should be responsible for overpopulation."

Robin said, "Yeah, but I don't think Matt thinks that at all, I think he's really proud. They all sounded so impressed."

Tricia called and said, "We decided to add a second story on to our house, and then Mom told us you were pregnant—perfect timing! So you all plan on staying with us when the new baby comes."

"I would love that! Would it really be okay?"

"Of course, baby sister."

Matt was feeling sick. I loved nurse-maiding him, bringing him aspirin and tissues and mentholatum and juice, and remembering how good it feels to be taken care of made me relish making him comfortable. Everyone likes to be babied when they don't feel well, and it's the rare opportunity when Matt lets anyone do for him.

He woke up feeling much better. He got up, stretched, and said, "I feel like slapping somebody around." He rumbled into the kitchen like a big shaggy bear and over coffee and a cigarette he asked me, "Got somebody you want me to slap around?"

Then we took the kids downtown to see Santa Claus. Chelsea looked all starry-eyed and Liam shook his baby head at the toy they rattled in front of him. Later, Liam was so tired he fell asleep between bites of his lunch. After we got home, I put the kids down for naps and Matt left to go shopping for Christmas presents.

Robin and Neil had a party. I sat with Liam asleep in my lap through all the noise. Sarah was taking pictures, and when she came up to me and aimed her camera, Matt hollered, ""Get one of her sideways!" But I just sat there and smiled.

I don't have to be anybody's clown.

As usual, I felt a little subdued by their recklessness, and wished I could have been as wild and witty, too. But then, an elderly aunt remarked on how beautiful the flames in the fireplace were, and Matt growled, "Look, it's just a fire, okay? It's not a painting, it's not a poem, it's just a fire!" I was so embarrassed for him, and mad at him, too, for being so rude.

Matt was sleeping in and I had just put the coffee on when Liam toddled up to the Christmas tree. He gently fingered it and then suddenly grabbed a branch in his little paw and pulled it over on himself.

His eyes wide with alarm, he bellowed as he crawled out from under the branches. "Baby in the tree!" I hollered, and Matt came storming out of the bedroom and we righted the tree and put it back in the stand, wiped up the water, and put the ornaments back on.

Last night I dreamed Mom was making a huge dinner, putting it all together. On the stove was a huge bowl of rising onion bread, and over the sink was a shelf with a smaller bowl on it with rising bread dough in it, too. There were plants in all the windows. Real homey and close and perfect.

CHAPTER TEN

FIRE
In which Matt saves Doug's life while I wait out my confinement

Matt skippered the *Destiny* again for Northern Pacific during that winter's king crab season. One Sunday before the season started, we were all sitting down for breakfast and I asked, "What are your plans for the day, Matt?"

"Oh not much—go down to the boat for a little while."

"A *little* little while or an all-day little while?" He frowned. I was not being diplomatic. "'Cause I'd like it if maybe you could…take the kids to the park for a little bit and then—maybe there'd be some time, it wouldn't take too long—could you mop the kitchen floor?"

"What is this? The kids don't have to go to the park."

"It would do them good to get out and run around a little. And be with you. And then the floor's so dirty and it makes the whole place look so much better if it's clean."

"Well, if you think it's so important, why don't you take care of it?"

I jumped up from the table and my chair flipped over backwards. "Because I'm seven months pregnant! And I'm tired!" And I went down the hall to the bedroom, threw myself on the bed and started crying.

His job is the boat, my job is the kids and don't question or think—you'll go crazy—just work.

Donna came to Kodiak from Larsen Bay. She left Andy with me while she went into town and when she came back, all the kids were napping. We made some tea and sat in the living room, watching the storm toss the little wooden swing into the tree branches. "It looks like a commercial about child abuse," I said.

"Nora, that's almost not funny," Donna said, laughing until the tea slopped over the side of her mug. "God, did I tell you about Angela? This little girl in Larsen Bay whose Mom lives with some man who beats her?"

"The mom or Angela?"

"The mom. Angela told me she was standing at the window crying one time because her mom was hurt and another time, she, Angela, had to run for help in the middle of the night when her mom slit her wrists."

"The poor little kid!"

"Yeah, I know, and I told her, 'It's good your mom has someone to cry for her because lots of times I've really been hurt and there's been no one to cry for me.' Angela asked me, 'Did anybody ever hit you?' and I said, 'Sure, they did.'"

"What's going to happen to her?"

"I don't know. It's really sad, and there's this other little twelve-year-old that's pregnant by her dad."

"How can people live like that? That's so sick and low."

"I don't know, but these kids really have it rough."

Later Donna went downtown, and got home late, and I babysat Andy with my kids. I felt resentful but I couldn't refuse when she asked me—I wasn't doing anything anyway. On Sunday she offered to sit with the kids so I could go out for a while. I hauled out some baskets of laundry (washing machine still broken) and washed and dried them at Robin's. She and Neil were house-sitting at Dr. Copstead's house on the channel while their new house was being built.

I'd just dragged myself up the stairs from the basement after I'd loaded the wet clothes into the dryer.

"I hope you used that non-phosphorus detergent. Here, have some raspberry tea, it's good for contractions," Robin put a steaming cup of tea on the table.

"I don't want contractions, they'd split my stitches. I got my date set for the Cesarean. Pretty teacup."

"Neil got that for me when he went to the environmental hearings in Anchorage. So how's it going with Donna staying with you? Did you know she came to town to have an abortion at Dr. Nelson's clinic last week?"

The tea burned my throat. "Oh no, poor Donna—how do you know?"

"Oh, she had some lab work done at Dr. Copstead's office. She didn't want us to know she was having another abortion because she had one at our clinic last October."

God, Robin, what a vile-tongued gossip! Where's your respect for your patient's privacy?

'I thought maybe our friendship and my good influence were having some effect on Donna's screwed-up life."

Robin hooted. "You think you're going to save Donna? Get real."

"Yeah, but when she moved into our rabbit house before Liam was born, and then when she went to your baby shower for me, she told me, 'I wish I had some nice good friends like you do.' And then she and Sarah are the same age and they got to be friends before Donna moved to Larsen Bay," I protested.

"But she can't overcome her upbringing—it's a pattern."

"I can't think that. I've got to believe you can change."

141

It sounds so snobbish, but maybe Robin's right. Maybe there is a class system and you're doomed to be frustrated if you try to pull yourself up by your bootstraps. I can see how Natives think, "Why even try?"

Donna told me she was getting involved with Tommy Zvorkin, who's married. She would be so much better off if she could get settled, get organized and get some good friends that want to do more than fuck her and drink with her. Maybe her sister's religion, the Worldwide Church of God, would be the best thing for her, even though it sounds a little wild-eyed to me. It just makes me despair for her and for our friendship—will she always be making a muddle out of her life, and for a nice person, why can't she see all the wrong turns she's taking?

But then look at me—I'm not sure who's making a muddle of their life. Donna seems to get a lot of enjoyment from life, though she sees a lot more crud. Like she was out late both Friday and Saturday nights—really late. But telling me about it, it sounded like she had a lot of fun, really enjoyed herself, while when I go out it's all so damp and sedate—and unfulfilling, a waste of desire and money. And when I babysit, I just do housework and oversee the kids; she plays with them and talks with them. So where do I get off feeling superior? For all my "good" life, who's the one who keeps her cheer and heals the hurt?

I feel so blah and sluggish. I guess it comes from all the excitement of the weekend with Donna and Andy staying with us. Matt left on Friday—the tanner crab season opens today. They say it's bad luck to leave on Friday, but Matt timed it to get through Whale Pass so he wouldn't be bucking the tides. Besides, he thinks that superstition is just an excuse for fishermen to be lazy.

Jake banged on the front door at six, waking me from dreams of survival suit drills on board Matt's boat. At the first try, the kids' suits didn't fit right and time moved slow, so we did it again and it felt safer, more reassuring.

I roused myself and put on a robe. It still looked like the dead of night.

"Nora, don't get upset. There was a fire on the *Destiny*. Matt wants you to call him on the radio."

"A fire? What happened? Is Matt okay?" It felt like the blood just rode a wave out of my head down through my legs.

"It's okay, Nora. Come on over and talk to him on the radio. The kids will be all right, I'll send my mom over—she's staying with me for awhile."

Over at Jake's, I stood beside him while he called over the radio. "Yeah, I got Hunter's wife here to talk to him," he said when the *Siren* finally responded. "Go ahead," Jake said to me. "Just push this button in when you speak and say 'over' when you're through talking."

"You there, Nora? Over."

"Matt, you okay?" Jake nudged me. "Over."

"Yeah, we're okay, I guess. Over."

"What happened? Over."

"Well, we had a fire, but the Coast Guard will be flying us in. You think you can pick us up at the hospital? Over."

"The hospital? Are you all right?" My voice broke and Matt jumped in.

"We're gonna be all right. Just pick us up at the hospital in an hour. I'll talk to you then. WXR914 *Siren* clear."

Jake took the transmitter away from me. "He's not going to talk any more, Nora. But they're all okay. It's just the boat. They were lucky."

"Do you know what happened?"

"No, just that the *Siren* and the *North Sea* called in that they saw flames and then later picked up some survi—some of the crew."

"What's going to happen to the boat?"

"From what I heard, it's gone."

Gone. The Coast Guard. The hospital. It felt so funny, so removed. I looked out at the channel where the sun was finally streaking the dawn sky.

It might just as well be one of those mornings where I'm getting up, making coffee, and turning on the radio to hear a Coast Guard announcement that a boat's gone, no survivors, names withheld pending notification of next of kin. It happens all the time. Somehow we just lull ourselves into thinking we won't be the ones. If you dwelled on it, you'd go neurotic and not be able to do anything. But we're all gambling with our security; our lives are hostage to the sea. There's not a thing you can do to change the outcome, not prayers or honor or right living. God has his reasons, but the sea doesn't.

And what if you're on the boat and you don't have what it takes? All the strength and power and know-how won't save your life if your number's up. What if you're overcome by fear and can't save yourself? What if you can't do the thing you must to be courageous, what if you're a selfish coward? Then you have to live the rest of your life hating yourself for not being strong enough but being alive. How can you go on living knowing that because of you, someone else slipped away?

Jake's mom stayed with the kids while I drove up to the hospital to pick Matt up. He was standing in the corridor in a tight red shirt and he walked sort of pigeon-toed in jogging sneakers—someone else's clothes. "We're going to drive Will and Eddie home, okay? Doug called Rita already. He'll stay at our house till he's ready to fly down to Seattle."

They looked like a bunch of sad sacks, all in scruffy clothes they'd borrowed from men on the *Siren*. Their faces sagged, without color. If I didn't know what they'd been through, I would have thought they were fighting bad hangovers.

We drove Eddie to a little shack in the Aleutian homes and Will to the small house he shared with his brother out by St. Mary's. They were both stone quiet, none of the usual wisecracking or fishing talk.

"Take it easy for a couple of days," Matt said, "then we'll figure out insurance and all the rest of it." He let out a deep breath as we drove towards home.

I was afraid this would be another event I'd never really know about, that Matt would minimize the whole thing.

"Where did the fire start?" I was thinking burnt fuse on toasters.

"Well, it was in the engine room, so it was pretty bad. We were out by Sitkinak Island when the season opened and had fished straight through till about 3 a.m., baiting the pots we'd already set down before the opening. At about 5 a.m. an alarm woke me up. The pilothouse was already full of smoke and it was hard to see and breathe. I ran down to the engine room, but it was all smoke and glowing, so I got everyone up and told them to get their survival suits on. I tried to get a radio message off back in the pilothouse but I couldn't—it was too hot and smoky.

"Will was the engineer. He ran down to the engine room below deck and tried to put the fire out with an extinguisher, but it was too far gone already. By the time he gave up he couldn't get into his cabin to get his survival suit on because of the flames and smoke. He was running around, screaming 'I know I'm gonna die!' He completely lost it."

That would have been me.

"Fuckin' Nellie," Doug growled from the back seat.

Matt continued. "By then I was out on the aft deck, catching my breath. I went back to the pilothouse and was able to find my survival suit by feel. Doug and Eddie and I had all gotten our suits on and Will started to climb the rigging to get to the roof of the pilothouse so he could launch the life raft. It's supposed to open upon contact with the water. So after struggling with it for quite a time, he got it launched but it landed upside down in the water and he was running around like a dizzy woman."

"That shit!" Doug yelled.

"Yeah, well, we're okay now," Matt turned around to say to Doug. I looked over at Matt and caught his eye. We drove home in silence, except for me telling him how Jake had woken me up.

When we got home I made a pot of coffee, and after smoking a cigarette, Matt told Doug he could take a shower in our bathroom. When we sat down at the table again, I said, "Matt, what is wrong with Doug? Tell me what happened."

"Oh man, he had it rough. We were standing on the deck in our survival suits except for Will—I guess he'd lost his and he started arguing with Doug about his suit. I was trying to get them to get the life raft loose. The embers and debris from the rigging had started falling on us, so the three of us in survival suits jumped off the boat into the water. Will was hopping and screaming around on the bow, still trying to get the life raft away.

"Finally he jumped in the water, but he landed right on top of Doug and knocked him out. I saw it coming and was able to get pretty close and dove for him—well, as best I could—when he went under. God, that fucker is heavy."

"Matt, you saved him."

"Oh, the hard part was bringing him back. He weighed a ton and I couldn't get a grip on him, like a jello truck. Meanwhile Will climbed on the raft— it had landed upside down.

"Thank God, just as I got Doug back conscious, I could tell some boats were coming, they'd seen the flames. We kept yelling to Will to hang on, it was just hanging on for a while. Eddie was getting rattled too. His survival suit was leaking in at the neck. I think it was too big and loose on him and he was getting scared."

"Weren't you afraid?" I asked.

"No, I wasn't about to go under. It was just something I had to get out of. The boats were coming. But it wasn't dawn yet and the *Siren* almost ran over us, misjudging the distance and the swells in the dark. Pissed me off."

I'd be scared. He was mad.

"When we got on board—the *North Sea* picked Will off the raft—we were mostly trying to check on Doug. He was weak as a baby and crying just like one, too. And we had to get Eddie warmed up. This is the third or fourth time he's been on a boat that sank. He says he'll never go fishing again." Matt chuckled, "He'll be okay—Will has some burns on his head and arms but nothing serious."

"What do you think happened?" I asked.

"Well, I don't know. Probably a fuel line broke on the auxiliary and sprayed fuel on the exhaust. Too bad, that was a good wooden boat, for being over thirty years old."

I put my arms around him and hugged him hard. "Matt, you are wonderful, and I'm so glad you're here. Don't leave me. Stay. I love you."

"I know, Mama, I love you too. I love you too much."

Doug came down the hall. "You hear how your old man saved my life? It just got worse and worse out there. I thought my number's up. Many times. Having to listen to that squealing asshole, and then he knocks me out! I owe you my life, buddy."

Matt huffed out his cigarette smoke and shook his head.

"No lie, Captain, no lie. My life is yours now."

"Well, shit, Bradley, you going out with me again?"

"On land, Captain—the only wet stuff I'll be dealing with from now on will be in a glass."

"That's okay, I guess. You try dancing underwater with two hundred pounds of pudding. I'm telling you, I had some hairy moments."

"It was too wet out there. Wet and cold and dark." Tears came to Doug's eyes and he put his head down between his hands. He trembled and looked up and said, "I'll never make it up to you. You saved my life." I held Matt's thigh under the table and tried not to cry.

After Matt took a shower, his parents called. "Just another character-building experience," I heard him say to his mom. "Nora, she wants to talk to you."

I took the receiver from him. "The cannery called us as soon as they heard that the *Destiny* was down. We knew Matt was okay and there was no way we were going to call you," his mom said.

For the sake of peace, I just assumed that they were thinking of my best interests, but I seethed to think I was competing for knowledge about Matt. *I have the first right to know about my husband.*

It seemed that the *Destiny*'s burning upstaged all concern about the new baby. I wanted Matt to be with me when the baby was born even more than ever, and even though he wasn't working, I worried that he might have to stay with a new job on another boat when the baby came.

Meanwhile, I loved having him home. It warmed my heart to see Liam trying to talk to Matt, and Chelsea being held in his arms after her nap. Chelsea told Matt she didn't feel good cause she ate too much junk. Matt said "What junk?"

She said "Oh, like breakfast and dinner."

"It would be so perfect if you could get six weeks of hard fishing in and then quit for six weeks when the baby's born. Oh God, it could be such a beautiful exhilarating spring," I told him, luxuriating in the sun streaking through the windows as we sat over our coffee.

"Our baby is sure kicking and moving around at nights. When I babysat in the church nursery last Sunday, there were about six one-year olds, and there was one little boy there with crossed eyes, glasses, and brain damage. He was so sad, Matt. Do you realize what miracles our babies are, what beauties?"

Matt talked to Robbie, Scott, and a bunch of other guys about fishing jobs. Robbie warned Matt that the insurance company would want to hold him liable for all the pots he put out for the *Destiny*.

"I'm kind of surprised at Robbie," I said. "You'd think he'd be glad you're alive."

"Nora, life isn't a tea party. Robbie offered to bring the pots in so they're not just left out there, but he would get the crab in them. He's thinking business."

"I guess I just expected him to have your best interests at heart."

A few weeks went by and the boats were bringing in crab, but Matt couldn't find another boat to work on.

Matt stayed home, mulling over possibilities, filling out the insurance forms. On top of everything else, he was driving the Jeep when it slid on the ice and plowed into a parked truck. So the bills mounted.

Robbie brought in Matt's pots after picking the crab out. "It's a business, Nora, not a family," I had to tell myself.

We walked down on the docks one morning and Matt pointed out the *Beaver*.

"Might run that for Tollefson, he's in Hawaii."

The *Beaver* was an old scow like the *Sea Lion*, but it looked heavier and there were no sides to it, like an old raft. It scared me. "Matt, there's no rails to keep the sea out."

"Oh that's no big deal. The engines are okay and the house is decent, but it might just be one huge hassle to fix it up." He sighed. "And after the days I spent refinishing the floors in the *Destiny*'s house!"

I was fuming to remember all the time he spent on the boat doing something as cosmetic as sanding the floors when he could have been home, and how he objected when I asked him to mop our floors.

Finally, Robbie asked Matt to run the *Sea Lion*, fishing the last few trips of the season and removing the *Sea Lion*'s pots from the fishing grounds and storing them away. As soon as Matt took the *Sea Lion* out, the electricity went out the length of the right half of the trailer, and the Harbormaster called about the damage the *Destiny* had done to a piling earlier this winter.

I get this longing in my soul. I just want something so much. The snow coming down is like heavy-textured rain. I should be glad Matt is running the Sea Lion *now, for the money, but I'm worried he'll have to honor the commitment to the end of tanner season even if it means not being able to come to Seattle for the baby.*

I had my five-minute bit of hysterical crying this morning when I saw what a mess the bathroom was—toothpaste smeared on the toilet with toilet paper for a "cover"—and then the dryer quit in a puff of steam that sent Jake's mom running into our house because the truck wasn't outside and she thought the house would burn down while no one was home.

So it's back to haunting the laundromat with Liam and Chelsea wiping their runny noses on my denim maternity dress. This is the pits.

CHAPTER ELEVEN

OVERWHELMED
In which I cut my hair and everyone asks me what I'll do with three kids

We left Matt to finish the tanner crab season on the *Sea Lion*, and flew down to Seattle.

It was party time for Chelsea and Liam, with Adam and Elizabeth to play with and a real neighborhood to play in instead of a mud-and-gravel driveway. Tricia and Lou expanded their household in an easygoing, natural way. I went to my old obstetrician, Dr. Gentler, who asked what date I wanted to have the baby. I went through the "Monday's child is fair of face… " rhyme in my head and decided on the Friday before Easter, so that my child would be loving and giving.

I feel like a pregnant teenager whose mother has to hold her hand because the boy copped out. It felt so urban and sinister up on Capitol Hill in the heart of Seattle when I went to the doctor. I used to walk up and down Broadway all the time, but yesterday I felt so intimidated, as if a sniper was on the roof of every building aiming at me. Time to deal with my fears before paranoia becomes permanent. The trouble is, I got away with so much recklessness in the past; it's hard to tell when I'm overcompensating now.

We were all crowded around the dinner table. I sat next to Lou and he started breathing real heavy, imitating me. I hadn't realized I was doing it and I felt so embarrassed.

Matt got in at midnight the night before I was to be admitted to the hospital, and I met him at the airport. He was walking towards me on the concourse. "You look like a bulldozer coming at me," he said.

The next morning I told Tricia, "I wish I could just wait for the baby to start coming on its own, so that I could be surprised. I'm afraid to go in to the hospital."

"Don't worry. It's no different just because you know the exact date you're going in."

"But I know what to expect—the preparation, the…."

"You don't want to be considered a troublemaker if you're going to be dependent on these people."

Matt and I went straight to admitting and the clerk clattered at her keyboard and shuffled through her piles of folders. "We don't have you in our records."

"Dr. Gentler scheduled me for a C-section for tomorrow."

She called Dr. Gentler's office and verified that I really was his patient, really was due to have a baby, really was scheduled for surgery the next morning. Wordlessly the clerk sat at her typewriter for ten minutes, filling in forms, talking to us only to ask for my signature on the payment form and the release form in case they killed me.

Then they put me in a room, and Matt said good-by. I was in the bed closest to the door, without even a curtain to draw around my bed. I was determined to be compliant. Finally they brought a curtain and hooked it up.

I was lying in bed by myself in the room with the muffled clatter of dinner trays outside. The sky to the east was dark and my anxieties about the day to come re-emerged. *What if the baby's deformed? What if the baby dies? What if the pain is unbearable and never-ending? What if Matt isn't with me?*

A nurse, crisp and solid, strode into the room and smiled brightly. "Your husband would like to take you out to dinner! Would you like to go?"

"You mean I can go and come back?"

"Just remember your C-section is at seven. Don't make a late night out of it. Nothing to eat or drink after midnight—but you'll be back before then."

We went to a fancy restaurant on the waterfront, the restaurant where all the rich boys took their dates on Senior Prom night.

"I can't shake the high-school feeling of this pregnancy."

"What are you talking about?" Matt frowned and looked up from the menu.

"I feel like everybody's looking at me and wondering if I'm married or not, if my baby's legitimate."

"For God's sake, Eleanor, you're a married woman. Remember me?"

"No…I mean…Matt—it's like coming down here by myself with Chelsea and Liam and all the trips to the doctor's office with you up in Alaska, and staying at my sister's house and now seeing all these skinny high school girls at their prom while I waddle around enormous…. I just feel so alone and uncertain. I'm so glad you made it, that there weren't any more emergencies."

When we got back to the hospital, the nurse said to Matt, "Be sure you're back by seven tomorrow morning."

The orderlies came for me at 6:45 the next morning. "I thought the operation wasn't until seven—can we wait until my husband gets here?"

"We're just getting you all set up." They wheeled me down the hall in a gurney.

They left me in the hallway, flat on my back, and I was so scared to go into that sterile steel-filled room again when I heard a nurse say, "Well, this must be him!" And there was monolithic Matt in his leather jacket leaning over me and giving me a big hug.

Then they took me into that white metallic room and rolled me on my side and stuck the anesthetic needle in my spine while I looked at the chrome fixtures and the tiled floor. They allowed Matt to watch the birth through a window.

"Just be over, just be over," I chanted to myself.

The draping, the anesthetic, the testing for numbness, the methodical procedures....

"It's a boy!" they said and took a sheet-wrapped lump over to a table where the pediatrician examined him.

"Can I see him?"

"Oh yes, we're just checking him out first. We're doing it a new way now."

Minutes later they brought my baby to me. He looked like a pastel flower petal, fair with downy blond hair and pale blue eyes and pinkie-white skin, so different from the rest of us dark-haired gypsies. He was beautifully made and perfect.

Tears of gratitude and relief filled my eyes. I only had two arms, but now I had two baby boys, and my little girl. I couldn't let this little creature overwhelm me. I had to be a Mom Machine, yet not try too hard. But he was so perfect, so peaceful, such a free gift. "Please be good," I whispered to him as I held him close. "I just can't handle anything else."

Matt was white-faced and worried-looking when I came out of the operating room. "You okay, Mama?" he asked quietly, respectful and a little in awe of me. I began shaking, little trembles at first, then harder until a nurse pushed Matt out of the way and put a heavy warm blanket on me. I didn't see Matt as they bustled around me, whisking me away in an elevator to the recovery ward.

The next day I felt the pain of healing more keenly. I sank back gratefully into the clean sheets after the nurse made the bed with me in it, and I welcomed the back rub she gave me after she gently and firmly got me up to walk. Visitors came and the nurse walked in behind them. "Now don't you wear out Mom."

That night percodan sent me into a fidgety, feverish sleep. I woke up startled from a nightmare and pushed the button for the nurse. "What is it?" came a foreign-accented voice.

"I'm scared. I'm having nightmares...."

"I'll be there." A minute later the nurse walked into the room with a syringe. "This is different, it should help you sleep. Sometimes percodan makes patients jittery," she said with a big smile.

The next morning I was still uptight when Matt brought Liam and Chelsea in to visit me. I was taken in a wheelchair to the visiting room, and Chelsea kept bumping into the chair and I felt so awful, being annoyed with her.

"We had a bottle of champagne at Peggy's this morning to celebrate."

"You were at Peggy's house this morning?"

"Yeah, well, I felt uncomfortable staying at Tricia's while you were in the hospital, so I took the kids over to Peggy's."

"Oh."

"I want to call the baby Matthew." Matt smiled proudly.

"But he looks so different from you, and besides, I want him to have his own name."

"Like what?"

"Well, like Brian or Michael or…. Chelsea, please don't bump into my chair. It hurts."

Liam started squirming and Matt picked him up. "I guess I better take the kids out of here."

"Okay Matt, thanks for coming, and for bringing the kids. Come close, Chelsea, let me love you." I kissed her and Liam. Matt wheeled me to the end of the corridor and I waved good-by to them and watched them walk down to the end of the hall and out the door.

A priest came into my room later. He had an extraordinary smooth face, almost Oriental, with huge brown eyes. He asked if I wanted to talk, and sat down before I answered. "How are you doing? Let's see, do you live in Seattle?"

"No, I live in Kodiak, but I wanted to have all my kids in Seattle, and keep the same doctor."

"Kodiak! How do you like living there?"

"Well, it's beautiful in a big way, but at home—well, there's lots of muddy streets and junky cars in people's yards. I guess Kodiak's a man's town."

"Well, then," he said, elegantly crossing his legs and making himself comfortable, "you'll just have to make it a woman's town."

Why do I have to make it a woman's town? I'm Pioneer Woman with three babies and a husband who saves other peoples' lives. I'm all alone and why do I have to make it a woman's town? What do you know about it anyway? What do you think you're even talking about?

Matt stayed in Seattle after the baby was born, working on the *Moonlight*, the Northern Pacific cannery boat that he had been running before we were married. We stayed at Tricia and Lou's, with Tricia letting me rest in bed and taking care of all of us.

When a neighbor came over to see the new baby, she asked me how long we'd be staying.

"Oh, I think about two months…"

"Two months! That's awfully good of you!" she said to Tricia in amazement.

"Oh, well.…" Tricia said, embarrassed for me, "Nora's my baby sister."

Tricia and Lou and their kids went out of town for a baseball tournament, and we had Matt's family over for a gathering before Matt took the *Moonlight* to Kodiak for the salmon tendering season. Liam had a fever and a cold and was so out of it. I felt so hot and ugly and terribly torn, with a new baby and a sick baby, I wanted nothing less than to be responsible for a party.

"Matt, should we be having this party with Liam sick and all? Maybe we should call it off."

"Well, if you don't want my family to see the baby that's fine, but this is the only day they can all come. We've already invited them and their feelings would be hurt."

"Yeah, okay, I guess."

Matt's mom rocked Peggy's one-year old to sleep, I noticed with resentment as I made a bottle of juice for Liam with the baby fussing on my shoulder while Matt handed beers around.

"So you finally gave in on naming the baby Matthew," Peggy said.

It was worth it when Matt put his arm around me and said, "Yeah, she let me have my way."

Matt was late getting home from work at the shipyard, really late. Chelsea was waiting for him to help her ride a little purple bike around the back yard. Liam wanted to run after him and hug his legs. I wanted to hand the baby to him and lie down on the sofa next to him.

When he finally got home, I was frantic. "Where have you been?"

"Out on the boat in the middle of the Sound."

"I need you home."

"Eleanor, we're racing the clock as it is. We just finished in the engine room and I had to swing the compass."

Swing the compass. I wish I had a neat professional term for my crises. All I know is that swinging the compass has something to do with navigation, and that it could have been done another time.

I stormed upstairs. A little while later, I looked out the white-curtained window through the tulip tree leaves and saw Matt doggedly pushing Chelsea on the bicycle, holding it steady for her.

Tricia said, "He's such a good daddy to take his little girl around and around the yard."

And I'm such a witch.

Matt left to take the *Moonlight* to Alaska. "It'll take about ten days to get up the Inside Passage and then across the Gulf of Alaska, a week if we just cut across the Gulf."

"How will I know which way you go, when you'll be in Kodiak?"

"I'll call you when I get to town."

After Matt left, Tricia and I and all our brood went to visit Mom at Shine. Tricia took her kids down to the beach and I settled in.

The kids tussled around the house. Liam stuck his head between the balusters of the staircase and Mom got after him and said, "Nora, you can't let him do that."

"What's wrong with playing on the stairs?"

"He'll hurt himself and break his neck."

"Liam, come here please. Liam, I'm going to count to three and then you'll have a time out. Liam, come sit with me and I'll read to you."

"Nora, you're spoiling him. Liam, come down here this minute and obey your mother!"

Oh God, please make her back off.

Tricia and Adam and Elizabeth came in with their healthy, cheerful faces while I was making spaghetti for dinner. I held the colander over the sink with one hand while I poured the boiling water off the spaghetti with the other. Only I spaced out and poured the boiling mess over my hand, not in the colander. I dropped the whole thing and stomped around the kitchen howling and Mom told Tricia, "That does it! You've got to take Chelsea and Liam back to your house and let Nora and the baby stay here and rest."

I felt defeated, like I should protest and assert my independence, but I just wanted to cry and sleep. I felt so bad, so weak and irresponsible, always the little sister, the incompetent. But I was too tired for pride and overcome with worry. How was I going to take care of my own?

With just Mom and the baby and me, it was restful. Matthew was such a tidy little baby and so beautiful with his flossy blond hair and sweetness. He rested in his basket outside while I lay on the grass and soaked in the green quiet of Shine. Mom would bring out meals on a tray and it was like a rest cure at a health spa.

When I got back to Tricia's I kept looking at Chelsea, trying to figure out why she looked so funny, something about her eyes, her eyebrows. Finally I realized she'd shaved off half her eyebrows. She must have found a razor in the tub.

A week later, Mom came over for tea and Tricia said, "Did you hear that they say that Skylab is going to fall on either Australia or California? They're having evangelical prayer meetings all over so that people will be saved."

I said, "Nothing like disaster to make people religious."

Tricia laughed and Mom clattered her teacup onto the saucer. "That's blasphemy."

"Oh, come on, Mom, you can have a sense of the spiritual and a sense of humor too," Tricia said.

"Yeah," I added, "After all the scandals we've put you through, why get rigid now?"

Tricia got up to answer the phone. "It's for you, Nora. Matt."

"Well, what's going on?" were his first words, and I could tell he was upset. "Are you in Kodiak now?"

"Yeah, I'm in town. Why aren't you here?"

"Matt. We're waiting for you to get home first and call us, remember?"

"No, I'm home and I thought you'd be here."

"Okay, I'll try to get tickets for tomorrow afternoon's flight. You know, after being here two months, it's not like I can pack up three kids and a dog and take off in a couple of hours."

"Well, you do whatever you want," he said.

Yeah, just call me Matt Hunter.

Later I told Tricia, "It's been fun, but I'll be kind of glad to get back home."

And she surprised me by saying, "I know, it will be nice for us to be just our little family again, too."

It will be a relief to be back in my own house where I can live my own life and don't have to be a polite guest. I'm not ungrateful for Tricia and Lou taking us in this long time, but it isn't a breeze being nine months' pregnant and having Lou make fun of my heavy breathing, or Mom cracking down on the kids, and everyone asking me, "How are you going to do it?" I'll just have to do it.

Lou took us all out to the airport in his van. The kids were sitting on top of boxes. He dropped us off—kids, luggage, baby basket, and Goldie in kennel. When the porter got our bags and kennel to the ticket counter, they told me that the plane would be delayed five hours. Thank God they had a big nursery at the airport.

The boarding gate was way at the end of the concourse, and with Matthew in a hand-carried basket, plus my purse, a diaper bag, and the two other kids, I was hoping someone would offer a hand. I stopped off to rest at a gate halfway down the concourse and asked a man sitting there if he could help me to the gate. Unfortunately, I picked a guy who had a sizable carry-on bag himself, but he took Babe in the basket.

Seven hours later, in Kodiak, Matt met us at the airport and took us home. It felt like the house was glad to have us all rampaging through it again. We had a beer and Matt told me that Jake had gotten married again.

"Wow, that was quick."

"Yeah, well, Jake—he doesn't mess around."

"Doesn't sound like he was much broken up over Tuffy, either."

"Yeah, well, who knows?"

We were getting the kids ready for bed and Matt was giving Liam a bath when he slipped and cut his eyebrow on the edge of the bathtub. At the sight of blood flowing from his forehead, I wanted to wrap Liam up in towels and rush him straight to the hospital, but Matt said, "Hold on, now. We can get him dressed."

The doctor was so cavalier about putting stitches in Liam's eyebrow. He goofed the first time and just ripped them out and did them again while I held Liam and Matt waited in the corridor.

I'm sitting down with a cup of tea, Matt and Liam just back from getting Liam's stitches out at the doctor's. So good to be home, though looking at all the work still to do is stupefying. Yesterday during naps, I actually organized some stuff. Wow! If I could really get organized, stuff that's been piling up the last three months.... Just a minute to gather my thoughts. Babe is fussy and upset, guess it's hardest on him. Sort of feel like my patience and even-handedness are gonna snap today.

CHAPTER TWELVE

SUMMER FEVER
In which we return to Kodiak and I find out what I do with three kids

Soon after we'd arrived back in Kodiak, Donna came to visit me. The Reverend Sun Young Moon's cult had leased the bright-yellow cannery building next to Northern Pacific's on the channel, and the local newspaper reported protest marches and other ways the town was opposing the Moonies.

Donna had found security and comfort in the rules of her sister's religion, the Worldwide Church of God. They observed the Sabbath on Saturdays, and disdained the presents and other unholy observances of Christmastime, although they were Christians.

As I made tea and sandwiches for lunch, I opened up a jar of peanut butter and found Liam had put thumbtacks in it. Down the hall, I heard the baby stirring in the storage locker we used for a bed. "Oh, there's Babe waking up," I called.

Donna said, "All the people in the village say 'Babe' or 'Baby' and I hate it. 'Go get baby,'" she mimicked the low Native accent. "I feel like saying, 'He has a name!'"

Ah! my second cup of coffee, my pen and diary—whoops, looks like the mad bubble blower doused that with her solution. I hear Babe squirming in the next room, so I'm not entirely at peace. Liam is having a bottle break and Chelsea is changing her clothes. A windy stormy night, and I woke up at three with dread, thinking about the Moonies. The town is heating up about them starting a cannery. Grey again today. I can't believe how quiet it is right now. Stevie Wonder on the stereo, Chelsea under a tent of blankets over the rocking chair, Liam bumbling around, me sitting quiet and watching. I'm drinking in the nothingness and wonder what I'm learning, what I'm teaching.

The scary thing about kids is that you can do them irreparable harm. They're something I feel I can't be noncommittal, let-it-be, about. The responsibility is absolute. What's the best way to maximize Liam's climbing instinct? Is he going to teach me how to cooperate on a problem?

Chelsea more a help—funnier, sweeter, and smarter everyday. Telling Liam to come into the "snake parlor."

There are piles of junk all over the house, and every time I go past one, I try to pick up something that belongs at my destination. "Cheeselovers" letters litter the floor, from a cheese-a-month buying club. They send me three dollar rebate checks for cheese I haven't bought. When I see the check I get all excited, and then deflated when I realize what they are.

I went across the trailer court to say hi to Jake's new bride. Jake answered my knock.

"Oh hi, Nora, what's up?"

"Hi Jake, I'd like to meet your…um…wife." So he took me into the kitchen and introduced me to Stella.

She had platinum blonde hair with long bangs falling into her big blue eyes and told me over a cup of coffee about their flight into Kodiak. "Want some Jack Daniels in your coffee?" she asked, then set the cup in front of me after I shook my head. "Well, I need some to buck me up, after that flight in to town. I tell you, kid, the wings were that close to the water and I dug my fingernails into Jake's arm. For two days in Seattle—it's not worth it!" I marveled that she had been able to spend the money just to commute to Seattle and back with Jake, as if flying back and forth were such a casual thing.

"Jake says you've got kids coming out your ears. Eli's around here somewhere. He's four."

"That's how old Chelsea is.…"

"Great! Send her over! Anytime! The more the merrier! We're gonna try and get Christie back here, too. That Tuffy, she's nuts—nuts!" She lit a cigarette and waved it around with her long, lavender-painted fingernails.

Back home I said to Matt, "I'd hoped we might be simpatico, but she's kind of hard."

The first opening for salmon fishing sent Matt across Shelikof Strait. One summer morning, I tried to devote some time to Chelsea. It took me an hour to make twelve color cards. Then Chelsea and I played "Concentration" five times and "Go Fish" once (high excitement). Then the cards fell by the wayside until she woke up from her nap.

I was nursing Babe while Chelsea watched "Sesame Street," when Pete and Sarah drove up to visit me. Sarah hugged me, her big soft freshness surrounding me. "Ooooh Nora, it's so good to see you! So good to have you back! You look great! Let me see your new little snickerdoodle!"

I made them some coffee and we sat in the living room. Sarah cuddled Babe and soon the other kids were trying to get her attention, so she handed the baby back to me and she and Pete played with the little kids.

"So how's it going? Is Matt out now?"

"Yes, he's back on the *Moonlight* with Northern Pacific, but maybe he can come in to town in between openings. He won't have much say this year. After the *Destiny* sinking, he's low man on the totem pole again."

Liam was back asleep and Babe was at my breast when Chelsea saw the cards again and in a manic bid for love and attention, grabbed them up and shredded them. "I'll come over and help you, Nora," Sarah said. "Would you like that?"

"Oh Sarah, I really would—mostly the company."

Pete beamed. "My Sarah is wonderful company, isn't she?" He pulled her to him and patted her rump through her heavy full skirt.

"Oh Buddha, you sweet teddy bear, you're the best!" Sarah grinned and kissed him.

After they left I was sitting in the living room. I could hear Liam up to something in the kitchen, but I was determined to sit still until I'd finished my cup of coffee, no matter how bad it sounded. When I went back into the kitchen, Liam had pulled apart the plastic parts of the coffee maker and broken the handle.

Stella knocked on the door. "Can I come in for awhile? I've got a rat in my trailer and I don't want to deal with it."

I said, "I saw a dead rat in the back yard yesterday—the second this week. We should call the building inspector."

The building inspector came and looked around. "Did you just move a bunch of gear or something like that?"

"Larson moved the last of his ropes and nets from our yard last week."

"He must have evicted a family of rats."

"What are we going to do?"

"Hell, this is nothing, in the Aleutian homes some kids have been bitten by rats, live rats. At least the one you saw was dead."

I said, "I can't live like this; this isn't New York City!"

"Well, rats belong in the great outdoors as much as they do in the urban jungle. Get yourself a big fat cat and sic her on 'em. And close up all the openings to your place where rats can come in."

Sarah came over to help with the house and kids. She looked at me like I was crazy when I asked her to change the light bulbs. "I hate climbing on a chair, breaking my neck craning up at the fixture, dropping the screws and getting dust in my eyes."

"Okay, Nora," she said, laughing, "but are you sure there aren't more important things to do here?"

"Probably, but it's driving me crazy stumbling around in depressing half-light. It's such an interruption, like getting gas in a gas station."

After Sarah installed the ceiling light bulbs and got down from the chair, she picked up Matthew and rocked him to sleep while I did housework. I wanted to say, "You do the housework so I can cuddle my baby," but I didn't have the nerve.

I feel nervous. The kids are making me tired. Liam is having a tantrum day. My neck is still kinked. Skylab fell in Australia today. I miss Matt and I'm lonely.

It's beautiful again tonight. I'm so dirty. The house is such a mess. Keep on keeping on. All three kids in bed, Baby just stopped fussing. Hope it's for good, that I won't have to get him up again. Felt so much better today than yesterday. I had 103-degree fever and felt odd, dizzy and achy.

If I can just keep calm. Like tonight, Babe was crying, Liam was crying, Chelsea was banging the rocker into the piano. I went over, played the bass to "Summertime," and started singing the words. Liam came over and pushed me off the stool. I picked up the toy chimes, rang them softly, and started singing, "Row Your Boat," with the

Row, row, row your boat, gently down the stream
Throw your children overboard, listen to them scream

verse in it. Chelsea started beating a stick on the rocker to keep time, Liam started banging the piano and singing, and Babe stopped screaming.

It's eleven at night, it's just beginning twilight, and I should go in, take a hot bath, and get some sleep. But I won't. I'll live it up and watch the cars and boats go by. Every once in a while, a boat steams into earshot and then into view. There aren't too many of them going through the channel tonight. Everyone gone fishing is making town so quiet. Got blue jeans, blue T-shirt, and blue blanket wrapped around me. This night is so full and immense. God, to be fishing on a boat! No wonder Matt loves it.

Stella came back with Christie. Tuffy had another bad breakdown and almost drowned herself and Christie in a pool, so Stella went to pick Christie up in California. Poor Tuffy. She's only three years older than me, but I feel like her life is over. I guess I shouldn't give up hope for her, but it seems like the possibility of her recovering would be fantasy. I hope Christie can come through.

I sit at the dining room table. The clock ticks, the front door is open, and the screen door blows back and forth against a rock I put on the step. I can hear the cars without mufflers cruising by and feel the bigness of the sea. And I don't really feel scared to be alone, though I do feel a little lonely. Wonder if I should shut the door. The night is so darn big and beautiful. Then the wind blows the grasses and I think of the rats and I feel less divine. But oh! the colors of blue in this sky that's begging the sun not to leave—the deepest old twilight.

Matthew's plastic diapers come thirty to a box. Tonight I left the box in Liam's reach and when I went to tuck him in, he lay there covered by diapers like square white leaves. He looked like a little gorilla in his cage—no wonder he went so quietly to sleep.

I took Liam out for some time all to himself. Down to the boat harbor, to the hardware store, the grocery store, the post office, the library, just him and me. Sarah was babysitting and made all this possible. I came home and she was bustling around the kitchen, cleaning the counter with bleach, the water running in the sink. "Aren't you glad we have all this water and don't have to worry about rationing it? Doesn't it smell clean?"

I looked out the front door and saw Stella and Christie standing by the fence, talking to the new neighbor. Stella was just absent-mindedly stroking Christie's hair, and I felt so happy for Christie's sake that she has someone responsible to care for her at last.

I asked Stella, "How do you stay happy? Don't you ever get lonely? How do you do it?"

"Yeah, I know, kid. It's like Jake gets home and in his mind, he's still fighting with the honchos downtown, then Christie has her problems and Eli needs some wrasssling time. We all stand in line when he comes home. I get him in the bedroom. That's where I hit him up and the horny bastard can't resist. Ha, ha, ha!"

It's 7:30 in the morning. Babe back to sleep after two hours up, and now I can just feel the birds and bugs waking up the world, as I sit on the front step with my coffee. Yesterday I cleaned house, today the floors and windows and light bulbs. Poor Matt. I wish he was bringing in lots of fish and having fun figuring out how much money he's making. Instead he's running a supply ship and appalled at how fast a little money goes. He must be tired, too, and we have so little life for each other.

I've got to pull this off. I've got to give Liam some space to be himself, to be spoiled and loved. I've got to let Chelsea know she can be a baby but she has to think of others sometimes, too. I've got to fit Babe and Matt into it all. And I have to have some left over for me. I'd just like a thick layer of sleep and rest on which to build.

The boss at Northern Pacific cannery here in town called me up. "I just talked to Cy, the cannery superintendent at Alitak on the phone. He wants you to get on the mail plane to Alitak this afternoon. Matt will be bringing the *Moonlight* there today."

"I've got the kids, too."

"Cy says bring them along. You can stay in the bunkhouse. So be there when the plane leaves in about an hour. It's at that ramp down in the boat harbor, ya know what I'm talking about?"

I jumped at the chance to see Matt and didn't even consider the complexities. I called Stella and asked her to hold the baby while I packed. Sarah appeared too, and she drove us into town and lent me her sweater when I realized I'd forgotten a jacket.

Nick McAllister was flying the plane. It was a beautiful day and I was so thrilled to be joining Matt.

"Are you still coach of the Little League?"

"Yeah, but that's over now for the summer. You got two little guys gonna be playing Little League before you know it, don't you?"

"I suppose so, they're still babies to me."

"I don't have kids, but boy, if I did, I sure wouldn't be a fisherman—you miss too much."

I nodded.

The *Moonlight* was just heading into Lazy Bay as the plane flew over the cannery and Nick said, "Let's give him a buzz," and before I could say anything, Nick put the plane into what felt like a nose-dive. I thought we were going to hit the radar or antennae on the boat and I could see someone's face in the pilothouse. The plane finally landed on the beach and I hurried out to the misty dock and waited for Matt to tie up.

Matt climbed up the ladder to the dock. "Well, well, I was afraid to hope that I recognized you in that plane." He stooped down and picked up Chelsea and Liam in either arm and leaned down to kiss me. "Come on, I'll take you down to Astoria House."

"Is that where we're staying?"

"Yeah, but I've got to get back to unload fish and pump the boat down."

We walked up the beach where the plane had landed to the old one-story dorm that had been nicknamed Hollywood. It had a wide covered porch and workers outside their rooms were hanging on the railings talking to the people that got off the plane. We walked under the bluff past the offices and bunkhouses to where a sidewalk led to the two motel-like apartments and the log cabin that Cy lived in. Still on the wooden sidewalk, we passed the summer mess and bunkhouses where the Filipinos stayed, although there was a lawsuit against the cannery charging discrimination because of the separation.

We stayed at the little apartment across from the summer mess. Our lodgings had a narrow sitting room with a stove and sink and then a short hall to a wide bedroom with two single beds on opposite walls. After we got settled

Matt came back to take us down to the boat to eat. We walked the kids down to the docks, past the recreation hall.

"When Daddy and I worked at the cannery, before we were married, they had parties at the rec hall when the fishing was slow and no fish were coming down the line," I said to Chelsea.

"Remember the time, Matt, that Cy turned off the electricity in the whole cannery so that everyone had to come to the party?"

Matt said, "Those were the old days. Things got too wild last year so the rec hall is locked up."

The crew had just finished their dinner and came out on deck to help us down the ladders from the dock. They held Babe and kept an eye on Chelsea and Liam while we ate.

"There's probably going to be another opening tomorrow night, and I have to change the filters and do some other work in the engine room," Matt told me.

"Okay, I'll take the kids back and get them ready for bed." We walked up the docks through the barn-like sheds of the cannery to the machine shops.

I was getting a real bad throatache. I went to the cannery nurse's door, but there was a sign on it saying she'd be gone until the next day. I grew feverish.

Bedtime was the usual musical chairs. I went to bed with Matthew and Liam and a little later Matt put Chelsea in with me and took Liam to the other bed with him and then we dozed and my throat hurt so bad and Matthew woke up to be fed and by the time I got through feeding him, I was crying. Matt got out of bed and came over and patted my back and said, "Just try to sleep."

But I was restless all night. In the morning Matt got up early while the kids slept and went down to the boat. When I heard the plane roar in, I went to the nurse's station and got some aspirin.

We walked out past the Filipino bunkhouse and the pot storage yard to where they used to burn the garbage. It had been converted into a helicopter landing pad and it seemed like we walked out along the gravel spit forever before we got to where the helicopter would land.

It came in while we were there. I crouched down with Chelsea and Liam and Babe in my arms, far outside the radius of the chopper blades. I felt like a Vietnamese war refugee. The helicopter was full of some Japanese corporate investors or something. Cy came out to pick them up in a clean truck, the only motor vehicle at the cannery. Then I walked back and everybody who'd come out to meet the helicopter passed us up on their way back. Because I was surrounded by kids and walking slow, everyone thought I was with someone. No one talked to me. Or maybe they didn't even see us.

I peeked in the Filipino mess hall to see if Benny the cook was still there. I remembered him from the summer I worked at the cannery.

It was hot inside and Benny was sitting at a table, whistling as he gently slapped cards down on the table. The water fountain gurgled endlessly at the end of the room and my eyes rested in the peace of the spare apple-green room with its grey benches and tables. I could hear the cooks chattering in the kitchen in Tagalog.

Benny saw us and smiled. "Sit, sit down, sit here." We sat down on the bench across from him.

"Hi, Benny. It's good to see you again."

"Me see you? Yes, yes."

"Yes, five years ago."

"You got kids! Ice cream, ice cream for kids?"

Benny called into the kitchen in his foreign language and the cooks babbled on for a minute and then stopped. Benny yelled some more and one of the cooks came out to the table with three bowls of ice cream for the kids.

"Thank you, Benny, thank you."

"Where you live—Seattle?"

"Kodiak."

"Aaahh, Kodiak."

When I got back to Astoria House, Matt came in with some food from the boat and cooked some meat and I gave Babe some mashed peas. "So, like I said last night, I have to head out tonight."

"Oh, Matt—okay."

"I don't know when we'll get back to Kodiak. They might send me after this opening, but I don't know. It may be back here or into Port Bailey. The season should wind up in a few weeks anyway."

That was all we said, in between getting ready to go and tending the kids. We walked him to the boat and he kissed me good-by on the dock. Cy came up to me standing there with the kids and he picked up Liam and carried him back to Astoria House with us.

"I wanted to get you down here for the Fourth of July, but the *Moonlight* was packing salmon in Bristol Bay then."

"That's okay. Actually, this is our fifth anniversary,"

"Well, I wanted to try to get you together. I wish I'd been home more when my kids were little. It makes it tough."

The next morning the skies were grey and low, but they lifted enough by noon for us to go out on the mail plane. Nick McAllister was the pilot again and I got the kids on the plane along with a Japanese businessman who sat in the front next to Nick. When we took off, Nick had the map on his lap and instead of heading north for Kodiak, he took off toward the east, heading toward the foggy Gulf of Alaska.

He had to know he was going in the wrong direction, but he continued east into the mist. Finally I leaned forward and said, "Isn't Kodiak north?"

He yelled back, "Yeah, but there's weather up there. We'll go around it and then turn back pretty soon."

Then the weather got rough and the plane ride more tumultuous as we flew through the mountains. I tried to joke with the kids like we were riding a bucking bronco horse, but I was spooked, and I rummaged in my backpack for belts to strap around the kids and tie them to me and tried to soften my body to cushion the blow when we crashed. Nick turned around to say something and my heart lurched into my throat. He took one look at my face and yelled, "We're okay!" and then the plane bucked and he turned back around.

When we finally landed on the runway and Nick brought the plane to the airport office and turned off the engines, he said, "I'm sorry I scared you so bad. Can I give you a lift back into town?"

Tears came to my eyes with the relief of being safe on the ground and his kindness. "Thank you, but I've got the Jeep waiting for me here. We should be okay."

"Well, here, let me help you load up. You've got quite a delegation here."

I'm sitting here at the table with Babe in his little infant seat. Liam climbed up on the table and shook salt on Babe's head and licked it. A beautiful bright blue morning that makes it easy to stay up for, though I've been up since five. So much to be thankful for—life itself, three healthy kids, a good man, a big happy house, coffee at my elbow, a blue afghan, and a five dollar rocking chair. Quiet and the ticking of a clock. Green ferns and a piano. Love in my heart and people to love.

At Eli's birthday party up at the park, Stella brought rum punch in a thermos. Leanne and Stella and I were sitting at the picnic table and one of the older kids was swinging on the metal swing and getting high and wild, but just normal for a kid. Then Leanne's little girl started walking straight towards the swing set and it was like slow motion. We all could see that baby was going to get conked but nobody could move. At the last moment, Leanne jumped up and grabbed her daughter and yelled for the kid to slow down. I felt hot and distracted when I got home.

Tuffy came back to town, demanding Christie back. Because of Christie, I have given up on Tuffy "seizing the reins" of her own life. I just want her to stay away and be crazy someplace else and leave Christie in peace.

Sarah and Pete moved into a little garage-size house off Mill Bay Road. Sarah calls it the Sugar Shack. I went to visit her last night and told her how I worked my way through college by being a guinea pig for medical procedures, like measuring my gag reflex or testing the torque of my body fat. Robin came over with a *Cosmopolitan* magazine and we looked through it together.

Robin pointed out a cartoon of the Leo woman which showed a man and a woman in a canoe, the man paddling, the woman sitting back, directing him with a pointed finger. "When I showed this to Neil, he just laughed and said, 'That's you and me all right.'"

We took a romance and honesty test and were talking deep and I was just enjoying myself and trying not to think about how I should go home. "Do you think the crisis clinic would look after my kids for four hours if my crisis was I just can't face going home now?" I asked.

A boatload of antiques was brought up from Seattle for an auction at Bells Flats. Since we were flat broke I didn't go the first night, but beautiful furniture was going for garage sale prices so I went the second night. I bid on a carved wood bed frame like the one Mom and Dad used to have. I sat behind Pam and Fred Nelson and Fred put his arm across the back of Pam's chair and casually put his hand on her neck and it just about killed me.

Neil had a surprise birthday party for Robin. I had a ball, drank three or four daiquiris and got really loose without making a fool of myself. All the women were wearing full skirts and screaming to the music and dancing in the living room while the men were all in the kitchen, leaning against the counters with beer bottles in their hand.

Leanne and Chuck were there. He'd just got back from herring fishing in Norton Sound by Nome. I walked past him and Leanne in the kitchen as they were kissing. Later Leanne said, "Poor Chuck—all his nets and gear were ruined. It was a total disaster. So I said, 'Okay, Chuck, you've had your turn. The next thing we're going to invest in is furniture for the house.'"

That summer, some of the kids from the Mission would ride their horse down to our place. Chelsea asked if she could ride with them, and she'd get up on the huge tall horse and ride without fear. One of the kids was a 14-year-old boy who seemed lonely and left out. He asked me if he could come in and talk to me and I felt my charitable impulses at war with my common sense. I told Robin about it and said, "Something about him makes me so uneasy."

She said, "I think he's mildly retarded."

"Of course, that explains his unfocused eyes and disjointed talk."

"I don't think he's dangerous, but you don't want to encourage him."

I finally broke down and called the cannery to ask when Matt was bringing the *Moonlight* back to Kodiak. I hated to call. I always got the feeling fishermen's wives with their questions and needs were so bothersome to the cannery. They weren't able to tell me anything anyway.

I called again later that week, and was told, "Oh the *Moonlight* won't even get into Ketchikan until tomorrow."

Ketchikan is closer to Seattle than to Kodiak! What's next? A trip to Seattle or San Francisco or Tahiti for nets? It's like a conspiracy.

I'm praying all the time. I guess it all got to be too much the night of Robin's surprise party. It gets to me, seeing couples talking together and laughing. How reasonable—your way and then my way. Taking turns. Sharing the load. It makes my life feel so futile.

Matt finally made it home after midnight one late August night.

"Oh, Matt, I'm so glad you're home! Let me get the kids up, they'll die with happiness to see you. Are you home now for awhile?"

"No, don't do that. I have to leave in a couple of hours."

I didn't want to scream my frustrations at him, so I took a long hot bath. I came back into the living room afterwards and said, "Matt, why can't you stay?"

"Look, I snuck in here as it is. I'm supposed to be back in Alitak tomorrow evening. I finally get home and what do you do? Disappear into the bathroom to cry and take a bubble bath."

"I need you. I need some help. I'm crying all the time. I'm not the kind of mother I want to be, not creating the kind of home and childhood I want my kids to have. I need you more than I need the money you make from fishing. The kids need their father in their lives, and I'm so scared I'm going to wind up like Tuffy."

Matt lit a cigarette. "Look, Eleanor, I'm trying to provide for my family. I'm not going to sit around the house and ask the government to give me welfare. I have no respect for men like that. I don't expect the kids to appreciate that I'm keeping food on the table and a roof over their heads now, but someday they'll thank me."

"Matt, please. I'm getting so depressed. Everybody has somebody but me. I just can't do it. Can't you just quit and do something else for awhile, take one season off, or set a personal quota for what we need and then stop fishing and come home?"

To my surprise he said, "Well, I've considered it."

I was floored, but I said, "I know it's a scary thought, but we would be happier."

"Well, listen—salmon will be over in a week. I've got to fish king crab for Northern Pacific till Christmas. Then we'll sit down and look things over."

" Oh Matt, I'd be happy if you were just home more, especially when Liam and Matthew are so young, and Chelsea's no old lady, either."

Matt grunted.

When we went to bed, I said, "I bet you loved me more when I wasn't so unhappy."

Matt said, "Yeah, it's pretty hard to keep patting you on the back and love you when you're so insecure."

"I know why you love me, but why do I love you?" I asked Matt.

He said, "Yeah, that's the real mystery," and I was too scared of what he meant to pursue it.

He left before it got light again, and I sat at the table watching the channel. *Sometimes I feel like I could write my own heartbreak song.*

When we met
You were weary of living
And you rushed
To be close through the night

At the time
I was weary of loving
And just wanted
A man by my side

Now you say
To live life
Like you have to
We must part while you go being free

And I can't
Bear the thought
Of nobody
Who knows what it is to be me

So now that you're free and you're lonely
Do you like how it's all turning out?
But I, I will never say nothing
'Cause you're what my life is about

Without me, you would never have no one
Without you, my life wouldn't be dirt
Ain't it sweet, this romance we got going
That's measured in heartache and hurt?

Ain't it hard
Ain't it hard to take lightly
The spins that we take
On this ride?

But for you—
Why you've got your loneliness
And me—well,
I still have my pride

Who says I don't like country western music? I can get into the heartbreak of it. If I had somebody to talk to, I would spill my guts. So maybe it's good that I don't. Nobody else is crying for help and begging for attention, except Chelsea, Liam, and Babe.

Ay, what a day I had today, and every day. Babe is crying his head off—I mean crying himself to sleep. Chelsea is fretting and I'm sitting here with a broken back and a cup of tea after catching Liam licking Spic'n' Span off his fingers and rolling a peach pit around in his mouth.

Then the summer was over and Matt was back in Kodiak, fixing up the *Wild One* for the king crab season. We ended each day collapsing in bed.

Matt put up the wood bed frame I got at the auction, and the first time we lay down on it, the slats collapsed under his side. We still have the gold satin quilt on our bed. The stitches are coming out and I'm constantly threading needles to mend it, but it looks pretty, even if it is flimsily made.

CHAPTER THIRTEEN

ALL IS THREATENED
In which the new baby is hospitalized

The seasons seemed to drift into each other as Matt began gearing up for king crab right after the salmon gear was stored. He took off for the south end of the island where he planned to set his pots.

One day soon after Matt left, Matthew had a fever all day and seemed groggy and listless. Chelsea was playing next door and after naps I took the boys with me to pick her up. I was uneasy at how quiet and hot Matthew was, and when we got back home I called Dr. Copstead's office and told Robin how Matthew had been feverish all day and how I couldn't get the fever down for very long with Tylenol or cool rags and how he seemed so out of it.

Robin suggested, "Try putting him in a cool bath. I'll come down to see him after work." When she came, she told me, "Go out and get juice and more Tylenol."

When I came back she said, "The only thing I'd be worried about is spinal meningitis. But look," she said, and pulled him from a lying position to a sitting position by his little hands, "the strain doesn't hurt his neck or he'd cry, so I don't know."

As she left, Robin looked at me sympathetically. "You're going to have a long night. Keep giving him cool baths and juice and Tylenol, and call Copstead in the morning if the fever hasn't gone down."

It was one of those nights where you're up and down, but not really tired because you've got this baby that needs tending, depending on you, and you're scared and you just go from one solution to the next, none of them working, but it's what you have to do and the baby's just out of it, slipping farther and farther away. But you don't cry because that would give life to your worst thoughts.

I took Babe to the clinic first thing the next morning. When Dr. Copstead pulled Matthew's hands and brought him to a sitting position, Matthew cried like a weak, wounded animal, barely able to force the pain out in a whimper. The doctor's face was so serious it terrified me. "Nora, I'm afraid it's meningitis. We'll have to do a spinal tap. It's going to hurt him. Do you want to be with him when we do it?"

I let them take Matthew to another room and heard his screams. My heart burned inside my chest in sorrow. I held myself physically, hugging my arms across my chest and pacing until they brought him back to me. Then I rocked and comforted him, trying to surround his hurt with my health. It comforted me to hold onto him.

They sent me across the street to the hospital, where Dr. Copstead explained they'd be giving him antibiotics through the veins in his temples. My poor little baby, lost in a big hospital crib, with intravenous tubes in both sides of his head, still scarcely rousing himself to whimper. I sat all day in a chair next to him, doing nothing but sitting, looking at my baby, patting him, humming and singing to him, trying to settle his and my pain.

Robin came in during her lunch hour and hugged me. "Robin, tell me, I can take it. Could I have done something to prevent Matthew getting sick? Did I do something wrong?"

"No, Nora, don't feel guilty. I know you're worried sick, but there was nothing you could do. Some kids get colds in their chests, or ear infections. He got the bug in the sheath around his spinal chord. But he's where he should be now. He probably feels like he has a terrific headache."

Dr. Copstead came to check Matthew's IV. "His veins are so tiny, it's hard to put the needle in and then to keep it from pulling out if he moves at all. We're giving him two kinds of antibiotics in case he doesn't respond to one of them. When we know which drug he's sensitive to, which one is working, we'll drop the other one."

When I asked Copstead how Matthew got meningitis, what went wrong, he said, "Matthew's probably got the most common kind of spinal meningitis, homophilus influenza type B. How he got it in his spinal meninges is anybody's guess."

I wanted reassurance about Matthew's chances for recovery, but I couldn't ask for them. I wouldn't be able to bear it if the doctor wasn't positive, or if his assurances were qualified. I was just one of those numbly waiting mothers who line every hospital corridor, fighting a war between hope and fear with nothing but my presence.

I called the Northern Pacific office in town and asked them to transmit a message to Matt, who was still at the south end of the island in Alitak gearing up his pots for the king crab season.

Then I drove home to hug the "big" kids. Sarah and Karen staggered arrangements so they could help me out with meals and babysitting. I went back to the hospital.

I spent the night in the chair next to Matthew's crib, listening to the night sounds of nurses murmuring and the radio crackling every once in a while to advise the hospital that the ambulance or police were bringing a patient in. Matthew was quiet except for a few whimpers and squeaks. I placed my hands on him and talked and sang to him. Just before dawn, I went into the corridor and lay on a plastic sofa as the hospital woke up.

Back in Matthew's room, the telephone rang. It was the marine operator. "I have a call for Nora Hunter from the *Wild One*."

"Nora, are you there?"

"Yes, it's me. Matt, the baby's really sick. He's got meningitis."

"I tried to come home when I got the message yesterday, but I spent most of the night bucking winds and getting about five knots before I had to give up and come back here. I'm going to try coming up the other side of the island today."

"Okay, just try to get here."

"Okay. You hang in there, I'll get there as soon as I can."

Dr. Copstead came in and told me that since Matthew was sensitive to both antibiotics, they'd eliminate the chloramphenicol. "Can I nurse him?" I asked.

"Oh yes, that would be good for him, even if he's not strong enough to get any milk. Just be careful you don't pull out the IV's." Though Matthew barely nuzzled at my breast, it felt wonderful to hold his little body across mine.

I remembered with shame how I'd always disparaged Kodiak's doctors and hospital. I'd always thought if anything ever happened, I'd get on the first plane to Seattle and take the kids to doctors down there.

I'm ashamed of my ignorance, smugly saying I would never trust Kodiak's doctors: I would do anything if I had to. I'm trying to assume that Matthew's on the road to recovery, that the worst is over. Thank God I can feed on that thought and coat my worries with a little hope, like dipping candles. Matthew's whimpers are infinitesimally stronger and he's moving just a little bit. God, let me trust that my baby's coming back to me. Thank you for ignoring my arrogance.

Another night in the hospital without sleep but without fatigue, because Matthew was rallying. Many of the nurses were Filipino who spoke minimal, heavily-accented English, but they'd gently coo and care for Matthew. At dawn, I got another call from Matt via the marine operator.

"Okay, Nora, I'm almost home, just rounding Cape Chiniak. I'll come right home."

"The baby's just a little better this morning. I'll be so glad to see you."

"Okay, I'll be there soon."

It felt like my boat had been tied to the dock with unrelenting iron bars, making me tense and rigid. Now the bars were turning to rope and there was a space between the dock and the boat, and the waves were lapping against the hull for the first time in three days.

The sun was rising when I walked back into Matthew's room from the hall. A nurse was holding the baby and walking him around the room. "Matthew wants to dance. We all want to dance with Matthew."

After I nursed him, his cry was much stronger, now a feeble wail instead of a whimper from the grave.

I went home to get Chelsea and Liam's day started. In the midst of everything, Matt just appeared. He looked haggard and his clothes smelled of diesel, the old reassuring smell.

He hugged me and the kids hard and then said, "I'm just going to get some clean clothes on, let's get up there."

When he held Matthew it looked like the lion with the lamb, vulnerable strength with naked weakness. Matt looked at me. "If this is stronger, I hate to think how weak he was."

"It was awful to see him so sick. We could have lost him, but now we won't. And you're home. We're going to be okay."

Two days later the king crab season was scheduled to start, but the fishermen struck for a better price. Matthew was still in the hospital when a reasonable offer was made.

"Matt, if they vote to accept the price tomorrow, will you go?"

"I don't know. I wish I felt like I had a choice."

The strike settled the next day and he left.

I just changed Liam and found three nails he had cached away in his diaper. Somehow it can't all be this gritty. Somehow there must be something sublime in all this.

Beautiful sunshiny day. Must get the kids outside.

My mom came up from Seattle to help. Liam's habit of getting up four or five times a night horrified her. "That's not normal! Something's wrong with him!"

"I know, Mom, but I don't know what to do about it. Everything's been in such an uproar lately…. I should get things on track. I feel so guilty."

"You shouldn't feel guilty! Just get him back in a crib."

"Isn't that bad for him, you know, like telling him he's a failure as a big boy, he has to be a baby again?"

"Oh, for heaven's sake! You think too much!"

Anyway, it is a relief to have Mom here. No big deal, just a helpful hand. Sometimes I feel like I'm not really here if no one is interacting with me. If I'm not seen at the post office or grocery store, how do I know that I don't just go through some reality warp when I walk through the door and life at home is just some figment of my imagination? It's like I could be dead for days and who would know?

The washing machine took Mom's visit as an opportunity to break down again, and it is a luxury to be able to haul the wash to the laundromat by myself while Mom stays with the kids. No sign of Matt. And I'm still praying, "Make me tough and tender."

Since Matt has been gone this time, I've prayed, not asking for it to be this way or that way, but praying for a blessing just the way it is now, that in some way I can't see, his hard work and my hard work, just plugging away, will make all our lives better.

But I've missed him so much and it seems so long since we've been together. I know we all would be so much better off if he were home. The little kids need him so much. I feel guilty laying this on him, sabotaging his boat dreams, but a part of me wants fishing to be such a bust that he'll give it up and come home and be with us. I can't even honestly say "just for a while," because we'll always need him. What kind of a family would we be if he were superfluous?

Stella popped in while Mom and I were having tea at the table. When I asked Stella to join us, she said, "Oh kid, no. I just had to tell you—God, you're going to kill me. Eli's got some kind of throw-up bug and since he and Chelsea are inseparable—I'm sorry, kid, but it looks like you're all in for it now. Just what you need. God, I'm sorry."

"Oh Stella, it's not your fault, and maybe they won't even get it."

She put her hand over her heart. "Oh, thank God! I told the old man, 'Nora will kill me!' but Jake said, 'Just go tell her.' What a relief!"

When Stella had gone, Mom shook her head. "What a tough one—'My old man!'" She imitated Stella's gruff voice.

"Yeah, I know, but Mom, she's so good to Chelsea. Stella always has Chelsea over to play with Eli. She's a good neighbor."

Mom came with me to a crafts meeting at Sarah's Sugar Shack. On the door, she had a Norman Rockwell picture of two kids cuddling. Underneath the picture it said, "Foolin' Around Sure Beats Fishing." Something about it ticked me off, like it was bragging about keeping your man at home; or like the woman who was able to keep her man home won over fishing.

Robin commented on Karen's new permanent, "You look so cute and fuzzy-headed!"

"Scott hates it—he says, 'Cut it off. I'd rather have a bald-headed woman than you, sweetheart. You're a frizzball!'"

"Does he ever say anything nice?" Robin teased her.

"Oh, you know, Scott is a different person when he's not fishing. He recites poetry to me in bed and walks up and down the house in his velvet bathrobe reading from his books. Work doesn't agree with Scott, but with him getting this new boat and Michael being so little, it's good for us to be in town."

"He and Pete were sure howling at the moon the other night," Sarah said.

"Oh, is that where Scott wound up? At your place? I thought maybe he'd drowned in the harbor, and I just thought 'I'm glad I've got good life insurance on him.' Then he had to wreck all my fantasies by coming home and moaning hung over on the sofa all day."

Sarah bit a piece of thread off. "Yeah, Pete did too, but first they came barging in at four, arguing and giggling at the top of their lungs. You know, Karen, they were really disgusting."

"Oh, they're just letting off steam, Sarah. It's not like I've never seen you drunk."

Sarah was getting righteous, and Karen's voice had an edge to it. I was relieved when Robin broke in. "The newspaper sent a reporter over the other day to ask about this castle we're building on the hill above the boat harbor. Like I want to tell the whole town our floor plan so everybody can copy it!"

"All four stories?" Karen said.

"Four stories, really?" I asked.

"Well, yes, because I want my weaving shop underneath, and then the main floor and then the bedrooms and then a top story tower where we'll put the radio and the stereo equipment. And this dumb reporter calls the house Victorian, just because it's got stained-glass windows!"

Oh a house, a house, be glad you got a house. Be glad or be quiet. You're putting your whole heart and soul into this and everything must be perfect, but it's not the only thing in life. So who cares if it's Victorian or Modern or Gothic?

Karen asked, "Did you hear the woman on Hotline saying she needed someone to look after her sick child? He couldn't go to his regular daycare because of the risk of making the other kids sick."

"God, lady, stay home and look after your own kid!" Robin said.

Sarah said, "That poor woman must be desperate to have to call the Hotline to find someone rather than take time off work. What if she loses her job? It must be awful not to have someone to turn to."

That's why I love Sarah. She always seems to get to the heart of the matter in a kind, non-condemning way.

"You've got to have a lot of self-esteem to stay at home and make peanut butter sandwiches and feel some dignity," I said.

"Yeah, we give all this lip service to how important mothers are and how kids are our bridge to the future, but it's almost like a leper colony," Karen agreed.

"If there was a war on, we'd be setting stars in the window," I said.

"Hey, Robin, that was you and Neil walking down Rezanof the other day, wasn't it?" Karen asked.

"Yep, that was us. I was walking to work and Neil was headed for the library to research the impact of offshore drilling on the fisheries for the Senate hearings on oil leases. And then when we get home we discuss it, and he's preparing a speech he's going to give when they have the teleconference about it."

Robin and Neil do everything right, everything the way you're supposed to. But they act so superior about it all.

When we got back home, Mom discovered that someone had painted some of her clothes in her suitcase with watercolors. Someone who'd escaped the baby-sitter's attention.

Mom said, "I think I'll just stay till Matt gets in to help you, and then I'll go home."

"Weren't you going to stay for two weeks?"

"Well, I know, but I'm too old for three little ones. It's hard being a grandma. I wish I could help you more, honey, but I was an old mother, and now I'm a cranky old grandma."

Matt got in a few days later, and the next night I talked him into going to the Russian Dancers' class with me. He wasn't very enthusiastic about going, and I could see that it would be many classes before he'd get the hang of even the stomping and boot-slapping and, most of all, the posturing that goes with Russian dancing.

But that gruff macho bearishness is such a part of Kodiak. Fred and Pam Nelson were there, and Fred was even more of a galoot than Matt, but I was glad the two men could look to each other. And I loved being there with my man. Matt and Fred looked at each other often in exasperation and camaraderie and at one point the two of them had their shaggy bearded heads together trying to stomp out the dance pattern with their feet. I could have kissed them both.

"Well, I tell Fred, turnabout is fair play," said Pam. "I go camping and hunting with him, he goes dancing with me. It's a two-way street."

That night, Matt threw himself onto the bed and his side fell through the slats to the floor again. "Goddammit, what the hell!" We got up and put it together again and he crept in gently.

The next night Matt suggested taking Mom out to dinner, but I couldn't get a babysitter and Mom said, "That's okay, I'd rather just have dinner here. You don't have to make a fuss."

"Well, how do you like Kodiak this time?" Matt asked her.

"Oh…well…" she shrugged, "same crummy little town, I guess," and she laughed.

While I made dinner, Matt gave the kids rides on his back and they squealed and wanted no end of it. Mom said, "Kids love it when a big man tosses them around. Do you know what a lucky man you are? Three darling kids and a beautiful wife. Aren't you worried to leave her alone in town all the time?"

Cool it, Mom. I wish Matt would think that, but hearing you say it only makes him suspicious.

At dinner, Mom asked Matt when the crab season would be over.

"Oh, it should wrap up within a month."

"And then Nora tells me you won't be fishing again until salmon next summer?"

Matt looked up in surprise and said, "Well, no, we have to eat. There'll be another opening for king crab in December, and then tanner crab starts after New Year's."

But first we're going to sit down and assess all this and make some changes. That's when we're going to start being a regular family.

Matt was saying, "Tanners in January should be a pretty good season, but I don't know what boat I'll be on.

You won't be on any boat. You'll be home with babies and a wife climbing all over you.

"What about the boat you're on now?" Mom said.

"The *Wild One* will go back to Seattle for maintenance for the salmon tendering next summer." Matt said. "Northern Pacific doesn't buy tanner crab, that's mostly the Japanese market."

"Mom's like me, Matt," I said. "You can explain it and explain it, but fishing never gets clear."

Being a fisherman is like being a traveling salesman or a gambler. The next roll is always the lucky one.

Robbie Wade called to say he had a proposition to make to Matt if he could fly down to Seattle the next day to talk to the owner of the *Poseidon*. Before he left, he rushed out to meet Robbie to "talk over business," which meant drinking all night.

All my life people tell me I have no right to be mad, that my anger is irrational. I'm mad because Matt doesn't discuss things with me, he tells me. No apology or explanation for breaking his promise to be home for a month, no recognition that he'd promised to re-evaluate fishing and to set aside time to be with us.

The kids have seen him about eight days in the last six months. Matt doesn't explain to them why he's going or how he feels about them, and it's left up to me to do it when he's gone.

The first thing he tells me about this boat deal is that he's leaving. He has this image of being so mellow and I'm the one ranting and raving, but he's the one rushing around setting the world on fire while I wait endlessly.

The baby's grown out of his storage locker, the truck doesn't work and I have to drive Chelsea's preschool group this week, the refrigerator isn't working, there's bills to pay and no money in the bank.

If I were in his position, if a record producer wanted to see me in Los Angeles, I would tell Matt all about what the producer said and share in the excitement and not make our life together such a drag. I would celebrate with the ones I love best before I went.

When Matt came back from Seattle he told me that the *Poseidon* is a 58-foot seiner. We went to the boat harbor to look at it. It was a clean-looking blue and white boat, but Matt said, "I don't know, the only time I fished salmon was that time I wrenched my foot on the *Maggie J.*"

Our refrigerator finally died on Thanksgiving. Looking at the expense and hating to see the money go to such a mundane item, I said, "Pioneers didn't have refrigerators. We should just put things on the back porch. They'll stay cool enough."

So after our bountiful Thanksgiving dinner, we put the turkey on top of the freezer in the shed.

After dinner, I took the kids down Mission Road for a stroll while Matt cleaned up the kitchen. I stopped in to see Robin and Neil, who were housesitting about a half-mile away, in a house with a beautiful view of the channel. I could tell they were nervous the kids would upset something, so I didn't stay long.

"Where's Matt?"

"Oh, he's cleaning up the kitchen." I said, proud that Matt helped out with the housework.

"Too bad he doesn't enjoy being with his family," Robin said sympathetically.

I could have torn my hair out.

This is probably the closest we've come in ages to being together, celebrating our own family, Matt being around after dinner to help clean up. Why do you have to make me feel so defensive and second-class about my life?

When I got up the next morning, Matt was throwing the turkey in the garbage and said, "Some varmint got into the turkey last night."

"So I guess we have to buy a new fridge, right?"

"Yeah, you can't pick that up at a garage sale. Good thing the seven-inch season is starting next week."

During the seven-inch crab season Matt ran the *Sea Lion* again for Robbie Wade. He made one or two day trips close to home, and when he came in he slept in between unloading the boat at the cannery and going out again.

Leanne had a Christmas party for the women in the babysitting co-op, and with talking about their fisherman husbands and their lives, so busy with kids and school and hobbies when the husbands are away, I was laughing at the things I cry about alone.

For all that we shared the same lifestyle, I wasn't close friends with a lot of fishermen's wives. Just when I'd start to be friends, their men would come home and Matt did his socializing with the men on the boat and at the bars—and no one invaded his home. "Scott and Neil and Pete, all those guys only want to talk to me to pump fishing secrets out of me," he would say.

That afternoon, word came over the radio that a boat sank in the Bering Sea. "Did anybody survive?" I asked

"One guy was picked up in a survival suit, the other two went down."

Leanne said, "Everybody knew that boat was in terrible shape."

"Matt says there's lots of those in Kodiak, but I can see some naive kid thinking, 'I've got a charmed life and somehow the boat I'm on can't sink.'"

"Chuck always says, 'A man's got to do what a man's got to do.'"

"I hate that, that's like people always say 'He was a fisherman when you married him' and I want to say, 'He was also my lover and my friend when I married him. He's not just his job, he's a person, too!'"

Leanne said, "Well, you must have all your kids on schedule by now," and I didn't know if she was joking or serious.

How can you keep to a schedule if your washing machine goes kaput and you have to go to the laundromat or if the kids get sick at an inopportune time or you have a big fight when you were planning to get some work done?

"The school Christmas pageant is later this week. Are you going?"

"I haven't heard about it."

"It's a big deal. The whole town goes to it. Sister Irene puts on a big production every year, and she's just amazing. My little Anna had a starring role last year and all the kids were so excited, and just as Anna was about to start singing she saw her dad in the back of the auditorium. She didn't know if he was going to make it or not, and he just raced in from fishing. Her eyes had stars in them and the whole thing was just so thrilling and innocent and full of love."

Matt came home from the boat harbor with tickets to the Fisherman's Ball.

"Oh Matt, I love it when you surprise me like that!"

"So you want to go?"

"Oh yes, I've wanted to go every year, but you've always been out fishing."

We went out to dinner before the dance. I wore my spaghetti-strap red dress for the first time since I got it three years ago, and high-heeled sandals. It seemed ridiculous in the snow.

"You might as well be out barefoot and naked," Matt commented.

"Well, I've got my fur coat, and my feet will dry out at the restaurant."

After dinner Matt handed me his wallet and told me to get the bankcard out while he went to the restroom.

The bankcard was wrapped in a car rental bill. I looked at it and saw that Matt had rented a sports car while he was in Seattle discussing the boat deal. "So what else did you splurge on while you were down in Seattle?"

"What about your shoes, Eleanor? I suppose going out once every three years makes them a necessity? Or are you the only one who can throw money away on luxuries?"

We treat ourselves to little extravagances, but always apart. I buy presents for him, but he never uses them. He does his own laundry when he comes home. He signs birthday cards with his name only. It's like we're really not married, like I'm a hidden wife that he's ashamed to associate with.

I was running away with these thoughts and realized if I wanted to, I could turn the evening into a fight and never make it to the dance. Or I could just shut up.

When we drove up to the Harvester Inn, it looked like things were in full swing. Gloria and Robbie Wade waved us over to join them at their table by the edge of the dance floor.

"How's Baby Matt doing?" Gloria asked.

"Oh, he's fine whenever I'm looking. Chelsea's going to preschool at the daycare center now, and trying to keep the car and the washing machine both running…. I wish I had some quality time with my kids."

"Oh Nora, that's bullshit, quantity is the only part of a mom's time that has any quality to it. They know you're the one who's always there for them," Gloria said.

Matt lit a cigarette, "'Bout time for us to have another baby if we're going to keep up with you guys."

"Oh, not the Wade Syndrome—another baby will make everything you already have to deal with easier? Forget it."

When the men went up to the bar for more drinks, Gloria pulled her chair up closer to me. "I know what your life is like, Nora. And the men don't think they can offer the kids what you can, so they're off fishing, so at least they can take pride in providing well for their family. They just don't realize how much their help would mean to you and the kids."

I was hanging on, waiting for her to divulge the magic secret to coping, when Gloria said, "All you can do is be a mother, not a teacher or a father or a friend. Just be a mother."

I was underwhelmed.

What's the rest? What about that saying in The Family of Man *about mothers, "She is a tree of life to them?" And the skinny African mama with her children clinging to her? Mother as survivor. Mother Courage.*

Stella and Jake were out on the dance floor. Jake looked so devil-may-care and Stella was glamorous in a slinky sequined gown. We were all watching them shimmy across the floor. "Well, well, didn't know old Jake had it in him," Matt said. "C'mon, Mama, let's see if we can bump into them."

Dancing with Matt was like shoving a big carcass of beef around in a meat locker, but he'd smile and dip me over his arm and never let me fall.

Just before Christmas we went to a party at Jake and Stella's. "This is turning into a social season that Madame Bovary would drool over," I rejoiced.

"Madame Bovary?" Matt asked.

"You know, the French woman who was stuck in the provinces and spent all her husband's money on clothes and parties and killed herself?"

"Sounds like your kind of heroine all right," Matt said.

We walked into the Iversons and parted company at the front door. All the men were exhausted from fishing all day, but had agreed to let their wives drag them along for a good time.

Stella introduced me to some friends of hers, saying, "Nora's got three little ones, the baby's as blond as Jake is. I wonder where that kid came from. I mean, I know Jake was unhappy with Tuffy and I know there's a couple of blond kids of his running around the villages, but the next-door neighbor? Couldn't you have waited for the milkman?"

I laughed and said, "Hey, I never even thought of Jake. But Stella, don't say that in front of Matt. He's kind of sensitive about that sort of joke."

"Oh God, Jake is terrible—I could kill him. Here we are in the heat of passion and he calls me 'Tuffy'! More than once!"

"He should just call you sweetheart."

Word had just come in that afternoon that the *Mighty Pride*, Chuck Hartwell's 110-foot boat, had gone down. Luckily, there were boats nearby to rescue the crew right after the boat rolled over. Nobody was hurt or lost, but the boat is gone. Chuck and Leanne had just moved into a nice little "real" house with a view of the channel on Rezanof Drive.

Gloria said, "Robbie thinks the boat was probably going too fast and the waves breaking over the pots on deck iced them up. So that makes the boat top heavy and it can't recover from a roll and flips over."

Stella said, "But if you don't go fast enough, you're dead in the water."

"So how do you know what to do?" I asked.

"You play it safe," Gloria said.

"But these cowboys can't play it safe," Stella complained. "It's not in their nature."

I started talking to Stella's friend, Elizabeth Brooks, and told her how much it disturbs me that Liam gets up in the middle of the night. "Last week he got up at four in the morning, ready for the day, and started playing with his toys. It really freaks me—I wonder if he's mentally disturbed."

But Elizabeth only said, "Oh, I just love my kids so much, and when they get up in the middle of the night, I get up too and we all play together and have a good time till they're ready to go back to bed."

What is this broad's problem? I wish Leanne were here to ask Elizabeth about her schedule.

"My husband quit fishing about three years ago, he says it's just not fair to the family to be out fishing where you can't be counted on. My husband is such a good man, he is such a great father, he takes the kids to church and he puts the kids to bed and he's always happy and tells me how much he loves me."

Even though Matt was home, Christmas was flat. We had tons of presents, no church, stayed home by ourselves all day, ate a big dinner, and went to bed. No fishing.

CHAPTER FOURTEEN

THE FISHERMAN'S BOAT
In which Matt achieves his dream; I wake up to a nightmare

On New Year's Day, Robin and Neil had a housewarming party for their new castle. Happily for me, Matt was home and agreed to go. We drove up the steep narrow driveway where already several trucks were crowded into the side of the hill. We walked across a short, sturdy wooden footbridge to the front door, which was surrounded by palladian windows. We knocked, then stepped inside to a long hallway with hooks jutting out at waist height, already loaded with heavy jackets and parkas. Underneath, mud and ice-caked shoes dripped dirty puddles on the floor. We stepped out of our shoes and hung up our coats, and walked to the end of the hallway to where three steps led to the main room, wrapped in honey-toned wood paneling and warm golden-rose carpeting. Floor-to-ceiling windows looked out to the boat harbor. On the far wall was a stone-faced fireplace with a large hearth for seating.

We went to the kitchen and got drinks, and I settled the kids at the kitchen table where the women were hovering over plates of food. Matt took his drink and sauntered into the living room where the guys were hogging the fire and talking about fishing.

I heard Matt say, "Flying a plane to spot herring this spring in Norton Sound by Nome may be a good little money-maker outside of fishing. I should be able to renew my pilot's license without any problem."

"I wonder if finding something to do in town so he can come home at night will ever have any allure for Matt?" Robin whispered to me. I nodded.

Karen talked about opening up a whorehouse with male whores so the wives could get sex when their husbands were out fishing. "It makes perfect sense!"

"Except even if they put paper bags over their heads, I don't know if I could warm up to some guy just to have sex. It's just not the same as it is for guys," I said.

"Oh Nora, for a hippie, you're such a square," Robin said.

When we left the party, Matt said, "Look, there's Robbie in his car." Robbie's head was bent over by the steering wheel, and Matt yelled, "Yo, Robbie!"

Robbie's head jerked up and there was white powder all around his nose. He looked startled at first, then rolled down the window and said, "Matt, my boy, come over here!"

Matt said, "Nah, I don't want to lick your face. That stuff kills people."

When we drove down the hill, Matt looked back and said, "Yeah, well, some day everyone's going to know that Matt Hunter is the best fisherman this town's ever seen."

So he's got the glory-hunger too. His crowning glory is not his wife or his kids or his happy home. His ambition is the mythical Highliner. I walk two steps behind.

Even though it's nice and secure to have him home, we just kind of roam through the day next to each other, not talking. He goes to the hardware store and I stay home, or I go visit my girlfriends and he stays home with the kids. His fishing buddies don't come to the house, even for just a cup of coffee, and Matt doesn't suggest I go with him on his errands. Always some kind of distance. Nobody ever tells you that hanging by a thread is a stage you'll probably go through in marriage. And be better off for it? That's what I keep telling myself, but I wonder if I should believe me. It's hard for me not to fight to change. Something in me doesn't believe that doing nothing may be the best thing to do.

Is it like Hesse says in Siddhartha, *the best mother learns to not care, to separate? Instead of just "get tough," now I am telling myself "think right."*

I went to bed before Matt, and when he got into bed his side fell down again. "Oh, shit," he sighed and fell asleep with the bed on a slant. Everyone slept through the night for a change. Matt woke up with a hangover and said, "Did I make a total fool out of myself last night?"

I smiled sweetly and said, "If it bothers you, why don't you quit making a fool out of yourself?"

Matt and the other fishermen were working on the boats in town, gearing them up and getting them ready for the tanner crab season. Soon after the party, Matt came home one night at dinner and announced he was leaving after midnight.

"But the fishermen haven't settled on a price with the canneries, have they?" I asked.

"I'm going to wait on the grounds, be ready for an agreement."

"What if they don't settle soon and you're stuck out there waiting for nothing? Can't you stay here in town?"

"I fish, Eleanor, I go when I have to."

"Yeah, and I sit here and tell the kids why they're never as important as fishing and your precious reputation." I wanted to scream, and the effort not to was choking my words out.

"Oh, fuck you," he said, and put his hat back on and headed for the door, his shoulders knocking the copper molds off the kitchen wall.

After he left, I sat at the table and finished my cup of tea, got the scissors and some black construction paper and scotch tape out, and went around to the photographs hanging on the walls. I cut off pieces of the black paper to cover Matt's face in all the photographs. Chelsea came in.

"What are you doing, Mommy?"

"I'm covering over Daddy's face. He's been bad."

"Is Daddy in trouble?"

"Yes, he's in big trouble with me."

We had a cold, miserable January, with storms sending waves crashing up over the road and winds knocking out the power lines.

I'd placed the red velvet curtain, out of use since the old poker parties, against the door to block the draft and the wind still blew the door open, so I moved the gold sofa against it. The only time we opened the front door in the winter was when Goldie would bark to come in.

Well, here I sit with a cup of tea, my kids gone to a babysitter and the house a mess though I spent most of yesterday cleaning it up. Got a kink in my neck and just feeling distracted. Maybe I'll get to playing the piano later.

I guess this is cabin fever. God, I hope it's a pretty spring in Kodiak, and I hope it comes soon. I wish our extended family was warmer. I wish I had a grandma, sister, or friend I could cry to without feeling guilty. I wish I didn't feel guilty or feel like crying. I feel like going to bed.

Another giant storm brought Matt home. The roof leaked all night in four places—the living room, Chelsea's room, our room, and the hall. I thought the roof would cave in along the "zipper," the long beam that runs the length of the house through the center of the trailer.

Chelsea wanted to sleep on the floor in our bedroom in her sleeping bag. I said okay and she lay there talking on and on; the last thing she said was, "Mom, I'm gonna tell you something and it's…well, it's really gonna break your heart."

"What is it, honey?"

"I just love sleeping in my red sleeping bag, but I wish I could sleep with you in the biggest bed."

"I know, I wish that too sometimes." Then Matt came in and I wanted to be close with Matt's arms around me and I told him I wanted to kiss him so he moved Chelsea and her sleeping bag to the bed in the boys' room and came back and Matt and I made fantastic love. He hadn't even noticed the blacked-out photographs.

The weather is so severe and awesome, extremely cold and ferocious. I shudder to think of being on a boat out there, like one of those boats that sank before Christmas. Do I have the courage? Would I be heroic or squealing? Could I live with the shame if I didn't? What if someone needed me and I felt if I helped them I'd die? Could I live knowing that about myself?

That night, with Matt home to babysit, I went to a co-op meeting. Leanne asked, "Is Matt doing really good, Nora?"

"Well, I guess so. I mean he doesn't talk much about it, good or bad, but he always says, 'It's okay' and seems to be bringing in a pretty consistent amount."

Leanne said, "Because Chuck said the fishing's been so poor, and he mentioned Matt's name when he was talking about the Highliners."

Matt won't tell me how well he does or how much crab he brings in. He's afraid I'll tell my friends.

It was so cold when I walked home, even though I had my fur coat and long underwear on. I felt frostbitten inside.

When I got home, I told Matt that Chuck said he was a Highliner, and Matt said, "All Chuck does is get on the radio and complain about the weather and how he misses his wife. What a lightweight!"

I bit my tongue, but later, when Ronnie Milsap sang on TV, "I'm a Stand-By-My-Woman Man" and Matt snorted, I turned on him. "Why do you find the concept of standing by your woman so distasteful?"

Matt just laughed.

So although Matt was home that week, we avoided each other except when I pressured him to look at two houses that the realtor had showed me. "These houses are the first possibilities in the eight months that she's been showing me around."

"Well, I don't have time and that's all there is to it."

Sloopy Don called and invited Matt over to watch the Superbowl.

"Promise you'll look at the houses with me when you get home afterwards?"

"Okay, Nora, I'll be back around four."

At eight I heard the Jeep roar up, and I grabbed the last pork chop off the plate and bolted it down before Matt sauntered in, drunk and slurry-tongued. "No dinner, that's great." He slammed around the kitchen making a sandwich and passed out on the sofa. I jostled his shoulder and said, "I'm going out. I'll be back."

Then I checked into the Kodiak Inn.

Boy, does revenge feel cold. And expensive. I don't want to be here and blow all this money, but I have to do something or else resign myself to being a doormat for the rest of my life.

I woke up at nine the next morning and pulled the curtains. It was a beautiful clear day. When I got home, Karen was babysitting. She said, "Matt just left an hour ago. He called me up when the weather finally broke—after a week of storms, they're all frantic to get out on the grounds."

I was hugging Liam on the floor and Karen said, "When the boat was going out the channel, Matt made a circle with it in front of your trailer—like he was apologizing?"

"Yeah," I said, "we had a fight."

It's funny—Matt makes such a big deal about other people knowing his business, yet he involves Karen. And he always accuses me of telling her our life story.

Karen laughed. "Yeah, well, when I came over he just said, 'Eleanor split,' and Chelsea said, 'Yeah, Mom split,' and snapped her fingers." Karen laughed again.

I could imagine her repeating the story to Robin and Sarah and anyone else who was bored and wanted a juicy story. But I would probably tell them myself, so what did it matter if Karen beat me to it?

Hardbitten: Mom split, Dad could give a rip. What if I hadn't come home? What if I'd really flown the coop? Fishing comes first.

Matt got in after two days fishing. He walked through the back door, knocking the aluminum jello molds off the wall, and after hugging the kids, he looked at me and said, "What's going on?"

I said, "What do you think I am that you can treat me like that?"

"Like what?"

"Hey, you can figure it out," I said, and sat down on the sofa with a book.

He came up to me and grabbed my hand. "Mama, I'm sorry. Come on, we can't be fighting like this all the time."

He knows what I'm going through. He just hates to deal with it.

The next Sunday, Matt took the day off to stay home with us. It was so nice just to have him sitting around the house. I made breakfast and cleaned up the house. I sewed during naps and made cherry pies, then cooked a German dinner while Matt watched the Olympics. Liam got to go down to the boat with his dad after dinner, and Matt wore the Russian shirt I made him. We were a family.

Later that spring Pam and Fred Nelson called to say they'd stop by to pick up the space rent. Matt said, "Have you seen Pam lately? She's really changed her looks."

We were overdue with the rent, but they weren't snippy about it. Pam was holding Matthew and cooing over him, and Fred said, "Pam's plumb crazy about babies. She just got back from helping her twin sister with her new one."

"So Pam's a twin, huh?" Matt said.

"Oh, yeah," Fred said, "I had my eye on Pam since she was a little girl. I married her with milk on her breath."

Matt was right; Pam really surprised me. She had her hair done up in a ratted beehive, was wearing tons of makeup, and had her pants tucked into high-heeled boots and was smoking a black cigarette in a cigarette holder.

She said they wanted to move and I thought of their big secure house and asked why, and she said, "We just feel that the Lord wants us to minister elsewhere—to bring together a new community of his people. The Lord is everything to us."

I said something like, "I wish I felt the Lord as a personal presence—I feel so lonely."

Pam said, "The Lord can even be a husband to you. Like it says in the Bible, in Jeremiah, 'I was a husband unto them, saith the Lord.'"

I didn't want to get into a Bible discussion but I felt uncomfortable just nodding my head. "Pam, I can't help it, that just sounds sort of silly to me."

"I know how it can, but you see, I've prayed over it and it means, if your husband is not as smart or as understanding or as kind as you'd wish, you seek those things in your relationship with the Lord, and then you're not looking to your husband for things he can't give. The Lord gives them to you, so he is your husband."

"Yeah, I can kind of see it when you put it that way," I said, and tried to make it my philosophy, but I wanted more than a spiritual connection with God. I wanted a flesh-and-blood helpmate.

I drove down to the dock to pick Matt up. They were unloading and storing the crab pots from the *Sea Lion*. Matthew was in the front of the Jeep in his car seat and Chelsea and Liam were strapped in the back.

I pulled up and waited at the end of the dock. Sloopy Don was driving the boom truck at the other end of the dock. Suddenly he came speeding straight towards our Jeep.

I don't know what he thinks he's doing

Is he playing chicken? Does he think Matt's driving the Jeep?

At the last minute, he swerved to avoid us, but there was a seven-foot square crab pot swinging from the boom. When I saw it heading for our windshield, I threw myself across Matthew and waited for the blow.

Luckily it didn't shatter the windshield, just banged the hood in.

I'm not waiting around for you to finish me off!

I threw the truck into reverse, got off the dock and hauled up Mission Road.

He could have killed us with his irresponsible little game! He could have wiped out my whole life—just having fun!

But behind my indignation there was shock and excitement. I could imagine him going up to Matt on the boat and saying, "Hey man, I'm sorry. I just hit your truck and your wife and kids were in it."

And Matt would be consumed with worry until he found out we were okay and he'd flutter over us like a mother hen making sure we were all right and making a fuss over us till we were placated.

I pulled into Karen's. Scott was there and they gave me a drink. When I told them what happened, Scott said, "They were playing chicken!" and laughed his head off. Karen joined him.

I wonder if Matt will come looking for us, if he'll think to look for us here. I wonder what he'll say when he tries to calm me down.

After a long while I called home.

"Where are you?" Matt answered.

"Did Sloop say anything?"

"No. Where are you? I thought you were going to pick me up."

"Matt, Sloop almost killed us, playing chicken with the boom truck. I'm really upset."

I shouldn't have to say that.

"Well, are you all right?"

"Yeah, I'm all right." *What a letdown.* "The truck's bashed in," I was happy to be able to say.

"Well, are you going to come home and have dinner or what?"

"I'm too upset to cook dinner."

"Well, I'll cook dinner, what the hell."

"I'm upset Matt, I want to go out. I need to calm down."

He sighed. "All right, well, I'll take a shower. Come on and pick me up, or are you too upset to do even that?"

When I pulled up behind the trailer, Matt looked at the damage. "Well, at least it didn't bust the radiator," he said.

Hell.

Stella called early on St. Patrick's Day and asked if Matt wanted to take her and me out to celebrate that night. We went to the gambling party at the Elk's Club and after a while, went over to Solly's to dance.

Matt asked Stella to dance, and she wanted me to dance with them too, but I said, "I'll sit this one out and wait for the next one."

"God, kid, why didn't you come out and dance with us?" Stella said, when they got back to the table. "Just because you and Jake had something going doesn't mean I'm going to steal Matt away."

I impulsively picked an ice cube out of my drink and tossed it at Stella and said, "I told you not to talk like that."

Stella got huffy and mad and said, "Well, thanks a lot, kid. What gives you the right to throw your drink at me?"

"Stella, come on. It was just a joke."

Tears started rolling down her face. "Well Jeez, lady, that's some way to treat a friend."

"I didn't throw my ice cube at you to start a fight."

Goddam it—why can everyone else brawl and carouse and go off half-cocked and I can't even throw a fucking ice cube?

At least Matt had the decency to speak up. "I think I have something to do with this. I give Nora a pretty hard time sometimes."

We sat there staring down at our drinks for a little while and then wordlessly got up and got in the Jeep and drove home.

Matt brought home *The Fisherman's News*, the big national newspaper, and there was an article with photographs about the *Princess Anne*, the fancy boat that his brother-in-law Glenn is building with his fat-cat partners, including the state senator. The article discussed Glenn's fishing career and how he's gone so much, and they quoted Glenn saying, "My wife's from a fishing family—she understands." They used that quote to headline the article.

Tanner crab season wound down and Matt finally decided to do something about the bed falling down all the time, so we went to the hardware store and he ran into an old fisherman and the two of them conferred about how to fix the bed while the kids ran around the toy department. I wanted to meet everyone and have everyone see that we do things together: we don't always fight, we have three kids, we share a bed, Matt likes us, our kids are cute, we're normal, we're a family.

Afterwards I went over to Stella's to return a dish I'd borrowed before the night we went out and she seemed rather cold, so I said, "You still mad about St. Patrick's Day?"

"Well, yes, I'm mad."

"Well, I hope you come over when you're not mad anymore," I said. I got all the way home before I burst into tears.

"What's wrong?" Matt said.

"Stella's still mad at me about St. Patrick's Day."

"Well, what's the big deal? She's wrong—screw it."

Neil called from Seattle and asked Matt to get some roses for Robin for her birthday. Matt said to me, "That's ridiculous—they're just going to die. Neil is so sentimental."

But when he came back home, he brought me a bouquet of roses. "Matt, you old softie, thank you for being so good to me, even if you were shamed into doing it."

Of course, then he had to wreck it by staying out all night. He rolled up at six the next morning. When I heard him drive up, I jumped out of bed and behind the door and poured the vase of roses and water over his head.

"All right, all right, okay! Okay enough! I'm sorry! I passed out at Randy's!"

I took the jeep and drove out past Monashka Bay to where the road ended. The sun was shining. I turned around and drove home and crawled into bed beside Matt for an hour before the kids woke up.

Sarah came over to talk about her wedding plans. "Pete wants to get married when the moon is full, so we set the date for June 28. I just wish he didn't always need to get high. I don't know what to do."

"Does he really get high a lot?"

"Every night, and Scott eggs him on. The two of them are either drunk or high or both at Scott and Karen's place, or on the boat."

"He never seems high to me, the times I see him."

"Well, he's a big guy, and—I don't know, it doesn't seem to affect him that much, so why does he need it? I can't accept his way of life; if he really loves me and wants me, he'll change."

"But even if he wants to it will be hard for him, if Karen and Scott and all his friends always get high."

"He's building a house out on Mill Bay and then he says 'I want to build a house for us, Sarah.' He's such a sweet old Buddha, so jovial and complacent. Would you play the organ at St. Mary's for our wedding?"

"Okay.... Why don't the two of you boogaloo down the aisle while I play *United we stand / Divided we fall / And if our backs should ever be against the wall / We'll be together / Together you and I....*"

"Actually, Nora, I'd thought of something a little more traditional," Sarah laughed. "And I wrote my mom and Pete's mom and asked if I could try on their wedding dresses. I want to wear one of them. What was your wedding like?"

"I guess I was afraid if I made a big fuss over it, it would never happen. Like one night, months before we got married, Matt said to me, 'Do you know what I'd like to do?' I knew he was going to say, 'Get married,' but when I said 'What?' too soon, he just sighed and said nothing. Then we were up at the cannery in Alitak and the way the fishing worked, Matt would be out on the boat whenever the cannery was quiet, and I had to work in the cannery when he brought the fish in. Whenever he was in, I was busy; whenever I was off work, he was out fishing. But one night he said, 'Let's get married,' and I remembered the time before and said nothing, and he said, 'C'mon, marry me,' and then he turned on the light and said, 'I want to see your face.'"

"Where were you?" Sarah asked

"We were in bed, in the captain's stateroom on the *Moonlight*," I continued. "Matt talked to Cy, the superintendent, about taking the mail plane out the next day. But Cy tried to talk him out of it, saying 'Fishermen's marriages never last,' and I thought, 'Well, thanks a lot for the good wishes.'

"But the next clear day that the plane came in, he said we could go into town. I was going to wear a frilly blouse, but I started getting sick, so I wore my long underwear and the blue jeans with the embroidered rose on them and we flew into Kodiak and got married at the Church of God with the minister's wife and next-door neighbors for witnesses.

"Then we got a room at the hotel and a bottle of champagne and the next day flew back to Alitak and went back to work. I thought now that we were married, I could go with Matt on the boat as the cook. But Cy had hired a 50-year old woman to cook on the boat and I had to go back to the cannery."

Matt called me from downtown and told me to come and join him for a drink. So I asked Sarah if she'd babysit so I could go down to the Mecca. When I got inside and sat down, Sloopy Don asked me, snickering, "So how'd you like your roses?"

"Ahab had a hard time getting home, huh?" laughed Robbie.

I looked at Matt across the table and he shrugged and smiled and blew me a kiss.

Matt and I looked at an Aleutian home that was for sale. It wasn't on one of the three parallel streets in the main part of the Aleutian home ghetto, but was off a little cul-de-sac. The woman who owned it said, "We decided if we couldn't live in New England, then we'd make it look as much like home as we could."

191

They'd decorated it with bay windows, candlewick bedspreads, calico cushions, and grandfather clocks. Matt and I discussed it in the car on the way back home.

I said, "It doesn't just look good, it's solid with copper pipes, thick insulation, and that large entry hall for all the boots and hats and mitts that clutter up everybody's entryway."

"They did a good job renovating it, you can almost forget it's an Aleutian home."

"Plus it has a fenced yard with real trees, and you can feel the respectable, solid vibes."

"Plus we can afford it."

Oh, I was so excited thinking that we might have a real solid house that felt like home!

Later I went up to St. Mary's to practice on the organ for Sarah's wedding. Sister Therese showed me how to work it, and Father Romeo from the Philippines came in and pestered us.

"Oh, you're playing for a wedding? I bet you like to play for a man and a woman who are going to be married. I bet Sister Therese wishes she could be married. Sister Therese would make a beautiful bride…"

Finally Sister Therese said, "That's enough, Father!"

Yeah, get lost, creep.

When I got back home, Matt and I continued to discuss buying the Aleutian home.

"It's really nice, Matt."

"Yeah, but it's still an Aleutian home, with no view of the channel or boat harbor."

"But a view! It'll be years before we get a place with a view, and this has a fenced yard the kids can play in."

The phone rang and Matt was on it so long that I finally started doing housework. I was folding laundry on the sofa when Matt hung up at last.

"That was Arnie Peterson at Northern Pacific. He wants me to fly down to Seattle to negotiate buying into the *Ocean Mistress.*"

"Buying into?"

"They'd buy three-quarters. I'd…we'd…buy one-quarter with the possibility of buying them out down the road."

"How much is one-quarter?"

"Around a hundred thou."

"We don't have a hundred thousand, do we?"

"Oh, they'd do some kind of financing, but this way they'd be guaranteed my interest in paying it off."

"The *Ocean Mistress*, huh? Do you think it's a good idea?"

"Oh yeah, I've just been waiting for a chance to get my share of something like this. It's stupid to fish for someone else, like giving them your money."

"So how much money would we have to put into it? I mean really have, like in the bank?"

"All of it, all twenty thousand."

We were both quiet for a while and Matt stared out of the window while I sat at the table. Finally I said, "But it sounds like a good deal, right?"

"Right." After another long while he said, "Well, anyway, I should go down to Seattle and see what the deal really is, what the fine print says."

"Yeah, you should. I should go, too."

I don't think Matt can turn this down, whether it's a good deal or a bad deal. He's wanted to own a boat for so long and now we have $20,000 saved towards it. Or towards a house.

I hustled and got Robin to look after the kids. I was packing in the bedroom when Liam toddled in and I told him we were going for four days, and he said, "Go on plane?"

"Yes, Liam."

And he said, "I come too?"—half-question, half-statement, and he looked so vulnerable with this hopeful, happy, scared look all mixed up on his face, that I didn't have the heart to turn him down.

When I told Matt that I'd told Liam he was coming with us, I said, "Robin can entertain Chelsea, and Matthew's just a baby, but Liam gets squeezed out so much anyway."

We stayed at the Towne Hotel. Liam slept with us and by some miracle didn't wet the bed. While Matt cinched the boat deal, Liam and I hung out at Tricia's.

"It's hard to believe just a year ago, Matthew was born."

"So you ready to go again?" Tricia smiled.

"With another baby? That's funny, Tricia, real funny. No, it's great not to be pregnant or worried."

"So Matt gets his baby now, huh?"

"Yeah, it's weird. If he'd gone herring fishing like he originally planned, this deal probably wouldn't have come up. But I made such a big deal out of him being home more, and so he was home when this opportunity came up. It's sort of scary to be committed this deep, but Matt's been at it for so long, I just have to trust his judgment."

One night we went out with Matt's family. Peggy had her tail tied in a knot about something and at one point the conversation had ground to a halt. Though I didn't want to acknowledge Glenn's devotion to Peggy, I told her I'd seen the article in *The Fisherman's News* about Glenn's new boat and how nice it was that he'd given her credit for being supportive and understanding. "That was really sweet," I said.

Peggy made a face. "Well, kind of corny, really."

Later we all started dancing, and it had just been husband with wife until Matt asked his mom to dance and Glenn asked me, and when we got back to the table Peggy was bristling. "Come on, Glenn, let's get out of here," she said, and they bustled away.

"What's Peggy upset about?" Matt said.

"Who knows?" said his dad. "She probably figured they'd owe the babysitter a fortune."

"Well, I didn't want to babysit tonight," Matt's mom said defensively. "I wanted to go out and celebrate with the kids. Oh, do you think now she's mad at me? She's so stubborn when she doesn't get her own way."

"Oh, leave her alone, she'll come around next time she needs a babysitter," Grandpa said.

When I told Tricia about it later, and how I can never get along smoothly with Peggy, Tricia said, "Maybe she's jealous of you?"

"Jealous of me? She's got everything I'd want—a husband who tells the world how great she is, a big beautiful house, money to burn, and parents who just love to babysit!"

Before we left Seattle, Matt's mom and dad took us out to lunch. We ate at a fancy restaurant downtown. I held my breath, but Liam was so good and endearing.

"He's a trouper," Grandpa said.

"Five grandchildren!" said Gramma. "I can't believe it!"

"Are you going to Europe on your vacation again this year?" I asked.

"Oh no, no, we'll probably just hang around the house."

"Why don't you visit us in Kodiak? Before you go up to the cabin in June? Matt won't be out tendering yet and the weather would be okay and we'd love to have you," I urged.

"Well, maybe we can. Wouldn't that be fun, Grandpa?"

"Oh, it would be great," I urged. "I would really like it and the kids would go crazy."

When we got on the plane, I said to Matt, "Do you think they really might come?"

"No, they'll never come to Kodiak," he said flatly. "It's too blue-collar for them."

Back in Kodiak, I invited everyone over on Sunday for Easter brunch, but the guys had planned a hunting trip, so Matt was the only man among all my friends and their babies. I wondered if he felt left out or if he'd wanted to be asked along on the hunting trip, but he never hangs out with those guys, just with the die-hard fishermen without families.

It started snowing in the afternoon, and Eli and Christie came knocking at the door with baskets of Easter treats for us. I was mildly surprised, as this was the first sign of a thaw from Stella. I scurried around the house raiding what goodies I could from the kids' stockpile of chocolate eggs and marshmallow bunnies and made a basket for Christie and Eli to take back to Stella. Trailer court diplomacy.

Matt went down to Seattle to get the *Ocean Mistress* ready for salmon tendering. After we'd put our share of the down payment on the boat, we realized we had absolutely no money to get through the month until Matt starts the salmon charter in June and we could draw on that money. We had to take out a loan from the bank to pay bills.

One day on my way into the grocery store, I saw Leanne wearing a funny little rabbit hat with huge pompoms dangling from her chin.

"How are you doing?" I asked.

"I broke," she said calmly.

"Huh? You broke?" Leanne with her routine, her exercise, her new house—Leanne broke?

"Yeah. After the *Mighty Pride* sank and we were trying to buy another boat and it just seemed so complicated and at the end we'd have to pull with all our might and main just to make ends meet to fish another boat, and I said to Chuck, 'Anna's never going to have another brother or sister if her father's never home.' Finally Chuck and I just looked at each other and said, 'What is so great about fishing and Kodiak that we mortgage everything to fish here?'"

"So what are you going to do?" *I hate my friends leaving Kodiak, and little phrases like "Chuck and I looked at each other" make tears come to my eyes.*

"Well, Chuck offered to move back to Seattle and I'm taking him up on it. This is our chance to get out," she said with finality.

"Oh Leanne, I'm glad for you, but I'll miss you. Maybe someday Matt will give it up, too."

Maybe someday like never.

And she walked off with her silly little pompoms bouncing off her shoulders.

The money is really tight. It's like when I was in college. I only buy broccoli and milk, and thank God for the canned salmon. Matthew gets so excited when I come back from the store, he jumps up and down on the back porch screaming, "Milk! Milk!" I'm embarrassed to take the kids visiting any of my friends, because they ask for food.

At our next sewing get-together, at my house, I was making a quilt for Pete and Sarah on the theme, "To everything there is a season and a time for every purpose under Heaven," but I couldn't show it in front of Sarah.

"Are you making a quilt out of jeans?" Karen asked her.

"Yeah, I've been picking up old jeans at garage sales," Sarah said.

"That's not going to keep you very warm for how heavy it is."

"Well, I'm going to finish it and see how it turns out. Look, Nora gave me the jeans she was married in, and I'm going to use the part that has the rose embroidered on it."

Karen said "My mother sent Scott a Royal Doulton teapot for his birthday."

"Did Scott like it?"

"Oh yeah, Scott likes nice things. He said, 'Well, sweetheart, if we get divorced, I get the teapot.'" Karen laughed. "You know, Nora, it's funny. You look around our house and you see things of Scott's—you can see a man lives there. But I don't see anything of Matt here."

"But Karen, there's the walrus skull and...the refrigerator...and the kids," I fumbled.

"So instead of Matt out fishing herring in Norton Sound, he's down in Seattle fixing up a boat," Karen said.

"Won the battle but lost the war, huh, Nora?" Robin said.

"Yeah, I want to go to a bar and get drunk and make a fool out of myself."

Robin said, "No, it wouldn't work. You're not in the right mood. Bartenders hate to see people like you walk in."

"What am I waiting for?"

Karen said, "I was talking to Scott on the radio and he says Wild Bill is driving the crew nuts, he's so stir-crazy. He insists on the forks being turned a certain way, practicing witchcraft. And when a plane passed overhead, trying to spot the herring runs, he grabbed a gun to shoot it down."

"Why?" we all asked.

"God, he's so crazy! He was yelling 'There's women in that plane!' and Scott practically had to deck him to get the gun away from him!"

"That's the kind of fool I'd like to make of myself."

When I told Matt about my conversation with Leanne outside the grocery store, he said, "I don't want to hear what Leanne thinks or how they couldn't take it and how she talked Chuck out of fishing. If they can't hack it, let them leave."

It's funny, Matt has always raved about Leanne and how competent, how good-natured, how attractive a fisherman's wife she is.

Sarah and Pete's wedding day grew closer while Matt was down in Seattle fixing up the *Ocean Mistress* for the coming salmon season. I went over to Karen's to visit her mom, Lynn, and Gramma Inga, who came from North Dakota for the wedding. Lots of their relatives came in from the Midwest, and Robin and Sarah's family from New York, too.

Gramma Inga was straight out of *Little House in the Big Woods*, baking cookies and supervising some tole painting at the table. She was so full of life and opinions, and was so kind to Liam and Chelsea and Matthew.

Lynn had braided Karen's long blond hair and wanted to do mine. I was sitting at the table and Karen passed me a joint. I shook my head and Karen lifted her eyebrows and took a drag.

Lynn said, "With all the stories you hear, it really bothers me that she still does that." I didn't hear what she said next, but I sensed she was waiting for a response from me.

"I don't know, I sure couldn't smoke dope in front of my mom," I dodged.

Lynn tugged on my hair as she was braiding it. "Hmm. Well, I wish I could say something to her." Lynn held up a mirror so I could see my hair braided around the back of my head.

"I don't look like me! I look like Jo in *Little Women!*" I said.

Robin glanced at me and said, "Right! Where'd the 'hippie mama' go?"

Fed up with all the disorganization around the house. Started clearing everything off the floor into closets. Then I got into a paring down, pristine mode and started taking down all the posters and calendars and photographs and mirrors on the walls. Simplify.

I had a tea party for Sarah, and Chelsea just had to wear her plaid skirt and sunrise shirt, just as she had every day that summer. Robin told her mom of staying with the two kids last spring when I went to Seattle, and her mom said, "Oh, that must have been hard."

"It was," Robin said quietly.

I felt anger coming out of every pore.

My kids are good and sweet. They could have made it a lot harder. I paid Robin money. Nobody pays me. Robin was here four days. I'm here twenty-four hours a day every day of my life. And most of all, Robin has a sister and in-laws in town and a husband who makes sure she gets roses if he's out of town.

When I was saying good-by to everyone after the party, Matthew was playing with the blocks by the window. He just walked up and slammed a block into the window and crashed it.

I grabbed him out of the way and put him in his crib, howling, while I picked the broken glass up. I stood by my "space," the kitchen countertop above the dishwasher that's the only place the kids respect as off-limits, and looked around the long living room, from the fireplace to the bookshelves, the piano, the sofas, the coffee table, the lamps, doors, and windows. My view swept around to the dining room table, chairs, and desk beside me. There wasn't one thing I looked at that didn't bear the mark of the kids' destruction.

I sat down at the table and cried.

Why do they have to destroy everything? Is this is normal, my frustration and the kids' destructiveness? This is too hard.

We had a stag-ette party for Sarah the week before her wedding, the night after the guys had had their bachelor party. Lynn, Karen, Robin, Sarah, Leanne, and a couple of others, met me downtown and we had drinks at Solly's before heading out to the Beachcombers for their wet-shorts contest.

Before the competition began, Lynn ordered Sarah a six-pack of gin and tonics.

What are you trying to do to your future daughter-in-law? If I drank that much, I'd disgrace myself for sure.

"Wow, that's a lot of booze," Robin said.

"If she's going to marry Pete, she better be able to handle it," Lynn said.

When the contest began, Sarah was a "squirter" to spray water on the guys who individually got up and danced, stripping to their shorts. I was too embarrassed to watch, so I hung back by the pool tables and wound up talking to a guy who'd been with Matt on the *Moonlight* when Matthew got meningitis.

"You don't know how hard your old man was trying to get home that night, the wind blowing him back every time. And then when we had to turn back to

Alitak, I thought he'd break from nerves, stuck waiting out the weather. I felt real bad for him. But your little guy turned out okay?"

"Yes, he's fine now, tearing the house apart."

"Well, that's good. You want to hang on to those little critters. 'Nother time, I got launched overboard in a crab pot."

"You mean over the side in the water?"

"Yeah. See, I'd been crawling in it getting the last of the crab out and setting the new bait in, but I took too long and next thing I knew, I was floatin'."

"Actually underwater?"

"Oh yeah, plenty cold and wet."

"How'd you get out?"

"Well, they saw right away what had happened so they were bringing the pot back up on deck and you'd better believe I was working my way out of that pot."

"Weren't you overwhelmed with fear?"

"Nah, even then, underwater and all, I knew I couldn't panic, even if I was gonna be dead in a minute."

Karen came up to me. "Hey, they're saying the guys are gonna crash our party. I knew they wouldn't have fun last night. Everybody's broke before salmon season starts."

"Well, they better not, this is the one night when everybody's single; nobody's husband is running interference."

"Or giving a ration of shit—yeah, I'm with you," Karen said.

The contest ended about three in the morning and Karen, Sarah, Lynn, and I were still there, so we took a taxi back down Mission Road to the Mecca.

About seven they chased us out and we walked over to Karen and Scott's place across from the Russian Church. Scott was asleep on the sofa, the TV set blaring at him.

"What the hell are you doing, Karen? It's almost noon and you come screaming in here like a bunch of banshees."

"Oh, shut up and go back to sleep. You're just jealous 'cause we had a great time and stayed out all night and you guys ran out of money before midnight!"

"Nora, where's Matt? Your old man gonna be in for the wedding? Salmon hasn't started yet."

"Matt's fixing up the *Ocean Mistress* in Seattle. He won't make it back in time for the wedding."

"Oh, too bad—he'll miss out on all the fun."

"Yes." *And he's so resentful of the fun I have with others, especially if any men are involved, but he's never around to be included, or if he is, he distances himself with work or superiority.*

Sarah and Pete's wedding took place in the little wooden church. I felt like a lost soul at the reception, though Karen called me over to sit with them. The parish priest was on vacation, so the priest from the Coast Guard base was standing in. Lynn was asking him about his duties, and he said he had to conduct way too many funerals for fishermen.

"Those ships sink because of one thing—greed. They either stack the pots too high, or fudge on maintenance, or ignore danger signals, because they're driven to make the gamble pay. Most fishermen are pretty desperate creatures."

Gramma Inga was dancing and having the time of her life with Scott, who was flattering her and flirting with her, calling her "my little Norwegian song bird." Everybody laughed about it, yet I sensed how, beneath the laughter, Gramma Inga loved dancing again, and the male attention, being treated as a sought-after female.

Robin said, "I really don't know how you do it, Nora. You're so strong and independent. I know I couldn't stand my husband gone all the time and my family not around and having to take care of everything on my own. How do you do it?"

Do I tell her how much I cry, how trapped I feel, how much I hate it, or do I let her say I must be quite a strong person. What does strong mean? What's strength, what's bitterness?

Some of the guys who played musical instruments brought them out and started singing. I was shocked when they sang "Cocaine." It seemed like such a slap in the face to the old people there. I don't know. Sarah came up to me and said, "Pete bought some cocaine; we've been sniffing it all day, want some?"

I declined and thought how sad and sort of sacrilegious to go through your wedding day and exchange vows and the rest of it, high on cocaine.

The next week I had that "Is that all there is?" feeling. I came home from church on Sunday, all dressed up and wanting to visit or do something to keep the day going past noon.

Then Matthew burned his arm on the iron and was howling. Liam lost the car keys, so I had him looking around the car for them. "Don't tell me you can't find them. You just keep looking till you do find them," I screamed at him while I sat on the front step holding Matthew, bawling his head off.

Sarah drove up and said, "Smile, Nora!" and I felt like throwing Matthew at her.

"What's wrong?" she said when she walked in.

"I hate my life! Everything's gone wrong this morning."

Sarah helped Liam find the keys and then she said, "Come on, Nora, Pete and I are going on a hike up to Cascade Lake. Come with us, we can help you with the kids."

We spent all day climbing through the tide flats and up the mountains and through the bush to Cascade Lake. It was beautiful, so serene and natural, no sign of man around. This is what people think life is like all the time when they move to Alaska.

Leanne and Karen and I took a field trip with the kids out to McAllister's Chicken Ranch. Nick McAllister's dad was showing us around all the hen houses and chicken coops with their six-foot-tall chicken wire fences, when he noticed a bunch of roosters had gotten out through a hole under the fence.

"Those goddam chickens!" he said. "Goddam it! I spend half my goddam life chasing those goddam feathered animals and goddam it, they dig holes and run off the goddam countryside!"

Leanne and I rolled our eyes madly at each other and the kids stood motionless, kind of shocked by McAllister's unbridled swearing. It reached a point where it was ridiculous to be shocked or offended. "Those goddam chickens!" I said, shaking my head with a grin.

"Where could those goddam birds be?" Leanne asked me, and then looked at the kids.

Liam was the first to seize the opportunity. He squatted down to the hole in the fence. "Hey, you goddam chickens!"

Soon we were all chanting like profane monks, having a grand old time marching around the chicken farm, swearing and laughing at the top of our lungs. Then I bumped my head on a low-lying beam. "God damn it!" I said in earnest.

"Now this sounds serious. Dad, you got customers complaining?" I stood up from my bashed-head crouch and stared up into Nick McAllister's blue eyes. "Oh, it's the children's crusade! You okay, Nora?" He put his hand under my arm, laughing.

"Oh yeah, Nick, I'm okay, just bumped the hell out of my head. We were kind of taking advantage of the atmosphere here...."

"You mean Dad's choice vocabulary?"

"Well, yeah, the kids are loving it, being so bad."

"It appears to me you're having the best time of anybody."

"Well, yeah, I am."

"It agrees with you, brings out your dimples. You should laugh more often."

The kids swarmed around then and we regrouped to leave. Nick said, "Next time we lose some poultry, we'll know who to call," and went off with his dad. I felt great, even with my throbbing head, and the kids faces' were glowing with defiant dirty joy.

For the Fourth of July, my friends held a huge picnic on Long Island. We all loaded up on Karen and Scott's boat for the hour-long boat ride out there.

Just as we hit the beach, a plane came buzzing down toward the water and flew almost at deck level between two boats.

"That's Eric Oleson—he's got more money than sense," Robin said. "He sold his sense for coke, and lost his wife in the bargain."

"You mean they just built that big beautiful house and she left?"

"Yeah," said Robin, "ran off with the carpenter because he talked to her."

"Who's the carpenter?"

"John Blanchette, you know him?"

"No. I thought maybe you meant Fred Nelson, he's the only carpenter I know of."

"Oh, Fred's got his hands full. Pam's been sick and they don't know what it is. She's just exhausted all the time and can't get out of bed all day and they don't know why, so Fred is doing all the housework and looking after the kids as well as his carpentry work."

"'I would love to pull that one off, if Matt would just come home and look after things and let me be too tired to get out of bed."

I'd made a huge pan of barbecued chicken, and set it down on a blanket with all the other food. Matthew just planted himself next to it and ate chicken all day. Everyone was laughing at him.

I hadn't seen Liam for awhile and so I looked all over for him, on the beach and in the grass and by the boats and finally I came up behind him, sitting on a log by his little round-headed self, looking out at the water and the horizon. "Whatcha doing, my little boy?" I asked.

"Waiting for Daddy to come," he said in a matter-of-fact voice.

"Oh, honey," I said with a sinking feeling, "I don't think Daddy can come. I wish he were here, too, but he's fishing."

"Why can't he come? Scott's here and Pete's here and Neil's here—maybe he can come, too."

When we came back to the main picnic area, there was Matthew, his mouth full of chicken, drumsticks in both hands and barbecue sauce all over his face.

Karen was getting drunk. I could tell because I could hear her voice clear across the beach. I walked over to the log where she was fussing over Michael.

She was wearing overalls and had stuffed a beer bottle in the front pocket on the bib. "Look at you, Michael, you're just a mess," and when she leaned over to wipe his face, the beer spilled out of the bottle and onto Michael's head. Everyone just roared.

"'Yes, Michael, you're such a mess. Let super mother Karen clean you up with a little beer!" Scott laughed. "Sweetheart, you're such a slob."

After we got back to town and tied the boat up at the dock, Karen invited everyone up to her house for fireworks. But I was just too beat, and I worried about the firecrackers scaring Goldie back at home, so I took the kids home.

Another drifting, nothing summer day. Karen brought Michael and a six-pack over and we sat on the front steps drinking beer. Karen said she and Robin and Sarah made lemonade and cookies and took them out to Bells Flats where the guys were all working on their shrimp gear. It seems so simple for them to do fun things—all these guys are friends, all their wives are friends, and it just all falls into place to stop work for cookies and lemonade. Matt being a loner makes me a loner, too.

I got a letter from him and he wrote, "I'm going to make this all up to you." It meant so much to me and I was all excited to tell Karen.

"I wonder what he has in mind?"

"Probably bed," she said.

"But bed would be for him, too. No, he means something more than that, for leaving me alone so much."

"Don't count on it," Karen said

Another night sitting here crying and hurting and all the people from the Beachcombers yelling and laughing outside. And tomorrow it'll just be more keeping on keeping on, keeping my voice from screaming, keeping from hating everybody who's happy or at least together. I just can't wait anymore. My babies can't wait.

Later that week I woke up to the sound of someone hammering on the back door at 4:30. It was Doug Bradley.

"Doug, what are you doing here?"

"Hey, I just got off the *Wet Willie* and got my settlement."

"You're fishing again? Does Matt know?"

"Ah, I came up in the middle of the season, had to make some money and get out of Seattle. Now I'm getting ready to go home, but first I gotta see Eleanor and her little babies."

"I didn't even know you were up here fishing. Well, come on in."

He went into the living room and sprawled on the sofa. Chelsea came pattering out of her bedroom and I pulled her on my lap. "Remember Doug?" I said to her. "So how long have you been on the *Wet Willie?* Matt's still out with the *Ocean Mistress.*"

"Yeah, I know. I heard him on the radio. Yeah, I came up here about a month ago and got right on. Needed money pretty bad and we kept pretty close to shore, so I guess my number's not up yet. You're looking good, Eleanor."

"Oh yeah, are my eyes open yet? Shall I make you a cup of tea?" I sat Chelsea in the rocker and went into the kitchen to make tea. Then I brought it back out to the living room.

"Ya got any Jack Daniels to put in it?"

"Oh God, Doug, yuk!"

"You getting too good to drink with an old friend?"

"No, Doug, but I have to function in the morning."

"Yeah, I'd like to function with you all right."

"Shall I call up a taxi for you?"

"No! God, Eleanor, can't you take a little shit off me? You used to think I was all right."

"I've always thought you were a friend, Doug."

"Well, all right then. Calm down, don't be so uptight."

Then Babe woke up and I went to change him and brought him out and made him a bottle and rocked him till he went back to sleep, Chelsea snuggled up on the loveseat next to my rocker with her blanket up to her face. "Okay, Doug, I'm getting everybody back to bed. You can sleep it off on the sofa if you want."

Doug lurched up from the sofa and staggered over to where Chelsea was. "Can I sleep with this little girl?"

I wish I'd kicked him out then, but I picked her up and said, "No, she's sleeping with me." When I got to the end of the hall I looked back and saw Doug already passed out on the sofa.

We all woke up again about three hours later and I was running around getting the kids dressed and making breakfast with jump-rope jingles playing on the record player. Doug woke up and lumbered into the kitchen. "Shit, it's really wild around here. My head's exploding. Hey Eleanor, would you give me a ride to the cannery? I don't know what happened to my wallet."

"Sure, Doug. C'mon kids, let's take Doug into town. Hurry up now, he's got to get going fast."

Matt got in a week later. Before we'd said more than "How're ya doing?" Chelsea piped up. "Daddy, Doug stayed overnight at our house."

Matt looked at me so cold I felt like a huge dirty wave had washed over me. "Hey, Chelsea, I just filled the tub. Why don't you jump in and I'll come get you in a little bit?" I said.

After she bopped off, I said to Matt, "Yeah, Doug came here dead drunk after getting his settlement. I let him in and then he passed out on the sofa a little while later."

"Well, that's a great story, Eleanor. I think it's great when a man comes home after working the whole goddam summer to find out his wife's making herself available to anybody in pants that comes knocking at the door." He picked up the silver box on the counter that I'd gotten from my grandmother and slammed it down so hard it collapsed under his fist.

"Matt, that's so unfair and mean! Here I am, so relieved that at last you're home, and you're blaming me for the fact that your friend comes knocking at the door and imposes on my hospitality."

"Your hospitality? You always have a grand word for your schemes, don't you?"

"Is it a scheme to invite old friends in when they come knocking at my door in the middle of the night? Is it a scheme to be juggling babies and running a hotel and taxi service for your drunk friends? If I wanted to scheme, I could do a lot better than that!"

"Oh, you could do a lot better! Then why don't you, instead of whining to me every time I walk through the door?"

"You don't understand me at all! And you have no idea of what I want, certainly not a drunk irresponsible loser like Doug. Why can't you come to me and say, 'I'm so lucky to know that you're keeping our home together when I'm out fishing, you make me so proud.' But no, you just want to accuse and blame. If you're so fucking insecure, why don't you just stay home and watch me like a hawk?"

"You just can't handle being a fisherman's wife and are out to get anyone who supports me."

"Right. That's why we moved to Kodiak. That's why I never knew for sure if you'd be with me when the kids were born, why we bought a boat instead of a house."

"Eleanor, you've really got to grow up and learn to go with the flow."

I couldn't let the blood boil in my throat. I had to control myself. I wanted to be like Jane Eyre and say exactly how I felt in a way that couldn't be misunderstood, but also wouldn't make Matt hate me even more.

"What is the flow, Matt? Am I being super-sensitive, or missing some connection? Have I hurt your feelings and you're trying to get back at me? Or would you just prefer not to have to deal with me? How can you just accuse me of cheating on you?"

I was sitting on the sofa with my elbows in my stomach, curled over myself.

"Doug and I have been through a lot together; I saved his life. You've always been jealous of our friendship, always throwing your little scenes, and now you're out to destroy it. Well, it won't work Eleanor. He'll always stand by me. You've stood in my way of getting a boat and now that I've finally got one, you can't stand not being the center of attention."

I looked at him. There was a cold wall of distance behind his eyes.

God, he really hates me. I'd been so sure he was crazy about me. I was wrong.

I looked in the mirror. I couldn't clear the hurt expression from my face. I sat down again on the bed.

The worst has happened. Matt wronged me. I thought about keeping Matt from the things that he loves. Well, we're married, for better or worse. Is it my fault things get worse and worse? Doesn't he want a family? Does he think he doesn't want us because it's all so troublesome?

Matt stormed out the door. I turned around and there stood Chelsea.

I thought we could get to the truth. To Matt, it wasn't a matter of clearing up a misunderstanding. It was a matter of dealing with someone he wants to mistrust. I thought we would clear the air of the sniping and innuendoes. Instead it's still all ugly.

I know I never did anything so bad to deserve to feel like this, so why do I have to? Why do I always have to be left alone while other women are raising their kids or building houses or enjoying life with the men they love and all I ever get to do is miss him?

There's no way I could explain to Matt what this past summer has been like, that we don't have a life together to share. I can't accept the idea of living our "marriage" apart and alone like this, but I can't accept the idea of leaving him either. This is driving me crazy. Why can't I just give up on it? Oh Jesus, this hurts me—there's no way it can be right to hurt this bad for this long.

CHAPTER FIFTEEN

THE FAMILY TUMBLES
In which my world collapses; Matt retreats to the Bering Sea

Matt was busy putting tendering gear away and rigging the boat for crab. One night around midnight the phone rang. Matt's mom called to say his dad had gone to the hospital with a suspected heart attack.

"Are you going to go down, Matt?"

"I'm going to wait and see what's going on. Maybe he'll be okay. They're going to do tests."

I knew his mom wanted him down there for her and his dad, but Matt hadn't seen his own kids in three months, either.

My better nature says that Matt should be with his parents, but my selfish side is gratified to see that he can't be there for them, either, if he's out fishing. Let them see how good it feels to support Matt's fishing—the name of our religion.

Whenever the phone rang, I felt bad news storming our way. The doctors had discovered that Matt's dad had cancer—three spots on his lungs. He was having surgery. His heart was in bad shape, too, but they felt it could withstand surgery.

"Mom says all these people are coming to the hospital, asking him how he is, telling him he looks great when he feels terrible. Why don't they just leave him alone?"

I knew I couldn't explain other peoples' motivation to Matt, their desire to just be there for someone they cared about who was hurting. I got a book from the library about cancer.

"Matt, it says here that all the family can do is try to make him comfortable and to let him know he's not alone. Maybe you should read this."

Read this. That's the best I can do for my husband and for my children's only grandfather—suggest books to read, and stay out of it.

More phone calls from Gramma and Peggy saying Grampa had survived the surgery and what the odds and percentages were, medical mumbo-jumbo. Sloop came over while Matt was on the phone and I asked him how his brother Frank was doing. Sloop looked dejected and said, "Not good, he shouldn't be up here working and he's not doing what he's supposed to do to take care of himself, and now he's gone and hurt himself. I tried to get him to fly home and now he says maybe he'll leave tomorrow. If I can get a reservation for tomorrow. I had a reservation for today, but he wouldn't leave today."

"Oh Sloop, I'm so sorry. It's so hard to feel responsible for someone who won't feel responsible for himself."

And he said, in his painfully slow way of talking, "Yeah…well…I'm…I'm just mad at him now."

When Matt got off the phone and started talking about fishing, Sloop was telling him how much he's in debt. "I just can't quit. Frank tells me our skiff's no good and we ought to just quit, and I know it's no good but it's all I've got and I can't quit."

"Yeah, I'm trying to figure out how long I can stay in Seattle before king crab starts. It might not even be worth it to fish around Kodiak."

When Don left, I asked Matt, "You wouldn't go out to Dutch Harbor again, would you?" To me, Dutch Harbor meant three months away and always the dread of another injury.

"No, Dutch Harbor's not supposed to be good this year, either. I'm looking at the Pribiloffs."

"The Pribiloffs! They're beyond Dutch, almost in Russia—you can't do that!"

"I've got to keep the boat working, Eleanor. I've got a $100,000 payment to make next year."

"Yeah, but you might as well get Russian citizenship. You can't go to the Pribiloffs, Matt. It's just too extreme."

I sounded so reasonable, so matter-of-fact, like it was all settled.

He didn't say anything, and I knew he was thinking, "Better not tell her what I'm planning," so I said, "Matt, we have to make these decision together, and there's no way I'm going to accept you going to the Pribiloffs."

He didn't say anything, and I felt like a defiant mouse facing a wildcat poised to spring.

Later that night Sloopy Don pulled up to the house again. "God, I finally got Frank on the plane out of here. You guys up for a couple of drinks downtown?"

"I've got to get the early morning flight out of here," Matt said.

"Well, just a couple then. Nora, you coming, too?" Sloop asked.

"No, I'd have to line up a babysitter. You guys go ahead."

"Get a sitter then, you want to send your old man off, don't you?"

"Well, okay then, I will."

At the Mecca, Darrell, one of Matt's deckhands, joined us. Matt grumbled under his breath, "First he screws up tendering and then we have to babysit him at the bar."

I looked around, but no one had heard Matt in the noise.

Darrell had already been drinking and was really snide and belligerent, and I could tell he was getting under Matt's skin. It was so obvious. Darrell was acting like a jerk, but I kind of liked hearing him give Matt lip.

Matt finally told him, "Why don't you either shut up or take a hike?"

Darrell said, "Oh, yeah. The big captain speaks. Well, this isn't your boat, Hunter, and I can say whatever I want." My blood raced at his words and I secretly cheered for him.

They both jumped up and Matt hit him. Darrell was stunned and staggered back, and then came charging. Matt just kind of shook him off. Darrell was uncoordinated from the booze and he just buffaloed off through the dark crowd.

After Matt got to Seattle, I called him up on the phone to ask how things were going.

"It's really bad, Eleanor. The cancer's spread. He's really sick. They can't do any more surgery. Mom and Peggy are just losing it."

He told me about conferences with doctors and specialists and social workers who gave him a lot of percentage figures and treatment options—surgery, radiation, chemotherapy—and nursing home and hospice referrals.

"Matt, I'm so sorry. Is there anything I can do up here?"

"No, there's nothing I can do down here. Are they meeting to settle on a crab price?"

"You mean the fishermen and canneries?"

"Yeah."

"They're having a meeting tonight. Matt, what will you do if the strike breaks?"

"I don't know. I have to fish. I'd have to leave."

Poor sad old fisherman.

Meanwhile, I was getting Chelsea ready to start kindergarten. *This should be her happy time, it isn't her fault Matt hates me and his dad is dying.* I got her ready and the brothers up and took pictures of her in her new school clothes and polka-dot umbrella and the boys in their pajamas in the front yard before the school bus came.

The strike settled. Matt called and said he'd told his dad he would have to go and Grampa had said, "I know," and Matt flew home. Peggy called and said Grampa died while Matt's plane was in the air. I sat on my bed and looked out the little window at the gloomy stormy waters of the channel. It felt like those dead-God Good Fridays of my childhood. Poor, poor Matt.

We all went to pick him up at the airport. Before I said anything to him, Matt said, "I know. He's gone."

When we got home Matt kicked a footstool across the living room and went back to the bedroom. I followed him and put my arms around him and said, "Matt, he was a good father and you were a good son, and now you will be a good father."

Matt accepted my hug and then turned his back on me.

With the kids babbling, it wasn't so noticeable that we weren't talking to each other. People who heard about Matt's dad called to say they were sorry. The next few mornings, Matt would go down to the boat and work until dinner. One night he took Chelsea and Liam down to the boat while he messed around; the next night he took them out for ice cream.

Meanwhile, we weren't speaking to each other or looking at each other. It was only when Sloop came over that I learned Matt did plan on going out to the Pribiloffs in October. I realized that even though the season might only last a month, with the time getting out there and back and waiting for crab season to open, the earliest he would be back was late November.

I can't believe he would go with all this anger between us and nothing settled. I'll just be swallowing tears till Thanksgiving. What's the answer? Treat Matt like he treats me? He's not going to make me live my life without joy and kindness just because he does. But I can't protect him from himself. He's going to cut his own heart out just like he's cut out mine.

But for me, maybe with my fire, my piano, my kids, my home, and my view, maybe I can be a Mountain Mama, wearing long skirts, making fires, telling stories, singing songs. Mother Comfort, Mother Courage.

I got up early. It seemed calm after blowing hard all night, and the sun was shining.

Karen came over. I couldn't let her know what disaster had descended on my life. I told her Matt was broken up about his dad's death and I was unable to reach him.

"What are you going to do while Matt's out fishing this fall?"

"I'd like to take the hula dancing class at the college, but I wonder if I'll have time to do it. I think I'd better anyway. I've got to get moving. Karen, do you notice something weird about Matthew's eyes?"

"What do you mean?"

"Just look at him and tell me."

"Come here, Matt-baby," she called and put him on her lap. "So Matthew, what are you going to be when you grown up?"

"A blue tiger-tamer."

"A tiger-tamer! How come blue tigers?"

"'Cause de're da mean ones."

"Are they mean to you?"

"Yeah, I'm scared a dem."

"Well, I bet they'll be scared of you all right, when you start taming them." She hugged him and laughed and set him down and he ran off. "Are you talking about his eyes crossing?"

"You can see that, too? Oh heck, I was hoping it was just me. It's not, huh?"

"They can fix that. You just have to take him in to see the eye doctor."

"Not the optometrist, he's just for glasses. I don't even think there is an opthamalogist here in town."

"No, but I think one flies in once a month from Anchorage."

"Oh, I just hate this."

"I know, he's got such beautiful eyes and he's such a sweetie—a blue tiger-tamer! They sure keep you entertained."

"Yeah, entertained, that's the word for it," and we laughed. It felt so good, and I realized I hadn't laughed or felt light-hearted in a long time.

Karen said, "There's always something to laugh about—that's what gets me through."

"Everyone thinks Matt is so mellow and good-natured, and I'm so uptight."

"That's not true! I was talking to the guys who came back from Alitak on the boat with Matt, and they said he was a real grouch."

"Really?" I went over to her chair and pulled her up and made her dance around the kitchen with me. "It's not just me?"

When Karen sat back down again, I said, "I don't know what I'm going to do. I'm just hoping someday he'll come home, his arms full of roses, and tell me how horribly sorry he is, and say 'I owe you an apology and I wouldn't blame you if you didn't accept it.'"

Karen sputtered, "But you've stood by Matt! Nora, he's not supposed to reject you!"

"I can't make him come to me for comfort if he doesn't want to."

"For all the fights Scott and I have had, when things get really bad, we have each other. We both know that."

"I wish we did, Karen. I don't know how to inspire that belief."

And I thought of Captain Fog with all his advantages and head starts and how I'd always thought Matt was so much better than Scott—but Scott trusted Karen.

She was still talking. "You just have to fuck him—I mean, take the high road. You can't let him beat you down. He's wrong. Someday he'll see how wrong. You just play the waiting game, kill him with kindness."

I remembered Mom's casual remark, "It seems like we're always waiting for something," and I thought how degrading and back-of-the-bus it is to always be standing in line for justice. And then the possibility that justice will never come no matter how long you wait. I felt hopeless.

Matt can stay away forever. If he doesn't want to come home, I don't want him. We don't need a man that gives us the scraps of his time and thoughts left over from his real dream. If he doesn't love us, I hate him. Poor little kids. I just know one thing anyway in all my sad confusion—this kind of loneliness isn't right for them to live in.

The kids love him, though, and so I guess that's the final toss of the dice. Can't say I do anymore, though. He's always grumpy and cold, materialistic and shortsighted, disrespectful to me. Wish I could just ignore him.

A year by the fire—I'm going to see what a winter by myself, just making a fire every night, will produce.

So I got two cords of mill ends, scrap wood that's gotten pretty wet already, and a cord of bigger wood—alder?—that's in the shed and should be getting dry now. Our fireplace doesn't really put out, but it's the making, the tending of the fire, that I like. Matt hates. Never once in this house has he had the patience to get a fire going.

Matt was going to go downtown to celebrate Leo Davidoff's birthday and for once I was ready to let him hoot at the moon, bond with his friends, whatever.

First Matt took Liam down to the boat with him, and I put on the black sexy dress I bought before we were married and my feather choker, put my hair up and make-up on and my black high heels and perfume.

When Matt came back from the boat he said, "What are you getting all dolled up for?"

"I just wanted to."

So Matt stayed home. I could tell he wished we were talking. I started the fire from trash and old kindling and it caught on with almost no trouble and I just kept building it up till, by the time the kids went to bed, I had the fire roaring.

CHAPTER SIXTEEN

THE BERING SEA TAKES MY CHRISTMAS
In which we are abandoned

Matt finally said, "Well, are we going to talk or not?"

I said, "If we start talking here, we'll start screaming."

So we went down to the Kodiak Inn, where we had to keep our voices down.

Matt ordered drinks and then told me, "I have to go out fishing."

I said, "This isn't about fishing, or what you do, or even about you being gone. It's about respect and trust and knowing each other and helping each other. You have to help me by believing in me, appreciating me, honoring me. Then you'll understand your priorities more clearly."

He smirked. "Oh, come on, Eleanor, this isn't some fairy tale. Besides, when do you honor me, appreciate me?"

"Do you really believe I'm unfaithful to you?"

"Well, you bitch all the time about being lonely. What am I supposed to think when Bradley tells me you come on to him? That he's lying?"

"It's you I want, that I'm lonely for. You're my mate, the father of my children. Bradley's a mean, irresponsible drunk. Don't you think I have any pride at all?"

"I don't know what you're capable of, but I saved Bradley's life. He's not going to lie to me."

"But I would?"

"I don't know."

"Matt, I moved up here. I've had my kids here, made my home here. We wait for you to come home and enjoy it, but all we are to you is a supply station and a banking stop. You're more to us than the money you bring home. We have to come to an understanding about where the kids and I fit in your life."

Matt was silent for a long time, looking out the window at the boats in the harbor and I thought he was mulling over what I'd said, formulating a solution or an apology.

Finally he looked at me and said, "Do you know, if we were sitting in Dutch Harbor, every one of those boats would be worth a million dollars?"

Roaming through the fabric store, I found some beautiful plaid flannel. I fingered the rich, sturdy, dark colors of red, green, and blue, and rubbed the comforting feel of the bolts of material with the palm of my hand. It came to me to make a quilt for Matt to have on the boat, instead of the rough Mexican blankets we'd bought on our honeymoon. The blankets were stiff and scratchy, harsh-colored yellow and orange.

Something in me still says, "You belong to me. Whatever happens, you're my responsibility, my destiny." There's nothing I can say to gain Matt's loyalty, but I can make a quilt for him, a talisman to protect him. My pride won't let me defend myself, but I want to do something honest and loving. I'm supposed to take care of him, not as a mother, but as a mate.

The pattern I used for Matt's quilt was simple: two triangles forming a square. One triangle would be of forest green corduroy, the other of midnight blue cotton-velvet, backed by the blue plaid flannel with a double border of the green and red plaids, with a thick layer of cloud-like washable filling inside.

As I cut the triangles out, careful that the nap was running smooth, in the same direction, I felt involved in a ritual that was almost religious.

I don't understand, I can't forgive, but I love like a quilt over all. Not a fancy one that will make me resent the unrequited time and care in the making, but a solid, straightforward quilt that Matt can casually say his wife made for him to keep him warm. I want him to wrap up warm in my quilt if he can't wrap himself in my love.

I won't think about it much, I'll just get the corduroy running straight and embroider charms into it.

I signed up for the hula classes at the community center. The only students were another fisherman's wife and myself, taught by a 300-pound Polynesian woman. The room was completely bare, except for the grey tweedy carpet and the narrow, foot-wide ribbon of window at waist height that showed the grey-green, mossy, wet Alaskan forest outside. We were barefoot and loose-clothed, wearing flowing skirts. Evalani played her Hawaiian records and positioned us. "Knees bent, shoulders still," she'd tell us. "Do like me. Bigger."

Then we'd just imitate her to the music. She'd dance in front of us and I'd hypnotize myself, watching her enormous figure sway and glide across the room. Occasionally she'd look back over her shoulder and smile impishly, encouragingly at us.

Evalani translated the Hawaiian words of the music for us:

Look at me
Look at me, lover
My hips, my breasts, my eyes, all saying
I exist to love you
Talk about sublimation!

I sewed the forest green and deep-sea blue triangles into squares and embroidered four red symbols in the patchwork—a tree for steadfast growth, an anchor for hope, a star for inspiration, and a heart for love.

I was doing my hula dance for the kids when Matt drove up so I quickly shut the tape recorder off and carefully picked up the quilt squares and stacked them in order before I hid them away.

Matt left the following Sunday.

I finished his quilt the day before he left. I went down to the boat before hula class, first stopping at the marine store where I spent my getaway savings of $350 to buy an emergency transmitter beacon. I crept on board the boat like a stowaway and wrapped up the transmitter in the quilt and left them on Matt's bunk.

I had a hard time wording the note. I didn't want it to be a request or an apology or a phony sentiment, so finally I just wrote, "Keep you warm" like in Aleut syntax. Is it a wish or is it a command or both?

The next night, when Matt called a taxi to take him down to the boat harbor, I said, "I'll drive you down."

"No, you won't even sleep with me."

He nervously watched for the cab, checking his bags to make sure he didn't forget anything.

'Oh, how can you go?' I silently pleaded. 'Please believe me. Please turn around and love me.'

Liam and Matthew bumped their heads and started hollering bloody murder just as the cab pulled into our driveway and tooted the horn. I stood empty-handed in the kitchen, with Chelsea bopping around me with a bright, unnatural smile. "Bye, Daddy." Matt picked up each of the kids and kissed them good-by, Matthew still sniffling.

Then he came up to me and grabbed my forearms, but that was all we could do. We both turned our heads and muttered, "Good-bye."

After Matt left, I went for a walk with the kids down Mission Road, looking out towards the channel. As we approached the old rabbit hutch house, I knocked on the door and a pretty blond girl answered.

"Hello, my name is Nora Hunter. I used to live here when I first came to Kodiak. I was just walking by and thought I'd say hi."

To my chagrin, she brushed her cheek with one hand as if dismissing tears. "Oh, I'm Catherine. Would you like to come in?"

It was strange enough to be back in the little shack again, but I was floored to see the pictures she had on her fridge, the little fridge that was shorter than me. The pictures were the exact same ones I had cut out of magazines and taped on the cupboard doors at home—women in Victorian dresses leaning out over flowered windowsills; a girl wading into the ocean with a shell up to her ear; a man and a woman embracing under a quilt on a hearth in front of a blazing fire.

While Catherine and I stood in front of the old oil stove, the kids left us to look around. Five steps in each direction and the whole house had been explored. "Do you have any children?" I asked.

"No, no, I'm...well, I'm single. Are these all your kids?" She seemed so flustered.

"Yes, but we just had my little girl when we lived here. Well, we're in danger of overrunning you, so I think we'd better be on our way. Thank you for inviting us in. Please come and visit me, we live just down the road, the first trailer past the Beachcombers."

I didn't make a fire that night and the next night I tried half-heartedly to make one with trash instead of newspaper and wood.

"Oh darn it, why can't I get it to go?" I sighed.

Liam stood at my elbow. "I'll go outside and get more wood, and look at the moon in the water."

I pulled him to me and kissed him. "Oh, sweet baby, maybe you're a natural moongazer like my daddy was."

The weather was wild after Matt left. I called Scott to see if he'd heard Matt on the radio. Scott said, "Matt pretty much disappears out there. Nobody ever hears from him."

Finally I called the radio operator who broadcasts the marine forecast to the fishermen. "I was wondering if you could contact my husband's boat and see if he's okay?"

"Do you know his call letters?"

"No."

"How about what frequencies does he use?"

"I don't know," I said, and felt hot with shame.

She called back the next morning and said, "I finally heard from him, he'd gone into Sand Point when the storm was brewing, but now he's underway again."

"Oh, thank you for checking for me."

"By the way, his call letters are QRJ392, and he stands by on 1250."

"Okay, I've got that written down."

A few days later Catherine came over after naps, and when we sat down to a mug of tea, she said, "I'd been crying and upset just before you knocked on my door the other day. You see, my husband died a year ago in a car accident. I was a little overwhelmed with the memory of it all."

"I'm so sorry. My first husband died in a car accident, too, so maybe I know how you feel. It's such a horrible shock."

"Yes, at first it is, and then the pain sets in and won't go away. You wonder what life holds for you anymore. I work part-time at the health food store and come home and sleep and watch TV and wonder how to get going again, how to live for just myself."

I was struck by the similarities in our lives. Her obvious discomfort at living unnerved me. All I could think of to console her was something totally off the subject of death.

"I was almost named Catherine till my dad decided against it at the last minute. It sounds like we have lots in common, and you know, someday life will change. Things will get better."

"I believe that, but grief takes so much longer than people think it should. Most days I just want to die and be with him, and nobody wants to be around you when you feel that way. Luckily, nobody *has* to be around me, so I just retreat into my little cocoon."

"I know how you feel, but if you ever just want to get out, do something, or sit around with someone else, I'm always here."

"I didn't even ask about you? Where's your husband? Out fishing, or are you alone?"

"Yes, he's out fishing in the Bering Sea now till around Christmas."

I dreamed last night that Ted Bundy was after me. I ran home and was struggling to shut the door and lock it. But he was pushing against it, forcing his way inside to hurt us. I woke up, startled, frightened. I thought sure I heard someone say "Shh—she's up." So I got the gun and went in the living room and cocked the trigger and said, "Who's there?"

Liam said from his bedroom, "It's just us, Mommy," so then I had to find a way to uncock the gun, and not knowing how, decided I should fire it out the door at a tree. But when I did, there was no bullet in the chamber. I checked the kids, all sound asleep again and safe in this flimsy trailer in Alaska where the wind howls, murderers haunt my dreams, and I roam my household with a useless weapon.

In the morning I woke up to hear Chelsea muttering, "One more day till Halloween and I can't wait." I got as excited and tired as the kids going out trick or treating. I dressed up in velour pajamas, hot pink and navy blue striped, and painted circles on my face with lipstick and eye shadow and went as the Cheshire

Cat, grinning madly. We knocked at the house two doors down and a man opened the door and hissed, "Get out of here." My face started to itch under the makeup and the kids got cold and tired.

The day after Halloween I got up, determined not to get depressed. The morning went slow, the house was a mess, and I had to scream to get it picked up. Then we went over to Karen's, where she greeted us with, "Did you hear the *Sea Spray* sank last night? That's the boat Pete was on."

"Is he okay? Does Sarah know?" The kids gravitated toward the TV set, which Karen had already turned to *Sesame Street*.

"Yeah, they're all back in town, the *Seeker* brought them in a couple of hours ago. Halloween night vibes." She shivered as she sat down at the table and reached out to hold Matthew. "Hi there, little Sven. This kid should be my baby, with his blond hair and blue eyes and husky little build. You look like a Scandahoovian, buddy."

"So what happened on Pete's boat?"

"They started taking on water—maybe someone left the lazarette open."

"What's the lazarette?"

"You still don't know? Doesn't Matt talk to you at all? It's that opening to the hold, like a drain at the bow. Anyway, if that's left open, the hold fills up with water and down she goes."

"God, scary."

"At least we have the satisfaction of knowing our worries are real worries and not what color to paint the bathroom."

So, a boat sinks, a plane crashes. You don't know today if you'll be here tomorrow. Have you lived the life you wanted, that you were meant to, or are you waiting to put it into motion until you have advance notice you're going to die and had better make each day count?

It turned out okay, nobody was hurt—maybe a fortune lost, but that's what fortunes are for, to be won and lost. It's just a thing, an event, not a historical marker, like "before my husband died."

A way to observe Halloween. Nobody's Christmas will be ruined, nobody's family is torn apart. This time the sea was satisfied with just a boat, no souls lost, at sea or back home.

We're so untouched if no one is lost, just a brief sigh of relief, but if someone dies, everything's changed for everyone who remotely knows that person. You'll just never see that person again.

After I drove Chelsea to kindergarten in the rain, I cried all the way to the post office, where I discovered I'd left my key at home so I couldn't even get the mail. So I went to the store, bought a *New York Times* and a box of cappuccino, and was going to buy whiskey and drink my blues away in the afternoon, but I forgot to buy the whiskey. Liam had his eyes on me the whole time as I cried, but he didn't dare say anything.

I knew in the back of my mind there was some reason why Matthew was not to be in the bathroom. But the little darling had climbed into the bathtub and it seemed such innocent fun. Only later did I remember about the toilet, after Liam told me they'd put a battery down it.

John Denver is singing on the radio:
> *Love is everywhere*
> *I perceive it*
> *Life is perfect*
> *I believe it*

Oh, shut up, John. A myth-making bummer day. I just took a shower and got the fire going and it smells so nice and woodsy, I can relax a little. It's real cold out tonight. Frost on the ground. I miss Matt and the old way when I still believed he loved me. I wish things could get better.

I know there are hedonists in the world. There are ski bums, beach bums, surfing bums: not so much that they're lazy bums, but that they live to indulge their passions.

I went over to Robin's house one afternoon to make jigsaw puzzles, which made me feel proud and competent. But along with the good feelings, something made me feel so blue, maybe the comparison with the past when I felt more secure and hopeful; maybe Neil coming home with a bag of shrimp and a bottle of wine for a warm dinner in the kitchen with his wife.

Chelsea said, "Mama, come quick, I have to tell you a secret. Quick before it's dawn!" and then a magical thing happened. Chelsea taught Liam how to play "Jingle Bells" on the piano, and my two little muffins in hooded sweatshirts sat together, playing "Jingle Bells" and warming my heart.

I had a beautiful dream last night where I flew in my own personal, umbrella-shaped helicopter, with flowers for propellers. Wrote a song called "The Fairweather Lover." God, to be a singer in a band! To howl at the moon and take it to the limit....

Karen invited me over for Scott's birthday party. By the time I got there, Pete and Scott had been drinking all afternoon. Sarah was glassy-eyed and Karen was loud.

Karen had heard Matt on the radio. "The *Ocean Mistress* was docked in Dutch Harbor. Did Matt call you?"

I shook my head, "Haven't heard a word from Matt. It's no big deal, he doesn't usually call." But it would have been nice to say I know what's going on. I am the captain's wife, and it would be nice to know what's happening in my life before friends tell me.

"Well, I hope he's getting crab out there, " Scott draped his arms around Karen and took a drink from his glass. "There's nothing around the island."

Pete was talking about the *Sea Spray* sinking. "I told that little weasel when he grabbed my survival suit, 'You've borrowed and used all my stuff this trip, but you're not taking my survival suit.'"

"Did he make it?" I asked.

"Oh yeah, he found another one."

"So are you looking for another job?" I asked.

"No, no more fishing for me. I'm staying home and putting Sarah to work—fooling around beats fishing. Down the lazarette." Pete saluted with his beer bottle.

"Sarah, are you still in school or are you working at the hospital now?"

"Both," she said, "I'm probably going to spend next summer in Anchorage as part of the nurses' training program."

"So you'll be a bachelorette?"

"Yeah, and hey! I heard that *Playboy* is doing a photo spread on "Girls of the Far North." Maybe I can get in it."

"Oh yeah, I can see it now," Pete groaned, opening up a magazine and pretending to unfold the middle page, "'Here, let me show you a picture of my wife.'"

Scott yelled, "Karen, change the record, and don't scratch any of my record collection!" I went with her to the bookshelves where the stereo was set up, and as Karen put a record on, I saw that she had the first two volumes of the *Tale of Genji*. I remembered when I'd read all five volumes telling of Japanese noblewomen who spent their lives writing poems, flying kites, dressing for court ceremonies—culture bums.

Back in the living room, Sarah was itching to dance but the men wouldn't get up off the sofas, so Karen came up, put one arm around me and another around Sarah, and we started dancing and singing and doing the can-can for the guys, who just sat there laughing.

It was so beautiful today, I made a fire at naptime that caught on slowly and it's just going out now, nearly midnight. The wind started up again about an hour ago.

Things won't ever be the same. No use looking back until I can do it without crying. So...dignity. It won't be any worse. It will be better. God give me wisdom. And patience? I don't think I could take any more patience.

Maybe Kubler-Ross would call it denial, but it feels like a cigarette is burning through my heart and chains go through that hole and wrap around my stomach and squeeze my solar plexus every moment of the day with an undeniable knowledge and an aching want.

My dream isn't sordid or selfish. It's right and noble—to have a family bound together by love. Matt gets his self-esteem, his applause from fishing; my stage is hidden in a trailer off Mission Road. Recognition is important. The whole town gets its Wild West identity from fishing but what about the women who are sitting at home, holding down the fort, when every night could be the showdown night between her man and nature. But if you think about it you might put it in the collective consciousness and make it happen, and there's nothing you can do about it, so why worry? Why think about the fight you had the night before he left? And when Matt gets home, he's home to touch and to care for and hold and fight with and make up to and be a part of my little empire called family.

Okay, so there you're sitting, being the beacon to come home to, and you've got these babies and your own childhood memories, and all the baby boom doctors who have popped out of the woodwork tell you how you are warping your child and it's good for a boy to take apart the clock if he's inquisitive but it's bad if he's destructive, so you walk in late for church and the kids' shoes don't match. Then you come home and because you're depressed you don't plan a picnic or do anything with your kids, and then you think they're watching too much TV so you turn it off and everybody's crying and screaming, so you turn on the radio and listen to the drama program where a kid badgers and antagonizes and provokes his mother to beat him to death just for some blessed peace and you think "No, no, no, this isn't what it's all about," so you take a walk with your heart in your throat as the kids run into the street. Then you start to cry and head for home because one thing you won't give in to is crying in public.

Karen came over for a cup of tea and said, "I hate to bring this up, but you should probably be looking at the fact that Matt won't get home for Christmas."

"Why?"

"Because all the fishermen say the fishing's been lousy and when it starts to pick up, he's not going to be able to leave when he's finally making some money."

I didn't say anything, because Karen's like my mom—too often right to even begin to argue with.

Matt called that evening and I told him what Karen said, and was heartened when he snarled, "Karen's always making trouble, thinks she knows more than anyone else."

But then I thought about it and felt uneasy again, because he didn't say she was wrong.

Gloria called to ask if I would play the piano for the school's Christmas program.

"Oh, I'd love to, that *means* Christmas to me—the music, the Christmas carols. I remember the parties my Mom and Dad had, where everyone would carouse around the piano while Mrs. O'Farrell would vamp away, nobody listening to anybody else, nobody trying. The noise was thunderous and everyone was happy. Gloria, do you think Matt will make it home for Christmas?"

"Gee, Nora, I don't know. I'm glad Robbie decided to fish around the island, though. I don't think I'd like Christmas without my husband, and the kids wouldn't stand for it."

Well, I don't like it and neither the kids nor I know how to not stand for something Matt does. We have to take whatever he dishes out.

For the next month, twice a week, I'd walk through the woods of the Baptist mission to Main Elementary School, where I accompanied the music teacher while she directed the children. The school was full of movement and anticipation, with the kids lined up in the halls with snow-frosted boots making muddy puddles on the floor, biting off their mittens with their teeth, and vigorously pulling their jackets on and off; their talk full of the excited laughter of kids at Christmas time.

Robin stopped by the house after work for a cup of tea. "So how do you like playing for the school kids?"

"It's great, I'm not responsible for the discipline, I just get to bang away at Christmas songs on the piano."

Robin asked "Would you play Christmas carols for the hospital staff's Christmas party at Dr. Copstead's house?"

"I'd love to, when's it going to be?"

"Next Saturday—I'm in charge of entertainment, and I think people would love to hang around the piano and sing Christmas carols."

I felt so damp at the party. I arrived by myself in a howling rain, walked across the slushy road in my boots, changed into heels at the door, plunked down at the piano while all these merry people drifted through. Only about four people gathered around to sing and everyone else was talking above the piano, like it was a nuisance.

Afterwards, I was kind of roaming around, trying to socialize, and all these husbands were there at their wives' gathering, getting along, making small talk. I felt so ungrounded, so diffuse, like I'd slowly melt into a puddle until I was just a drink somebody had spilled. I tried to shake myself into a happy mood.

The psychologist for the Native association was holding forth in the dining room with a group of people who were talking about the Native attitude.

"Why is it they seem so doomed, that they drink as if to drown themselves?"

Dr. Copstead said, "Well, look at their heritage. Starting with the Russians, the Natives have been told over and over that their ways are no good or that they offend God. If someone says something often enough, you believe it. The power of spiritual erosion added to physical and political bullying finished them off. Their only escape is alcohol—dulls the pain and everything else."

Then the psychologist butted in. "I have Native clients that come to my office for counseling and just sit in front of me for an hour, not saying anything. And I sit there in silence too, because that's the way they communicate, and I respect their ways."

I didn't believe him. He could never sit in silence for an hour with another person without interjecting his ego. Other people were arguing with him and he said to me, "You don't need to speak to communicate. Right now, just look into my eyes and tell me what message I'm giving you."

I looked directly into his eyes and felt that he was thinking, "I'm not giving you any message, I'm just looking at you blankly." The room was silent, watching us. He said, "Did you get the message?"

I said, "Yes, I think so...."

He slapped his knee triumphantly and said, "There was no message!"

I babysat Michael for Karen. I made popcorn for the kids and dropped the bowl, so there was popcorn all over the living room.

"Don't eat it off the floor, let me pick it up!" I scrambled to pick up the kernels, while the kids were gobbling it up by the handful. Then the phone rang.

"What's going on?" Matt growled over the static.

"Where are you Matt? Are you headed home? "

"No, I'm in Dutch Harbor." He sounded so wary and aloof, my heart sank before I could remind myself not to imagine things. "Look, Nora, there hasn't been any crab, we've just been sitting out here. But it's starting to pick up."

I was watching the kids scrambling around, eating popcorn off the floor, instead of from the bowl, and thinking, "I'm so tired, I'm so tired." I didn't want to face this. Why can't he put his tail between his legs, come home and borrow from the bank or his folks or anyone?

"Please head home. I need you for Christmas. Please, Matt."

Chelsea got on the extension. "Please, Daddy, listen to Mama."

"Chelsea, I have to work."

"Mom's important, Daddy. Listen to her."

"Okay, Chelsea, now you hang up the phone and let me talk to Mom."

When she hung up, Matt said, "I thought you didn't care if I came home or not."

"Is that why you're not coming home? To punish me for being angry?"

He sighed. "No, Eleanor, but I can't just drop everything and go on welfare, much as you'd like me to."

"But Matt, wasn't Christmas important to you when you were a little kid? Can't you remember how it felt? I can't pull it off without you."

"We're not little kids, Eleanor. Life isn't one big party."

Suddenly, Michael started choking.

"Oh God, Michael's choking! Gotta go, call me back, Matt!"

I dropped the phone and patted and shook Michael till whatever he was choking on seemed to go down his throat. He breathed again, but kept coughing a dry little hack.

Michael continued to cough off and on till Karen came back, about an hour later. She seemed pretty unconcerned about the popcorn-choking incident, and stayed to talk.

I told her about Matt's call.

"So he's not coming home?"

I shook my head and tears welled up in my eyes. "Damn it, I am not going to cry. How do I get a thick skin? How do I get to where it just doesn't matter, that I don't need him to be happy?"

Karen shrugged. "I guess you just do it. There's good Christmases and great Christmases and crummy Christmases, and the sad ones make the happy ones that much better in contrast."

"Why do my kids have to have the crummy Christmas?"

"Oh, Nora, I don't know. I'm sorry." Karen hugged me and her eyes were red, too.

I'm so tired of always sublimating my desires, of rationalizing my unhappiness as a necessity, but feeling my wants poking through my maturity like sharp, meatless bones.

Stella called. "Hey kid, d'ya just get home from church?"

"No, I didn't go to church today. The kids are sick, so we're just holed in."

"You remember my friend Elizabeth?"

"The one who was so goony at your Christmas party last year? She was going on and on about her great husband and her wonderful kids…"

"Yeah, well, she lost her husband yesterday, out hunting."

"Oh no, what happened?"

"He was on a trip with some other guys and took the skiff back to the boat to get dry socks and he never came back. They started to look for him and found the skiff, but no sign of him, so…he's a goner, drowned."

"Poor Elizabeth, the way she worshipped him, she must be bad off."

"Oh, she is, totally struck down."

The day before Christmas Eve, there was a knock at the door just as the kids woke up from their naps. Sarah and Pete rushed in dragging a Christmas tree through the door. "We were out getting a tree and Pete said we should get one for you," Sarah said.

She was so proud of Pete, and I realized how tired I was of carting the whole show down the road and how wonderful it was to have someone just help out instead of saying, "You must be so strong, how do you do it?"

Sarah said, "Did you hear what happened to Karen's baby? I guess he's been coughing for a few days and finally the doctor x-rayed his neck and found out he has a nickel lodged in his throat."

"Oh no! That happened over here the other day. I spilled some popcorn and the kids were eating off the floor before I could stop them."

"Oh yeah, Karen mentioned that."

"Is she furious at me?"

"No, she was pretty philosophical about it, like 'What next?'"

I drove up to Karen's to apologize. "Karen, I'm so sorry. I was watching the kids, but then Matt called, just as I dropped the popcorn bowl, and before I could put Matt off for a minute, Michael was choking...."

"It's okay, Nora, really. Dr. Copstead said this happens a lot, that it's a pretty routine operation actually."

"Yeah, but at Christmas time...."

"Scott's in from fishing, we can all go together. It's okay Nora, don't worry."

I feel so careless and guilty, like my "misery loves company" attitude is infecting everyone. Now Karen and Scott and Michael will spend Christmas Eve in the hospital and Christmas Day in a hotel, if all goes well.

When you have kids, they are your life. You're hostage to what fate has in store for them. If I hadn't babysat or if I hadn't made popcorn, if I hadn't dropped the bowl, if Matt hadn't called.... What do you have control of, once you accept responsibility for someone else's life?

I spent Christmas Eve morning at the laundromat and wished Izzy a Merry Christmas when we finally left. "Oh, kid, I never celebrate Christmas. Fifteen years ago my husband dropped dead on Christmas Day, and it's just another day to me."

Robin and Neil came over on Christmas Eve to spend the evening with us, and Neil played with the kids while Robin and I talked.

"How're you doing with all this?" Robin asked me.

"It's pretty awful. I just can't believe Matt wouldn't be home for Christmas."

"Yeah, Nora, he should be here. Neil and I used to think that it was just you having trouble adjusting to whatever a fisherman's wife has to go through, but Matt's obsessed. His kids need him. He should be here."

I said, "Yeah, well, I guess the pioneer women had to do it. I'll get through it. When I feel real sorry for myself, I think of Elizabeth."

"That's what I was just thinking of, too."

But those kind of thoughts seem almost wicked to me. Does Elizabeth's husband's death make me feel any better that Matt's gone? Was there any point to him dying? What kind of cruel power makes Elizabeth and me both suffer, but in comparison to her, I don't feel quite so bad off? It's not like Elizabeth's misfortune brings relief to my situation.

Matt's mom called late Christmas Eve, after coming back from Peggy's, to wish me a Merry Christmas.

Sure, merry. But she knows.

She said, "Light a candle in the window and maybe Matt will make it home."

"I've had one burning all week," I said and I got all wobbly-voiced and tearful.

"Now don't start that, you'll be okay."

"Yes, we'll be okay."

"Now take care."

"Okay."

On Christmas Day, Chelsea went over to play with Eli. Liam was sick.

While the boys napped, I walked around the house. It was immaculate, with every corner squared away, and I went around taking pictures of the cozy scenes—the brown teapots and crab-shaped shortbread cookies, the gingerbread house and the manger scene, the tree and the train set. Damn, it was beautiful.

Animal, Matt's old crewman, called from Seattle to wish us a Merry Christmas. "Ahab isn't home?" he said, amazement in his voice, "What are you doing?"

"Well, we're having Christmas and…." I started crying in the peace and the snow falling and the holiness, "and then we'll go to bed." I was crying.

"Hey, kid, it's okay. You'll make it and he'll be home and you'll be okay. He'll be home," Animal floundered. "It's gonna be okay."

No, it's not going to be okay because it's not okay now and I will never forget how awful it feels now and how he abandoned us.

When Animal hung up, I sat down at the clean table and looked around at the beautiful Christmas I'd created, and cried my heart out, waiting for it all to be over. When the boys began to stir, I washed my face and cleaned Liam and Matthew up.

Liam seemed real woozy and out of it with a low fever, but I still bundled them all up and we went over to Robin's for dinner.

I had my usual nervous breakdown getting the car up the narrow winding hill to her house. Inside was a loud group of people who were all drinking and smoking dope. Robin showed me all the presents she and Neil had bought for each other, endless toys and trinkets and novelties and books and records and candy and clothes and jewelry.

It all seemed so pagan and commercial. I felt snobbish and ungrateful, but everyone was so out of it. I fed the kids, and Liam stood up from the table and threw up all over the kitchen floor. I wiped it up, and put a cleaned-up Liam in fresh pajamas and though he was tired, it seemed like all the poison was out of him. Then I asked Pete to drive our car to the bottom of the hill while we walked down, and the kids and I got in and drove home.

Just before I went to bed, the phone rang. It was Tricia. "Well, we're home from Gramma's," she said. "How'd it go up there?"

"Oh Tricia, thank God it's over."

Before New Year's I ran into Stella at the grocery store. I asked her what news she had of Fred and Pam Nelson. She said, "It sounds like Pam's got whatever threw Tuffy off course. She's reverted to being a teenager and goes out at all hours, driving to Anchorage to party, just doesn't care about the kids. Fred's worn out tracking her down, and then when he finds her, arguing with her to come home." Sounds like Matt and me, except he's got the justification of working to support us.

How scary to snap so completely—and to jeopardize your kids' lives like that. What goes through someone's head to turn your back on what people have meant to you for over ten years, or your own children? Your need must be so desperate. And I always saw Pam's strength and her bedrock of faith—what happened? Did she just snap, or was it a planned decision?

Back to the old grind. As long as I keep the broom, mop, and dustpan in my hands, the house is clean. Chelsea said to Liam, "First comes your birthday and then my birthday and then your birthday and the world never ends!"

Finally got Matthew in to see the eye doctor. The clinic was packed with people from around the island that needed to see the specialist who came about every six weeks. He said the course of action for crossed eyes is to patch them alternately, the right and left eyes each day.

So I tried a black pirate's patch, but it wouldn't stay on even if Matthew would have left it alone, so then I went to the pharmacy and got the kind with adhesive on the back, that pulled his tender skin when I had to take it off. The poor baby hated it, running to hide when I'd come at him with a patch.

Poor Matthew, I feel like I'm torturing him. He hates having the patch on and he hates taking it off and he runs and hides and I get impatient and I feel so anxious about him I feel like crying, too. Rain. Rain on the rooftop, rain on the parade, soggy dreary rain. Go. Grow. Escape fate. Grow green and tall and not so hard, so brittle.

CHAPTER SEVENTEEN

MAKING A LIVING
In which my floor gets fixed

Matt has been gone three months now and I'm just digging in, keeping on, trying not to think too hard until my next move becomes apparent.

When they released the American Embassy hostages in Iran, I sat in front of the TV, crying, and the kids asked me what was going on. It's like waiting is a prison too, how being tied to someone, for better or worse, makes you a hostage to their fate, to their decisions, and you can say all you want about choice or about acceptance, but it's not like it's a black-or-white, absolute thing. Yeah, it's your choice to stay with them, but that doesn't make acceptance automatic; or yeah, you can choose to break apart from them, but that doesn't mean the heavens open up and the birds start singing—maybe you've just made things worse. And when they're not bad or sadistic men but just your ordinary run-of-the-mill insecure guys, and you know that you're insecure too and you just go around and around till you're crazy and.... Matt has work to distract him, but I have the kids to constantly remind me that their dad should be there.

I drove into town with Liam and said, "You know what you are, don't you?" Just to see what he'd say.

And he said, "Yeah."

I said, "What are you?"

And he said, "A brat."

Sloopy Don called almost daily to see if Matt would get home in time for Don's wedding to Jessie. She is the only daughter of some pillars of the community—wonder what they think of Sloop.

Finally I got word from Matt, via the marine operator, that he was headed home. Late afternoon, I saw the *Ocean Mistress* go by in the channel. I didn't tell the kids—no need for them to get excited and yammer at me to go down to the boat harbor to pick Matt up.

Instead I waited for half an hour for the taxi to pull into the driveway and Matt to emerge. "It's Daddy!" Chelsea and Liam went tearing out the back porch and then Matthew scrambled behind. Finally they dragged Matt into the kitchen.

"Mama," Matt said, "it's good to see you," and he gave me a hug.

We seem to be operating on a truce mentality, with Sloopy Don's wedding and the tanner crab season all looming in the near future. Maybe we'll sit down to talk, maybe Matt's done some thinking. Maybe I will get an answer to the question that keeps running through my mind—"What do I want if I can't get what I want?"

"What do I want that I can get for myself?"

I'm glad Matt didn't have too much time to think about whether he wanted to wear a powder-blue tuxedo in Sloop's wedding. Matt's way of getting even was not combing his hair.

After the wedding, Father Tiernan came up to Matt and asked him how long he had been gone fishing, and when Matt said three months, Father said in his usual snotty way, "Hmmm—sounds like you have a lot of making up to do."

I wanted to jump up and down and dance around Matt and the priest and say, "Yes, Yes! You've got a lot of making up to do! What are you going to do? How are you going to make it up?"

But Matt just snorted and said, "Yeah, that's right. A lot of making up to do."

At the reception, Gloria and I were standing outside at the top of the stairs into the hall when Gloria said, "Robbie's got some coke—go out on the deck and get some."

"Nah, Gloria, I can't afford it."

"It's free, silly."

"No, I mean I hate myself the next morning."

"I'm pregnant or I'd be out there myself—go snort some!"

"I can't." Some man was coming up the stairs.

"Gloria, who are you pushing—well, well, if it isn't the profane Mrs. Hunter!" and Nick McAllister smiled at us. Somebody caught Gloria's attention and called her back into the hall.

"Last time I saw you, you were chasing kids and chickens. How've you been?" Nick nudged into me with his shoulder but I didn't recoil, I just stood there like a shock absorber, welcoming his touch.

"I've been okay. What have you been up to?"

"Oh, I did some flying down in Arizona and New Mexico before Christmas."

"Dope flying?"

"God, no—there's no romance in that for me. Stakes too high and I'm not a gambler at heart."

"What are you at heart?"

He leaned back against the railing and said, "I'm a flyer. I soar like an eagle—and I party with turkeys."

We laughed and he said, "But I always come back to the nest."

"Yeah," I sighed and leaned back, looking at the stars.

We were quiet and he said, "Isn't that beautiful? You don't know how hard I've tried to stay away from you. Well, actually you shelter yourself pretty good. I used to go out on the town, hoping you'd show up at one of the bars, but you never do, do you?"

I shook my head. "I can't drink—it just leads to fights. I'm a lover, not a fighter," I said, scared that I'd said something so bold.

"Is your husband in love with you?"

I scoffed, "He did that already. He doesn't think about 'to love, honor, and cherish' anymore."

"He should." Nick just said it and looked at me and I couldn't stand it.

"Oh, I give him hell," I said. "I'm always crying and nagging him to come home."

"Why wouldn't any man want to come home to you—you're one hell of a woman."

My heart was in my throat and suddenly I was aware of myself thinking, "Just don't touch me. Just don't touch me," when Matt came out on the porch with Sloopy Don and Robbie, reminiscing about who'd killed the fifth of whiskey the last herring season in Bristol Bay.

They saw Nick and started asking him if he was going to fly to spot the herring runs the next spring.

"Oh, yeah," he said. "I'm going Outside with my dad buying poultry equipment and then I'll be back in April before herring."

Thank God everyone was too absorbed in themselves to be aware of the vibes between Nick and me.

Later, Matt and I sat with the other members of the wedding party at the raised dais in the Elks club. When we danced together, we had a good time. I was really pushing and shoving Matt and he'd hardly move and then he'd push me and I'd go flying half way across the room but he never let me fall, though it was close.

When Matt asked Gloria to dance, she said, "No, you two go ahead; it looks like you have a lot of fun together."

If we could just be left alone, just be hippies and dance and sing, we could be happy—if Matt didn't fish, if he didn't have to prove to the world that he was the greatest fisherman, if we lived in paradise and were free of the world. If we were dead. Instead the double hurt of

231

disloyalty and distance makes this ugly monster, this mistrust, appear, and Matt's way of dealing with it is to deny me.

Gloria has always been so competent and practical, I was surprised when she leaned over to me and said, "Robbie and I aren't doing so good. It's all business and fishing and numbers to him and he doesn't see the kids needing him, doesn't hear a thing I say."

"Oh God, I know. What is it with these guys? It's like they want us to be totally tied to them as long as they can leave whenever they want and we cease to exist for them."

"Robbie's getting old and he drinks too much. He and our oldest are always fighting. It'd be easier if Robbie never came home. He's gone home to pass out now," Gloria said.

I thought of Gloria's huge family in Kodiak and how she grew up in town and had so many friends, but she's still lonely for Robbie to be a husband, still raising her kids alone.

"Do you want a snort?" And she handed me a small vial.

"No, it wastes my nose too bad and I don't get anything out of it," I said.

"Oh, come on. It's subtle—that's what makes it so good."

"You mean so expensive," I laughed. "No, you go ahead. I don't like it."

"Sure you do—c'mon. Here, go ahead."

"No—you have it. It just makes me sick."

Gloria left the table and I felt fastidious and prim, like a real goody-goody.

Matt, sitting on the other side of me, had heard our exchange. He said, "That was good. I wish I had the discipline to say no."

It's stuff like that that makes me feel so together with Matt—like I'm the star he steers by. At my funeral they'll say, "He worshipped the ground she walked on."

Maybe Matt was right about the anger and bitterness, the less said the soonest mended. The tanner crab season is due to start but the fishermen are striking for a higher price. We can't talk about it. Matt's home now, but the malignant silences continue, burst only by angry sparks.

Five days running of headache, eye ache, throat ache. We took Liam's Goop Group for a field trip—to the jail. I left Matthew with Karen and didn't look where I was going on my way back out, and I ripped my cheek on a steel girder hanging out of Scott's truck. God, it hurt, but I just put a butterfly bandage on it.

We're so starved for cultural experiences around here that we take field trips to the jail behind the police department. I didn't realize how inappropriate it is to haul 3-year olds around the yellow-painted steel bars of the jail cells till after we'd seen the miserably hung over men in the drunk tank, and the guy with bruises and welts all over his face from a fight, and the man in abject shame, hanging his head and turning his back to us so he wouldn't have to face our innocent domesticity. With my bandaged face and emerging black eye, I looked like I should be one of the inmates.

Robin showed me all the finishing work and decorating they've done on their house. I saw a photograph in the bedroom of their neighborhood in New York where her Gramma lived right down the road, and the quilt that her mother had made for Robin and Neil.

"How do you do all this work?" I asked her.

"Every day when I get home from work we run around the high school track and then come home and have dinner. Then we'll do a project, like installing the weaving room floor or sanding and staining it...." When she turned around, tears were running down my face. "What on earth is wrong?"

"You've done so much—and my house is in shambles." But it was the "man in the house" effect, the obvious signs of Neil living there, that got to me.

Robin poured me a cup of coffee and we sat down at the table. "Look Nora, what do you want done? You just have to start one project at a time. What do you want to change the most in your house?"

"The dingy kitchen floor."

"Okay, just go pick out what you want, go to the hardware store, ask them how to do it down to the tiniest detail, act dumb so they don't take anything for granted, and just get started."

Every night I go to bed freezing. Even if the house is warm, when I turn down the covers, the bed is icy cold, and I climb in and scrunch my toes up in the hem of my nightgown and my knees are stone-cold and bony and I lie in bed and shiver and hold myself till I warm up a spot and go to sleep.

Last night I thought, "I'm not going to hold myself, I'm just going to see what happens if I shiver unrestrained." So I shivered and shook and shivered so hard that finally I sneezed and started laughing. So I won't shiver to death! At least now I know what's behind that door.

Matt left before dawn to go fishing but later that afternoon, I saw the *Ocean Mistress* steaming through the channel back towards Kodiak, as I was driving the kids to the book store and candy shop. When we went down to the harbor, we found the boat in its slip. We climbed on board and walked into the galley just before Matt came down the stairs from the pilothouse.

"I've got to muck out my stateroom."

"What happened with fishing?"

"Oh, a big wave caught us." He turned and climbed back upstairs, or topside, or whatever the official term is.

I found some cereal and poured dry bowls of it for Chelsea and Liam. "Stay here now while I go talk to Daddy."

Matt look annoyed as I opened the door to the pilothouse. "What happened today?"

"Oh, we took a big roller and when I looked back on deck, I couldn't see the men, just the deck under water. When the water finally cleared off the deck, the crew was all clinging to the rails and the machinery."

"Is that why you came home?"

He nodded.

I wished I could have talked to him about life and death and how glad I was nothing had happened to him or his men, but then one of the crew came into the pilot house and I felt out of place with a baby on my hip and Matt standing aloof and reserved, like I'd caught him being vulnerable.

He left again the next morning.

Sarah came over one night just as the kids and I were finishing dinner. She was pissed at Pete for taking off to drink with friends.

"Yeah, it's humiliating to wait at home, not knowing if you're being stood up, competing with the good old boys."

Sarah said, "Nora, how can you keep on? I would just leave."

"And go where? Back home to my mom, who picks on the kids and yells at them and keeps me in a constant state of tension? Hire a lawyer and change the locks and kick Matt out when he's gone most of the time anyway, and make my kids completely fatherless?"

"But what keeps you going?"

"I just have to work harder to keep my family together. I feel like a monk in the Dark Ages that copied the Bibles by hand so beautifully. If they hadn't individually kept the faith, with the plague and barbarians all around them, then when the printing press was invented, there would have been no link between the ancients and the Renaissance, no inheritance worth surviving for."

Sarah said, "You're so strong."

"Damn it, I'm not strong. I hate this—it's not ecstasy or fulfilling. I wish I could break down and just not face another day, but that hasn't happened. Maybe I can't stop the tide, but damn it, I can keep bobbing to the top."

"Can you keep bobbing to the top forever, or will you go down?"

"I don't know, but I have this primitive faith that one day Matt will appreciate me for hanging tough, will honor me for being the tree of life to our family."

Then Sarah and I looked up "subconscious" and "subliminal" in the dictionary and figured out that we should not suffer from Pete's or Matt's rejection, or from their impaired consciousness.

Feeling better, we started singing to the radio and dancing, and called up Robin to come over with some beer.

Of course we acted like normal in front of her, because Neil is such a sterling husband. Later, after Robin went back home to Neil, Sarah borrowed a nightgown and climbed into bed with me, like when Tricia and I used to sleep together.

In the morning we got up, had breakfast and went to the Lutheran church. Father Tiernan at St. Mary's is such a turnoff and Pete was raised Lutheran anyway, so Sarah is checking out the other churches, which makes some people in town mad. They write to the newspaper about church-hopping like it was the height of promiscuity.

Everyone at the church was so neat and shiny. I was impressed by how many men there were who were church-goers and outgoing and secure, like expressing a belief in God or a higher being doesn't diminish them.

It's funny how self-righteousness and eccentricity are supposed to co-exist here in Kodiak. You'd think it's the easiest thing to recognize how flawed and human we all are, and be tolerant of weakness. But the police chief got caught driving drunk after he'd sat in the bar all evening drinking beer. When he left, a police officer pulled up behind the chief's car and the chief whipped around the corner and pulled into a parking lot and turned off his lights and hid under the dashboard, where the officer caught him.

But it's not like that hasn't happened to half the town. The chief just represents us. Why is this fierce moral standard imposed on him, when the whole town is half-rotten?

And he might have ridden out the storm except the newspaper exposed the story of how he'd shot a robbery suspect and had an inquest before coming here from Outside. The police chief said he wouldn't go through that again, resigned, and left town.

Later that spring, Matt was in from fishing and we were going to see the taxman. I changed my clothes and was putting on some perfume when Matt said, "Why are you getting yourself all done up for the accountant? I suppose he was the one you were with when you got that dent in the car?"

I said, "What dent?" and went out to look at the car. There was no dent.

When I came back in, I said, "The only dent is in your head. What kind of crazy are you? Don't we have enough problems without you making things up?"

Matt got up from the table and sat on the sofa reading the paper, ignoring me. I couldn't stand it. I stood there and yelled at him and he wouldn't answer, just sat there with the paper in front of him. I bashed my fist through the paper, stopping just short of his face. He jumped up and came chasing after me and I must admit I got a real charge out of his reaction. But as I turned the corner into the kitchen, I realized he was mad enough to hit me. So I pulled a chair behind me to slow him down and ran out the door.

When I got home a couple of hours later, he put on his coat and walked out the door.

When he came back he apologized for being such a bastard, and I said, "If you're sorry for being such a bastard, why do you continue to be one?"

Matt threw up his hands and said, "Eleanor, I am not responsible for your happiness. You spend your days feeling sorry for yourself, and I'm trying to earn a living."

"I know I'm a creep to keep feeling sorry for myself, but what else am I supposed to do? Sure I could be big-hearted and fun-loving if I wasn't overwhelmed and worried and lonely and maligned."

Matt slept on the sofa that night and the next morning, went out early to the boat. When he came back around lunchtime, he grabbed my elbow and said, "C'mon, let's go to the hardware store and show me what kind of floor you want."

So we went out and picked out squares of flooring, and he worked all weekend laying the floor, and then it turned out cock-eyed. It goes off on an angle in the hallway and makes you dizzy to look at it.

Karen came over to visit with Michael. As the kids played, I told her how down I've been, just going round and round the same old thing. Matt has no involvement in my feelings, absolves himself of the commitment to our life together with "I'm not responsible for your happiness." But doesn't he have some responsibility to the life we pledged to live together?

I asked Karen, "What is a nervous breakdown? Is it irreversible? Is it always a dramatic statement like running naked in the streets? Doesn't crying through the day indicate something? I feel like one of those cases Paul Harvey reports where someone hears a baby crying and comes into the house where the mother has been dead for days and no one knew anything was amiss."

Karen said, "You've got to get recognition, even if it's not as a wife or as a mother. Trying to make Matt respect you is draining you."

"But where there's a will, there's a way."

"That's fine as far as you go, but you can't impose your will on someone else. Matt gets his recognition from fishing, not from his marriage or fatherhood.

Isn't there something you've wanted to do that you can do, whether Matt wants to or not?"

I thought of how I've wanted to live in France, drink coffee and eat croissants, wear black dresses with white lace collars and talk and laugh about life with a gang of friends, sit in smoky cafes and sing the blues at night.

Karen invited me to go out on the town with her and we made the rounds of all the different bars, and it was just my night. I was knocking them dead, left and right. People would come up to talk to Karen and ask who I was and everybody said, "Oh, you must be new in town," and I'd tell them I'd lived in Kodiak for five years. It just reinforces my idea that I've been invisible or non-existent. "If nobody knows a tree fell over in the forest, then did it?"

So Karen and I were dancing and having a ball being the center of attention. And finally about one in the morning we walked into the Beachcombers. The band quit playing and there were only about 20 people there.

Karen's cousin came up to her and she said to him, "God, don't go out with this girl if you don't want to get an inferiority complex. I'm so sick of people coming up to me and saying 'Who is this beautiful woman?'" Karen is so generous to me.

When the band got back up to play, Nick McAllister walked over to us and asked Karen to dance. When she hesitated, he clapped his hands and said, "You wouldn't have come here if you didn't want to dance—now get out here!" So Karen jumped up and danced with him; he was really good. After the song Nick brought Karen back to the table and said, "Who's next?" And held out his hand to me.

It was so fantastic—he danced fast and twirled me and caught me, smiling and laughing the whole time—sheer abandonment. The whole place caught his spirit, and everybody started dancing again.

When I called out to the band, "Play 'Stagger Lee!' they said, "We will if you come up here and sing."

So I got up to the mike, scared and trembly-voiced at first. I had that feeling of singing with all my might and not being able to hear my own voice. But I remembered all the words and just wailed and people started dancing again. Every song the band played, I knew, and when I suggested one, they picked it right up and backed me up tight and I was sailing—it was just so much fun and they just took me in. All the band was singing different parts harmony and back-up and people were singing and dancing and one guy said to me in between songs, "When did you get to town?"

237

When the band finally stopped playing, we had drinks and listened to the jukebox, and then people started coming in for coffee and breakfast.

Nick was really interested in what I had to say, and when I dropped my head, he'd lower his eyes so I had to look at him. We were sitting in a dark corner, and then he asked me to drive him home.

When we got to the baseball field, he told me to pull over and we started kissing, and I thought, "This is incredible. Here I am, necking in the baseball field."

Nick said, "Come home with me," and I said, "I can't," and he said, "Come on, you don't have to sleep with me if you don't want to."

And I said, "But I do want to," and he said, "Well, good," and I said, "But I can't," and he said, "Okay, I'll just leave you alone on the sofa," and I said, "No, you won't," and he said, "I will, I promise," and I said, "I better drive you home."

When we got to his house, he said, "Please come in with me; we could be so happy," and I said, "No," and he said, "Okay, but Nora, remember, you're a real sweetheart."

As I drove home I thought, "Well, now I've done it. I'm one of those cheap fisherman's wives who fools around." I looked at myself in the rear-view mirror and started grinning. "I'm a sweetheart."

Sloopy Dan's boat, the *Charmer*, lost radio contact. Sloop didn't go out on the boat that trip and everyone was glued to the radio and called around after the Coast Guard report every hour to see if there was anything more that anyone knew from contact with other fishing boats. The guys out fishing were trying to close in on the area of the ocean where the *Charmer* was last heard from.

Karen called in whispers, "Jessie is up here, listening to the radio reports and crying her eyes out. Nobody knows anything, they haven't seen the boat or heard from it for almost a day."

The next day they found the boat, a washed-up wreck on a rocky beach, no one aboard. Karen called and said, "Sloop is just stricken."

Silly old Sloop, always goofing off, and now his boat took four lives...more widows and fatherless kids, childless mothers.

I answered an ad in the newspaper for a piano accompanist for the music teacher at school. The music teacher said, "I knew there was someone out there who was just what I wanted, and then you appeared."

I can reinvent my music career, produce musical versions of Tisha *or "Scheherezade" or* A Tree Grows in Brooklyn. *Work starts at the beginning of next month, and I need to line up a sitter for the boys while Chelsea's at kindergarten and I'm at work.*

238

I took the kids to church, and there was Sloopy Dan next to Jessie. I was going to tease him about being in church, but when he turned to wish me peace, he had such a cowed expression on his face. I looked at his gold earring when I said peace back to him. One of the outlaws reined in.

I spent the morning looking for daycare. I didn't want to take the kids to the daycare center, Shine Bright, because there are so many kids there, like a children's army without a general.

Robin told me about a lady who's married to a policeman and looks after kids. "She just had her fifth child, took a day off, and was back in business the next day."

"Somebody should tell her to get real," I said. But I went to see her, mainly because I knew that the lawyers and nurses and people who you'd think care about their children take their kids to her.

Her house is right down Mission Road from us and she was friendly, but her house was tiny and just crammed with kids—maybe only ten, but everything was so little, it seemed like the house was a maze of small animals.

One of her own daughters came up to her and said, "Mom, I'm thirsty," and she patted the little girl on the head and smiled vacantly and murmured, "That's a wonderful thing to be. Aren't you glad God gave you a body to hunger and thirst with?"

A file of kids came through from one of the bedrooms and the last kid was holding a white rat and sat down next to me. I jumped up as the kids started to put the rat in my lap, and I said, "What happened to the rat's eye?"

"Oh, it was hit by the corner of a drawer a long time ago," the mother said breezily. "What's wrong?"

"I really don't like rats," I said. "I've always been kind of scared of them." And I thought of a rat running under my clothes and felt nauseated.

"You're scared of little rats. Aren't you cute?" she said and chuckled gently. "The Lord God loves them all," she quoted.

"Well, thank you for taking the time with me," I said. "I think I'd like the boys to be where there aren't quite so many children for one person to look after."

I took Liam and Matthew back down the road and when Chelsea came in from school, we all went out for pizza and I almost cried looking at their bright-eyed little faces and thinking how much I loved them.

I went to see another daycare lady, a young mother with a little boy younger than Matthew. Her kitchen was white and clean and I felt good about leaving the kids with her, but mingled with my relief was a little bit of envy that I needed to work to keep my sanity and self-esteem.

Robbie Wade called and said Matt will be home Tuesday morning and leaving again right away for the herring season in Bristol Bay. I had hoped so much Matt would be able to spend this time at home like he promised. I can't live this way anymore.

Last week Matthew burned a towel in the oven, pulled a flaming newspaper from the fireplace onto the rug, and broke the living room window again with a toy. Liam knocked the black rocking chair on the hearth and broke the back. Chelsea tried to shave her chin in the tub and has little cuts all over her face. I need some help with them, some help for me, even if it's just a pat on the back.

Matt's been gone more than ever. Things are piling up. I can't even establish radio contact with him, and I worry about him. We have nothing together but kids and bills —no fun, no togetherness, no friends, no support, no religion or faith or whatever you call that daily justification for what you're doing.

So there are all those needs and holes in my life. On top of them, I have to bear Matt's attitude toward me. He has never stood by me and I don't care how strong a person is, that hurts.

CHAPTER EIGHTEEN

MAYBE
In which Matt and I are reconciled; we go to sea

After the kids were in bed and I was cleaning up the kitchen, I told Matt, "It's time to make some kind of plan to change some things."

He brushed me off with, "I can't change anything right now. I've got a $130,000 boat payment to make in June and I can't just quit fishing."

"Well, then," I said, "I guess it's time to separate. Things aren't getting any better by ignoring them, and if I'm going to have to do it alone anyway, I want you to move out and separate for a year." The blood started racing to my throat and I thought, "If I hadn't said that, would he have told me how much he loves me, and how he knows it's hard for me and that he thinks I'm the best woman that ever lived and he doesn't deserve me?"

Matt picked up his cup of coffee and headed for the sofa. "Forget it, Eleanor, I'm not going for that separation shit so you can fool around. I've got my pride. It's divorce if anything."

In for a penny, in for a pound. "All right, Matt, divorce then."

His face didn't register anything and I continued, "But tell me, when does your pride enter into it? Is it when some man fixes the furnace, or has a long talk with me, or gives me a hand with the kids, or goes on a hike with me, or gives me a hug? I have my pride, too. How do you think I feel when my kids' father won't even make it home for Christmas, or won't stick up for me when I'm bad-mouthed?"

He turned around and his face had a puzzled expression, his brows knitting together. "If you hate Kodiak so much, why do you want to separate and live here alone for a year? Why would you want to stay if we split up?"

"So it won't be such a wrench for the kids all at once. Besides, I might like it. Give it a try, anyway." I felt so flippant, and it felt strange.

Matt set his mug on the counter and folded his arms across his chest.

"I think you're really talking yourself into something here that you're going to regret. You're just babbling that Women's Lib line. I'm not going to sit around while some other man bounces my kids on his knee."

"Matt, that's almost funny—what have you cared about bouncing the kids on your knee? Why should you resent somebody doing something that you obviously have no desire to do yourself?"

"You just have some guy waiting in the wings and you're trying to work me out of the picture. Well, lady, you can go to hell."

"No, Matt, I'm tired of going to hell; you go this time," I said quietly and took my jacket off the hook and walked out the door. I walked out past the mission to Spruce Cape. At first I just stormed along, then I slowed down and started crying, but as the moon rose, I thought, "I can't waste my life like this. Some time I've got to start living it."

When I walked back in the door, Matt was sitting on the sofa, staring at the floor. I went to bed, wondering what would happen next.

In the middle of the night, Matt woke me. "Hey, wanna talk?"

I sat up in bed, waiting.

"You really rattled my cage," he said. "I don't want to lose you. What do you want me to do?"

"I want you home more, I want a husband and a father and not just a provider, not just a paycheck. I want a definite commitment to be home more, to talk to me, to be with the kids."

"I'm a fisherman. I have to work. I can't take months off."

"I've never asked you to do that, Matt. I'm asking for you to get a relief skipper, or some time off between seasons, or come home a day early each trip."

"Well, that would be okay. I thought you meant the whole season."

"Why do you just assume that I'm making unreasonable demands, why are you so afraid to talk to me? Why are you so angry with me?" He didn't say anything. "You've always expected to run a boat, but maybe you need to adjust your expectations."

"Yeah, well, I'm not going to give up my expectations. I think people who compromise their dreams are weak losers. When the going gets tough, you just get tougher."

"But Matt, that's what I've had to do, give up my expectations *and* get tough."

"It's different, you're a woman. Your job is to stay home with the kids. You don't need ambition for that."

It made me cry. Matt sat beside me like a stone. "You can see that I'm hurting. Don't you care? Don't you want to comfort me?"

"It makes me mad. You're always crying and it never solves anything."

"I cry because I'm lonely and overwhelmed and you could solve something by staying home more and addressing some of these problems."

"I've already told Robbie and the cannery I'd go herring fishing in Bristol Bay but then I'll find an engineer to do some of the boat maintenance for me and I'll look around for a relief skipper so I can get some time off, okay?"

I put my arms around him, tears streaming down my face. "But Matt, we can't always fight like this before you'll talk to me. You can't ignore me or wish my frustrations away. You have to be here in spirit, too. I need some support and enthusiasm, not just your grudging presence. Do you know what I'm talking about?"

"Okay, okay. I hate to say it, but I need you. I love you too much for my own good."

I have never seen him look more miserable.

It's just that Matt's steaming towards his goals and doesn't have room for anything less than a doormat in a wife. If I really wanted Matt's happiness, I'd be more accepting. But how could anyone short of a martyr be accepting about my life? I think Matt loves me and understands what I'm saying, but just wishes he didn't have to. Like I'm his conscience and unless I threaten—and threaten leaving him, not my cracking up or the kids' neglect—he won't listen. It's so easy for him to walk away.

If I just hang in there, someday Matt will see I'm right and be glad I didn't give up my values for our marriage. But now the question is, is that all I want out of our marriage? Life together could be so many things and they shouldn't all be a proving ground.

Another winter was over, spring was in the air, I had a new job, and some changes were going to be made. Matt left for the herring season in Bristol Bay.

The job at school was a lifesaver. I got dressed and the day began on an official basis, a schedule. I went from doing everything at home with no recognition to just banging on the piano at work and being praised as a genius.

I went to the fabric store and was inspired when I saw some beautiful grass-green calico material. I bought some to make a quilt for our bed and matching curtains, and sewed it up quick on the machine. It looked so fresh and airy and spring-like.

"Sloopy Don is a janitor at school now," I told Karen.

She announced, "Yeah, I know. Jessie's thrilled he's home, but Don's aching to go fishing again."

"I don't know if I believe that, Karen," I said.

"Why?"

"Well, one day we were talking outside the classrooms while I was waiting for the kids to hang up their coats, and I told Don, 'Matt just seems obsessed—talking to him is like talking to the walls.' And Don said, 'I know, he's driven all right. Why do you think they call him Ahab down at the docks? I'm just glad to go home every night.'"

I went swimming at the pool one evening. I put on the new purple suit I got from a mail-order catalog and preened in front of the mirror in the locker room. As I walked to the pool, two high school girls who'd caught me looking at myself in the mirror said, "You have to take a shower, Mrs. Purple," and I was so embarrassed, but I wasn't going to obey them, so I went to the pool, hoping to jump in before the lifeguard caught me.

I'd just limped through a lap of the crawl, which I hate anyway, getting my face wet, when a guy in the next lane started talking to me. "You've got to flex your ankles more. You'll get more strength that way."

"Oh…really?"

"Yeah—you've got to be strong. You know the *Odyssey*?"

"You mean the boat that sank two years ago?"

"Yeah. Well, I swam away from that, and I'm the only guy that made it. But I never would have survived if I wasn't a strong swimmer. See, you got to…." and he grabbed my shoulders and started moving my arms in a forward stroke. I was more shocked than insulted, but something restrained me from protesting. Our bareness and the wet discomfort of the water made me terribly uneasy. I couldn't wait to get out of the pool.

I want to go home to my man, to have him wrap me in a clean white towel and keep all the existential threats at bay. I shouldn't have to be confronted by a wet, half-naked survivor. I want Matt beside me, but he's gone to Bristol Bay for three weeks and the herring haven't yet even started to run.

Matt called me from Dillingham. "Ah, there's no fish here yet, haven't hit. Gloria's flying out here, why don't you get on the plane with her? I really want to see you."

"I want to see you too, Matt, but what if the herring start to come?"

"Well, that's a possibility all right, but right now we're just sitting around waiting."

"I wish we could have known, that you could have stayed at home. We really don't have the money for me to fly out, and I don't know who I could get to babysit."

"Yeah, I guess you're right."

The next week, after Gloria flew home from Dillingham, she came by with a letter from Matt for me and one for each of the kids. *At least he's trying to connect. And he asked somebody to do something for him.*

He got home later that month on a beautiful spring day. That night was the annual dinner at the daycare center and Matt went with me, actually tagged along to my world. Matt met people I'd been talking about for years. And I got elected to the board of directors for the center.

The school music program was part of the King Crab Festival that year. I was gone all morning with my job, Matt would take off in the afternoons to collect his settlement from the herring season, and then I would have to return to school in the evening for rehearsals. I hardly ever saw him. Karen told me she'd seen Matt at the doctor's office with Chelsea, who had an ear infection, and Karen remarked to him, "Nora's pretty busy these days, isn't she?"

Matt said, "Yeah, but she enjoys it so much—I'm proud of her."

"If he could just say these things to you!" Karen said.

I was waiting for Matt to come home and take over so I could go to an appointment with the music director. Matt was a half-hour late when he walked in and he tried to sweet-talk me by saying I looked nice. I said, "Matt, I was supposed to be at school at two."

"I'm sorry, Mama, I just got hung up."

A simple apology from Matt was so rare. I said, "I always complained about you being gone, and now I'm the one leaving all the time. We're never together and your time is so precious; I feel like a hypocrite."

Matt said, "You worry too much. I don't mind looking after the kids. Besides, I have to go to Alitak next week to get ready for salmon season."

I stopped dead in my tracks. "Salmon season? Aren't you going to be home for a while? I thought this herring trip was going to buy us a little time."

"Eleanor, you know what the bills are, and besides, now we're paying every babysitter in town because you don't want to look after your own kids."

I had to bite my tongue to keep our argument on track and not respond to his babysitter crack. "You made an agreement to be home more. If we're going to be married, I have to feel married, and I don't when you're gone all the time."

He sank down into the sofa. "God, you're hard to live with. Look, I can't afford to hire someone to run the boat. So I guess you'll just have to come with me. You can be my cook and weight-taker when I charter the boat to Alitak for the salmon season," he said with a grand, resigned air.

Be a boat family? It suddenly dawned on me that the reason we couldn't go out with Matt in the past had been because it wasn't his boat. Even if he'd wanted us along. Whenever I told the kids I was crying because I missed Daddy, they'd say, "Let's live with Dad on the boat." I want them to know their father, to claim that part of their heritage. I can cook on the boat, I can sing, I can read. We can hit the beaches, travel to different canneries, explore different parts of the island. Most of all, we'd be together, and away from the laundromat and the dusty roads and the longing for Matt.

"And the kids too?" I asked.

"Matthew's still in diapers," Matt protested.

"I'll change him," I said. "Big deal."

Matt ran his hand through his hair. "Well, I guess we can try it with everyone on the boat." He pulled me to him. "I can't lose you, Mama."

"Oh yes, yes!" I said, wriggling in his arms to feel him more, to feel his arms tighten around me to keep me close. "It will work out. We can do it. The kids will love it."

The next night Matt and I took the kids down to the boat after a trip to the ice cream parlor. The kids ran around, picking out their cabins and bunks. I would be with Matt in his tiny cabin off the pilothouse. The engineer, Ken, had the other cabin up above deck, with a tiny bathroom—toilet and sink—between the two cabins. The kids shared a small cabin off the kitchen, which Matt insists they call the galley and mess. The boys would sleep feet to feet in the lower bunk and Chelsea had the upper bunk.

"Who'll have the other stateroom on the other side of the pilot house ladder, across from the bathroom—whoops, I mean head?" I asked Matt.

"Oh. Randy will be the other deckhand."

Liam and Matty pulled the cushions off the benches along the mess walls and rummaged through the tin cans and climbed in and out, playing hide and seek.

"What's going on?" Matt said.

"The crew needs to play," I tried to humor him. "And I've bought tapes and books and color crayons for the kids to play with while the crew is busy on deck."

I know there'll be tension, but we're no strangers to tense times, we have them all the time at home.

At last the boat was stocked up with groceries and ready to go. I dashed home from school, where they had let me leave a week early. The administration was used to tailoring attendance requirements so that the kids could crew and the teachers could fish in the summer months.

Matt and the crew and the kids were already on the boat, just waiting for me, so I changed out of my nylons into jeans. I accidentally threw the bag with my extra underwear in the trunk of the car, so I had to keep washing out the underwear I had on that day.

We pulled away from the dock around ten o'clock and saw the city lights along the waterfront fade away—a totally different perspective, seeing Kodiak from the water, like a grand God's-eye view instead of the reality of dusty roads and trashy yards. We steamed towards Cape Chiniak, headed down the east side of the island. I passed out doses of Dramamine and the boys conked out in Matt's bunk.

Once we passed Cape Chiniak and were in unprotected waters, the boat started bucking. I took Chelsea down below with me. She was moaning and turning green in her bunk in the little cabin off the galley. I lay in the lower bunk, my stomach churning too from the boat's rocking, added to the close diesel smell from the work clothes and the wet rubber sea-smell of the boots in the closet. Chelsea said, "Mommy, c'mere, I need you."

From the lower bunk, I said, "I can't come, honey, I feel sick, too," and then I thought, "What kind of a mother are you?" so I stood up, leaned over her, and vomited in her bunk.

After a while, Matt carried Liam down and put him in the lower bunk. He leaned over us in the top bunk with a big grin and said, "How's it going, girls?" Chelsea had gone to sleep, but I groaned. "Come out on deck and get some fresh air," he said. So I went out on deck and it was still dusky blue at midnight, but it was cold and a slight drizzle was falling.

After Matt brought Matthew down to his bunk, Matt went back up the ladder to the pilothouse and I could hear him talking to the cannery on the radio speaker that broadcast on the deck.

Well, here I am, I'm a fisherman now, too. It's so great to be on the boat—limited, boring, crowded, nauseating—but Matt is here, no bills are coming in the mail every day, Matt can see the endearing things the kids do, and I can sit back and ponder it all—Happiness!

I wonder if I'll have to put on rubber overalls and gloves and hat and get down in the tanks below deck where the salmon are kept on route from the fishing grounds to the cannery, if I'll have to crawl around in the fish slime with the rest of the crew, if I'll have to cook while the boat is rolling and keep my stomach in my mouth and if the kids will keep their life jackets on or if they'll get caught in the machinery or tossed overboard.

If the boat started sinking, they're little enough that we could each take one in a survival suit, the suits are big enough for that. There's always a way out, they won't have to swim, just stay calm and tread water and keep your head.

But my fingertips go numb if I don't wear gloves and my feet are like blocks of ice at the end of a winter day at home. I remember reading in Alaska *magazine about the woman who was shipwrecked on a wintry beach with her husband and how he just wanted to give up and die, and she said, "Even if we lose our feet and hands, we can still go to the library, we can still see our families," and I think I'd be like her, but I don't know.*

Then I started shivering, so I went back up the ladder to the pilothouse. Matt got out of his chair and adjusted the compass and said, "It's better now that we have Sitkalidik Island between us and the Gulf." It had calmed down a little, and was as dark as it gets on a midsummer night. The engineer was driving the boat and he had put a Billy Joel tape on. Matt put his arms around my neck and said, "C'mon, Mama, let's try and get some sleep. We'll be in Alitak around noon." So Ken took over the watch and Matt and I slept like spoons in his thin bunk, and we were all under one rocking, rolling roof.

I woke up with the boat pitching from side to side. Finally I nudged Matt awake. "I'm scared we're going to roll over."

Matt said gruffly, "Don't be nervous." He put his head down to sleep again momentarily, then raised it to say again, "Don't be nervous."

Then he got up, pulled on his jeans and T-shirt, and left the cabin. He returned moments later to say, "I checked everything and we're okay. Don't be scared."

Then he climbed back into the bunk and put his hand up under my nightgown and when it was all up at my neck, he pulled it off and held my hands with his, with the nightie all bunched up and the boat rocking with us, bounding over the waves. I thought of pirates who flew the skull and crossbones but had a heart of gold.

We arrived at the cannery in Lazy Bay on the southernmost tip of the island late the next morning. As soon as we tied up to the dock—at midtide, so there was about ten feet of ladder to climb to the docks—the crew immediately began installing the refrigeration pipes to keep the fish alive in the tanks. After I made breakfast and set it on the table, Matt helped me get the kids up the ladder to the docks and the cannery. It felt great to stretch our legs and breathe deep lungfuls of open air, to see the lookout mountain looming behind the cannery buildings.

Since the fishing season hadn't started yet, all the cannery machines, the iron chinks, the belts, the retorts, were silent. The warehouses were empty of the pallets of canned salmon, the boats were on the ways waiting to be repaired and painted, and the crews were fixing nets and skiffs for the purse seiners.

The men spent three days tearing the deck apart and installing the refrigeration system. Then they replaced the battery pack and painted. Battery acid and paint meant keep the kids away, so we spent all day on walks in the hills where the wildflowers were emerging, splashes of color and delicacy in the spongy grey-green tundra. We returned to the boat only for meals and naps, but I was getting paid cook's share anyway. Matt said, "Just don't let the superintendent catch you off the boat too much or he'll get suspicious."

The little cannery store was open almost all the time so villagers from Ahkiok and Old Harbor came in for gear and groceries. I talked to Sparky, the laundry woman, and she told me of seeing bears on the beach. I got a week-old copy of *Time* magazine and read all about Prince Charles' marriage as I rested halfway up the mountain, lying on my back with wildflowers all around me, listening to the kids throwing rocks in the lake, and scanning the hillside for bears.

Matthew is the most beautiful sweet-tempered child—curly blond hair and pink skin and robin's-egg blue eyes. The other night when I tucked him in before I went to bed, he was chuckling in his sleep.

As I squeezed into the single bunk next to Matt, I said, "Matthew's eyes are bothering me."

"What do you mean?"

"One eye seems to be definitely turning in, crossing."

"Oh, it's just baby eyes, the way their pupils are so big, you can hardly see the whites of their eyes anyway."

"No, it's not just that, Matt. His eyes are crossing."

The next day, it was high tide after dinner and Matt and I were sitting on the dock drinking coffee, just a step off the boat, the kids playing on the buoy swing Matt had hung from a boom, when the superintendent came down to the boat and said, "You ready to take a trip? They're opening Cape Igvak tomorrow, so you might take a stroll up that way and see what they come up with."

"Is this it, Matt?" I asked.

"Yep, Cape Igvak."

"It looks pretty quiet."

"There won't be any boats unloading to us until tonight."

Robbie Wade's kids came over from the *Sea Lion* in a skiff to take us for a ride to the beach.

We came back to the boat and the crew was napping, so Matt sat at the table coloring with the kids while I cooked dinner. "Home!" I sighed happily. Matt groaned.

Just as we were finishing dinner that night, the first boat came alongside us to unload. I was in the cabin and heard someone outside hailing us, so I ran out as the crew was throwing lines to the seiner to tie up next to us. I headed back into the galley to clear away the leftovers from dinner. Matt was there giving the kids Windex and sponges to wipe down all the cupboards. It was kind of crowded, so I went back out on deck for a few minutes until Ken came stomping out, looking for his rubber boots. I was praying furiously to Saint Anthony to find them before the kids got blamed. Sure enough, Ken found only one and came back into the galley and said to Liam, "Did you throw my boot overboard?"

Liam said "No," and Matthew said "Yes."

Matt jumped on Liam and said, "Don't lie!"

I said, "Well, Matt, don't call him a liar until you know for sure what happened."

Matt glared at me, and Ken started laughing and said, "Liam, did you throw my boot over the side? You did, didn't you?"

And Liam said, "No."

I said, "It must be around here somewhere," and I went to look outside on deck. *I can't expect Matt to treat the kids the same as I do, but it sure is hard to bite my tongue sometimes.*

Randy came out on deck and threw the cigarette dangling from his mouth overboard and said, "Hey look, did you give those kids bottles of Windex?"

"No, Matt did."

"Well, do you know they're spraying each other with the sprayers? They're going to get it in their eyes and blind themselves."

So I went inside and took the Windex away from Chelsea and Liam and sat them down at the table with some schoolwork. Randy sat down with a cup of coffee and said, "It's tough having the little ones and being out fishing. I know my kids would be into everything and it's just tough—I'm never home, either." I could have kissed him for understanding and wished he didn't pour half the sugar bowl into his cup of coffee.

Matt and Ken came in and Matt gave Ken his own rubber boots and said, "That's $60 you owe me, Liam," but I still didn't think he threw the missing boot overboard.

The boat delivered about 140 red salmon. I took the weights from the scales and ran in to the galley table to record the weights. Just as we were finishing the first boat, two more boats pulled up alongside, and then the fish were flying and I was taking the weights from the brailers on both sides of the deck and calling out the weights before running inside to record them in the weight books on the galley table. As I flew past the galley, Matt and the captain from the first boat were standing next to the stove smoking cigarettes and drinking coffee and talking.

"You keeping those weights straight, Eleanor? Wanna make sure everybody gets paid for what they bring in," Matt said to me as I heard the hydraulics lifting the brailers and ran out to record the new weights.

Out on deck I glanced up at the scales, and from the corner of my eye, saw Liam scurrying about on deck, near the hatch. He was throwing stray fish into the hold with his bare hands, teeth gritted, wiping fish guts from his forehead. "Liam!" I hollered. "Keep out of the way!"

"It's okay!" Randy yelled back. "We're just finishing up this boat, and I got my eye on him. He's a great helper!"

We worked all night, and then lifted anchor to come back across Shelikof Strait at dawn. Just after Matt turned his watch over to Ken, and climbed into bed, squeezing me halfway up the wall, Liam came into the stateroom and threw up on the rug.

Matt jumped out of bed. "Goddammit!"

I got a towel from the bathroom and wiped it up before Matt started gagging. *The big strong man.*

"I'm going to put you all on the plane in Alitak," he growled.

"C'mon, Matt, it's not that bad."

"I can still smell it."

So I washed it over again and put everybody back in bed and prayed for strength.

We anchored in Bumble Bay, just south of the village of Karluk. "Look, you can just barely see the tiny blue onion domes of the Orthodox Church," I pointed out to the kids.

"Yeah, it's one of the few buildings that didn't get washed away in the tidal wave after the big '64 quake. But the people were okay here. Old Harbor, on the other side of the island, wasn't hit very hard, but the villagers went up the mountainside to be safe and some of the old folks and the babies died from exposure."

While we were waiting for the seiners to deliver, the crew set lines off the stern of the boat to jig for halibut. When they'd hook one, the fish would flail on the deck and the men got a club and bludgeoned the fish until it was still. It made me sick, especially to see the kids so excited by it.

We went back and forth across Shelikof Strait a few times between the Alaska mainland and Kodiak Island. The kids got seasick and claustrophobic in the 18-hour run for the cannery at Alitak, at the south end of the island. At first when I got seasick, I tried to fight it.

For two years now, you've wanted to just lie down and let someone else take over while you sleep. If it takes being seasick to justify it, why knock it? So this is my rest cure. Matt takes over the kids, and at least he's getting an idea of what his children are like; I just try to live with a "let the children's father handle it" attitude, trying to hold out for a time when I feel some love in my heart for him again. I know you can't change easily or just by wanting to, and I'm afraid his promise to be home more was just words said to keep the status quo. No time off in sight, no relief skipper, still talking about leaving on long trips, still rejecting any unpleasant discussion with either a stoic, put-up-with-it attitude or else an easy, pat solution: "I'll put you and the kids on the next plane."

Just like our marriage, he thinks of his decisions as faits accomplis: the kids are on the boat, either it will work out automatically or they'll have to go, but no piecing together solutions or, heaven forbid, compromise.

I took the kids off the boat to take a walk and ride the tricycles that had been left outside by the mess hall. It's the first cold day, and the kids sneak in and out of the mess hall to cadge sugar cubes from the mug-up tables.

When we got back to the dock, once again the crew was mixing paint. Then Matt announced, "We're leaving for Port Bailey."

So we headed up to the north end of the island, only five hours from Kodiak.

On the way, Matt showed me how to steer the boat and adjust the automatic steering and I watched the grey immensity drop off to the right and roll and drop off to the left, with a surge from below in between. Slowly the headache and nausea started. I'd thought I'd have a natural affinity for boating, but this drawn-out mental nausea is insufferable. I went to lie down on the bunk and I could hear the kids rattling around in the pilothouse with the tape recorder playing Oscar the Grouch and I worried they might be destroying something. When I heard the horn blow, I jumped up and there was Matt in the pilot's chair with Matthew on his lap, honking the horn, Liam crawling on the chart table and turning the knobs on the radios, and Chelsea in the other chair, leafing through the *Playboy*s. "Why does Daddy like to look at these?"

"Because they remind him of Mommy," I said, and took it away from her. "Isn't Liam messing up the radios?" I asked Matt.

"Nah, he can't hurt anything."

We arrived at Port Bailey about seven in the morning, and it was strange to see trees outside the pilothouse windows, instead of the low scrub on the south end of the island. We beached the boat so that when the tide went out we could clean the bottom. The boat shifted and settled and finally the engines, which were water-cooled, shut off. The world assumed a huge, total silence.

We climbed down a ladder to a rowboat and hit the beach. From the beach, the boat looked like an eerie monolith, with the bottom of the hull, usually hidden under water, now exposed. Like doctors to a whale, the crew rowed about, scraping and scrubbing the hull.

Later that morning, I took to the hills, exploring with the kids. When we got back, Matt said, "Did you take my gun?"

"No, I wouldn't want to have your gun around the kids."

"Well, you were lucky. I was watching a mama bear and her cubs with the binoculars all morning. They hang around pretty close and raid the cannery garbage cans."

After Port Bailey, we were sent to Kodiak. After traveling for eight hours, we finally pulled into the boat harbor. It felt great to be back in town.

Matt and I sat down at home, and he said, "Well, it's not really working out, is it? The kids are throwing up and getting in the way and if we get sent to Bristol Bay or Prince William Sound, it will be a long trip and a real mess."

"Yes, but...." I started, and then I couldn't think of any objections to what he said. But the thought of another lonely summer of waiting and hoping for Matt to come home filled me with dread. "Matt, since you'll be gone from Kodiak so much of the summer, can I take the kids to Seattle and stay with Tricia?"

His eyebrows went up but his face was expressionless and he said, "Well, you've got about eleven hundred in wages coming to you. I don't care, you can do what you want with it."

So Matt left and I kissed him good-by, for once not feeling forlorn at being left behind, because I was leaving town, too.

We walked off the plane, but there was no one at the gate to greet us, so we walked towards the baggage area and I headed for the down escalator, holding Matthew by the hand, with Liam and Chelsea trailing behind. Mindlessly, I stepped on the grilled steps going downward and Matthew took one look at the disappearing stairs and me descending and screamed as Liam, who was throwing his own fright-fit at the top of the stairs, vanished from our view. A man with a briefcase almost tripped over them before I grabbed Matthew in my arms and raced back to the top of the stairs against the current. Always. I pulled the kids to the side of the escalator and crouched down, hugging them and drying tears, on the verge of hysteria myself, when Tricia appeared. "Sorry we're late. I was at a soccer game."

We stayed at Tricia's house and caught up on her life, working at a school and playing on a soccer team and painting with a group once a week.

Tricia and I went to an arts festival and when we got home, I asked Chelsea if anyone called.

"Just Daddy," she said.

"Oh! What did he say?"

"The babysitter said it was long distance and not to talk anymore so I told Daddy I wasn't supposed to talk to him."

I wondered how that sounded to Matt, coming from his six-year old daughter. *I hope he won't be mad, will give us the benefit of the doubt, like consider maybe there's a mix-up, but even if he decides he's been snubbed, I feel a "consequences be damned" kind of bravado. Let him be responsible for his own fears and anger and frustration instead of me translating all his emotions for him. Let him think what he wants, let him put up with all the things I do, or he thinks I do, that hurt him. After all, when have my feelings been a matter of concern to him?*

We walked to the neighborhood pool, and after we goofed around a little in the shallow end, Liam asked me, "Is Daddy still on the *Ocean Mistress*?" and then he stopped cold and said, "I said it right!"

All along he'd been stuttering over the name, saying *"Ocean Mistiss"* and *"Osean Shistress"* and today when he said it right he almost shot out of the pool with pride.

Later that afternoon, Tricia and I were in her kitchen, making another pot of tea. The kids were playing in the backyard.

"These beautiful summer days remind me of the Garden of Eden," I said.

"You're so in tune to the lush greenery and the smells and sights of nature."

"Well, that's what living in exile does to you."

Suddenly my eyes fixed on the scene out the back door. Liam had been climbing on the two-foot high rockery. He reached up to the clothesline and wrapped it around his head, then teetered on the edge of the embankment, about to fall forward with the line snapping around his neck.

I ran out to him and grabbed him, loosening the rope and disentangling it from his neck. "Liam, you scared me!"

"And we were just standing there watching it happen!" Tricia said. "Oh baby Liam, you live so dangerously!"

"Kids are just an accident waiting to happen. You have to be constantly vigilant. It makes me believe in guardian angels."

I went to visit Leanne in her new home in Seattle. She was seven months pregnant and big as a house. Chuck was flying back and forth from longshoring jobs in the bush in Alaska, but she said, "We are so happy when Chuck's home. We just sit and eat ice cream and look at TV and watch my belly grow."

"Chuck's not lost without fishing?"

"No, he doesn't miss it at all. We're getting along so great. When he left last week, he kissed Anna and me good-by and patted my belly and said, 'You're my life.'"

Matt called in the middle of August. "Well, what's going on?"

"We're having a good time, swimming and playing in the yard and visiting Grandma. Are you going to come down?"

"No, we're still delivering salmon to the cannery. I'm in Kodiak for the first time since you left."

"Why didn't you write me?"

"Hey, when I call and get told that I'm not supposed to talk to my own daughter, I can get the message pretty clear."

"And did you ever think that it was the babysitter giving the message, or that you got the message wrong, or is it more satisfying to feel sorry for yourself?"

Sigh. "Eleanor, are you coming home or what? Everyone's talking about how you ran out of town the minute I was gone."

"Oh, and couldn't you trouble yourself to set them straight, or is it just easier to be mad at me?" It felt good to get mad. "Are you going to take some time off fishing when we get home? Can you get a relief skipper?"

Sigh again. "Well, I'll call you back after I talk to Randy. I guess he can handle the boat. Then will you be coming up?"

"How long till king crab starts?"

"Three weeks."

"Okay then. This will work out good. And it's what we agreed on, isn't it?"

His answer sounded like a growl.

The next day was the first day of 100-degree temperatures in one of Seattle's rare heat waves. It was also the day the air traffic controllers struck.

I called the airline repeatedly throughout the day to make sure the plane to Kodiak would be taking off and was told that, as far as anyone could tell, it was leaving on schedule.

But when I got to the airport, I was informed at the ticket counter that the flight had been canceled 15 minutes earlier. The airline flew over Canadian territory and the Canadians wouldn't give clearance to the striking US flights over Canadian airspace.

"Are the other flights to Alaska flying over Canada, too?"

"No, they're flying over the ocean, and they're still on schedule."

"Can you transfer our tickets for one of their flights?"

"No, you'd have to buy new ones and then apply for a refund for your unused portion of the ticket with us."

I called Kodiak and Matt said, "Well, this is great. Now I'm stuck in Kodiak and where are you?"

"Okay, I'll try to get tickets on the other airline, but I'll have to charge them to the credit card."

"That will put us over our limit."

"What do you think I should do?"

"I don't know Eleanor, you should have thought of this before you went skipping off to Seattle."

Of course. Well, the bank isn't at a congested airport with three kids in this torrid heat waiting out a strike to get home to my darling husband.

Even with our new tickets, the flight was delayed two hours on the runway after the doors had closed, delayed again taking off from Anchorage, and again for 45 minutes before we could complete the 30-minute flight from Kenai to Kodiak.

The kids were wilted when we finally landed in Kodiak. "Oh Matt, I'm so glad to be home, in drizzly grey Kodiak—so glad you're here to pick us up!"

Even though Matt fumed about buying an extra set of tickets, I knew he would have done the same, and I brushed off his complaints. "We'll get a refund," I said.

"It'll take years."

"But at least we're home."

Home. Good old cool Kodiak, where Chelsea would start first grade at St. Mary's with all the other beloved little girls who were the apple of their daddy's eyes. St. Mary's, where the whole school joined in the Christmas program and where the little innocents were sheltered.

Matt was torn between humoring me and fearing that we'd all turn into wild-eyed cultists. "Do you realize how much harm the Catholic Church has done? In the Inquisition? My God. I read Dostoevsky's *Grand Inquisitor* in college. Have you ever read that?"

I had to bite my tongue to keep from saying, "Have you ever read anything since?" But I couldn't lose this battle, so I said, "You're right, Matt, but I just want them to go to St. Mary's. I want them to be a part of that community and besides, with you being an atheist and me confused, and them going to Catholic school, they'll grow up questioning. If they decide to go in a different direction, okay, but I think it's better for them to go to St. Mary's than public school for now."

So our three weeks home were a boon, except for calls from the bankcard office demanding immediate payment on the overlimit. Matt refused. "Tell them we'll pay them when the airline pays us your refund."

"But that's blowing our credit record."

"You should have thought of that before you bought the tickets."

Oh well, the bank officer doesn't know it's all my fault.

'I'm sorry, but my husband is adamant. He just refuses to write a check for the overlimit."

I tried to create in myself the Woman Aglow who accepts her husband's dominance and rejoices in submission, and it felt very calm to be in the army of the humble: just following orders.

We found the grass road to Cliff Point and took the kids on picnics where they played in a tent, explored the marshes, and fried their shoes in the campfire, resting their feet on the flame-licked rocks.

We saw the outdoor production of the boring historical drama, "Cry of the Wild Ram." We had dinner at both Jake and Stella's and Karen and Scott's.

Karen casually turned to me after dinner and said, "Oh Nora, when you were in Seattle did you hear the news? Now, what is her name? She moved down there about a year ago? Oh yeah, Leanne Hartwell! Her husband died in a plane crash—Chuck Hartwell."

"No!" I said, "I saw Leanne! When? She was having a baby!"

But it was true. Chuck had died in a small plane crash in Alaska and Leanne had her baby by herself a few weeks later. I imagined her frail, enormously pregnant body in a black funeral dress with a bewildered Anna by her side.

Why? Has she angered the gods by moving Outside? Wasn't she supposed to be happy?

We visited Robin and Neil. "So, are you two having a good time?"

"Oh yeah, it's been fun," Matt conceded.

"Well, good. After all, owning your own boat should have some payoff."

"Yeah," I agreed, "it's been a pretty tough go." And I sat there in the August twilight on their deck overlooking town and the boat harbor and slapped a bug from my arm and said, "I am never going to have it so hard again."

This is only the beginning. I've won some time with Matt as a family. We're finally getting somewhere.

CHAPTER NINETEEN

REBEL FISHERMEN AND OUTCAST CHILDREN
In which I am tested

Really enjoying my time at home with Matthew and Liam and Chelsea now. We went into the woods today and entered a magical world of greenness and moss. Chelsea and Desiree galloping around singing,
> *I'm free as a monkey*
> *Free as a horse*
> *Free! Free! Free!*

Liam showed me his fort. His face registers such pleasure when he feels my approval. We went up to the buoy swing that's tied to a tree bough in front of one of the Mission houses and swung out over the hill overlooking the pasture and trailer court and channel.

I made an appointment for Matthew to see the ophthalmologist when he came in from Anchorage. The dread in my stomach was like a block of granite and I wanted to just pretend there was nothing wrong. But I made the appointment. I drove into town with Matthew, only to find the doctor's office locked up with no note or any explanation. I returned home and the airline called to tell me that there would be no refund since the air traffic controller's strike wasn't their fault. As if they overheard us, the credit card company called soon afterwards to hound me about paying the overbalance.

When the boys were napping and Chelsea was playing over at Eli's, I sat at the table with a cracked cup of tea, tears streaming down my face as the tea wept out of the cup. Sarah drove up in her big sedan, walked in, and gave me a big hug. She felt so slender and cool. "Oh, Nora, I'm so glad I came. What's wrong?"

I told her all my troubles and she said, "Nora, all you can do is one thing at a time. Just make one step and then build on it, one way or another. All these things are complex and cold. The only gratification you'll get is when they're over and out of your hair, but you can't solve them in one day. But now, you've got to take a break. Even if it's just coming over to the Sugar Shack with me to look at magazines, or to quilt while I study."

I spent a long time on the phone trying to get a sitter, but Sarah wouldn't let me give up. She played with the kids and made sandwiches for dinner, and finally one of Robbie Wade's daughters gave me the number of her friend who agreed to baby-sit.

Sarah told me about her nursing program. Her sister, Robin, is the coordinator and it just seems so easy—academic nepotism. Sarah will be an excellent nurse and, like teaching, I wonder how much your training really prepares you for the job, but I think of the nursing students at the University of Washington when I went to school and how rigorous it seemed—calculus, physiology. Sarah said the psychologist who's the head of Alcoholics Anonymous in Kodiak is teaching a sociology class by having each student take a chapter from the text and presenting a lecture to the class based on that chapter. "Pretty easy way to teach a class," I groused.

"I know, I wonder about him. He told us he used to be a heavy drug user, shooting up and all and then he finally got straight when a friend of his died from shooting up an overdose in front of him."

"Is that what it takes to get straight with your life?"

"Oh, Nora, you're being judgmental."

"Well, yes, it is a judgment. You know, everything isn't beautiful. I know I'm getting more conservative as time goes by, but his profiteering from his own degradation just irks the hell out of me."

A few days later I was looking after Karen's little boy Michael. When she got back, late, she told me that a couple of guys from Scott's salmon crew had come to her door drunk and yelled at her because Scott hasn't paid them their crew share yet.

"I told them as soon as Scott got the receipts from the cannery he'd pay them, but we haven't even paid ourselves yet. Scott has to get ready for king crab, and I told them, just get off my back. They can't get anything out of me if I don't have it."

"Yeah, and harassing you when Scott's not there, what a bunch of bullies. You want to spend the night in case they come back and bug you?"

"Ah no, we'll be okay."

"How about dinner, then?"

"Well, yeah, that sounds good. I'll go get a bottle of wine."

She stayed till it was late and past the kids' bedtime. We were discussing gossip and rumors and friendship and I said, "I don't believe anything I hear unless I'm the one who said it, and even then I have my doubts."

Karen laughed and said, "Yeah, things get twisted in the telling, all right." She gave a kind of wry little smile and said, "Yeah, well, there's a little rumor going around now about the *Ocean Mistress* fishing early."

"What? What do you mean?"

"Well, I guess when Scott was out prospecting he saw some *Ocean Mistress* buoys on the deck of the Fish and Game boat."

"What were the *Ocean Mistress* buoys doing on the Fish and Game boat?"

"Well, they must have got them from a line of baited pots that Matt had set out. You know, evidence."

"You mean Matt was fishing early?"

"Yeah."

"And they caught him?"

"Yeah." We were both quiet while the kids chattered and then she looked at me and sighed and said, "They caught him." She added, "And if he did go out early and they caught him, I hope they sock it to him."

"Karen, why would you say that?" I asked, stung by her bluntness.

"Because he's taking crab from Scott and all the other fishermen who wait till it's legal to go out and bait their pots," she said heatedly.

But if they sock it to him, where does that leave us?

Karen turned to Matthew. "Hey Matty, you want to come spend the night at our house?"

Matthew looked uncertain, and I sure didn't want him to go, so I said, "Oh Karen, I think it's just too late. I think we all just need to turn in." After they left, I was beat and the house was a disaster, so I decide to follow my own advice and ignore the rumor about Matt fishing illegally.

The eye doctor examined Matthew again. "Well, we'll need to try glasses. These patches aren't having any effect." He went into all kinds of technical jargon about what was wrong, about functional vs. physical blindness, which scared me silly.

"And if the glasses don't direct his eyes in the right direction...?"

"Then he'll need an operation. In fact, that's probably how it will turn out. The glasses are a long shot, but sometimes the correction for far-sightedness is all a kid needs. That's what we'll try next, anyway."

And he wrote a prescription for glasses and dismissed us.

Ten days later, I was doing the dishes when I looked out the kitchen window and saw a man coming up our back steps. It was Matt, and he bounded in and hugged me, and I said, "What a nice surprise! How come you're home in the middle of the day?"

"Well, I've got some good new and some bad news."

"What?"

"The good new is that I hit crab. I've got 65,000 pounds of crab on the boat! And the bad news, well, Fish and Game found my pots about two weeks ago…before the season opened."

It all clicked at last. "You mean you were fishing early? Oh no." I felt like a sledgehammer got me in the stomach. I went around the kitchen corner into the hall and began to cry, hugging the wall.

Matt pulled me back into the kitchen and said, "C'mon now, what are you so upset about?"

"Oh Matt, after all the hassles and troubles and trying to get somewhere and now this."

I felt Matt stiffen and he said, "Well, hey, don't you worry about it. It's not your problem."

"Matt, we're in this together. This is a big deal. Now what's going to happen?"

"I don't know," he said. "I have to go downtown this afternoon. Fish and Game have the boat. Sixty-five thousands pounds! I couldn't believe it! This might all turn out for the best."

"For the best!" I exploded. "Don't be naïve, Matt."

Robin was having a tea party, and I wasn't going to be chewed up and spat out in absentia, so I went, denying that Matt was home, refusing to feel anything but the immediate reality of tea and cakes and kids.

When I got back home, Matt seemed more serious. "Well, they're keeping the boat, they've impounded it, and levied a stiff fine too. I called Cy and got the name of a company lawyer in Anchorage so I gave him a call, but he says there's nothing he can do for me. So I called up Harkins here in town and have an appointment with him Monday morning. Damn. I need to get back out there." He looked out the front window at the stormy channel and his lips started moving as he muttered to himself.

Oh shit, if only I'd opened my eyes when Matt left, but he's never listened to me, it's not like I have any weight to throw around. But when we talked about other guys fishing early, I'd never acted like I was horrified at the prospect, or demanded a promise that Matt wouldn't go early. I know if I'd said anything, it would have been, "Don't get caught."

But we have gotten caught. I thought, like Matt, that most serious fishermen sneak out early, that it wasn't a big moral thing. I really hadn't thought that there are fishermen who chafe at playing by the rules, whose catch is diminished because they wait until the season officially opens, but they wait anyway. I just thought they weren't as gung-ho as Matt, that was all. I know there are other fishermen who fish early and never get caught, but now the moral weight of the fishermen who resented waiting for the legal opening and watching guys like Matt leave town early struck me. Matt's reason was always "to gear up," and since his gear is at the south end of the island, even I didn't know for sure that he was fishing early. And if I ask him anything, he brushes me off.

The next night, the Board of Directors for Shine Bright had their annual dinner at the chairman's log cabin on Monashka Bay. I had to keep up, to save face, and it was a diversion from our horrible predicament. Matt took the kids to Sloop's cabin at the top of the steep winding hill that led down to Monashka Bay, where they could watch cable TV, and then I went on to the dinner alone.

Of course no one mentioned our downfall, but one board member who worked at Fish and Game sat next to me on an old-fashioned porch swing that was hanging from a beam inside the house and he went on and on about all the problems he was having remodeling his kitchen. He was kind enough to ignore my lack of response. Thanks to him, I was able to keep from thinking of my problems, which would have brought me to tears.

Karen came by on Sunday while Matt was changing the oil in the Jeep, and I was like a polite stranger to her until she said, "Well, what's going to happen with the boat?"

"Oh, Karen," I looked up from the cake I was mixing, "they might take the boat away from us." I didn't want to cry and have her comfort me, while inside she was licking her chops over this great piece of gossip, but I was close.

"Oh, now, they won't do that. They'll lower the fine. He's got to make a living. You'll see. Are you going to the lawyer tomorrow?"

""Well, Matt has an appointment at nine with Harkins."

"You bring the kids by. I'll watch them so you can go, too."

That evening Robbie Wade called from downtown and asked how things were going. "Robbie, please come over. It's like a funeral here. Matt can't talk without getting mad and neither can I. We need you."

So Robbie came over and we all sat around. They talked about the Fish and Game officers and how decent they were about the whole sorry mess. Robbie said, "Yeah, but those guys, they just love playing policemen, turning the screws."

"Well, what about you guys?" I said. "Isn't half the reason you're fishing because you love the gamble of it, the pirates getting away with your plunder? You're playing your game, they're playing theirs, and this time they won."

Monday morning I was getting ready to go to the lawyer's and Matt said, "I'll go by myself and come back and tell you what's going on."

"No, Matt, I'm going too."

"I don't want you sitting there getting upset and crying."

"Matt, you know I can hold it together if I have to. I promise I won't lose control."

I sat there while Matt and Harkins tried out the legal defense possibilities: that it was beyond U.S. jurisdiction, that the pots weren't really his, but finally Harkins said, "The facts are, this is your second violation, and they caught you red-handed. There's really no recourse but to try to negotiate the fine with the prosecution in Anchorage."

"What are they talking about?" Matt said.

"Impounding the boat and $150,000."

I looked out the second-story window at the rainy, indifferent streets. *That's right, sock it to us. Make us leave town. Nobody wants us to be here. Run us out.*

Matt and Harkins were waiting for a phone call from Anchorage. I tried to formulate my question so I could say it without emotion. "Who makes the decision regarding the fine?"

"The prosecutor's office in Anchorage."

"Would any understanding of our personal situation affect their decision?" I asked.

"No, I'm afraid not. Things have been pretty tough, have they?"

We went home, and I paced up and down the living room while Matt looked out the window. "What are you going to do?" I asked him.

"Well, I guess I'll just have to work harder and get out of this. If I could just get out there," he insisted.

I broke down. "I've been dealing with this for years and I just can't get anywhere. I'm so tired of being alone and tired and struggling and now you're saying it'll have to be even more so. How am I going to do it?"

"Okay, okay, okay," was all he could say as we stood with our arms around each other.

Karen brought the boys home and after I put them down for naps and Matt went back downtown, I sat by myself in the rocking chair. I drank in the big living room and the view of the front yard and the channel, and realized all I had. It all became so precious to me, and so threatened.

Matt came home from the lawyers and said that they accepted the $80,000 the crab brought in and a $40,000 fine. Northern Pacific would loan us the money for the fine. The trailer would be collateral, and Matt and Harkins had discussed the possibility of the company absorbing the fine. "If I'd gotten away with it, they would have patted me on the back and taken the profit with a big smile on their faces," Matt growled.

But at least he could take the boat back out once the papers were signed.

The next afternoon the Fish and Game officer came to the door with the legal documents. Chelsea had just presented Matt with some school papers to look at, and while he read the legal papers, she fussed at him while I felt my nerves being torn to shreds.

When the officer left, I said, "Matt, Chelsea wants you to look at her schoolwork."

"Okay, but I have to read these over before I can see her scribbling."

"Matt, her work is just as important to her as those things are to you. I understand you, I understand her, and I feel like the top of my head is going to blow off with understanding."

"Okay! I'll look at her papers, but I can't stand your whining!"

Well, thanks a fucking lot. It's all you, isn't it? You're the only one who's been dragged through this thing.

Karen had us over for dinner that night, along with Sarah and Pete and Robin and Neil. Matt and the guys were standing around the kitchen having drinks and Robin said to me, "Well, are Matt's gambling days over? Everybody in town is talking about it."

"I just feel smashed, I never realized how financial disaster could just devastate you. At this point, I could care less who's talking about it, for God's sake."

"Well, you have to accept the consequences of your decision. You can do anything if you're willing to accept responsibility for it. You can kill somebody if you're willing to go to jail for it."

I just kind of nodded dumbly and walked out of the room.

Wait a minute. No, you can't. You can never kill somebody. And what's that got to do with humiliation and impoverishment and my pile of troubles?

I was back in the den picking out records when Sarah came in and said, "Nora, I don't really know what's going on, but I'm so sorry. Can I do anything?" She put her arms around me.

"Sarah, I just feel so rotten, but I know Matt needs to get out fishing. I feel like his mother. I want to comfort him and protect him from those big meanies, but I know the best thing for him is to get back out there."

"Oh Nora, I'm so glad to hear you say that. It's terrible, but I was so afraid you'd be furious with him."

"No, I should have hashed this out before, but I didn't."

264

I hated Robin and Neil for sitting together on the sofa, so legal and happy and smug and together. They hadn't the foggiest idea of how cruel life could be. "Nora, I'm teaching a class at the Women's Resource Center on dealing with stress. You should join it. It would help you a lot."

At the first class, I took the test of stressors in your life that says if you score over 300 your body is going to break down, get sick, or get in an accident or something. I scored 560. The dryer quit working again.

Reading a magazine article, "Luxury is the Only Defense," about French "splendor" and marble and porcelain and only the finest, when Matthew emerges from his room with poop dangling from his pants and we go to the bathroom with the stains in the toilet, the horrid smells, and the rotting floor.

How can I get out of this? I've been asking that one for years. Never have I been sure of anything but that I'm alone.

How do people escape that prison of responsibilities and desires to become insane, or do they get ensnared by insanity? How bad does it have to get before you can crack? There's just a raw hurt at the bottom but I want to get out, not go crazy or hurt people. I want to be victorious, happy. How? One thing I know for sure—it has got to be an adventure, not another crisis for me.

Matt was out fishing. I went to pick up the babysitter before my next stress-management class. She lived out by Mill Bay and I had all three kids in the car.

As we were coming back home on the cutoff road, there was a truck stopped in the middle of the road. I swerved to go around it and the Jeep skidded on the ice and the brakes didn't work. We rammed into the rear of the truck.

I hit my neck on the steering wheel and the thought raced through my brain, "I can't be hurt. I've got to get everybody else home okay."

The babysitter screamed, "My leg! Oh God, my leg!" and I jumped around to her side, opened the door and held her. "We're gonna be all right. The hospital is just down the road. You're gonna be okay!"

She cried out, "I can't breathe, you're smothering me, stop hugging me!"

Then I heard the kids crying in the back and I ran back around to the driver's side and pulled the seat forward. Chelsea's glasses were broken but she seemed all right, and Matthew had a bloody nose, but I wasn't afraid for him. Liam was crumpled in the corner and I pulled him towards me and was sick with fear. His head was dented in at the temple and bulging above his nose.

I just felt wild. I had to get him to the hospital.

The driver of the truck came up to me. Some teenage kids pulled up in a car behind me. I said, "I've got to get my kids to the hospital."

The driver of the truck said he'd stay with the babysitter until the ambulance came, and the teenagers helped me get Chelsea, Liam, and Matthew in their car. All I could think about was Liam.

The hospital was less than a quarter-mile down the same road, but we had to go slow because of the ice. In the emergency room, the high school kids stayed with Chelsea and Matthew and I hovered over Liam. A nurse cleaned the blood off my face from where I hit the steering wheel. "You don't want to frighten your little boy when he looks at you."

Liam never lost consciousness or seemed disoriented, but he moaned that his head hurt. I was just barely aware of Chelsea and Matthew waiting on a sofa in the hall as I went back and forth with Liam to the X-ray rooms.

I felt like a grenade was in my stomach, with the pin pulled out, just waiting for some blood vessel to burst in Liam's head and explode our lives.

They put us in a room for the night for observation, Liam in his little boy skivvies and distorted brow. The doctor told me that it looked okay, they'd just have to watch and wait for awhile. He drove the other kids and me home to wrassle up pajamas and find Liam's "angel blanket." Then I took Chelsea and Matthew to Stella's, and as she took Matthew in her arms she said, "Oh, kid, when is your luck going to change?"

Back at the hospital Liam dozed, groaning occasionally. Someone came in every hour to check his pupils and see if he was coherent. Liam said, "I want Daddy to come home so I can sing, 'I See the Moon' to him."

I started crying again. I called Karen and asked her to radio Matt and she called back to say he told her he would head home as soon as he'd moved some pots.

I was sitting in the dark chewing my lips when Gloria Wade came in the room. "Eleanor?" she said. I think I overwhelmed her when I fell into her arms, sobbing my head off.

"I just feel like God's up there seeing me pick myself up over and over and trying to walk around normally and saying, 'Hasn't she learned her lesson yet? I'm going to smash her a good one this time.'"

"Now, now. It sounds like you're a little depressed."

Bless Gloria's understated heart. She makes it sound so simple. "Just be a mother." "You're a little depressed."

The next morning I took Liam home from the hospital and around noon Matt walked in the front door. The next few days I was almost oblivious to the fact that Matt dealt with getting the wrecked car towed to town, talking to the baby-sitter's parents (she had a broken leg), and squaring things with the insurance company. I wandered around the house day and night, trying to keep up some kind of normal function, but I couldn't sleep at night and was distracted all day.

I took advantage of Matt being home to jump all over him at the slightest provocation. Making dinner one night, I discovered the gas element in the oven had gone out again. I slammed the oven door. "The goddamn propane heater won't stay lit! I'm tired of nothing working right!"

"For God's sake, Eleanor, it's no big deal. Would you relax?"

Matt arranged for the VW bug to be shipped up from Seattle. When it arrived on the container barge, Matt drove us there in the neighbor's car and followed us home while I drove the Volkswagen with the kids. Halfway down Mission Road, the headlights went out and the accelerator jammed. Thank God it was a stick shift, but the engine roaring away full throttle in second gear terrified us all. The worst thing was Liam screaming in the back seat.

We finally pulled in the driveway and I turned off the ignition. I pulled the kids out of the car as Matt drove up. "My life is nothing but crisis! I want out!"

"Oh God, Eleanor, what now?"

"This damn car is trying to kill us. The accelerator jammed!" Liam was still roaring and now Chelsea and Matthew joined in.

"Jesus, you're a nervous wreck!"

"You noticed!"

Finally Matt brought home some tranquilizers from the doctor's office so I could sleep at night. The swelling in Liam's forehead went down and we were safe at home.

Sarah pulled into the driveway and burst into the house one afternoon just as it got dark. "Nora! The weirdest thing just happened. Oooh, I've got the ickiest feeling!"

"What?"

"I was driving down Rezanof towards the college when I saw Dr. Copstead jumping around naked in front of his house!"

"Oh, come on, Sarah...."

"No! I couldn't believe it either, but I mean he was naked! Totally! In the cold and everything!"

"What!"

"Jeez, I don't know, but he was like dancing around like some ceremony and I didn't know what to do, so I went to the clinic and told them, they said he wasn't there, and then somebody else came in and said the same thing, and they called the police."

"Oh my God, really?"

"Yes! And when the cops got there, Leslie, his wife, wasn't home, but their little kid, their little three-year old, was locked in a closet inside, and the cops said Copstead was chanting to rid the house of the devil!"

"What happened to him?"

"He must have taken some bad acid or something."

"Sarah, I can't believe that. You just don't get more straight-arrow than Dr. Copstead."

"Well, he flipped out, and now they sent him to the mental hospital in Anchorage. He can't remember his own name and is just totally out of it."

"This is really creepy."

"Yeah, he's the last person you'd think of would freak out, or be on drugs or whatever it is."

I was baking Christmas fruitcakes when Chelsea, who was sitting at the dining room table doing homework, threw her pencil at the wall. "I hate school!"

"Honey, what's wrong?" I pulled her onto the rocking chair while she sobbed away.

"I hate it, Mom, I hate it. Please come to school with me. Other moms do it."

"They do?" I asked. "What does Sister Irene say?"

"It's okay. She talks to them and likes them and she never yells at their kids."

"Honey, does she yell at you?"

"Yes, she told me if I don't speak up she won't let me be a toy for Christmas."

"A toy for Christmas—you mean in the play?"

"Yeah—oh Mom, I hate the play and please come Mom!"

My poor little grown-up girl fighting Sister Irene! She's so proud of her bad temper, calling herself "Kodiak's Grouchiest Bear."

I called Sister Irene and asked if I could help with the Christmas pageant.

"Well, you could play the piano for me."

So the next afternoon, I left the boys at daycare and went to Chelsea's school and watched Sister Irene whip the children into shape.

"My God," I thought as I heard her drill the children, "what army did I draft my baby into?"

"Tina, you dummy, step forward! Ben, don't be so clumsy!" A lot of the kids were oblivious or jittery, and a lot more were wary and nervous, waiting for their share of official wrath.

On the way home, I tried to bolster Chelsea up. "Honey, she's just an old flea-bitten bear. Don't listen to her when she's grouching. I'll be there and if she goes after you, I'll nail her hide to the wall."

So we got through the rehearsals and the highly touted Christmas program fast approached.

Matt went out several days before the program to set pots down for the seven-inch king crab season that would open three days before Christmas.

"Matt, don't go out now. If the weather comes up, you know you won't make it back in time. Please—Chelsea's had such a hard time with this."

"Look, I'll be there."

"Matt, I'll be so mad if you aren't."

"Okay! okay I'll be there! I promise!"

The morning of the show, Cy called from the cannery. "Yeah, uh, Matt says he's not going to make it in. The weather came up."

That night I struggled with my composure as the kids sang my favorite Shirley Temple song in the show:

Make my mother's life a song
Make my father safe and strong
Keep him with us all year long
That's what I want for Christmas

Matt got home Christmas Eve day. I said nothing to him, nor he to me, and after the kids went to bed, I dragged out boxes of trikes and playhouses from the closets and under the beds and we assembled toys and wrapped presents wordlessly, ignoring each other, till three in the morning. I remembered old Christmases with eggnogs and laughter and unexpected company and hushed whispers.

The new pastor of the church where Shine Bright was housed dropped a bombshell at the January board meeting. He said that the church governing council had met and decided they wanted to use the church basement as a teenage drop-in entertainment center. "So we've decided that Shine Bright will have to vacate the basement as of June 1, this year."

One of the board members leaned on his crossed arms across the table and harangued everyone. "Well, isn't that just great? Not only does the high school have the only paved parking lot in town so the teenagers can park their new trucks that they get from salmon fishing, but now they have to drive the poor little kids out so they can play their acid rock music!" His head bobbed and weaved as he talked, and he slurred his words.

I could sense people drawing away, but it was comic relief to hear his speech, daring to say what everyone else was too diplomatic to voice.

Sandy, the Shine Bright director, said, "I don't think it's productive to consider this as an eviction. However, Pastor Wentright, is this decision final? Could we perhaps work out some compromise, or at least persuade the church to defer their decision?"

Wentright said, "Frankly, the Board of Governors is not happy with the noise and the mess of Shine Bright. Further, the teenagers roam the Plaza and the harbor and downtown streets at night. They need a place to go after school and work hours."

"But the little children need a place to go *during* school and work hours," Sandy said. "We provide that, and our program has assistance from the government programs set up now to provide hot lunches and other benefits for the children."

"Well, that too is a problem," the pastor said. "Does our church want to contribute to government welfare, especially for children of families who are not even church members?"

I said, "I would really like to see the community's daycare housed in a building of its own, where its existence isn't always dependent on some other organization, at someplace permanent and independent. Here's our opportunity to exist on our own."

The chairman said, "That's an excellent suggestion. Would you like to be in charge of the committee to locate such a place for Shine Bright?"

"Well, all right, I'll try."

The chairman asked for hands of people who would volunteer to help me. Sandy, the director, and one of the dads, who was a carpenter, offered. Afterwards we met for a minute, and both the director and the dad were steamed.

"That pompous…!" the dad fumed.

"I think we've got to have the attitude that it's for the best, and we should move onward, heads held high and all that," I said.

"Lady, do you have any idea what you're up against?"

"Well, what else can we do? Too many people need daycare. There's got to be a place for it."

We started at the Legislative Affairs Office in the Town Hall, but they didn't offer much help. Sandy and I went to a state budget meeting attended by the city councilmen and when I told them what I was there for, they shook their heads benignly and said, "With oil revenues going down this year, you don't have a chance, but if you want to butt your head against the wall, why go ahead."

Matt smirked at first when I told him of the plan for an independent daycare center. "I thought you felt that mothers should stay home with their kids."

"I do, or a dad or a gramma or somebody that cares about that kid above everything else, but if the mom's the one who has to work to buy groceries and pay rent, the kids still need to be taken care of, to be safe while the mom's making money."

"You always talked like going on welfare was the perfect solution if there wasn't money for food and rent," Matt said.

"Oh, Matt, I did not. There's a difference between working to pay for necessities and working to avoid going home to your family. There's kids in daycare, like Donna's Andy, who'd never get above poverty level if his mom couldn't work and raise their standard of living. They would be stuck on welfare."

"What about all the teachers and principals and doctors and attorneys where both the couple work and slam their kids into daycare?"

"Look, Matt, I don't know about everybody, I don't even know about me, but I just think the kids need to be someplace safe during the day, and in this town, Shine Bright is the place where they can go."

Sandy and Carl, the carpenter dad, and I met about daycare and went over state requirements for the cost per square foot and space contingencies and other dry money matters.

I sighed and said, "I hate these kind of details because it's like they're in a different language, and they always seem to change."

Sandy said, "Oh, you get familiar with them after awhile."

Carl said, "Now, how come the City Council isn't interested in this? After all, they have votes to consider."

Sandy said, "The council thinks they're always bailing Shine Bright out. Last year we had a big accounting error, and we're still paying them back a loan they gave us to get out of that pickle. And then there's the upright citizens who think that women should stay home with their kids anyway, even though it's often the grandkids they're looking after. It's just not the good old days, and you can't make it so."

"So how can we get them interested in us, supportive of us?" I asked.

"You know, they're having a seminar this Saturday on budgeting for non-profit organizations. If we went to that and then called on them for advice, they'd probably be more willing to take us seriously. Can you go?"

"Yeah, I guess we better."

Matthew's glasses arrived and he looks like the absent-minded professor, with his horn-rimmed spectacles and his shock of chicken-feather hair.

I went to the budget meeting yesterday and looked at everybody's hair. Either I'm the only one getting grey hair or everyone else does a great dye job.

Matt's been out since Thursday morning. He went out Tuesday when the season finally opened and came back the next day with a broken-down engine and worked on it for 20 hours straight. Poor guy—his eyes were so red and his dirty old pores looked like they were oozing oil grease. And he'd worked on that engine for six weeks before the season opened.

Karen had a Valentine's party for all the kids and it was wild. Michael went on a rampage and hit his mom and stomped on Matthew's glasses. No apology or offer to fix them from Karen. She just said, "Oh Michael, you're just a little wildman like your daddy."

Leanne had moved back to Kodiak. Her baby looked just like Chuck, but Leanne looked so skinny and haunted.

"Are you glad you came back to Kodiak?" I asked.

"Well, I just felt that Kodiak was Chuck's town and I want to make my peace with it. Maybe then I'll be able to go on...." Big tears welled up in her eyes.

It was a beautiful sunshiny day when we went over at one, but when Scott came home about four, he said the temperature had dropped 20 degrees in one hour. That evening it was 15 degrees and still falling.

CHAPTER TWENTY

DEATH, DESTRUCTION, AND WINTER
In which I sound the depths

Minus two degrees this morning with a wind chill factor of minus 30, and the furnace went out. Not till this morning though, so it was 60 degrees in the house when we got up. A hard morning, but no screaming. Progress.

Everyone's furnace went out because the oil company had delivered oil that froze at minus five degrees. So the oil trucks went around filling people's tanks with "Arctic" oil that won't freeze. Meanwhile, everybody in town had broken-down furnaces and frozen pipes.

I called a plumber to thaw our pipes but they told me to call a welder. The welder said they had about 120 people before me but they'd get to me as soon as possible.

Sarah asked me if we wanted to stay with them till our furnace got going again. At first I said, no, we'd wait for the oil delivery, but the house was icy, except right in front of the fire, so we went over there late that night and slept in their big sofa-bed in their front room.

The next morning Sarah stood at the sink as we made up the bed again and got ready for the day. "Nora, you can stay as long as you need, you know that."

"Thank you, Sarah, but we need to keep to our schedule as best we can with school and all, and then I need to try to get the furnace working again."

So we began a different routine of getting out of my bed, warmed by an electric blanket, grabbing a jacket to change one or more wet babies, bundling them up and then getting myself dressed in layers of warm but confining clothes.

I told Karen I was afraid of freezing to death.

"Nora, that's sick."

"It's not like the days when it's freezing outside but I'm snug inside with long skirts and gleaming copper molds on the wall and the smell of food cooking. It's icy toes and fingertips and noses *inside* the house. This is miserable, and I don't know when it's going to end."

Jake came over and "bled" the fuel lines and got the furnace started again and the trailer started heating up, but the pipes were still frozen and the welding company hadn't worked their way to us yet.

Then at school Sloopy Don stopped me to ask how things were going.

"Oh, Don, our pipes are still frozen and I'm hauling buckets of water from Jake and Stella's."

"Tell you what, Nora, I'll come over and look after work today."

"How about you guys, doesn't Jessie need you home?"

"We were lucky there. She went down with the baby to visit her relatives in Seattle before this storm came."

When Don came over he crawled under the trailer. "Nora, come on outside for a minute and see this."

I stood at the front door while he crept underneath again and shone a flashlight at some pipes. "See that pipe?"

"Yeah."

"And see how it's got insulation wrapped around it?"

"Oh, yeah."

"And see the electric cord coming from the end of it?"

"Yeah, is that plugged in? How come it's not keeping the pipe unfrozen?"

Don yanked on the cord and pulled it out of the dirt. "Somebody buried it."

"Why?"

"Who knows, some genius."

"Great," I said and went back inside to get boiling water off the stove to wash the dishes.

I'm wearing my fur coat and wool pants and sweater and wool tights and fur boots, and still my feet and nose get cold. The poor kids that have to come to school from Bells Flats and further. If it wasn't for my job, I'd like to get on a plane—if I had the money. I just think people shouldn't attempt to live and function in this weather. Karen said, when I told her about hauling water, "I couldn't stand that. How can you live without running water? You must be so strong."

Strength has nothing to do with it. It seems to me she's saying, "You must be such a wimp to sit there without water and not be able to demand something be done about it. I wouldn't stand for it." But what would she do?

Don brought some big space heaters from school and set them under the trailer. Even after going full force all day, the ground was still frozen. The temperature is still below zero.

Don came inside the house as Chelsea was asking me to fix her record player. I said, "Chelsea, I don't know how to fix that."

Don said, "Oh, you could figure that out if you applied yourself."

I felt like saying, "I don't have the fucking strength left to apply myself to fix a cheesy record player. I'm not that strong."

I am so sick of this cold. It fills me with dread weight. All my plants and beautiful six-year old ferns have died and look like brown skeletons. I can't believe it still hasn't warmed up yet, it's like nuclear winter. Still no word from Matt. He is probably waiting the weather out in some bay.

The floor is cold from the moment my feet slide out from under warm bedcovers. I walk with my toes curled under all day. If one bare knee touches the other, the icy knobbiness of it sends chills up my spine. My face is burned raw from the cold wind. I guess this is one of those character-building experiences. I'd give up a little character if I could be warm again.

In the midst of the cold snap, there was a big city council meeting to apply for federal revenue-sharing funds. I got up, all prepared for the different objections from the council members, and used the terms like "internal controls" and "self-regulating agency" that I learned at the budgeting seminar.

One councilman said, "Didn't we bail the daycare out of some financial crisis last year?"

I said, "Although I wasn't on the board last year, it's my understanding that that was a matter of accounting, collection, and cash flow. Since then, we've installed internal controls into the system to prevent a reoccurrence. What we're faced with now is a logistics problem—simply, if we don't have a place, we can't operate."

I'm beginning to understand how politicians love the power of abstract jargon.

The committee got out early and I took the opportunity to drop in on Karen and Scott. They were having a dinner party with Neil and Robin.

I felt like I'd blundered, just walking in, and like they were thinking, "Poor Nora, she's sublimating all her need for a husband in this rabid child care issue."

Robin said, "Don't you resent all your time this takes up?"

I said, "Someone needs to do it and at least it takes my mind off frozen water pipes."

I decided today that if the weather is going to be so miserable, at least I am going out in style. I put on my fur coat and gobs of makeup and took the kids out for breakfast before work and splurged on a big pizza for dinner, paying for both meals with bad checks. Don said he thinks we may thaw out and get water tomorrow. I'll be so glad. It's hard pulling off Auntie Mame.

We got the water going and discovered where all the pipes had burst—under the sinks, the lines leading to the dishwasher and to the plumbing in the back of the house. So we shut all the water off again, and Don crawled back under the trailer to try to plug the leaks.

It is so nice of Don to work so hard, day after day, on my stupid problems. I don't think I was meant to have running water. I think this is a message from God saying, "What makes you think that just because you live in times where running water is a common household feature, that you are entitled to it?" Gee, I don't know. Just naturally arrogant, I guess. Spoiled rotten. Strong.

Finally, it appeared that things would get back to normal. The pipes were unfrozen and the leaks were fixed. Don turned the main water valve on. We were both so elated, like we'd christened a ship or something, and then we saw water flowing from the toilets onto the bathroom floor.

"Why are they overflowing?"

"Oh shit, they must be still frozen, blocked."

I mopped up the messes and sent Don home. He was finally ready to give up.

Matt arrived at dawn, finally able to get home because the weather was warming up. I told him the story of our frozen trailer in gory detail. He called the plumber and demanded they come out that day. Of course they did.

The plumber spent all afternoon and said he'd come back the next day to finish up if we wrote him a check for $800 to pay for his work so far. I said, "Matt, that's outrageous. We don't have that money in the bank!"

He said, "Look, it's got to be done. Your little boyfriend isn't coming around now that I'm back in town."

"What a cheap shot, Matt. If Karen or Robin had to go through what I went through and you didn't help them, I'd think you were terrible. And if you didn't offer to help just because I was out of town and you were concerned with how it looks, I'd have no respect for you. Wouldn't you offer your home or your help to a friend?"

"You could have called a plumber."

"I did, and I was 200th on the waiting list! Do you think I manufactured this crisis so I could have a little rendezvous with Don?"

"I don't know Eleanor, but I'm sure you had your plans."

I am not his dog to kick.

I took a deep breath and said, "Okay, Matt, it's time to level with you. I've tried for years to hide it from you, but you always knew the truth down deep. I've never been true to you. There've been men in and out of here every time you went away. I never missed you. I was so glad to see you go. All that begging for you to stay home was one big act.

"Jake and I have been carrying on from the beginning. Why do you think Tuffy went away? He'd come over and we'd spend your money and have the best time.

"And Sloopy Don, when we couldn't meet here, we'd meet on his boat. I could hardly keep my hands off him when you were around.

"And Neil O'Hara—he'd come over whenever he was in town and we'd go out in front of everyone and laugh at you and Robin.

"I thought I could hide it, but I never really had you convinced, did I?" I was shaking with rage and choking on my words. I wanted to hurt him so badly he'd torture himself with remorse for the rest of his long, spiteful life.

Matt just sat there. We both knew it wasn't true, but he'd brought it on himself. He looked stripped, like I'd exposed him. We both knew what a scared bully he was.

I threw a plate at the sink for emphasis and walked out the door to its satisfying shatters. "This nails the coffin. Go fishing. Go fishing and don't ever come back."

That night he slept on the sofa and left the next morning after paying the plumber.

A week later, he came back to town and I made him go with me to see the eye surgeon from Anchorage, Dr. Fleming.

"Your son is seeing double, which is why he squints and crosses his eyes. What we'll do is cut the muscle to reposition his right eye, but if his brain doesn't send the message to co-ordinate his eyes, they'll cross again. It's really quite difficult surgery, like trying to sew a wet noodle together. It's successful about 80 percent of the time."

"Is surgery the only recourse now?" I asked him.

Fleming sighed and said impatiently, "I just spent half an hour explaining the situation to you. You have to make the decision."

I felt so damn stupid.

CHAPTER TWENTY-ONE

CAREFUL LOG CABIN QUILT
In which I succeed

I took my old satin quilt up to the Community College where I could lay it out flat in the home-ec room and work on it. I was mending the tears and re-tufting it when Leslie Copstead came in to work on a project beside me.

I was apologetic about the ratty appearance of the quilt. Leslie said, "Sometimes our first attempts have a rustic, heartfelt beauty that can't be duplicated. Its flaws give it a unique character."

I looked down at my "bordello" quilt and felt proud—that I still had it, that it was so ornate and vivid, that its imperfections weren't what stood out in the overall effect.

I told Leslie I was escaping from home and my cares. She talked of her attempts to keep her family together. Dr. Copstead had been sent to Texas, still rehabilitating from his 'stroke,' as she called his naked-dance episode last winter. "He's little more than a vegetable."

"Did you have any warning signs before?" I asked her.

Leslie looked funny at me and said, "I thought everybody knew he'd been taking the drugs in his clinic, and street drugs as well. He destroyed himself, and us too."

I'd always pictured him the soul of propriety and upright ways.

Leslie said, "People tell me I'm so brave and strong, but I'm so tired of hearing that!"

"Oh yeah, I hate that, too," I said. "For some reason, it's no compliment."

"It's so uncompassionate, so distancing. I just tell them, 'What's the alternative?' It's not like I'm making a noble choice."

"Yeah, I thought the choice was making a home for my family, my children and their father. I'm trying to keep my family together, but it's like riding a bike with one wheel missing," I said.

Leslie said, "I have a friend who's a lawyer. She always wanted to practice law, and visualized her own office and her own stationery and all the rest, down to the fine details. She knew no one would give it to her, that she'd have to go after it herself. And she finally made it—now that's strength, to keep on trying."

"I know I have to get what I want by myself, but I don't know how to be a fatherless family," I said.

"Sometimes there isn't a path, you just have to hack your way through the wilderness," Leslie said.

Getting Matthew to wear his glasses was a struggle. He would take them off and misplace them and then we would be in a rush to go somewhere and his glasses were nowhere to be found. "Oh, Matthew, don't you realize that if these glasses don't work, you'll have to have an operation? Please wear them, please don't lose them anymore."

But he didn't understand.

The relocation committee put together a budget for Shine Bright to send to the Legislature for a grant application. It was the one thing in my life that was clearly defined and I was beginning to understand and retain the figures.

Sandy asked me, "Aren't you getting burnt out with your kids and your job and Matt being gone and now this?"

I didn't tell her that Matt's been gone from me for a long time. I just said, "I'm learning to compartmentalize my life and deal with one thing at a time. Besides, no one's indispensable and I'm going to be gone in the summer. I'm going back to school in Seattle to finish my music degree so I can teach piano and write musicals."

"Up here in Kodiak? Like Rodgers and Hammerstein?"

"I mean, this is my long-range plan, while Matt is fishing his life away. First I have to finish my undergrad degree, then I can teach music. I'm happy at the piano, and I feel free when I sing."

That spring, Chelsea brought home picture after picture of houses—with curtains in the windows, with flowers in the garden, with smoke coming out of the chimney. Her drawings inspired me to make a neat, cheerful log cabin quilt.

I figured out the dimensions and started cutting out the yellow squares and red cabin parts from calico scraps.

This is one quilt I'm making carefully and deliberately, not slap-dashing the pieces together or taking the easy way out. There's no rush to finish it, and it's going to reflect order and simplicity.

After naps, Robin and Sarah came over with a *Cosmo* magazine and we took the emotional stability test.

Robin was "A Rock—be careful you don't petrify." Sarah was "A Plant—centered and flexible." I was at the bottom of "The Walking Wounded," but at least I wasn't "A Mess—get help now!"

I told Sarah, "I'm so tired of having only sadness and troubles to offer people."

She said, "That's not true! You don't just mope at home feeling sorry for yourself."

"Oh yes, I do."

"But you like to party, you're great with the kids, you play the piano, you get people organized—you're not just a sob sister."

"Yeah, but I scored "Walking Wounded!""

"That's just because of the turkey you tied yourself to. Besides, Nora, you were home with your babies. Now they're little kids, and you're going to recapture yourself while the rest of us are just beginning."

I feel a bundle of contradictory feelings—grateful to Sarah for her encouragement, guilty that the kids' babyhood has been so filled with disappointment and unshared joys, powerful at the thought of getting on with life, and little-kid terror, not knowing what lies ahead.

I went to visit Karen but she was preoccupied, packing boxes for their trip to the boatyard in Seattle. Scott was drunk and making horrible cracks about Michael, who was sick. "Oh, if he dies, we'll just have another baby," he snickered.

I drove home with the kids, feeling at odds with life, when a taxi pulled in front of us. "Maybe that's your Dad," I said to the kids. "Let's follow that taxi." So we followed the taxi out Mission Road past our house to the end of Spruce Cape Road when the passenger got out.

"Nah, that's not Daddy," Liam said.

"But maybe he's getting into one right now downtown at the boat harbor," I said. "Shall we go see?"

"Yeah!" screamed the kids, so we spent about an hour before bedtime tailing cabs around Kodiak.

Matt came into town a few nights later just as the kids were getting into bed.

"So, you guys eat a good dinner?"

"Yeah, really good. They had frozen hot dogs and pickles for dinner. Yeah, I know it's the nutritional pits," I said as his face registered his disapproval.

As Matt was getting ready for bed, I told him the latest about Matthew's eye problems. "We're using both the glasses and the patches until Dr. Fleming's next visit."

Matt grunted and climbed into bed.

"Fleming said there's a 20-percent chance they'll overcorrect in surgery and instead of crossing, Matthew's eyes will focus outward. It makes me really scared."

"Look, Nora, there's nothing I can do about it now and I'm trying to sleep."

I went out to the living room to sleep on the sofa and cried. I realized very clearly and coldly that I would be making this decision alone, too, weighing the information, making the arrangements, and living with the results.

I can't burn out on tears or I won't be able to function for the kids. I hate the social responsibility of being straight, but I know drinking or dope would just put me out of commission. I don't want that. I want to be happy. I'm a fool to count on Matt for that.

Don't be envious. Be what you're envious of. Be happily married? Be yourself?

Grab your mind by its shoulders and steer it away from troubles. Make your own luck. Reach in the darkness of your unhappiness and misfortune, grab something, and make that something you've grabbed be the thing you want. A blues singer in a smoke-filled bar? Too lowlife for the kids. A music teacher at school?

I met with the new minister in Shine Bright's church to ask if the daycare could stay in the church basement until fall. After he showed me pictures of his new baby, his first child, I told him we were having a hard time finding an alternative location for the daycare center.

He said, "For any campaign to succeed you need one person who believes heart and soul in its importance. How does your husband feel about your involvement in this?"

His comment threw me, but I said, "Frankly, this is my interest, my campaign. My husband doesn't oppose me, but like most people in town, he considers the children's situation to be the concern of their mothers."

"Well, naturally," Wentright said.

I came home to find Matt bumping around, squinting through one eye with a patch on the other. "I made a deal with Matthew to wear one as long as he does," he said. "This isn't easy, you know."

I went to the City Council meeting and reported on everything we'd done—asked all the churches, set up petition-signing tables, talked to city offices and to all the government people, participated in teleconferences with state officials—and said, "Though everyone supports us, nothing has materialized for Shine Bright to relocate except the Mormon church, which would be perfect, but it costs $250,000."

Then some throw-weight bureaucrat got up and said, "Did you talk to the Teen Center? Did you talk to the Episcopal Church, to the Parks Department?"

"Yes," I said.

"Go back and tell them that I said to talk to them," he said. "Tell them I'd like to know their answer."

I was so frustrated. Aside from the fact that we'd already checked them out and they were unsuitable or unavailable, the idea that his influence—which after three months he's deigned to bestow—is going to make the difference was so insulting.

Tanner season ended and Matt came in from fishing. We had scheduled Matthew's operation in Anchorage later that week, but then the kids came down with sore throats and strep infections. I called Dr. Fleming's office to reschedule the operation.

Matt said, "Don't worry. We'll go next month and everything will turn out okay."

I put the kids to bed and from the kitchen I could hear Chelsea singing:

Me and my dumpster
My dumpster and me
We both get along so famously

The next night the girls were having a party for Karen's trip to the boatyards and for Sarah's completion of the schoolwork for her nursing degree. I got dressed to the hilt with my stiletto-heeled sandals, and as I left, Matt looked at me and said, "How come you never get dressed up for me?"

I said, "Well, why don't you join us in town later?"

"Nah, you go ahead with your girlfriends."

Everyone was giddy that night. Sarah was making popcorn and spilled oil on her dress. She was running around, asking how to get it out. I got some stale bread from Karen and started rubbing it against Sarah's dress to soak up the oil when Robin walked in and saw all the breadcrumbs on the floor. "Nora, you're making a mess!"

I wanted to say, "Oh, lighten up," but I just laughed and said, "Bring on the ducks—they'll clean it up!"

After awhile Scott and Neil showed up and we all went downtown. It was the same old dark, damp, yelling-across-the-bar scene. Karen went up to the bar and Leanne and I were sitting together when this guy walked up to us and said to Leanne, "God, I'm sick of looking at your sad face. Why'd you come back? We loved Chuck more than you did. Your were always nagging him, making him mad."

She jumped up and stumbled away and I just grabbed the edge of the table and flipped it over on him.

"You jerk! You stupid fucking jerk!" I yelled at him and ran through the crowd to where Leanne had disappeared in the bathroom. She was clutching the side of the sink, retching her guts out.

"Leanne, it's okay, it's okay, he had no right. He's just too drunk and stupid."

"I loved Chuck! We were happy!" she sobbed and broke my heart with her skinny body feeling like a crushed delicate bird fluttering inside her dark coat.

I tried to celebrate Matt's birthday the next week by making a Black Forest torte. It was pouring rain, and I'd already made two trips to town for ingredients, when I found I'd forgotten the whipped cream. Matt came home then and I was feeling so ornery and mad. When he saw how flustered I was, he offered to get some whipped cream.

He brought home the kind they use on the boats, that is basically lard, so I went out again in search of real whipping cream.

When I finally got the cake together with liqueur and sour cherries and whipped cream and chocolate shavings, it just kind of held its breath for one minute, then let it out and started crumbling apart. We were all so grubby and at loose ends by then, we just ate it with our hands.

Sandy called and said, "The city has a lot we could build a center on, right downtown. And the elders at St. Herman's are interested in talking to us. Can you go meet with them while I meet with the city?"

She came over after our meetings and we looked over the city planner's plots and talked to contractors and figured out it would cost just about as much to build new as to buy an existing building. "This is narrowing down to a quarter million dollars, anyway you look at it," Sandy said.

"Yeah, when I met with the Russian Orthodox guys at St. Herman's, they were dead earnest about cooperating on a daycare center. I felt a little uncertain, because I know they think women shouldn't concern themselves outside the home, but I was all I had to offer. And you know Ivan Rostoff, one of the elders? He's a fisherman who remembered me from last summer on the boat, and he was very nice.

"What they have in mind is co-ownership of a building on their property for a daycare center during the day and a recreation hall on nights and weekends. But they'd need a tremendous amount of money and haven't started any planning or construction and we still wouldn't be an independent daycare center."

"Well, something better go our way soon, or I don't know what's going to happen," Sandy said.

"I wish we could put a daycare tax on all the fishing boats every time they come back from a trip. It's to the whole town's benefit to have a good daycare center. It's funny, more and more I see the little kid in adults, wanting their own way and wanting to be seen as the good guy or strong guy, but everyone really as fragile and self-interested as the kids."

The kids and I made May baskets out of construction paper and left them on Stella's and Karen's doorsteps. "I love spring," I bubbled over to Matt. "I'm going to grab joy at every chance I get."

We looked at a house for sale later that day. It was actually the shell of a house with wallboard still to be put up. The builder showed us the wallboard paneling he'd picked out—fake wood, stained blue with ducks flying out of marshes imprinted on it. He'd chosen paneling for the other rooms that was just as bad. He said proudly, "Yeah, this is one house that won't have plain white walls like a doctor's office."

I said, "But I like plain white walls."

"You do?" he asked in disbelief. "Well, you can decide what kind of wallboard you'd want this summer when you get to that stage," he said.

Matt said, "I'll be out fishing and Eleanor has made her plans for the summer," and he looked at me and smiled. It was the first I knew that he didn't feel I was running out on him, or being irresponsible, that he wasn't mad at me. But he just said I'd made other plans, like we'd discussed it, it was a fact he could live with and we were in agreement about it.

The state legislature voted to give Shine Bright $250,000 for an independent daycare center. Sandy called me and came over with a bottle of champagne.

"Did you even know they were voting?" I asked her.

"Well no! I knew it was coming up sometime soon, but then maybe they'd table it or send it to a subcommittee for further study or some political thing, but they just passed the appropriation! It's ours! Nora, you were great!"

"Oh, Sandie, all I did was grunt work and make noise."

"But they heard you. You made them hear us!"

"Yeah, and after all the suits telling us we were wasting our breath, and little kids couldn't vote...."

"And we didn't understand the legislative process and oil revenues were down...."

"And we were just banging our heads against the wall!" Sandie and I clinked our glasses.

"Sandie, I'm done, someone else can navigate this move. This has been the best thing for me, to battle for something outside me, to grasp hard cold certainties, and to plan on leaving instead of getting involved forever. I feel like an Olympic champion."

I had the best birthday in years. We took the kids out to Cliff Point for a picnic. Matt gave me a scrimshaw pendant etched with a bird sitting on a tree branch. It reminded me of the saying, "You have to hold out a green bough before the bird of happiness will land."

Then we took the kids to the babysitter's house so they could sleep there and we could stay out all night if we wanted to.

We went to dinner at the Village. Afterwards Stella and Jake came over to our table and had a drink with us. Stella asked me about my summer plans. I told her about school in Seattle.

"So you're not going out on the boat?" When I shook my head she added, "I've got to hand it to you, kid, you've hung in there when a saint would have screamed."

"Oh, I scream."

"Yeah, but you've tried everything. For a while there I thought you were going to wind up with Captain Kangaroo. That reminds me—Elizabeth is getting married again—to a great guy. He takes her boys fishing, a real family man. I told her, 'I want to be the first to dance at your wedding,' and she said, 'Most people think I should wear black for the rest of my life.'"

Stella laughed and got up and I wondered how to digest her comments about me. Did I feel proud for persisting, or ashamed for being a martyr? Was it worth it? Would I sink back into the pit or would I break through to the other side?

After dinner we went over to the Mecca and Matt's cronies sat down with us and were talking fishing. I'd had two drinks, then switched to ginger ale, and just wandered in and out of the conversation.

Two old Russian-Native fishermen who never take their wives out to a bar—or anywhere—sat down. I felt like, in their eyes, no lady would be in a bar, so I was pretty quiet. One of them turned to Matt and pointed a finger at me and said, "Well, this lady is turning the town upside down trying to shake a place loose for the daycare center. My grandson goes there and his mom didn't know what she was going to do if they closed. Your wife did a great job."

Matt said, "Yeah, she's quite a lady—too much for me sometimes," and everybody laughed.

Later we got up to dance. I had my high heels on so I could almost look Matt in the eyes. I felt so strong and whole and gently powerful, like I wasn't a body of bones and muscle, but a force of nature and harmony that drew respect. I didn't even have to protect myself from Matt.

We took a taxi home at four in the morning and stood in the kitchen, realizing the kids weren't home and we could fight or party or swing from the chandeliers for all anybody cared.

"I've been dreaming about this all night," Matt said. He pulled me down the hall by the hand and we lay on the bed, him running his big strong hands up and down my body. "God, I love the way you move," he said.

I was purring and moaning my heart out, so scared and protected at the same time.

"You little witch," Matt said, and then we just kind of went spiritual and animal and good and bad all at once. I kept saying, "Don't go, don't go." I wanted to keep him sweet and tender forever.

After things quieted down, I lay enfolded in his arms and slowly started crying.

"What's the matter, Mama?" Matt said gently.

"Oh, Matt, we've tried so hard and gone through so much and I love you and care for you, but I have to leave. I can't live your life anymore."

"Shh, Mama, shh. I know. I can't make it without you, but I know you have to go."

I turned around and saw tears streaming down his cheeks for the first time in my life.

Goddam it, it happened again. We were all packed and ready to go to Anchorage for Matthew's operation when I got strep throat. I called the eye doctor and asked his nurse what she thought, if we should go ahead anyway. But she said, "No, this happens all the time with families. We'll just reschedule again."

In bed afterwards, I realized that rescheduling meant Matt would be out fishing. I knew that I'd be going through this alone, too. I started crying and straggled out of bed and grabbed a blanket. I lay on the living room sofa, crying hard like the old way.

Finally Matt came out. "Hey, c'mon back to bed. I can't sleep."

"You can't wait and come with us before you go out salmon fishing, can you?" I asked.

He looked puzzled for a minute, then said, "There's no way," and I just felt abandoned again. I sat there in my flannel nightgown, like some stray animal, looking ahead as stoically as I could. "I can't afford this, I can't cry like this, it just brings the end nearer, I'm glad he's leaving before us, I'm glad we're going without him, this is all for the best," I told myself.

"You're upset because I'm leaving before you and won't be there for Matthew's operation and to see you off to school," Matt said.

"No, I'm glad you're going," I said, and actually felt a glimmer of truth.

"Why?" He looked startled.

"Because then I won't be the one who's leaving you—you've already left me."

Matt left a few days later for salmon fishing. I called up Sarah, who'd entered the nursing program in Anchorage. She agreed to pick us up at the airport and find somewhere for Chelsea and Liam when Matthew was having his operation. After that we'd head straight for Seattle so I could start school.

Then I called Matt's mom and asked if she would take Chelsea and Liam for the weekend when we first arrived in Seattle so Matthew and I could recuperate.

She said, "No, Peggy's having a big family party that day, and Matt's going to be out fishing, isn't he?" And unspoken, "Without Matt, you're not family."

"Oh," I said, "I see. Yes, Matt will be gone fishing."

Sarah met us at the airport on a beautiful warm evening, and drove us to the hotel. Chelsea came up to me as I registered at the desk. I put my hand on the top of her head. It felt sticky and I looked at it and it was blood red. I knelt down to her and said, "Oh darling, what happened?" Her face was twisted up, trying not to cry, and she turned around and pointed to the stairs. They were suspended concrete slabs with iron bolts joining them to the railing.

"I scraped my head running underneath the stairs."

Are there no angels to watch over us?

The next morning, I gave Matthew a sip of my ice water and we went to the hospital at 6:30. Chelsea and Liam went with Donna's son to his daycare while Sarah was at school.

I sat with Matthew at a bunch of booths in a waiting area and filled out forms. At the third interview when a nurse asked me if he'd had any food or drink at all, I said, "Well…yeah, a little ice water," and suddenly we were pulled off the morning surgery list. They told me that anesthesia could make Matthew choke on anything in his stomach, so they'd take him last instead of first.

So we sat all day in the main reception room of the hospital. They wheeled white-robed people on gurneys from one clinic area into the operating rooms and then wheeled them out later.

A little after noon I delivered up little white-gowned baby Matthew to them. He went calmly into their crib and I walked out the surgery area doors.

Then I waited. I glanced through magazines and looked at the clock every few minutes. The waiting room emptied out. I sat pretty still and made myself feel okay. Finally, about five, they opened up the recovery room doors.

A nurse came out with Matthew in her arms. His eyes were blood red, the pupils looking outward instead of crossing. I staggered as she gave him to me. I felt sick, like worms were crawling inside me. I was trying so hard not to cry but I was so tired from playing a losing hand.

While we waited in the lobby for a taxi to take us back to the hotel, the anesthetist came out. He gave me his phone number in case Matthew had any problems that night, and told me that the blood in his eyes was normal, that I should have been warned to expect that. He also gave me a card for his colleague in Seattle. He patted me on the shoulder. "Don't worry, he'll be okay."

When we got to the hotel, I paid the taxi driver and got out with Matthew in my arms. The driver sped away. As I carried Matthew up the steps, he started vomiting.

I tried to get inside the doors, but two people hustled up the stairs in front of me into the lobby. 'Why don't they help me?' I wondered. 'Were they too embarrassed, or afraid they'd get bloody eyes, too?'

When Sarah and Donna brought the other kids back to the hotel, Donna said, "God, Nora, head lice is going around Andy's daycare. I hope your kids don't get it."

I waved at the air with a hand. "Don't worry, after all we've been through, lice sounds pretty innocent."

I was starved and I didn't want to lay awake hungry so I ordered chicken dinners from room service. I gave Chelsea and Liam a $20 bill and told them to get change for pop at the front desk. They rode the elevators and worked the pop machines till 10:30 when I walked to the end of the hall to get them.

A man stood there, getting ice, and asked me if I wanted to join him in the bar for a drink, and I said, "No thanks, I've had a rough day at the hospital with a friend." I don't know why I said 'friend,' except maybe if I'd said, 'with my little boy,' I would have broken down again.

I was so afraid of lying down and being overwhelmed or going to sleep and waking up in the dark with all the exaggerated traumas the middle of the night brings. I paced and packed our suitcases over and over and flipped the TV channels and looked out in the street. I wrote a letter to Matt telling him how much I hated his family. In the morning I ripped it up.

It was foggy and cold as winter when I took a taxi to the doctor's office for a 7:30 appointment. He looked at Matthew and said to his nurse, "They're a little X."

I wanted to grab him by his white lapels and scream in his face, "A little X!! His eyes are turning *out* now, you arrogant fuckhead! Don't try to codify your mistakes with 'a little X.'"

Of course, I just sat there like a dumb ox.

I took the kids back to the hotel for breakfast and sat with them at a round booth in the dining room. I ordered for them and sat there gulping tears. The kids were either oblivious or afraid for me, but they left me alone. After awhile, the waitress said something was wrong with their griddle or wafflemaker or some damn thing and it would be a while.

After she left, the tears started streaming down my face and every once in a while a kid would crawl on me or stroke my hair. The man who'd invited me for a drink got up from a party of businessmen in the next booth and said, "Hey now, you're gonna be all right. It's gonna be okay." I nodded and he knew not to touch me. He said, "He'll be okay, won't you, buddy?"

Matthew stopped opening the sugar packages and said, "Yes."

Sarah came to the hotel on her lunch break to drive us to the airport. She sat next to me on a bench beside our gate while the kids bought candy bars from a machine. I looked at Sarah's thick braid and the gold threads in her shirt. Her hands were cool and strong as she held mine, and I knew she'd be a good nurse.

It's 3 p.m. Thursday and everyone's asleep on the plane.

Is there no right decision to be made, just any decision? I don't believe in wise men.

I believe my heart. It's wrong to be divorced from a man I love and am committed to, but it's wrong to be committed to a man who can't share himself. With divorce, will Matt have to wake up or will I be glad to be free?

I am going through a crisis but I am going to escape—not footloose, but with kids, suitcases, operations, and commitments. The sun is shining and we're headed for home.

On one hand I'm screaming for the right to live my life, and on the other hand wondering if I'm selling my soul for that privilege. The remaining possibilities are, I'm selling my soul for nothing, or doing exactly the right thing. I can see why people find comfort in fanaticism.

I cringe at observations like "she's so strong" or "she tried so hard." If I'm strong, or if I put concentration and effort in my life, I want it to amount to something that makes me feel good, joyous.

I'm worried about stressing out under coming events, feeling so alone. But I don't have to be understood, even by Matt, to stand by my decisions, my judgments. I am more powerful than anyone thinks, including me. I can do it and I will, and I'll learn and I'll grow and conquer this lonely, put-down feeling. I'll work so hard I won't even think.

I may cry, I may scream, I may laugh, but I know I have the strength to save my family. It may not always be pretty, but I'll be there.

0-9761099-0-5